INCHES FROM LOVE

"You can open your eyes now."

Petra wondered why Vorador's voice sounded rather choked. She cracked one eyelid open and saw the wizard's face only inches from her own. She snapped her eye shut again. Of all the places in the universe, she had to end up practically on top of him.

"Are you feeling dizzy?" he asked.

She could feel his warm breath caressing her cheek. It was all she could do to stop herself from turning her head those few inches until their mouths touched. Gads. She'd better get a grip on herself. She peeked at him again. Yup, he was still there.

"What're you doing?" His voice rumbled over her.

"Nothing. What're you doing?" She opened both her eyes and stared into his dark gaze. It was a struggle but she managed to look away before too much time passed. Geez, he smelled good, a combination somewhere between ocean fresh and just plain man. "You can back off any time."

He quirked an eyebrow at her. "I will gladly remove myself. As soon as you release me."

Petra yanked her hands away from his hair. "Why am I sitting on your lap?"

Vorador looked as if he ran down a mental list of possible answers before he simply said, "It's where you landed."

SPELLBOUND IN SEATTLE

GARTHIA ANDERSON

LOVE SPELL NEW YORK CITY

LOVE SPELL®

March 2003

Published by

Dorchester Publishing Co., Inc.
276 Fifth Avenue
New York, NY 10001

ISBN 0-505-52537-2

Printed in the United States of America.

Visit us on the web at www.dorchesterpub.com.

ACKNOWLEDGMENTS

All my love to Doug, Chris, Jenn and Josh. Thanks for putting up with a mom who'd rather read and write than clean house and cook. Love and thanks to Niel, who's always been supportive of my writing in ways too numerous to list.

I can never give enough thanks to WITTS, the best critique group ever. Susie Crandall, Esther Hedges, Brenda Hiatt, Pam Jones, Alicia Rasley, Laurie Sparks and Betty Ward, you are indeed Women Inspired To Tell Stories. And I can't forget Emily Alward, Deanna Sanders and Vicky Harden, past members of WITTS who have moved on but are sorely missed.

Thank you to all the wonderful crazy people who used to hang out at the Highlander Fantasy Board and Magic Springs on AOL. Thank you for sharing your wit and wisdom, and for the many hours of fun and laughter. Thank you, Draxen—you started the madness with your hilarious Phone Call Thread. And special thanks to Teresa for giving me Kerstie, who wasn't really evil, just misunderstood, or maybe only slightly confused.

SPELLBOUND IN SEATTLE

Chapter One

The present—but not quite here and now . . .

Petra W. Field needed to get the blood out of her rug.

She'd spent the last three hours scrubbing, yet nothing had removed the bright red stain from the middle of the large area rug that covered her living room floor. At least the numerous cleaning products had accomplished one thing: The slightly rotten smell was gone. Although she wasn't so sure the mixture of lemon scent, April fresh flowers, and mountain pines, combined with a dash of hospital disinfectant, was much of an improvement.

Her housewarming party was due to start in less than an hour and she had magic blood on her rug. Only magic could explain the way that darn stain kept reappearing. She had no options left. Squaring her shoulders, she picked up the phone and dialed.

"Good evening. You have reached the offices of Rapid Renovations. Please choose from the following menu to ensure you are connected with the proper department."

Petra made a sound of frustration. She hated these answering systems. Sure, the technical wizards had managed to make them slightly more intelligent, but the menus they offered never seemed to have any selections even remotely close to what she needed.

"Press One if you want a spell cast. Press Nineteen for a love spell.

"Press Two if a spell has been cast on you and you need it broken. Press Twenty-nine if it's a love spell.

"Press Three if you need to hire a sword master. Press Thirty-nine if you prefer an Amazon.

"Press Four if you need the services of a wizard. If you wish to request a specific wizard, please—"

Petra caught a flicker of black and white out of the corner of her eye. She dropped the phone, lunged for her cat and scooped him up just before he pounced on the bloody stain. She hated to think what might happen to Bosco if magic blood got on him. Despite his protests, she shut him in the bathroom.

Oh, crud! The phone. She got back just in time to hear, "If you wish to repeat the menu, please press Nine."

"Drat." Petra jabbed the proper button. "Yes, I want to hear it again, you stupid piece of junk." She'd been ready to punch a number but couldn't remember which one. "You should've stopped when you heard me drop the phone."

"Thank you for thinking of Rapid Renovations. Please choose from the menu to ensure you reach the proper department."

Tuning out the first part of the message, since she'd already heard it, Petra had to remind herself why she'd left Albuquerque and moved to Seattle. The first scientist-wizards had discovered how to combine the laws of physics and sorcery nearly fifty years ago. Since then, not all cities or states had passed laws favorable to the use of magic. However, Seattle had quickly become the West Coast center for magical activity. The city remained on the cutting edge of incorporating wizardry into mainstream life. Much as Starbucks Coffee had slowly infiltrated the rest of the country, the magic community hoped to do the same with their skills and talents.

She'd wanted some excitement in her overly mundane existence. Plus it was a good place to hide from Harold. Knowing her opinion of wizards, he'd never expect her to willingly subject herself to living smack dab in the middle of Magic Land. So, here she was—in Seattle for only a week and already up to her eyeballs in magic. Chalk it up to temporary insanity. It served her right. Considering her past experiences with magic, she should have expected this disaster. Oops, she'd forgotten to listen again.

"—if you need them tomorrow. Press Seventy-eight if you need them immediately."

She pressed 78. Whatever it was, she definitely needed it immediately.

"Thank you for choosing Rapid Renovations for your magical needs. Please select from the following menu to guarantee you reach the proper department."

"No," Petra shouted into the phone. "Just let me talk to a real person."

"Press One—"

She pressed 1, not up to going through the whole thing again. She really hated wizards, but everybody knew it took magic to remove magic. It just had to be magic blood, didn't it? Too bad she didn't have any sorcery skills, or she could do the job herself. Now she'd run out of time. Her guests would start arriving in less than an hour. She had to do whatever it took to get rid of that blood.

The phone clicked and whirred. She actually felt a small amount of hope. Nope, no such luck.

"All our operators are busy at this time. Please hold until the next available operator can take your call."

Trying to be patient, Petra mentally ran down her list of things-to-do. Thank heavens she'd hired a caterer rather than try to fix the food herself. The house was clean—except for the stupid blood. She only needed to change clothes before her first guest arrived. Everything was under control. Ha! Who was she trying to kid?

"Listen here, you dumb hunk of junk. I told you I needed help immediately. That means now. Let me talk to a real person

3

or I swear I'm going to come down there and yank all your tiny little wires out of the wall."

Silence greeted her threat. With a sigh, she picked up a business card beside the phone. "RAPID RENOVATIONS. WE FIX IT, QUICK AS A WIZARD'S WINK. NO QUESTIONS ASKED."

Evidently wizards winked pretty darn slowly here in Seattle. On the up side, they promised to ask no questions. She didn't want to get involved with the police, filling out reports, going in for questioning. Not that she had anything to hide—about this, anyway—although recent portions of her past wouldn't exactly stand up to inspection. Unfortunately, an official investigation, possibly one involving murder, would surely bring those other aspects under scrutiny.

Why did this have to happen to her? Other than the spot, nothing else disturbed her house. There were no bloody footprints, no smears where someone might have walked or crawled away or been dragged off. Just that blasted stain sitting there in silent accusation. She hated to think the word *murder*. Since she hadn't found a body anywhere, maybe assault?

She wished cats could talk. Her newly adopted pet had been a perfect gentleman since he'd shown up on her porch last week. When she'd arrived home from work, Bosco had been in the front window, napping in the sun, his black and white fur pristine. He might not be the culprit, but he must have seen something.

She supposed things could be worse. If she'd had a normal childhood, instead of being raised by two wizards, she'd probably be having a nice case of hysterics right about now. But years of coming home to Mom and Dad's experiments had pretty much made her immune to attacks of screaming fits. She couldn't quite recall if it had been the ogre in her closet or the fire-breathing dragon in the basement, or maybe the pink dancing elephants, that had given her nerves of steel. No, she remembered now. It had been—

"Thank you for calling Rapid Renovations. This is Bob. How may I assist you?"

"Oh." It took a moment to comprehend that she finally had a real person and not another recording on the line. She blurted,

4

"I have blood on my rug. I came home from work, and there it was."

"Thank you. We'll have a team there as soon as possible."

"I need—"

The line went dead. Petra held out the receiver and looked at it vacantly for several seconds. With slow, careful movements she hung up the phone and struggled to control her rising panic. "But you didn't even get my address."

She hated how forlorn her voice sounded. What the heck should she do now? At a loss, she glanced around the room, hoping another solution would present itself. Where was inspiration when she really needed it? How did one disguise a manhole-sized spot, anyway? Why couldn't it at least be smaller, easier to hide?

If she'd thought of it earlier, she might have rolled up the rug and stuck it in the back bedroom with the unpacked boxes. Now there wasn't enough time. She'd have to move the furniture out of the way, wrestle with the rug, then put the sofa, chairs and table all back in place. Besides, what if, after all that, the blood had soaked through and stained the floor underneath as well?

Should she just rearrange the furniture to cover the spot? No, her sofa smack in the middle of the living room would raise nearly as many uncomfortable questions as blood out there for all the world to see. Considering she worked for an interior design company, folks would be likely to wonder at her unusual decorating style.

There remained only one thing to do: She would lock the doors, turn out the lights, hide her car around the corner and pretend no one was home. When she went to work tomorrow she would invent some emergency and lie. Bosco's loud complaining yowls from the bathroom should add a nice touch to her story.

The doorbell rang and she nearly jumped out of her shoes. She shot a glance at the clock. It was way too early for her guests. Nobody came to a party forty minutes early, did they? She hoped they would all be fashionably late. She tiptoed to the door and peeked out the peephole. Her jaw literally dropped in amazement. Gathering her wits, she opened the door.

"Good evening, Miss Field. I'm from Emerald Renaissance Garments and I'm here to clean your rug."

"Emerald . . . what?" Petra stared at the man outfitted in a long green robe standing on her front porch. She had the fleeting thought that he'd escaped from a convention of Merlin wannabes. Even weirder, he looked exactly like the actor Val Kilmer. "I didn't call you."

"I'm aware you called our competitors, Rapid Renovations." He offered her a dazzling smile along with his business card. "However, we at Emerald Renaissance Garments can deliver faster service at a more reasonable price."

The printing on the card had so many curlicues it was nearly impossible to read. She managed to make out the company name and THINK GREEN WHEN YOU GO TO RENOVATE. This didn't make any sense. "But . . . how—?"

"Magic, miss. That's our business."

She lost her train of thought when he smiled again, his brilliant white teeth flashing in the last of the evening light. Impressive. She decided he must use a super strength ultra-charming spell to enhance his physical appearance. What a great way to recruit new customers. Especially female customers. Too bad he had to waste it on her.

"How much—?"

The squeal of tires cut off Petra's words. A neon orange panel truck careened to a halt in front of her house. Three people in orange overalls piled out. They raced up the sidewalk, tool belts jangling, buckets clanging. It didn't look like they meant to stop. She stepped back, fearful of being trampled.

The man in the green robe blocked the way. "This job's already been taken. Go back to your hole, fellas."

"Dugan, what the devil are you doing here? This is our job."

"Not anymore. And the devil had nothing to do with it. Miss Field simply prefers to use a more efficient company."

Petra tried to tell them she hadn't hired anybody yet.

"Stop wasting my customer's valuable time," Dugan insisted. "Get a faster truck if you want to stay on top."

Petra wasn't surprised to see the crew in orange turn around and go back the way they came, although at a much slower pace. Mr. Green Robe had been quite authoritative and intimidating. She hoped he did as well with the spot. "Thank you, Mister . . . ?"

"Dugan," he told her with another of those wide smiles.

She nearly told him not to squander a perfectly good spell. Considering her record with wizards, she was the last woman he should waste his talents on. To be fair, though, he'd come here to do a job. Maybe he'd turned on the charm in hopes that he could charge more money for what he surely must have realized was an emergency situation.

"Very well, Mr. Dugan."

He whipped out a piece of paper and pen from nowhere. "Just sign on the dotted line."

In too much of a hurry to argue, she glanced at the contract. The fee seemed a little high, but not outrageous. She quickly scrawled her name and indicated she'd pay by credit card. "Please come in. And please, tell me you can get this stain out."

Tucking the paper back wherever it had come from, he followed her into the living room. "No prob—"

When he stopped abruptly, she got a sinking feeling in the pit of her stomach. "No problem?" she asked hopefully.

Dugan knelt beside the stain and removed a device from his pocket. It looked like a small handheld video game. He waved it over the blood, intently studying whatever the compact screen told him. It didn't take a genius to read the look on his face. Petra knew he wouldn't give her good news.

"I'm afraid you've got a real problem here, Miss Field."

"Great. Just great. So you can't remove it?"

"Well, yes. But—"

"I thought—"

"Please don't interrupt. We don't have the time."

Even though he'd done the same to her, Petra apologized. As long as this guy got rid of that blood, she would play nice. "Sorry."

"This can be removed, but it's going to take longer than the thirty minutes you have until your guests arrive."

"How do you know—?"

7

"I told you, Miss Field, it's my business to know. Now, do you want to continue this unnecessary questioning? Or do you want to hear my plan?"

"Sorry," she said for the second time. His charm spell must have slipped. Now he looked more like a young Ron Howard. Was it too late to call back the guys in the orange overalls? "Please, go on."

"As I was saying, this can't be removed right now, but an invisibility spell can be used on it. Since the spot has such strong magical properties, that spell will only last until midnight. Will your party be over by then?"

"Tell you what—I'll just invite everybody to stay until then so they can watch a puddle of blood magically appear in the middle of my living room."

"There's no need to be sarcastic, Miss Field. A simple yes or no would suffice."

"Sorry," she told him yet again, not caring how surly she sounded. "Trust me. Everyone will be gone long before midnight."

"Very well. We'll return then and begin the removal spell." Dugan headed for the front door.

"Where are you going?" she demanded. "I thought—"

"I'm going out to the truck to call my wizard on our radio. She can be here in two minutes to cast the invisibility spell."

Petra let him go, not wanting another lecture about time management. She wondered why he'd arrived at a job minus his wizard. Surely it would be more effective to have the expert present right from the beginning. On the other hand, that undoubtedly explained how he had gotten here so quickly. Interesting that Mr. Dugan wasn't a wizard himself. What was his position with the company? Public relations, probably.

When the doorbell rang twenty-five minutes later, Petra took a deep breath, hoping the extra oxygen would help clear her mind. Pausing with her hand on the doorknob, she made one last visual sweep of the living room. Everything was in order. It even smelled nice, thanks to the spicy vanilla candles scattered around the room.

A quick glance down at her dress gave her morale another

much needed boost. The short skirt and thin straps of the red silk dress made her feel attractive, sexy even. Although, all things considered, she would prefer a color other than red. Well, she was as ready as she'd ever be.

Opening the door, she smiled at her boss and welcomed him. She hoped Dugan and his wizard shut the back door tight on their way out. And she hoped Bosco would stop meowing from the spare bedroom.

Chapter Two

"Gads, I didn't think they'd ever leave," Petra said to the empty room.

She leaned back against the front door and glanced at her watch. Eleven forty-five. Never in her wildest dreams would she have imagined everyone would have such a great time they wouldn't leave. She always gave boring parties.

Of course, she had never worked with such an eclectic group of people before. Being office manager for an interior decorating firm that included a wizard, a psychic and a witch on the payroll constituted quite a career change for her. Taking up skydiving or bungee jumping would have counteracted her boredom with much less stress.

Without warning a figure suddenly appeared in her hallway. With a yelp Petra leapt away from the door. "What are you doing here? How did you get——?"

"Actually, Miss Field," the blond man in the emerald robe explained, "we never left."

Mr. Dugan had been here all along? Where had he been hiding? Her house wasn't very large. It contained only front room, kitchen, bath and three bedrooms. A shady old-fashioned porch wrapped around the house and gave it a sense of welcome she hadn't been able to resist.

"I like your pigs."

"What?" Petra had heard him. She simply didn't want to believe what he'd said.

"Nice pigs."

"Mr. Dugan, what were you doing in my bedroom?"

"I wanted to be close by in case something happened."

She reminded him, and herself, "What could you have done? You aren't even a wizard."

Speaking of wizards . . . The wizard he'd brought in to work the invisibility spell had not inspired confidence. Petra had never seen anyone who looked less like a wizard. The girl, Caylin, appeared to be about twelve years old, playing dress up in her mother's clothes.

"I was here too, Miss Field."

Caylin stepped into the living room, and Petra couldn't help but smile. The little sorceress looked so darn cute in that long green robe. No, Petra refused to be sucked in by those innocent blue eyes. She didn't need cute. She needed competent.

"Good. Now finish the job and get that blood off my rug."

The two ERG employees exchanged a glance.

"You can get rid of the blood, can't you?" Petra asked.

Another glance flew between them.

"You promised you'd remove it after the party." Petra hated the edge of desperation that crept into her words.

That spot had to come out. She couldn't go through the rest of her life tiptoeing around a bloody spot the size of a manhole in the middle of her front room. A permanent invisibility spell was not a viable option either. All during the party people had circled the bewitched area, avoiding it and talking about the cold draft. With all the psychic power that had surrounded her house tonight, she'd held her breath in fear someone would volunteer to investigate. Thankfully, they'd all been too polite to offer.

Dugan said, "Caylin isn't certain she has enough power to do

11

an effective job." A knock sounded at the door and he grinned. "Ah, here he is now."

"He who?" Petra asked, but Dugan had already turned away. He whipped open the door with a flourish. She actually gasped at the figure standing on her front porch.

A man in yet another long green robe glided into her house. Seeing him move was like watching water flow. His very presence filled the living room, a room that suddenly seemed smaller. The air seemed to take on a crisp, clean scent like a refreshing breeze straight from the ocean. Even a non-talent such as Petra could feel his electric presence prickle along her arms and tingle at the base of her spine.

"Wow," she breathed in an awed whisper. He was as dark and forbidding as Dugan was light and charming. The power seemed to roll off the wizard in nearly visible waves, even to someone as magic blind as she. His long dark hair was secured in a tidy braid that hung halfway down his back. His eyes reminded her of bottomless pools of water, deep and mysterious and scary.

"Miss Field, I'd like you to meet Emerald Renaissance Garment's senior wizard, Vorador. Now that you're our client, you can trust him with your life."

The tingle along Petra's arms turned into goose bumps. Gad, what if she wasn't a client? Could she not trust the wizard then—with her life or anything else? Her newest guest dominated the room, demanding all her attention. What had happened to Dugan's charming spell? Next to Vorador, Dugan looked about as appealing as the Creature from the Black Lagoon.

Not quite certain she meant it, she said, "Nice to meet you."

"You have a problem." His pronouncement echoed through the room like the thunder of doom.

His words were like a splash of cold water in her face. "Gee, tell me something I don't know."

Vorador turned his piercing gaze in her direction. He was just like every other wizard she'd ever known: arrogant, judgmental and a pain in the—She managed to hold his look for a

12

few seconds before she glanced away. Her eyes fell to the spot of blood, once more visible on the rug.

"It's back," she told them, just in case nobody had noticed.

"It will continue to come back until the victim of this crime is laid to rest and the villain brought to justice."

Vorador's deep rumbling voice raised goose bumps on top of Petra's goose bumps. Or maybe it was what he said. Or it could be the fact that he stood there like a statue. She couldn't even tell if he was breathing. She did know his assessment was not what she wanted to hear.

"Just great. And I'm supposed to live with this?"

Without speaking, Vorador studied her for several long moments, then asked in a deceptively bland tone, "You don't want to see justice done for this poor troubled soul?"

"Truthfully, not tonight." Petra knew that sounded callous, but it had been a long day. She was exhausted.

"Now that I've had time to think about it, I doubt anyone was killed here today," she said. She definitely didn't want these guys to call the police. She had no intention of making it easy for Harold to find her. "The blood must be left from some older crime. Surely it's been solved by now anyway."

Petra could feel the weight of the three silent condemning gazes on her, but she plunged onward. "Magic has obviously been used to conceal it. And that makes me an innocent bystander."

Depending on your point of view, she was either one of the cursed or blessed beyond measure. On a scale of one to ten, her magic potential registered right about zero. Until meeting this wizard she had never before felt anything even remotely magical. No matter how disappointed her parents had been, or how hard they had tried to teach her some magic, any magic, she couldn't weave a spell to save her life. That meant she couldn't be involved in whatever crime had left enchanted blood on her rug.

"Why don't you just take the rug with you? Bring it back when it's clean."

"That is not an option," Vorador informed her in his doom-and-gloom voice.

13

Well, she had tried. She sighed, knowing he was correct. Too often magic was tied to the place, as well as the object.

"All I want right now is to go to bed and forget about blood and wizards. So, just do your job and get the dang spot out."

"It will take time," Vorador said, although he looked as if he wanted to say more. He wore the same expression Mom and Dad had when they'd finally accepted they had given birth to a magical dud.

"How much time?" Used to dealing with people's disappointment in her, Petra ignored it in this man.

"As long as it takes."

Petra barely restrained herself from rolling her eyes in frustration. He still stood in the exact same spot by the front door. He made a gorgeous statue, but he also made her nervous. Yeah, that's what it was . . . it couldn't be attraction she felt simmering just below the surface of her skin.

Starting to pace, simply to counteract his immobility, she asked, "How much extra is this going to cost me?"

"You've paid your fee, Miss Field, and signed the contract," Dugan answered firmly. "We at ERG stand by our word. We won't rest until you're satisfied."

She wouldn't debate the state of her satisfaction. Surely she'd been plain enough that right about now it was nil. Stifling a yawn, she wondered exactly how far Dugan meant to carry his promise. Or was it a threat?

"I can't deal with any more of this mumbo jumbo tonight. I haven't slept well since I moved. All things considered, maybe I ought to pack some clothes and Bosco, head out to a hotel and leave this whole mess to you wizards." She wondered if she could afford that extravagance. There was no telling how long it might take to clear up this predicament.

"That's your decision, Miss Field," Vorador said. "However, it will not hasten the end results."

"Maybe I should have followed my first instincts and hired the guys in orange. At least they promised rapid renovations. All you guys have done is parade around in ridiculous green robes you probably buy in bulk at some discount warehouse."

Neither man responded; they both merely stared at her. She

14

couldn't decide if they were stunned into silence by her bluntness or trying not to lose their tempers.

"Can you be a bit more precise about the time frame, fellas?" Petra knew she sounded as disgusted as she felt. Too bad for them. "I have a busy day tomorrow."

"Miss Field," Caylin spoke up in a timid voice, "tomorrow is Sunday. We don't do magic on Sundays."

Everyone looked at Caylin. Under their scrutiny she seemed to shrink even further into her oversized green robe. Petra had a feeling the junior wizard wished she hadn't brought Vorador's attention her way. Petra understood exactly how she felt. Out of sympathy, or stupidity, she broke the thick silence.

"Whatever. Listen, Mr. Wizard, do what you can right now. Tomorrow, come back after I've had some sleep. Because I will not wait until Monday to get rid of this blood."

"I don't think—"

"She has pigs." Dugan interrupted whatever Vorador had been about to say in that oh-so-serious, I-disapprove-of-this-whole-situation tone of voice.

"Really?" Vorador asked.

"Yes, really," she snapped, ready to smack the wide grin off Dugan's face.

The temptation to do violence doubled when Vorador actually smiled at her. She had a feeling the wizard rarely used that expression. No, she refused to be distracted. She didn't care that his dark eyes gleamed with roguish mischief. No, she didn't care that he had a hint of a dimple in his lean cheek. No, no, no! She didn't care one little bit that his smile transformed him from foreboding to fascinating.

She attempted to steer the conversation back to business. "Now, when—?"

"What kind of pigs?" Vorador wanted to know.

"All kinds," Dugan assured him. "Stuffed, glass, wooden, porcelain, china, carved—"

"Listen, my pigs are none of your concern."

"Flying ones?" Vorador asked with great interest.

Dugan laughed. "Oh, yeah."

"Can we just stick to the subject of this blasted blood?"

She jabbed a finger in the direction of the spot. The two men shared one of those superior, long-suffering masculine looks that had always infuriated Petra. As if she was the biggest problem they had to deal with. At least they shut up about the pigs and turned their attention to the problem at hand.

Now she, on the other hand, had plenty to complain about. She had magic blood on her living room rug, an unsolved mystery of unknown age, an unhappy cat locked in the bedroom and three weirdos in green robes threatening to hang around indefinitely. She unquestionably had more problems than either of them, especially since they were part of the problem. Problems, with a capital *P,* and that rhymed with . . . whatever.

Chapter Three

Yawning, Petra came out of her bedroom. Bosco did his usual morning dance between and around her feet, doing his best to trip her. Coffee; she needed coffee. Thank heavens it was Sunday and she didn't have to go to work. The thought reminded her of last night. Her gaze darted to that spot on her rug.

It was gone! Vorador's spell had done the trick in spite of his protests that it would take stronger efforts. Not quite believing it herself, Petra rubbed her eyes. Nope, the spot was definitely gone.

Wait just a minute. It took nearly that long before her mind could comprehend what she saw. Oh, this was great. Instead of a bloody stain, a large hole now gaped in the middle of her living room rug.

Gingerly tiptoeing closer, she leaned and peered over the edge. A dry, dusty odor similar to sagebrush tickled her nose. Having lived in New Mexico, it was quite familiar. She squinted into the gloomy interior of the opening. Not only was the circle of rug gone, but the floor too. She should have been able to gaze into the basement; instead only thick, impenetrable blackness was visible.

As Bosco cautiously slunk toward the rim of the void she snatched him back.

"I don't think that's such a good idea, kitty. You don't want to fall in there. Wherever there is."

Apologizing profusely, Petra locked Bosco in the bathroom. He was extremely vocal in his dissatisfaction. She grabbed the phone and dialed the emergency number Mr. Dugan had left.

"I swear," she muttered, "if I get an answering machine, heads will roll."

"Good morning. You have reached the offices of Emerald Renaissance Garments. Please—"

"Let me talk to Mr. Dugan. Now!" The line buzzed, clicked and whirred. "Put me on hold and I'll call Rapid Renovations."

"Good morning, Miss Field. This is Annie. How may we serve you this fine lovely morning?"

"It's not fine. It's not lovely. And you can serve me by getting Dugan or either of his two incompetent wizards to my house right now. I have a hole in my floor!"

"I'm terribly sorry, Miss Field. We'll have someone there immediately, if not sooner. We deeply regret the inconvenience and hope that this will not affect your future use of—"

Petra hung up, not willing to be pacified. She wanted to yell at someone, such as a certain wizard. If not him, then preferably the one responsible for this disaster. Yeah, she would really enjoy yelling at whoever had done the dirty deed and stained her rug in the first place.

The door bell rang. Petra flung the door open and glared at the tall dark man standing there. He really should look ridiculous in the flowing green robe. Somehow he managed to appear regal and imperious. The dark length of his braid glinted with blue highlights in the sunlight. She refused to be intimidated, or impressed.

"You screwed up, wizard boy."

"Indeed?" Vorador's voice was quiet and one eyebrow quirked upward.

She barely controlled an urge to giggle. Bet he'd learned that

18

expression while watching Mr. Spock on old "Star Trek" reruns.

"Well, somebody messed up. I have a huge hole in my floor. It's not exactly the improvement I asked for when I hired you to get rid of the bloodstain."

"Of course not. May I see this hole?"

Petra started to move out of the doorway. Oh, crud. She still had on the oversized T-shirt she slept in—the one with the trio of baby pigs in bright pink blazoned across her chest. She glanced farther down and saw her favorite fuzzy piggy slippers on her feet.

Gathering what dignity she could, she led him to the latest development in her magic crisis. He'd better tread carefully. She would push him in if he said one word. When she dared glance at him, his face was impassive.

"Well?" she demanded.

"Interesting." Vorador leaned out over the darkness. He righted himself just when it seemed certain he would lose his balance. "Have you been down in the basement?"

Petra shook her head, still fighting the urge to give him one tiny little push. Even stronger was the urge to lean closer to him so she could get a better whiff of whatever cologne he wore. How could his scent remind her of the ocean without being the least bit fishy or salty?

"May I see it?"

"Help yourself. The door's over there." She waved in the general direction.

He started to go, then turned back. "You can let your cat out. I find that noise very distracting."

"I don't want him to fall in."

"Cats are highly intelligent and agile creatures. I can assure you, he won't go near enough to fall in."

Since Bosco's yowls were getting on her nerves too, Petra went to release him. Vorador headed down into the cellar. She carried Bosco to the kitchen and opened a can of food she saved for special occasions. His suffering deserved a reward.

While cat and wizard were both occupied, she hurried to her bedroom and grabbed the first thing out of her closet. Back in the living room, dressed in her oldest ratty gray sweatsuit, she peered down the hole. It looked like Vorador hadn't made any progress yet.

"Yoohoo! Mister Wizard."

There was no answer.

"Hey! Are you still down there?"

A dead hush was the only response.

"Well, for crying out loud." She moved closer, trying to see into the pitch-dark interior of the hole. "What the heck are you doing down there?"

Petra sighed in frustration—and just a little bit of worry, if she was perfectly honest with herself. She guessed she'd better check out the basement and see what her wizard was doing. She turned and saw a streak of black and white race out of the kitchen, heading straight toward the hole.

"No!" She made a grab but missed by a mile. Bosco launched himself in a running leap and disappeared into the void.

Petra fell to her knees beside the opening. She plunged her whole arm inside the darkness. Tiny tingles of electricity shot from her fingertips up to her shoulder. Then it hit her. It was gone! Her arm was gone! Screaming, she jerked herself away from the hole. She collapsed in relief when she saw her arm still firmly attached to her body.

Gads, disappearing limbs would terrorize even the most stoic of skeptics—which she never claimed to be. She would give anything not to have to, but quaking with fear, she slowly slipped her hand, then her whole arm back in the circle of darkness. Even though she expected the unnerving sight, she squealed in fright when her appendage vanished.

The tingling jolts of energy returned and continued to increase in strength until the sensation became downright uncomfortable. She expected to smell burning hair and flesh any second now. She desperately felt around for any sign of her cat. Nothing!

"What are you yelling about, Miss Field?"

Petra jumped to her feet and spun to face the green-robed wizard. "It's all your fault, you faker."

"Exactly how have I misrepresented myself?"

"You told me it was okay. You said he wouldn't go near the

20

hole. You told me he had too much sense to jump in. In other words, you don't know what the heck you're talking about."

"He who?"

His dark eyes no longer looked mysterious, but warm and caring. She wanted to smack the look of concern off his handsome face, certain it was false. Besides, she knew from experience that no wizard of Vorador's power would be interested in someone as magic blind as herself.

"My cat," she practically screamed at him.

"Your cat fell into the hole?"

"No." Petra gritted her teeth. "He *jumped* in."

"That's impossible."

"Right." Turning her back on the wizard, Petra hurried toward the basement stairs.

"Where are you going?"

"To get my cat. You better hope he landed on his feet, because your company is liable for any vet bills if he didn't."

"Your cat is not in the basement."

Petra halted with her foot on the first step. She slowly turned. "Then where is he?"

Vorador gave her a stern look. "That I am not positive of."

"What the heck is that supposed to mean?"

"It means you haven't been honest with me, Miss Field. How can I perform my job efficiently if you withhold information?"

Petra couldn't believe her ears. He dared to scold her? "Hey, I'm the wronged party here. Besides, you should just know stuff. Oh, wait . . . did you forget your crystal ball, wiz boy?"

"Dugan was correct. You do use sarcasm too freely. It's quite inappropriate. Besides being rude."

"What in the blue blazes gives you the right—"

"I really wish you hadn't said that," he interrupted.

Petra was ready to give the wizard a huge piece of her mind when she noticed something unusual. "What the heck?"

Vorador actually looked sheepish. "Sorry. It's an involuntary reaction."

She stared at the crown of blue flames flickering around his head. "You aren't going to set my house on fire, are you?"

He shook his head, causing the small blaze to flitter from side to side.

She'd never seen anything like it in all her life. That said a lot, considering she had grown up in a house that overflowed with magic. The blue flames were obviously not hot since nothing seemed to be burning. Nor did she smell anything remotely like fire. If anything, his fresh, natural scent seemed stronger.

"Did I do that?" she asked, teetering between amazement and amusement.

Vorador nodded and the small conflagration danced down his hair and over his cheeks, as if he'd suddenly sprouted a fiery beard. "I have an affinity for fire, and this happens when someone uses it in a curse."

Petra knew all about curses and how even the most innocent words could cause problems. Her parents had taught her that. If a strongly magical person had a bond with a particular thing, even a nontalent such as herself could activate those properties. Which was why she avoided the more common curses of hell, damn, and any word related to excrement. The lesson had been reinforced when her unthinking exclamation had caused a student to be covered in human waste. Considering the girl's personality, Petra should have guessed she had a rapport with sh—

Vorador mumbled an incantation and the blue-blazing crown disappeared from his head with a snap, crackle and pop.

She smiled in appreciation. He must indeed have a powerful kinship with fire to control it so completely. Pushing aside her grudging admiration, she got back to the matter at hand.

"Impressive, but not exactly helpful in getting my cat back."

"Your cat wouldn't be gone if you'd been honest with me."

"What're you talking about? I haven't lied to you."

"Then you admit you called in another wizard?"

"I did not," Petra defended herself.

"Yes, you did," Vorador firmly maintained. "That's why you now have a hole instead of merely blood. Someone else's magic corrupted the spell I placed last night. This is the result."

"Well, duh." Petra was tempted to smack him in the forehead. "Of course there was some other magic involved. Do you think I bought the dang rug with all that blood on it?"

He took a deep breath and appeared to count to ten. "I took into account any previous spells. Only something recent— something powerful—would explain this result."

"Besides your assistant, Caylin, no other wizard entered this house."

Vorador's stance relaxed and he looked at her with some consternation, his eyebrow doing that Spock imitation again. "You didn't call Rapid Renovations."

"Ahhhh," she said, as understanding dawned. "You thought I called in the competition after you left."

"It seemed a logical assumption."

This time Petra laughed out loud. No, she wasn't going to ask him if his favorite show was "Star Trek."

"So, where's my cat? And how do you intend to get him back?"

If he had any curiosity about what she found humorous, he concealed it. "There's only one solution."

"Which is?"

In answer, Vorador moved to the edge of the hole and without hesitation stepped off into open space.

Stunned, Petra held her breath. He seemed to hang suspended in midair for several seconds. Then he disappeared with a loud whoosh.

In spite of her astonishment, a stray thought intruded. It would have been nice if when the wizard had dropped out of sight his robe had billowed up. It might have answered the burning question of whether he was a boxer or briefs man. She bet the whole house he had a lean muscled frame hidden under those plush green folds. Her mind played with the notion that he might even have been naked underneath.

Oh, boy. She had to get this wayward attraction under control before she made a fool of herself. Hadn't she learned her lesson with Harold? She scolded and lectured herself while she waited for Vorador and Bosco to return.

Fifteen minutes later she began to get worried.

Fifteen minutes after that she went in search of a rope.

Fifteen minutes after that she found something sturdy to tie it onto.

Fifteen minutes after that she actually tied the other end of the rope around her waist.

Thirty seconds later she decided if she didn't take the plunge now she would lose what small amount of courage she had scraped together. Taking a deep breath, Petra stepped off the edge of the hole.

Chapter Four

Petra knew she was falling. A gentle sage-scented breeze rippled across her skin and through her hair. The absence of light inside the hole made it difficult to tell how fast she fell. She didn't seem to have gathered much speed. This must be how a feather felt as it drifted to the ground.

Floating downward through the darkness, it was impossible to discern anything—not the speed of her descent, not how far she'd fallen, where the bottom was, or when she might hit it. In spite of her earlier confidence, she hoped she didn't go splat. She didn't want to see any more blood, especially not her own.

Strange. The dry, woodsy smell had been replaced by that bracing sea breeze scent she was coming to associate with a certain wizard. She clutched the rope with both hands, reassured by its solid texture. For some reason, it didn't feel as rough as before.

"You can open your eyes now."

With a squeal, Petra tightened her grasp on her safety line. She cracked one eye open and saw the wizard's face only inches from her own. Of all the places in the universe, she had to land practically on top of him.

"Are you feeling dizzy?" he asked.

She could feel his warm breath caressing her cheek. It was all she could do to stop herself from turning her head those few inches until their mouths touched. Gads. She'd better get a grip on herself. She peeked at him again.

"What're you doing?" His voice rumbled over her.

"Nothing. What're you doing?" She opened both her eyes and stared into his dark gaze. It was a struggle, but she managed to look away before too much time passed. "You can back off any time."

He quirked that eyebrow of his at her. "I will gladly remove myself. As soon as you release me."

Prodded by his words, she took stock of her position. She no longer clutched the rope. She had a stranglehold on him, her arms wrapped tight around his neck, her fingers tightly gripping his long black braid. "Oops."

Petra yanked her hands away from his hair.

"Why am I sitting on your lap?"

Vorador looked as if he was running down a mental list of possible answers before he simply said, "It's where you landed."

At least she hadn't gone splat. One second she'd been falling. The next, settled on his lap snug as a bug in a rug. "Hope I didn't hurt you."

"Not at all. And you? Were you injured in any way?"

"Nope," Petra assured him. "I feel just fine."

"Then perhaps you could get up?"

She hadn't thought she could get any more embarrassed. She'd been wrong. Scrambling to her feet, she wished a hole would open up and swallow her. No, never mind. That had already happened. She busied herself brushing off nonexistent dirt and straightening her clothes.

"Sorry," she mumbled.

"Glad to be of service."

When she glanced at him, the wizard's face remained as unreadable as the Sphinx. A tiny part of her admitted to some disappointment. He didn't appear to be the least little bit af-

26

fected by being close to her. Unlike herself. This rapidly increasing attraction must be one-sided. Her to him, not him to her.

"What happened to the rope?"

"What rope?" he asked.

She stared up but saw nothing except blue sky. No sign of the hole hovered overhead. No rope dangled down, offering rescue. "Never mind. So, where's my cat?"

"When I couldn't return through the hole, I postponed my search. You're predictable. I assumed it would only be a matter of time"—Vorador motioned toward the sky—"until you dropped in. I waited for your arrival so we could search together. Otherwise, you would be lost, as well as your cat."

"All right, Mr. Smarty Wiz—Hey, wait a minute. You can't get out of here?"

Vorador shook his head.

"Why?"

"My magic doesn't work here."

He said the words in a flat, unemotional voice, but Petra could guess how much that bothered him. A wizard without his magic was like a . . . well, it was pretty bad.

She thought of at least a dozen things she wanted to say to him. Deciding to exhibit a rare burst of restraint, she instead turned her attention to their surroundings. They stood in the middle of a paved road. Not a new road of fresh asphalt, but one patched and repaired many times. Beyond the concrete, desert stretched as far as she could see in every direction. There were cacti, small stunted bushes and trees and large boulders. It reminded her a lot of New Mexico. Coincidence?

No sun hung in the blue sky, but light came from somewhere. A cool breeze lifted her hair, making the heat less oppressive. As far as she could tell, they were the only two living creatures that inhabited the strange landscape.

"So," she said at last, "no magic? None at all?"

"No."

"Which means an even stronger wizard than you set up this whole trap."

"Yes."

She could tell how much that admission pained him. She'd bet he was used to being the best. "Narrows the field, I imagine."

"It is a rather short list."

"Got any enemies on it?"

"None I was aware of."

Petra's chuckle didn't go over well with the wizard. Geez, the man had absolutely no sense of humor.

"Okay, Mr. Wizard, we might as well look for Bosco. Any idea in which direction he went?"

Vorador pointed, gesturing toward one leg of the road.

"How can you be sure?"

He indicated something near where he stood.

Hesitating briefly, she inched closer to see. "Oh. Okay."

Without another word, the wizard walked away, following the set of little paw prints in the sandy dirt beside the highway. With a sigh and a shrug, Petra fell in behind him. She knew it was only her imagination, but her tongue already felt dry and swollen. How long did it take to die of thirst?

What seemed like hours later, Petra couldn't stand it any longer. If they trudged along in utter silence for one more minute she would go stark, raving mad. She had to do something to take her mind off the view. Walking behind the wizard like this, one thing filled her sight—him. Her fantasies had become downright lewd.

"Will you stop it?" Petra's shout echoed, then slowly faded away in the distance.

Vorador, halted and turned to face her. "If I stop walking, how will we accomplish our goal of rescuing your cat?"

Petra couldn't look at him. There could be only one explanation for her behavior. He must have used a powerful charming spell, maybe even a love spell. But why would he waste a perfectly good spell when he didn't seem to notice her? Could such a spell even be in effect with his magic nullified?

She wasn't about to discuss the matter with him. If he *wasn't* using a charming/love spell, she would look the fool if she admitted how attractive—attractive? Heck, he had become darned near irresistible. Petra took a deep breath. She would take charge of her own emotions. She would—She shouldn't be staring there!

She had no interest in anything to do with romance at this point in her life. It would take months, not weeks—and certainly not just a few short hours—to wipe out the ugly memories of Harold and—

"Hey!" She spun back to face Vorador. "What did you mean when you called me predictable?"

"I beg your pardon?" He looked utterly confused at her unexpected and unrelated demand.

She jerked her thumb over her shoulder. "Back there. You said you didn't want to search for Bosco until I arrived. How did you know I'd show up?"

Vorador looked at her, an irritating eyebrow cocked skyward.

"No." She pointed a finger at him for emphasis. "Just because you waited, and just because I showed up, does not make me predictable."

"Perhaps you know a different definition of the word?"

"I am not predictable," she insisted with more force.

"Why does the idea distress you so, Miss Field?"

Petra wasn't about to tell him. "None of your business."

Vorador stared at her in a speculative manner for several moments. "I understand," he said, then turned and continued on.

Grateful for the reprieve, Petra fell into step behind him. She didn't know which frightened her more—the thought that Vorador might be able to read her mind, or the way she couldn't stop staring at his butt. Because she was doing it again. His robe might be loose, but with every stride she managed to catch tantalizing glimpses of his rear and she continued to hope for more.

Forcing her gaze to the ground, she plodded along and contemplated her behavior. She had never reacted to a man like this before, never had such a strong physical reaction. Oh, she'd found men attractive in the past, but this mind-fogging lust was a first. There had to be some very strong magic in play.

Well, duh. Petra smacked herself on the forehead with the heel of her hand. Since she was nonmagical, spells tended to affect her in unexpected ways. No wonder she was ready to wrestle Vorador to the ground and make wild, passionate love to him.

"Thank heavens," she said.

"I beg your pardon?"

"I am so glad. None of this is my fault," she blurted without thinking.

He stopped abruptly and she nearly ran into him. She looked up at Vorador's angry glare and took a step backward.

"Oh, no. I didn't mean . . . That is, what I meant . . ." She gave up. "Sorry."

He nodded stiffly. "If you have nothing more to add to this scintillating conversation, I suggest we continue on our way."

"Sure," she agreed, glad he didn't press the issue. Hurrying to match his long strides, she had to ask, "Mind if I take the lead for awhile?"

She breathed a sigh of relief when he waved her to go ahead. As she walked, she became conscious of the wizard behind her.

What was he looking at while they walked along? Did he stare at her butt? She wished she'd put on jeans instead of these old sweatpants. Was he staring at her hair? Then again, maybe he didn't even like light-brown, almost-blond, wavy hair. Maybe he preferred short hair, not shoulder length like hers.

Maybe he was a leg man. What if he speculated about the shape of her legs hidden inside the baggy gray sweats? Petra suddenly wished she'd kept her New Year's resolution to spend more time at the gym. She carried only a few extra pounds but knew she was in horrible physical condition.

Incredibly self-conscious, Petra tripped, even though nothing blocked her path. If not for Vorador's quick reaction she would have sprawled face-first in the sandy dirt.

"Thanks."

Vorador simply nodded and motioned for her to proceed.

She shook her head. She couldn't go on like this. "Listen, why don't we walk side by side?"

"As you wish."

Grateful he agreed so easily, she started walking again. It didn't lessen her intense awareness of his presence beside her, but at least he was out of her direct line of sight.

30

"Do you see that?"

Vorador's voice startled Petra. In spite of her best efforts, she'd been lost in a daydream that could only be rated NC-17. At least he had interrupted her before it became pornographic.

"See what?" she asked.

"There, up on that small hill. Do you see lights?"

She squinted in the direction in which he pointed. There were several flickering points of light. "Yeah, I do."

Petra picked up her lagging pace. With any luck they could find Bosco, discover some way out of this hellhole and she could return to her nice boring life. Well, once her house was back to normal it would be boring. Which would suit her just fine. The past twenty-four hours had more than convinced her; adventure was vastly overrated.

"I don't believe it." Petra stopped on the stairs.

Vorador moved onto the rickety porch. "Why would you disbelieve this more than anything else that has happened?"

It was a valid question, she supposed, but his matter-of-fact tone irked her anyway. Following him, she demanded, "Isn't this just a little bit *too* weird?"

He paused to survey their surroundings. "Perhaps."

A pink neon sign announced their arrival at THE HOTEL CALIFORNIA. Why a hotel? Under her house? She didn't live in California. Even magic should make some sense. Shouldn't it?

Paint, faded to gray, peeled off the weathered walls. The front of the one-storied wooden building looked more like a motel than a hotel. She could see several wings angled off in different directions. Everything looked slightly out of kilter, not quite the right size or shape. There was something familiar about the place. With a shudder, she made the connection.

"Gads, it looks like *Psycho Meets Picasso*."

Before Vorador could answer, the office door slowly creaked open. Petra sidled closer to her companion, her heart pounding. If Norman Bates appeared, she was out of here.

A tall figure stood in the doorway.

"Who is it?" Petra whispered, clutching Vorador's sleeve.

He didn't answer, all his attention focused on the stranger.

It had to be the wizard who'd created this place. Petra prepared herself to either duck or run. The silhouette moved forward. He certainly knew how to make an entrance.

"Well, well, well," Vorador said.

His soft words, spoken in an amused tone, made Petra want to smack the smile right off his lips. The newcomer was a woman, not a man. "You know her?"

"I do. You may release me now, Miss Field. There is no danger."

Not at all sure about that, Petra let go of his sleeve and eyed the other woman. She was tall and statuesque. She filled out her skimpy leather outfit admirably. Her legs looked never-ending, the muscles well defined. She obviously never missed a day at the gym. Her long black hair hung past her hips. Her lips were bright red, her eyes so green they looked fake. Pale, flawless skin completed the picture. Petra hated her on sight.

"It's about time you got here, Vorador," the stranger said. "I've been waiting."

The woman's voice drifted through the air, low and sultry. She had no visible flaws. Petra suddenly realized what her adversary was. Oh, it just kept getting better. She was stuck in a hole with an Amazon.

"Hello, Kitty. How're you doing?"

Petra glared at Vorador, dismayed by the fond tone he used.

"I've been better," Kitty said.

"We were worried about you," he said. "No one has seen you since—"

"Excuse me." Petra interrupted the tender reunion. "I hate to break this up, but could I possibly have a drink of water?"

Kitty waved a hand toward the door. "Help yourself."

Indignant at being so easily dismissed, Petra shot one last glare at her wizard, then stomped inside. Well, wasn't this a revolting development?

Chapter Five

As he watched her go, Vorador knew Petra would hate his delighted grin. She amused him in such unexpected and enchanting ways. He'd never met anyone quite like Petra W. Field before. Kitoka made a crude noise, interrupting his thoughts.

"You damn well better remember my name is Kitoka. I never want to be called Kitty again."

Used to her brash manner, Vorador led her to a bench under the office window. "Where've you been? Dugan's been worried about you."

"Damn him!"

Vorador ran a soothing hand down her arm, ignoring the outburst. There had been bad blood between Kitoka and Dugan ever since Dugan had met Medora, Kitoka's sister, at a charitable event two months earlier. Instant attraction had zinged between Dugan and Medora. They had started dating, even though Amazons didn't generally indulge in casual relationships with men.

Vorador had heard rumors of the sisters' arguments. Kitoka hated Dugan for coming between her and Medora. Matters had come to a head when Medora had been attacked during a robbery three weeks ago. He supposed by Amazon logic it was understandable that Kitoka blamed Dugan for her sister's injury.

"He shouldn't have taken Medora," Kitoka insisted.

Following the out-of-sequence jump in the conversation, Vorador said, "Dugan had to act fast. He couldn't take time to ask questions and wait for permission."

"I know your friend stole my sister's body after she was murdered—a murder that was his fault."

Startled by the direct accusation, Vorador leaned forward, his voice intense. "How do you know that?"

"He's a man, isn't he? They're to blame for everything."

His tension eased. For a second he'd forgotten he was talking to a man-hating Amazon. "Of course."

Bright enough to pick up on his sarcasm, she punched his shoulder—hard.

The fact that his arm remained attached to his body told Vorador she wasn't really angry. "Have you found any clues about who committed the crime?"

Kitoka opened her mouth to reply, paused, then slowly slumped against the wall behind the bench. "I don't remember."

He gave her time to collect herself, and himself time to think. The two sisters had wielded much of the power in the Seattle Amazon Kingdom. Only the queen ruled above them. Medora was the clan's chief wizard. Kitoka commanded the Amazon Guards but had limited magical powers. That meant somebody else had put her here in this magic realm. Normally she was the fiercest of warriors. Mourning her sister had apparently weakened her.

At least he could relieve that much of her worry. "I'm sorry. I thought you knew. Dugan didn't steal Medora's body. He brought her to me."

"To you? Why?"

"When he arrived at her apartment, she wasn't quite dead. A small part of her spirit remains in her body. I can keep her in that state. Which gives us time to find the culprit."

"She's not dead?"

"She's mostly dead, but not completely dead."

34

"You can fix that?"

Vorador nodded. "Once we discover who tried to kill her, I can use some of his blood to construct the proper spell and bring her back to full life. Until then I'm using a general spell. Which is enough to keep her stable for now."

"She not dead!" The joy shone through her exuberant shout.

Vorador turned away to give Kitoka privacy until she conquered her emotions. He studied the hotel with professional curiosity. The entire landscape was a complex construction, which hadn't wavered even once since their arrival. Why Hotel California? That had to be a clue.

He didn't know many wizards in Seattle who had enough power to work the spell. As Petra had pointed out, it was a short list. Medora was on it, but hardly a likely candidate. The others were Landru, Zyrillus, Balok and Kollos.

Oh, yes, and Fytch. Her power might, or might not, be strong enough to pull off these spells, but he couldn't exclude her. If he listened to his own personal prejudice, he'd put Fytch's name at the top of the list of suspects. Although he couldn't imagine why she would do this, or what she hoped to gain.

"What a mess," Kitoka said.

Vorador returned his attention to the Amazon beside him. "Where have you been for the past three weeks?"

"You aren't going to believe where I've been. It's been the worst torture. I don't know how I've managed to remain sane."

"Tell me." He compelled her to hold nothing back, purposely making his voice calm and soothing. He might not be able to use his magic to cast a spell, but the principles remained the same.

"Somebody turned me into a cat," Kitoka said, her voice flat.

A cat? They were searching for a cat. It was too much of a coincidence.

"A *male* cat," Kitoka spat out.

He couldn't help it. He laughed. He regretted it when she punched him, then again and again, but he couldn't stop. He held up his hands to ward off her blows. "Play nice, Kitty."

When she came at him, nails extended and teeth bared, Vorador beat a hasty retreat. "I'm sorry, Kitoka. Please forgive me."

When he saw the battle lust had faded from her eyes, he allowed her to back him up against the wall. Her hand closed around his throat. He didn't think she would kill him. At least she wasn't wearing her sword or dagger, or he'd be dead already.

"I'm sorry. That was in extremely bad taste."

"Yes, it was." Applying more pressure to his throat, Kitoka hissed in a low, harsh voice, "Do you have any idea what it's like to be trapped in a male body? To suffer the indignity of all those raging hormones? To endure uncontrollable mating urges? To have those disgusting ba—"

She halted abruptly, jerked herself away from him and wiped her hand against the wall as if to get the very touch of him off herself. "Never mind. I guess you have a pretty good idea."

Fighting the urge to laugh again, Vorador saw the situation from her point of view. It would be the worst possible torture for an Amazon warrior to be trapped inside a male body—even a male cat's body. Whoever cast the spell on Kitoka had wanted to punish her in a cruel, sadistic manner.

His thoughts returned to Fytch. He always had thought her sneaky and underhanded. In spite of that, he wasn't sure she was capabable of murder. She might spread damaging rumors behind Dugan's and Medora's backs, but direct confrontation wasn't her style. Plus she had a squeamish streak a mile wide. It wasn't conceivable that Fytch had stabbed Medora. Fytch couldn't stand the sight of blood.

Nor did she have any motivation. True, Fytch and Dugan had been a hot item at one time. When it ended several years ago they had managed to remain friends. Maybe because Vorador had kept his mouth shut and never revealed to Dugan just how horrible he knew Fytch really was.

Kitoka had calmed down, so he asked, "Who did this to you?"

"I don't remember." She slammed her fist into the wall beside his head.

Apparently not calm enough. Not moving, Vorador considered her words for a moment. "An amnesia spell?"

"It must be. I remember I found Medora's body. After I called 911, I made a blood vow to find her killer. I heard the sirens and left, certain she was safe."

36

"Where did you go?"

"I . . . I think . . . there was some clue in Medora's apartment."

"What? An object the killer left behind? A footprint or a trail? A scent? Were you a cat? Or still a woman?"

"Damn it. I told you, I don't remember."

"All right. What happened next?"

Silence hung heavy as Kitoka struggled to pierce the darkness in her mind. She finally shook her head. "When I went to the burial hall—"

"As a cat?"

"Yes, damn you!" She swallowed hard and fought to regain control. "Medora's body wasn't there. My sisters talked about how Dugan had stolen her. I remember searching for him, to kill him."

"Only him? You didn't search for anyone else?"

"No, only Dugan. I know there was an important clue in her apartment. I just don't remember what it was. It has to lead to him." She punched the wall over and over.

Afraid she would do serious damage to herself, he slowly made his way back to the bench, hoping she would follow him. It frustrated him not to have magic available to help him manipulate people. Until now he'd underestimated how dependent he truly was on his spells to get things done.

"Do you have any idea why some wizard would set up this elaborate trap?"

Kitoka stopped trying to knock down the wall with her bare hands and joined him. "They didn't."

Even though it made him uncomfortable to have her towering over him, Vorador allowed her the advantage. "Then how—?"

"It was—"

"Never mind," he cut her off. A few of the pieces fell into place and Vorador shook his head. He should have recognized the work. Damn it, he should have recognized the rug.

It had been staring him right in the face, but he'd been too blind to see it. Dugan had undoubtedly figured it out last night. Why hadn't he said anything? Well, actually he had. It all revolved around Petra's stupid pigs. "The rug."

37

"Exactly," Kitoka confirmed. "I thought you knew, since you said you took Medora from her apartment."

"I didn't. There was something familiar about Petra's rug, something that nagged in the back of my mind, but I didn't put it together until now."

"Gee, and here I thought the Grand Vorador was infallible."

If only. Even now it made him uncomfortable to remember why he hadn't been in top form. When he had walked into that house last night, it had only taken one glance to turn him into a bumbling, tongue-tied, sweaty-palmed imbecile. *Stunned* was too mild a description for his reaction to one Petra W. Field.

He had caught a whiff of her light, fruity perfume lingering under the scent of the vanilla candles. She'd been a mouthwatering sight in her slinky red dress. He'd wanted to peel it off and spend hours exploring every inch of her lush body. He still wasn't sure what had caused the explosion of intense sexual heat. It had slammed through his body like a bomb blast. It'd been a long time since a woman had turned him into an idiot.

Although his stupidity could just as easily have been caused by the shock of discovering Petra had no magic. Absolutely none! Not a drop. Ninety-nine percent of the population had at least a trace of skill or talent, even if it remained latent. Totally nonmagical people were quite rare. It had been years since he'd run across any. He firmly pushed those memories away.

"I only saw Medora's rug for a few seconds that night," he said. "The paramedics had their equipment scattered everywhere. The rug was barely visible underneath it all."

"Make you feel better to justify your mistake, wizard?"

Vorador would have liked to believe Kitoka was teasing him, but he couldn't quite pull it off. More likely she wanted to take a knife to him for his mistake.

"Listen, I've looked everywhere and there's no sign of Bosco." Petra clomped across the porch and rejoined the couple. "Can we get out of here now?"

Vorador exchanged a look with Kitoka, who very deliberately shook her head. He nodded his agreement at her. Petra didn't need to know Kitoka was really Bosco the cat. Under normal circumstances he wouldn't have worried too much about keeping Kitoka happy, but Petra was no match for the warrior. Nor did he want Petra involved in this attempted murder case any more than necessary.

He slanted a glance sideways at Kitoka.

Petra smiled. Was Vorador afraid the warrior would try to pound her into the ground? Amazons would never do serious physical harm to another woman, especially not an unarmed one. True, Kitty might want to hit her, and might even give in to the urge, but she would die herself before she caused Petra serious injury. That was the Amazon way. Petra supposed she should tell Vorador, but she kind of liked having him worry about her.

"Oh, brother," Kitty murmured and turned away.

"Well, excuse me," Petra shot back. "By the way, why don't *you* get us out of here?"

"Me?" The other woman looked surprised at the suggestion.

"Yeah, you," Petra said. "After all, it's your fault we're stuck here."

"I didn't invite you to come along. I just wanted Vorador—"

"Ladies." Vorador moved between the two of them, as if prepared for the worst. "Petra, I think you misunderstood Kitty's part in this adventure."

Petra looked the Amazon up and down. "I don't think I've misunderstood a thing."

"She's not a wizard."

"Oh." Petra considered that revelation. "Well, if she's not the wizard, and she didn't cast the spell, then who did?"

"We can discuss that once we return to your house." Vorador started toward the office.

"Where are you going?" Petra demanded.

"The registration desk." He paused in the doorway. "Maybe we can check out."

"What about her?" Kitty jerked her head in Petra's direction as she followed him inside the hotel.

His voice floated out to where Petra stubbornly held firm on the porch. "She'll catch up once she figures it out."

"Are you certain she's capable?" Petra heard Kitty ask.

"I don't doubt it," came the wizard's voice. "She's a bright girl."

What could she do after that compliment? Sighing, Petra followed them.

Chapter Six

"I still don't understand." Petra flopped down on her couch and scowled at Vorador as if it were his fault. Which it was. "We shouldn't have been able to get out of that stupid hotel so easily."

"Disappointed?"

She scowled harder, wishing she dared utter one word and send him up in flames. If only it would leave him a smoldering pile of ashes. Unfortunately, as she'd witnessed earlier, his flames were cold.

They were in her living room. After he had completed the form to check them out at the hotel's front desk, they had popped right back here. The abrupt shift had left her dizzy and confused. Even more so upon discovering that the wizard held Bosco in his arms.

"I've already explained it to you. That spell wasn't constructed by an enemy in an attempt to trap us. I believe it was placed there as an aid in solving another mystery. One that has no connection to you."

41

Ah ha; she had guessed right last night. The blood was from an older crime. It had nothing to do with anything that had gone on in her house. However, it obviously was a crime that Vorador was familiar with.

"You couldn't get us out the way we went in, but we could check out?"

"Exactly."

Curious, both about the crime and whether he would actually tell her anything, she asked, "So, did you find any clues?"

"I was able to gather some information."

Bosco jumped into Vorador's lap.

"What kind of information? About the blood? The rug?"

Vorador merely nodded with a grimace, while the cat used his leg as a scratching post.

"Can you get rid of the bloodstain?"

"Not at this time."

"For some reason, Wiz Boy, I like it that you don't have all the answers."

"How gracious of you."

"Now who's being sarcastic?" Petra teased him.

Vorador didn't respond.

"So, about this other mystery . . . ?"

Bosco renewed his efforts and the wizard winced when sharp claws dug into his leg. He picked up the cat by the scruff of its neck. "Behave yourself, Kitty," he ordered, before dropping the animal on the floor.

"Are you trying to avoid my question, O Mighty All-Seeing All-Knowing Powerful Wizard?"

"It doesn't concern you, Miss Field. Which is why I was reluctant to mention it to you in the first place."

She grinned, enjoying his dilemma. "I guess you don't know me well enough yet to know I won't drop the matter."

"Hope springs eternal."

"Then gets dashed on the rocks."

"Of your stubbornness."

Refusing to be insulted, since he was absolutely correct, she went back to his original statement and his reluctance to talk.

"About this other mystery—once you told me about it, you knew I would get involved."

He nodded.

"You really don't have much choice, though, do you?"

He slowly shook his head.

"Because you don't intend to close up that hole just yet, do you? You plan to pop in and out until you solve this other mystery, don't you?" She laughed at the surprised look on his face.

He recovered much too quickly, then went on the attack. "Where did you get this rug, Petra? Did it come with the house? Or did you purchase it elsewhere?"

Irritated by the fact that he still hadn't responded to her questions, she nonetheless answered his. "I bought it. At a flea market."

"Here in Seattle?" Vorador disengaged the cat climbing his leg.

"Yeah, at that big one they hold out at the fairgrounds."

"Do you have the person's name from whom you bought it?" He wasn't as gentle this time in getting rid of Bosco. The cat landed several yards away.

"Nope, and I paid cash, so there's no canceled check or credit card receipt."

When he made no comment, Petra strolled over to stare down at the rug with its offending hole. It was just an ordinary-looking rug, rather worn in places. A country design of various colored pigs bordered the pale blue center. It had been that design that prompted her to buy it. Her decorating tastes ran the gamut, no one particular style dominating. However, she did follow one consistent trend: she couldn't resist anything with pigs on it. Even if the item was ugly as sin, she thought with a rueful smile.

Thinking out loud, she repeated what few facts she knew. "It's the rug, huh? Somehow that blood created this hole. Somebody was killed on the rug." Petra spun to face Vorador. "It was a wizard, wasn't it?"

"No one was killed." He grabbed the cat by the scruff of the neck, pulling the animal out of his lap before its claws found some very sensitive part of his anatomy. He brought the feline up until they were face to face. "Why don't you go chase a mouse or something?"

"A wizard was murdered on my rug. Great balls of fi—"

Vorador dropped the cat, shot out of his seat and slapped his hand over Petra's mouth just in time. She looked up at him, her eyes wide with surprise. Comprehension dawned and she realized what she'd almost said.

She silently mouthed *oops,* her lips moving against his palm. She took a deep breath and immediately regretted it. Standing this close to him, his fresh ocean scent surrounded her. A shiver ran down her spine. She felt light-headed. Nothing in her life up until now had ever felt more wonderful. Without thinking, her tongue flicked out and lightly tasted his skin.

He jumped back as if he'd received a jolt from a live wire. Petra waited to see if he rubbed his hand against his robe to wipe off her touch. Instead he curled his fingers into a fist, as if he held tight to the memory of her small caress. Either that or he fought the urge to punch her.

Hardly daring to blink, she stared up at him, and a warm thrill shot through her. His breathing came harder and faster too. He wasn't as unaffected as he wanted her to believe. They might have stayed like that forever if the doorbell hadn't rung.

Vorador broke eye contact first. "That must be Dugan. I called him while you were in the bathroom."

Petra made it to the couch right before her knees folded. Her breath whooshed out in a loud sigh. She just about had her wits gathered by the time the two men entered the room.

Once again Dugan's overwhelming charisma struck her like a sledgehammer. It literally pressed her back in her seat. After that first blast it settled down to a dull roar. He was handsome enough, but his blond good looks appeared almost washed out and colorless next to Vorador's dark vibrancy. Dugan's charm might have been on high, but the wizard's was by far the more potent of the two.

She wondered . . . "Why—?"

Bosco streaked out of the kitchen, yowling at the top of his lungs, and launched himself straight at Dugan's face. Lucky for

Dugan, he had quick reflexes and managed to get an arm up to block the attack. The cat twisted in an amazing acrobatic movement and dug into Dugan's chest with the claws on all four paws.

Lightning quick, Vorador grabbed the animal by the back of the neck. Carefully removing each claw from Dugan's robe, and the skin underneath, Vorador pulled Bosco away. The wizard was the only one who didn't look unnerved.

"What in the world?" Petra had to speak over the enraged snarls, growls and hisses coming from the unhappy feline as it twisted in Vorador's grasp.

"I don't think your pet likes me, Miss Field." Dugan held his ground but kept a watchful eye on the cat. "Think you could lock him up somewhere?"

She jumped to her feet and started to take Bosco, but Vorador froze her with a look. A look that warned her to sit back down. A look that immediately rubbed her the wrong way. "Don't you tell me what to do in my own house."

He held the angry cat at arm's length and merely cocked that one irritating brow at her.

Moving closer, Petra glared at Vorador. Her shoulder whacked into his chest and she got distracted. Gad, the man was as solid as a brick wall. Her insides went all wobbly. She was in sad shape if such brief contact could turn her into a complete basket case.

"Doggone it, will you stop doing that?" She reached around the cat and poked Vorador on the chest. Okay, not so much to emphasize her point, rather to check out his muscles a little more closely.

"Your face is all flushed and you're trembling, Miss Field."

"No, I'm not." She hid her unsteady hands behind her back.

"Nor is this the first time you've displayed such a reaction. But to what, I wonder?"

"Well, don't wonder any longer. It's an allergic reaction."

"To what?" he softly repeated.

"To wizards."

She glared up at him, defying him to question her further.

Bosco gave a plaintive meow, reminding the humans he still

dangled there in midair in a very undignified position.

Again, Vorador was the first to break eye contact. He handed the now calm cat to Petra. "Perhaps you should put your pet in the bathroom until Dugan leaves."

She nodded, not trusting her voice to come out steady. Darn it. Why did he have to affect her like this? She hated it. Yeah, right. She buried her snort of self-disgust in Bosco's fur, then carried him away to exile.

Chapter Seven

"What's with the cat?" Dugan asked as soon as Petra left the room.

"I'll tell you later," Vorador said. He knew she wouldn't waste any time getting back to ask the same question. The answer he gave her wouldn't be the same one he gave Dugan.

He was right. She returned in seconds. "Maybe you should widen the spectrum of that charming spell to include cats," she suggested to the room in general.

Dugan shot a questioning glance at Vorador, as if he wondered if such a spell was possible.

Vorador refused to take her bait. He didn't intend to discuss spells and magic with her. If she wanted an argument, she could go elsewhere. He would wait her out, certain she would break the silence first.

"Is there something wrong with my charming spell?" Dugan finally asked.

"Not if you don't mind being beat over the head with a two-by-four," Petra said. "It isn't exactly subtle."

Her analysis impressed Vorador. "I told you it was too much," he reminded Dugan.

Petra gave a huge sigh. "Well, I'm glad to know I didn't totally misjudge you after all."

For some reason, Vorador was glad to hear her say so. Yeah, he had cast the charming spell for Dugan, and it was too strong and overbearing. He'd only done it because Dugan had insisted. His friend just didn't understand subtlety.

Dugan smoothed his robe, his expression one of insulted pride. "Nobody has ever complained about its strength before."

Petra merely smiled.

Vorador itched to cast an honesty spell on her. What wicked thoughts put such a mischievous gleam in her eyes? He'd done similar spells in the past with other women, wanting to verify their intent before he pursued a relationship. For some reason he hesitated to use his enchantment skills on Petra. Could it have something to do with her lack of magic? A fact that both tantalized and repelled him. It forced him to recall matters long buried. Matters he refused to think about.

She was different in other ways too. For starters, she had absolutely no respect for his status as a sorcerer. Her disdain must stem from being raised around magic. He'd done some checking and knew both her parents were registered as wizards. Most people treated a wizard with wary deference. The general population tended to tread with caution around those with strong magical powers.

Not Petra W. Field.

"Maybe that's what Bosco objected to," Petra finally said.

It took Vorador a moment to figure out that she meant Dugan's charming spell. He sincerely doubted that was all Kitty had in mind when she tried to kill Dugan. Good thing she was still in cat form or she might have succeeded.

Dugan repeated his question. "Why did her cat attack me?"

"I don't know," Vorador lied through his teeth.

No way he wanted their client involved in this situation any more than absolutely necessary. There was a murderer running around Seattle and Petra had no powers with which to protect

48

herself. Or enough sense to know she might be in danger.

Whether she realized it or not, Dugan's statement last night was completely true: All ERG customers remained under Vorador's protection until the job had been completed. It was a vow he never broke. No one would ever again be harmed while under his care.

With grim determination, he pushed painful memories aside.

"Oh, by the way. I almost forgot." Dugan held out an envelope to Petra. "This was stuck in your front door."

Petra opened it and withdrew a business card. Turning it over, she found a handwritten note on the back.

"Who's it from?" Vorador asked, curiosity overcoming good manners.

She showed it to him.

He read the note. With a vile curse, he ripped the Rapid Renovations card into shreds and tossed the pieces into the air. They burst into flames, then vanished with a puff of smoke. "You will not call her."

Petra glared at him through the lingering wisps of smoke. "Don't even begin to think you can tell me—"

"You're no match for her, Petra. She is—"

"Who're you guys talking about?" Dugan interrupted them both.

Vorador's voice was cold with distaste as he said, "Fytch."

Dugan grinned at Petra. "Don't listen to him. For some reason—which he's never bothered to explain—he doesn't like Fytch."

"She's your business competitor?" Petra asked.

"She's a conniving witch. Don't trust her," Vorador warned, wanting to say more. As always, friendship held him back. The truth would hurt Dugan, so Vorador kept his secret.

"We're amiable rivals," Dugan said. "We get together every so often and trade war stories about the cleaning business. At one time she and I even dated, but it ended on friendly terms."

Petra looked from one man to the other. "Okay, which one of you should I believe?"

Vorador sighed in defeat. Petra walked a very fine line and could easily fall into dangerous territory. She just didn't know it yet. With Fytch nosing around, it looked like it was up to him to keep Petra safe after all. He didn't like Fytch, didn't respect her, but mostly he didn't trust her.

In the past she'd proven she would stoop to almost any depth to get what she wanted. He'd been vastly relieved when Dugan and Fytch had ended their romance. She'd done everything in her power to suck Dugan into her web of lies and deceit. And managed to snare him as well, Vorador grimly acknowledged. He couldn't allow the same to happen to Petra.

He realized Petra had said something he'd missed. "What?"

She sighed and rolled her eyes. "Try to keep up, wiz boy."

Irritated by the entire situation, his control slipped. "That might be easier if your logic followed a straight line instead of meandering off into unchartered lands."

"Well, at least I play with a full deck."

Unable to pass up the challenge, Vorador waved his hand with a flourish and snatched a card out of midair. "No, I think you're one short." He held it out for her inspection.

Petra chuckled. "Very appropriate if it's supposed to represent you."

He tried for a humble look. "Why, thank you."

Suspicious when Dugan turned a snort of laughter into a cough, Vorador looked at the card. For a moment he simply could not believe his eyes. He stared at it as if he'd never seen such a thing before. Truthfully, he hadn't. He'd meant for it to be the King of Hearts. He held a Joker. He had conjured the wrong card!

One look into Petra's laughing blue eyes almost made him call for fire to incinerate the offensive image. Instead he slipped the leering Joker into his pocket.

"Now, as I said, before you so rudely interrupted," Petra continued, unrepentant, "I'll talk to Fytch if she shows up, but I don't feel any burning need to give her a call."

Vorador held his breath for a few seconds. Would her "burning need" cause problems? He felt the familiar tingle. Of course it had. She'd set his balls on fire. Hoping nothing showed under the robe, he quietly and quickly vanquished the magic flames. He feared his resulting hard-on wouldn't disappear so easily.

"I have to wonder why you dislike her so much, Mr. Wizard," Petra went on, oblivious to his discomfort. "Bet there's an interesting story behind the whole thing."

"So," Dugan said in an obvious ploy to change the subject, "what's with this hole?"

Vorador ignored Petra and answered Dugan. He had a few bones to pick with his boss about this assignment. "That's what happens when somebody else's magic interferes with one of my spells."

"Hmmm. Interesting," was all Dugan said before a high-pitched beeping sound came from his pocket. He fumbled around until he pulled out his pager. He quickly read the message.

"I gotta go."

"What's wrong?" Vorador followed him to the door. "Do you need me?"

"Hey, wait a minute." Following in their wake, Petra protested. "I've still got a bunch of questions for you, slick."

"No," Dugan answered Vorador, "I can handle it. Zaylin's got the scissors again." He hurried out the door, speaking over his shoulder. "Vorador can handle you, Miss Field."

Then he was gone.

Petra stared at the wall after Dugan's final command. "Don't even think about it," she muttered.

A small smile tugged at the corners of his mouth. He could tell she had tried for a stern warning, but her breathy tone fell short. Instead of a reprimand, it sounded like an invitation. Did she think about him handling her?

"Are you hungry, Miss Field?"

She steadied herself against the couch and a soft groan slipped out. "How did you know?"

A jolt of electricity shot down Vorador's spine at her velvety tone. Great googgly-mooggly! Was she purring? He'd been playing with her up until that moment. All he wanted to do now was say a few words and make that ugly sweatsuit disappear.

"Lunch," he managed to croak. "Will you join me for lunch?"

"Sure." Her voice wavered as much as his. She cleared her throat. "As long as you pay."

51

"My treat." Yes, it would be a treat to spend more time with her. Vorador turned to go before things could deteriorate any further. A small sound from Petra stopped him. "What?"

"I guess I do have one other condition."

"Which is?"

"Could you lose the robe?"

He glanced down at his clothing. "You don't like my robe?"

"Well, it's okay. If your goal is to impress the clients with that Merlin look."

"I have a condition of my own, in that case."

"Which is?" She sounded much more leery than he had.

"Could you lose the sweats?"

Smiling, she spread her arms. "Don't like sloppy casual?"

"Well, it's okay," he repeated her words with a smile. "If you're trying for that Gladys the maid look."

She laughed. "All right. I'll change if you will."

"You've got yourself a deal." He bent and grabbed the hem of his robe. He started to straighten up.

Petra felt several things happen all at once. She couldn't catch her breath, her heart started to pound, her palms got sweaty and her eyes widened until they felt ready to pop out of her head. He meant to disrobe. Right here. Right now. The burning question would be answered. No room would be left for doubt. Briefs? Or boxers?

The velvet hem rose to his calves . . . his knees . . . mid-thighs. Her breath caught in her throat. Everything else in the room faded except that bunch of green cloth clutched between his hands.

In one swift movement Vorador whipped the robe up and over his head.

She blinked and it was too late. The wizard stood before her dressed in stylish black slacks and a lightweight black V-neck sweater. At this point she couldn't have said if his legs had been bare during the unveiling or already covered by pants. Not a strand of his long dark hair was out of place. He looked good enough to be an advertisement in *GQ*. Disappointment left a bitter taste in her mouth.

"Tell me, wiz boy, can you really work a spell that fast? Or were you already wearing those clothes under your robe?"

"You don't expect me to give away trade secrets, do you?"

She sent him a disgusted look and headed toward her bedroom. With no magical powers of her own, she would change clothes the old-fashioned way, and behind closed doors.

Chapter Eight

Petra stood in the foyer of the restaurant, waiting while Vorador parked the car. He hadn't trusted the valet to park his precious brand-new Jaguar. What was it with men and their cars? Looking around, she wished she'd worn a blazer with her jeans and silk shirt. She felt a little too casual for the decor.

At least waiting gave her a chance to gather her wits after being in the close confines of a car with the wizard. The rich smell of new leather combined with his tangy ocean scent had left her rattled. She needed to remember why she'd agreed to this lunch—besides the fact that she couldn't resist the opportunity to spend more time with Vorador. She had quite a few questions. Some answers would be nice.

If only this doggone lust didn't poke its head into every conversation she tried to have with him. She needed to keep her wits instead of melting into a puddle of yearning hormones. Okay, that was it. No more.

"Business before pleasure," she reminded herself.

"Is that a promise or a threat?"

Startled by the question whispered in her ear, Petra jumped. She jabbed her elbow back into Vorador's ribs.

"Don't sneak up on me."

"Then I suggest you not get so involved in talking to yourself that you aren't aware of what's going on around you."

"At least I'm sure of intelligent conversation."

She didn't need to see him to know he cocked that irritating eyebrow at her. Without waiting for him, she yanked open the door and entered the restaurant. He greeted the maître d' like an old friend. Even though several people were waiting, they were ushered to one of the best tables by a large window that framed a fantastic view of Seattle's skyline. For once, no clouds marred the glorious sunny day, and Mt. Rainier was visible in the distance.

Seated across from the wizard, she feared this would be a very long lunch. She wanted to smack him, and shake him, and kiss him—all at the same time. That thought made her smile. Now wouldn't that be an interesting way to spend the afternoon?

"What's so amusing?" Vorador asked.

"Nothing."

What did it hurt to indulge in a few innocent daydreams? Oh, good grief, what was she doing? She couldn't hold her resolve for five stinking minutes? So much for the pep talk. It was strictly business from this point on.

The waiter appeared with a bottle of wine and offered it to Vorador for his approval. After the wizard nodded, the waiter busied himself opening it.

"Can I just have a Diet Coke, please?"

"Of course." Vorador waved the waiter to leave the bottle. He poured himself a small amount, tasted it, made a sound of approval, then filled his glass.

"Am I going to get to drive your spiffy new car home after lunch?" she asked.

For a moment he looked bewildered; then his expression cleared and he chuckled. "No, I'm not going to get drunk. I'm

55

having one glass. I'll take the rest home to enjoy later."

Before she could respond, a different waiter appeared with a plate of fresh shrimp on ice. Another waiter delivered her soda. Still another brought cocktail sauce and lemon wedges.

"Gee, must be expensive when it comes time to tip them all."

Vorador simply smiled. "Would you care for some shrimp?"

So it went for the entire meal. As soon as their plates were empty, waiters served them more food. Glasses were refilled the second the last sip was taken. Nothing was ever ordered, yet when it arrived it was exactly what Petra wanted. For the most part conversation was limited to "Please pass the salt" and "Oh, this is good."

"I ate way too much," Petra said when the last dirty dish had been removed. She leaned back in her chair with a satisfied groan, wishing she dared undo the top button on her jeans.

"Are you ready to discuss business now, Miss Field?"

"You did that on purpose, didn't you?" She realized he had steered their limited mealtime conversation away from business.

When all he did was smirk and cock that blasted brow, Petra barely managed to control her temper. It certainly hadn't taken him long to learn how to push her buttons. That thought helped her remain calm. "I hope you're ready for this, Mr. Wizard."

"Ready when you are. Fire away."

"How did—Hey! You just said fi—you know what."

"Did I?"

"You know darn well you did. So where is it?"

Vorador couldn't help but be amused by Petra's combination of belligerence and curiosity. He was beginning to understand that was a basic contradiction in her personality. Wanting to keep everybody at arm's length, but dying to know all the facts. "I said, 'Fire away,' thereby sending any nearby flames—"

"Away," she finished. She cocked her head to the side. "When did you find out you had an affinity with fire?"

This wasn't a subject he wanted to discuss. With her, or anybody. "Weren't you going to ask me about Dugan?"

A long silence settled over the table. Finally she sighed. "You win. This time."

He heard her mutter, "Chicken," under her breath but let it pass. There was too much truth to that accusation.

"So, tell me, O Mighty Wizard, how did Dugan get to my house before Rapid Renovations when I didn't even call him?"

"A magic eight ball?"

"That's not an answer."

"Pure luck," he offered as second choice.

"Not good enough." She started to get up. "If you're not going to cooperate, I might as well leave. I have better things to do with my time."

Vorador's hand shot out, griping her arm, stopping her upward motion. Doing his best to ignore the tingling sensation where his skin touched hers, he said, "Don't go."

She froze for several seconds, half out of her chair. Finally she slowly sank back down.

He released a breath he hadn't even been aware he'd been holding. No, he didn't want her to leave. Even though she was certain to ask some uncomfortable questions, he wanted her to stay. He was definitely getting in over his head.

Miss Petra W. Field was big trouble. He was more attracted to her than he'd been to a woman in years. That was bad. First because she was a client. Second because . . . Was there a second reason? Other than his own reluctance to get involved in another relationship doomed to failure? He hadn't been able to make any of his previous relationships work. Would it be different with Petra? In spite of everything, he still wanted the storybook ending that fairy tales promised. Too bad reality wasn't as tidy.

Oh, yes. There was a second reason: she possessed no magic. That was enough to complicate everything.

"Excuse me, Mr. Wizard. Can I have my arm back now?"

"Please forgive me. I seem to be somewhat distracted."

"Distracted? By what?"

He didn't care for the gleam in her eyes. Oh, he liked her eyes well enough. They were a clear blue that reminded him of the ocean, or a mountain brook. He just didn't like the intense way she scrutinized him. For some reason, he didn't want her to know of his growing attraction to her just yet. It made him feel vulnerable, not a good position to be in around Petra.

"Business matters." He hoped that would appease her.

"Fine. If I have your full attention, how did Dugan get to my house so fast? How did he know to come in the first place? How did he know my name? That I was having a party? How—"

"He intercepted a radio transmission from Rapid Renovations to their crew in the truck."

"Quite by accident, right?" Petra gave a snort of laughter.

He smiled back at her.

"Rapid Renovations gave all the pertinent information when they sent their truck to your address. Dugan just happened to be closer than they were."

"I still don't understand how they got my address. I never gave it."

"Ever hear of caller ID?"

Petra nodded sheepishly.

"From there it's easy to tap into all sorts of records—realty, employment, financial, recent retail purchases."

She didn't look too happy with the idea of them poking around in her private affairs but moved on. "Exactly what does Dugan do, anyway? He's not a wizard. Why does he need that charming spell?"

"He owns the company." Vorador wouldn't mention that Dugan's own personal charm had been sufficient until he'd met the lovely Amazon, Medora. He'd been so eager to win her that he'd gone a bit overboard. "It never hurts to entice prospective clients."

Petra nodded, as if she agreed but didn't necessarily approve. "I'm still confused about this whole magic blood spot."

"Such as?" He would never admit it to her, but he had some questions himself. Dugan had been avoiding him ever since they left Petra's house the night before.

This morning you seemed surprised about the hole. As if you didn't know somebody else's magic was there and interfering with yours."

58

Yeah, that about summed up his questions. Petra definitely had brains to go along with her good looks.

"So?" she prompted when he didn't immediately go on.

He reluctantly admitted, "Dugan lied to me."

Chapter Nine

"He did what?"

Vorador couldn't blame Petra for sounding both outraged and confused. He felt the same way. "Dugan wasn't entirely truthful with me about the nature of the blood on your rug."

"But . . . why would he mislead his own wizard?"

That was another question he had for his friend and boss. "I don't know, but I mean to find out. Dugan told me Caylin's magic had backfired. He led me to assume it was her inexperienced invisibility spell that made the spot reappear. He never mentioned other magic had been previously involved."

He would never admit it to her, but from the first sight of her his thoughts had been so muddled it was a wonder he'd been able to remember his own name. "Let's just say there's a lot of misinformation floating around and leave it at that."

"No," Petra said firmly, "let's not."

Vorador sighed. He should have known she wouldn't buy that line. "I won't have any definite answers till I talk to Dugan. There must have already been an invisibility spell on the rug. I don't imagine even you would buy a bloodstained rug."

"Is that an insult?"

"No." He wisely decided to say nothing more on that matter. "The original spell must have failed for some reason."

"Yeah, I bet whoever sold the rug to me put an invisibility spell on it so the spot would disappear long enough to sell it."

"Perhaps."

"Or," she went on, apparently getting into the story, "maybe whoever had the rug in the first place also put a spell on it. The spot showed up and another spell got put on it just long enough to sell the rug again. Gads. There could be layer upon layer of spells. No wonder you were confused last night."

He supposed that was an improvement; he'd gone from being a total incompetent to the victim of major fraud.

Petra wasn't done yet. "When Caylin cast her invisibility spell it further clouded the original spell to the point that you could only discern her magic."

He rather liked having her create suggestions to cast him in a better light. It proved she wanted to think the best of him, didn't it? She must have at least a small amount of interest in him. He could only hope.

"No wonder I ended up with a hole. The spell you put on it must have been the final straw and broke through . . ."

Falling silent, Petra sat frowning at him for several long moments. "Okay, let me get this straight. You thought Caylin's was the only magic and . . . Then how did you think that blood got on my rug in the first place?"

Damn. He'd hoped to avoid this particular question.

Seeing the look on his face, she sat back. "You thought I killed somebody and was trying to cover it up?"

Neither confirming nor denying her accusation, he asked, "Why don't you want the police involved?"

She squirmed in her seat. "Okay, I see your point."

"Well?" he prompted when she didn't volunteer any further information. He didn't seriously think she was guilty of a major crime, but there had to be a fascinating story behind her reluctance. "Are you in trouble with the police, Petra?"

"Not exactly."

What the devil did that mean? He couldn't imagine what crime she could have committed, but how else to explain her wariness? His concern increased a notch. "Unpaid traffic tickets?"

"No, nothing like that."

"Any outstanding warrants?"

"Stop harassing me."

"Then what?" Her evasiveness reminded him of a child trying not to admit breaking something without lying.

She sighed. "Let's just say I've had some . . . ah, difficult encounters with the police in the past and would rather not get involved with the criminal justice system if at all possible."

He sat there and stared at her, waiting for more. He wasn't sure why he didn't simply cast that honesty spell. Maybe because he couldn't remember when he'd enjoyed an interrogation so much.

Petra finally gave in. "There's no need to call the police. Because once they find out magic is involved, they'll bring in a wizard anyway. Then they'll know I'm not involved."

The Seattle Police Department would do exactly that. He should know. He was on their list of wizards approved to help solve magical crimes. In fact, he was already assigned to Medora's case. Technically he supposed it wasn't necessary to call the cops. He wasn't quite ready to let Petra off the hook, though. Let her squirm a while longer. If not now, eventually he would find out why she preferred to avoid the authorities.

She was also correct in her assumption that her lack of magic pointed to her innocence. His stomach felt queasy. It had nothing to do with lunch. It had to do with nonmagical people. He remembered the feeling all too well from his childhood, even though he hadn't suffered from it since he'd been twelve and left—

"Any idea whose blood it is?" Petra asked.

He grimly pushed the pain away before it ripped open scars that never had healed properly. How much should he tell her, he wondered, then shrugged. It served no purpose—other than to irritate her—to hide the truth. "It's Medora's blood. She's Kitoka's sister."

"Kitoka? The Amazon at the hotel down the hole?"

"Yes."

"That makes this Medora an Amazon, too."

"Naturally."

"So who cast the whole weird hotel spell?"

"Medora did."

"Medora? You mean the Amazon's sister is also—Gads! She's an Amazon wizard! That's a whole lot of power in one package. And somebody managed to kill her?" Petra shivered.

She had a good point. It would take somebody with incredible power to overcome Medora, someone with a combination of great physical strength and high magical powers. "I told you, nobody was killed."

"Oh, come on, Vorador. With that much blood? Somebody bled like a stuck pig and died."

"No, she's not dead."

"Then where'd all the blood come from?"

"She was wounded."

"So, she's in the hospital?"

"Not exactly."

When he didn't offer any further details, Petra continued to ask questions. "Well, why did she put a spell on her own blood in the first place? Why Hotel California? Who sold her rug after the crime? And why?" Petra rubbed at her forehead. "This is all getting very confusing."

Vorador agreed with that. He had all the facts—such as they were—and he was still confused.

"I think I want that rug out of my house."

Vorador considered her request. Why not use that option? He could take the rug to his laboratory. It would be close at hand if he needed to enter the hole again. Petra would be removed from any further involvement. Of course, there was no guarantee the magic would work elsewhere. It would . . . Hold on just a minute. It would also take away any logical reason to ever see Petra again.

"That's a possibility, I suppose. ERG would supply you with a comparable replacement, of course. Although finding one with pigs on it might be difficult."

63

Petra blushed. "What is it with you guys and pigs, anyway?"

Vorador allowed himself the barest hint of a smile, knowing it would drive her crazy. "I'm not the one who has dozens of pigs in my bedroom."

She pushed back her chair and stood up. "Which reminds me. I just remembered I left Bosco shut up in the bathroom. Poor kitty."

Barely managing to hold back a snort of laughter, Vorador silently agreed. Poor Kitty, indeed. She would be one pissed off Amazon cat when she finally got free. He didn't think he'd go to Petra's after all.

Petra waited on the curb while Vorador went to get his car. The rest of the lunch crowd had already gone and it was too early for the dinner rush to start. In the quiet afternoon, she had the street and sidewalk all to herself. She closed her eyes and raised her face to the warmth of the sun. It had been an interesting lunch and fairly successful. Most of the time she had managed to keep her mind on business. Perhaps the attraction had only been fleeting and was already on the wane.

"Give me all your money!"

A hand clamped over her mouth, sealing in her squeal of fright. In the next instant she became aware of something long, cold and very sharp pressed against her neck.

"Scream and I'll slit your throat."

Petrified, she could hardly breathe. This couldn't be happening. It was broad daylight.

"Give me your money."

Petra held her hands out to her sides, indicating she didn't even have a purse.

"Don't move."

Something wet—blood?—trickled down her neck and she whimpered. Her knees began to tremble. There was a ringing in her ears. Bright dots danced in front of her eyes. No, she couldn't faint. Who knew what this maniac would do to her then?

"I said—"

The man's low threat ended abruptly. A hot, burning rush of

something streamed past her face. Her hair blew across her eyes, blinding her. The air crackled as if full of static electricity. She felt the man behind her jerk. The knife bit into the tender skin along her jaw. This was it. She was dead. She said a swift prayer and regretted she hadn't acted on her impulses toward—

Suddenly the man and the knife were gone. Petra staggered and nearly fell without the support. Strong arms caught her, steadied her and pulled her into a comforting hug.

"You all right?"

A deep voice rumbled from the chest under her ear. The air took on a salty tang and she realized she was nearly buried in Vorador's tight embrace. Dazed, she managed to nod.

"Stay here."

Suddenly she was alone again. She took a small step sideways to right her balance. With trembling fingers she brushed the hair out of her eyes, then touched her neck. The small track of blood had already begun to dry. She hadn't been cut badly after all. A nearby yell broke into her befuddled daze.

She turned, eyes opening wide at the sight. Someone—her attacker, she supposed—was pressed up against the brick wall of the restaurant. His feet dangled about three feet off the sidewalk. Her wizard stood in front of him, not physically touching him. The force of his fury alone kept the man pinned in place. Vorador's clothes billowed around him, as if he stood in the middle of a windstorm.

"Holy Toledo," Petra whispered. She swore she could see sparks shooting from Vorador's wildly flying hair. She almost expected lightning bolts to come zinging out of his eyes. She had never seen such a display of raw power. Not even her father could restrain another person without being in direct physical contact with him.

"Who sent you?" Vorador snarled the question at the terrified man.

She barely recognized the wizard's voice. The mugger seemed to press even farther back against the wall. A high-pitched scream was his only answer. The bricks began to crumble under the pressure.

"Tell me who sent you."

Petra shivered and realized she had to stop this before someone got hurt. Moving hesitantly, she approached the wizard.

"Vorador."

There was no answer.

She cautiously placed her fingertips on his arm. His muscles jumped and twitched under her touch. "Vorador? Can you hear me?"

"I hear you," he growled.

"You have to let him go."

"Not until he tells me what I want to know."

The man rose a few inches higher. His feet thrashed urgently at the air, seeking solid footing where there was none. His hands clawed at his throat, desperate to remove the invisible force choking him.

"Vorador, listen, you can't kill him. Dead men can't talk."

"Oh, yes they can."

His words uttered from between clenched teeth sent fear fluttering down Petra's spine. She'd heard dark rumors about such possibilities but never known of a wizard who dared.

"Vorador, look at me."

He gave no indication he heard her.

"Damn it, you pigheaded wizard. Look at me!"

His head slowly swiveled toward her. Even though his attention was now focused on her, the man stuck to the wall didn't drop an inch. "What do you want?"

She very nearly fled from what she saw in Vorador's eyes. His pupils were dilated, only a thin rim of brown showed around the blackness. She had a feeling that if she looked close enough she would be able to see his power swirling in their depths. For one brief spark of a moment she longed to touch that indescribable something and let it consume her.

Instead, she said, "I want you to let him go."

"No!"

His roar washed over her, and Petra took a step back. Gathering the shreds of her courage, she moved closer, holding his attention. "Listen, I'm not hurt. He barely nicked me. Let him down and we'll call the police."

"As you wish."

A loud bang followed his terse words. The force of the shock wave actually drove her back a couple of steps. She shook her head, trying to stop the ringing in her ears. When she could focus again, the man was gone. All that remained was a faint impression in the bricks where his body had been.

"What did you do with him?"

"I did as you asked."

"You let him go?" She looked around but didn't see any sign of the man.

"No. I sent him to the nearest police station."

She gave a sigh of relief.

"You're hurt," he said, as if noticing for the first time. "You have blood on your neck."

"Well, it's a good thing you're not a vampire then, isn't it?" she said, in a weak attempt at humor.

She didn't expect him to laugh so wasn't disappointed when he didn't. Instead he grabbed her arm and dragged her toward his car, parked haphazardly by the curb. She tried not to flinch at the too tight pressure of his fingers.

"I'm taking you home." He shoved her in the car.

"Good idea," she muttered.

Home sounded mighty darn good right about then. Once she was there, she intended to lock the door in his face and try to gather her poor scattered wits. This was one dangerous wizard. Besides, if she let him in her house she just might rip off all his clothes and make mad, passionate love to him.

"Well, isn't this a fine mess?" She watched him walk around to the driver's side. In spite of everything, she wanted him more than ever. "What the heck am I going to do now?"

Chapter Ten

"What's this?" Petra motioned out the car window. They were parked in the driveway of a large house in an upscale neighborhood. "This isn't my house."

"Very observant." Vorador got out and went around the front of the car.

She watched him through the windshield, her breath catching at the pure masculine beauty of the way he moved. He didn't simply walk; he flowed, one movement blending into the next in a smooth, liquid motion. A smile tipped up a corner of her mouth. She'd pay big bucks to walk behind him again—if she could keep him in those pants and out of that stupid green robe. Gad, he had a great butt.

When he opened the door, she sat there, refusing to get out. Mainly because she wasn't at all certain her legs were steady enough to support her, but partly on principle. Just because he could send people zinging any which way didn't mean she intended to let him intimidate her.

When she noticed his eyes narrow with a speculative gleam,

she knew exactly what was on his mind. It would take very little effort on his part to zap her where he wanted her to go. She warned, "Don't even think about it, Mr. Wizard."

When it became obvious she wouldn't get out under her own power, Vorador answered her question. "This is my house."

"Really?" Petra looked at it with a more observant eye.

Built out of natural wood and pale brick, the house blended into the large wooded lot. She wondered why a guy living alone needed such a big house. Smiling, she noticed a turret room rising from a back corner. She'd bet her whole pig collection he had his lab/workshop in that room. She liked the touch of whimsy. Somehow it didn't clash with the contemporary style of the rest of the house.

"It's nice, but why are we here?"

"Because it's not safe for you to go home."

"How in the world did you jump to that conclusion?"

"Petra—"

With a shiver, she missed whatever else he had to say. Oh, just the way he said her name. That low, deep, rumbly voice turned her to Jell-O. What would it be like to have him say it under more intimate circumstances? She fanned herself with her hand in an attempt to cool her steamy fantasies of king-sized beds and rumpled sheets.

"Are you listening to me?"

She smiled at the disgruntled expression on his face. "Depends on what you're saying."

"I was attempting to make you see why going to your house isn't a good idea."

"Okay, never mind. Just take me home."

"You could at least pretend to give my opinions minimal consideration."

"Duly noted." She paused for about two seconds. "And considered. Now, let's go. You're being ridiculous."

Oops! She shouldn't have added that last comment.

With a fierce glare, he bent down and scooped her out of the car. Ignoring her squealed protests, he carried her up the sidewalk. At the front door, he merely ordered, "Open," and it did.

Once inside, he kicked the door shut with a resounding slam before setting her down.

She immediately started to leave.

"Stay."

Petra turned, ready for battle. "I am not some sort of pet to command—" Her ire evaporated. Without any real force, she muttered, "You charlatan."

"Who me?"

How could she stay mad at him when he grinned at her like that? "You don't play fair."

His grin widened. "Didn't your parents ever tell you life isn't fair?"

"Yeah, all the time. That doesn't mean I like having my nose rubbed in it."

"Until I find out what's going on"—he reached out and tucked a wayward strand of hair behind her ear—"will you stay here? At least for tonight?"

Her insides went all wobbly. Spend the night. With him. She knew he hadn't meant the words that way. With trembling fingers she skimmed the same place on her hair, imagining she could still feel the heat of his caress. It took all her resolve not to reach out to him, but nothing could halt the fantasies unfolding in her mind.

"Well?" he prompted.

"I think you're making a mountain out of a molehill."

"No, I think someone sent that man after you."

The suggestion startled Petra. Surely the wizard was only trying to frighten her into listening to his instructions. Funny, he didn't look like he was kidding. "Who do you think sent him? And why?"

Instead of answering, Vorador went into a room off the main hallway. Left with no other choice, she followed him. At the threshold she stopped and stared.

The room was full of stuff. Her first impression had been to call it "junk," but many of the items were antiques, and expensive. The obligatory L-shaped bachelor leather sofa dominated the center of the room. Instead of the expected black it was a rich, buttery cream color. Petra's fingers itched to touch it and see if it was as soft as it looked.

Bookcases, shelves and end tables in a wide variety of styles lined the walls and filled any open spaces between the furniture. Every surface was covered with . . . stuff. Fascinated, her gaze jumped from one item to the next until she felt almost dizzy.

A collection of microscopes, ranging from antique to modern, sat on a large end table. Beside them was a carved Waterford crystal bowl filled with seashells and polished stones. Colorful art glass paperweights were scattered in front of the books.

An old-fashioned telephone hung on the wall. The table under the phone held a vast array of action figures—*Star Wars*, GI Joe, *Star Trek*, Transformers. Her eyes widened at the sight of a full suit of armor standing guard beside the phone. A huge bank of high-tech stereo equipment took up most of one corner.

She saw Coke memorabilia beside an old phonograph with the huge trumpet speaker, a brass telescope beside a window, a rack of handmade quilts, and crossed swords over the fireplace. There was pottery as tall as she was, and delicate carved Southwestern pots, a Tiffany stained-glass lamp and track lighting. In spite of the extensive furnishings, not a spot of dust was in sight.

She finally managed to see past the things to the room itself. The high wooden ceiling supported exposed beams. Pale misty green paint covered the walls. The large room was bright and sunny thanks to several floor-to-ceiling windows, offering a stunning view of Lake Washington and Mt. Rainier.

This was not how she had pictured his house. She'd imagined something spartan, very modern, with lots of gleaming chrome and contemporary art. This was so . . . homey and lived in.

Giving in to the temptation, she settled on the couch. Sinking into the cushions, she ran her hands over the leather. It was as sinfully soft as she'd hoped.

Vorador sat on the opposite end of the couch. "We have to consider the fact that you're in danger."

"Why?"

"Because you now own Medora's rug. It's possible that whoever tried to kill her found out and thinks you're a threat."

71

Petra mentally chewed on that for a moment and couldn't come up with any plausible connection. "Why a threat?"

"Because you have the rug now," Vorador repeated in a tone that implied she should have figured it out for herself.

She still didn't understand.

"I sincerely doubt the greasy, beer-bellied hick who sold me the rug has any possible ties to Amazons, wizards in general or Medora in particular. How would the murderer even know I have the rug?"

"The possibilities are endless, Petra. Maybe the rug was sold by accident and the murderer only now discovered its whereabouts. Perhaps the murderer was watching your beer-bellied hick to see who he sold it to. Maybe the murderer listens to radio dispatches for any mention of bloody rugs. It's even possible the murderer put a tracking spell on the rug and has been aware all along that you have it."

She wasn't about to admit his suggestions scared the beejee-bers out of her. She hoped her voice sounded calm. "So you think the murderer sent the mugger?"

"Yes."

"It's not possible it was simply a random act of violence?"

"Petra."

That was all he said. Just her name. Spoken in that low, intimate tone, it was more than enough to shut her up. If she hadn't been sitting, she would have melted at his feet. Irritated he'd picked up her earlier reaction to his using her first name, she pouted.

"Unfair advantage."

"Is it?"

Now that was a fascinating question, coming from him. Petra searched his face, but he had on his bland professional mask, as if regretting his confession. Did he really go all mushy inside when she said his name? Liking the idea, she didn't feel so bad.

"So, what's your real name?" she asked.

"I beg your pardon?"

She could tell she'd taken him completely by surprise. He couldn't quite manage his usual Spock elevated-eyebrow look.

"I'm assuming Vorador is your professional name. Probably one you took when you got your wizard's license."

He neither confirmed nor denied her guess.

"Is it some sort of family name?"

His glare turned into a frown.

"Well, it won't be too hard to check records and find out." She pointed to a frame on the wall. "I see by your diploma that you went to the University of Washington, right here in Seattle. How convenient."

His only answer was to glare some more.

"Did you have Professor Helios?"

"Yes," Vorador admitted cautiously.

"He's quite the character. He was my father's teacher, too."

Evidently feeling this was a safe topic, he loosened up enough to add, "He was my adviser. We still meet for lunch once a month."

Her expression softened with memories. "He used to come for a visit every summer—and to teach a seminar. It was like a two-week-long party. Students, professionals, teachers, grad students in and out of the house all hours of the day and night. Gads, the house nearly exploded with magic."

"It must have been a wonderful way to grow up."

Snapping out of her trip down memory lane, Petra couldn't miss the wistful tone in Vorador's voice. Because of that she didn't disagree with him. For her it had been an extremely painful way to grow up—surrounded by the greatest magical minds in the country, yet having not a smidgen of that power herself. She'd always been the outsider, the one looking in, the one not quite getting the jokes or stories the rest shared so easily, the one used as the guinea pig for countless experiments since nobody else wanted to miss any of the real action.

"Were your parents magical?" she asked.

"No."

"Brothers or sisters?"

"No."

"Grandparents?"

"No."

"Aunts? Uncles? Cousins?"

73

"No. No one."

Those meager words spoke volumes. Petra heard echoes of her own pain, only from the other side. All his power, yet none of those closest to him could share his true nature. "I'm sorry."

He jumped to his feet and paced to the windows. He stood with his back to her, hands in his pockets, a long silence stretching between them. Finally, he said without turning around, "Will you stay here while I file the police report?"

"Can't I go with—"

"No."

"What about—"

"I'll send Caylin over to let out your cat."

She stuck her tongue out at his back, hating the way he was beginning to easily read her thoughts from just a few words.

"Oh, all right."

"I'll be back as soon as I can." He headed for the door but paused to look over his shoulder at her. "Don't touch anything." Then he was gone.

Petra fumed as she heard the front door slam, then his car roar to life. Even after quiet settled over the house, she sat there, the rapid tapping of her toe the only outward sign of her agitation. Just when she had started to think he might see her in a flattering way, he said or did something to thoroughly demolish her morale and self-confidence.

" 'Don't touch anything,' " she mimicked.

As if she was a child, or an utter dimwit who had to be warned. She knew countless spells undoubtedly filled this house. Disturbing them could be disastrous. She didn't need to be told. Was he afraid she would go snooping in his private . . .

A slow smile spread across her face. It would serve him right if she just happened to innocently set off a few of those spells. Getting to her feet, her gaze leisurely swept the room, looking for her first victim.

She sauntered over to the suit of armor. It gleamed so brightly, she could see her reflection in it. It would only take one fingerprint in the center of that shining breastplate to announce her disobedience. She slowly reached out a fingertip, relishing her defiance.

74

"Milady fair, kindly remove thy finger."

Petra smiled at the courtly English tone issuing from the armor. Mr. Wizard had definite class, no doubt about it. Unable to resist, she left another fingerprint next to the first.

"I beg of thee, milady, kindly do not touch. Or the consequences will be most dire indeed."

She giggled. Who could resist the challenge to find out exactly what those consequences would be? However, she wasn't stupid. She backed up a couple of steps, then leaned forward and touched the armor again.

"Prepare to die!"

Clanging and squeaking, the armor came to life. Petra squealed and stumbled away. In her haste, she accidentally tipped over the nearby shelves holding all the action figures. The armor took a step forward, the battle ax in its hands beginning an upward arc. Gads, had that last warning been serious?

Suddenly, all the spilled action figures came to life. Before she could blink, several miniature battles erupted. Luke Skywalker and Han Solo fought the Borg. GI Joe soldiers skirmished with the Klingons. Spock and Captain Kirk brawled with Darth Vadar. Princess Leia and C3P0 ran from the forces of C.O.B.R.A., while Yoda meditated serenely in the middle of the chaos. Captain Picard and Data struggled with Storm Troopers.

Petra stared at the scene in openmouthed amazement. She couldn't help smiling as a diminutive Worf bellowed a Klingon battle cry and dashed into the melee to rescue Dax from Jabba the Hutt. As the conflict raged closer to her feet, she moved out of the way. Could the tiny phasers, light sabers and blasters do any actual damage to her?

A loud clang abruptly reminded her of the larger danger in the room. Spinning, she saw the suit of armor practically on top of her, battle ax raised high overhead. Yikes! Afraid to take her eyes off it, she backed up and tripped over another table. Knick-knacks scattered everywhere and she landed on her butt. Scuttling backward, she winced as the armor stepped on a Japanese cloisonne vase, shattering its delicate design.

Stunned, she could only lay there while the ax whistled downward. It hacked through the Persian rug and thudded into the wooden floor only inches from her toes. It was really trying to kill her! Scrambling to her feet, she dashed to the door. She heard the ax being ripped from the floor and heavy footsteps pursuing her.

With a scream she shot through the door and slammed it shut. Leaning her weight against it, she screamed again when the suit of armor banged into the closed door. The wood vibrated under her shoulder. Several loud crashes sounded inside the room. She put all her strength into holding the door closed.

Petra gradually realized her panting was the only sound disturbing the silence. She slowly slid down until she sat on the cool marble floor, her back pressed against the door.

Wow! Vorador was deadly serious about his spells. True, she'd expected spells, but something more along the lines of her parents' scolding lectures or innocent punishments. As a child she had disliked being doused with cold water or covered in polka dots whenever she disobeyed her mother or father's instructions. She'd take those childhood disciplines over being chased by a murderous knight any day of the week.

Finally she felt composed enough to stand. Cursing her curiosity, she simply had to look. She turned the knob and eased the door open barely enough to take a peek inside. What she saw made her groan and quietly shut the door. Leaning her forehead against the wood, she knew Vorador would kill her himself when he saw the mess she'd made.

The battle ax remained buried in the door. The suit of armor lay scattered in pieces. The spell must have been broken when she exited the room, causing the knight to fall apart. She'd seen a dent in the polished helmet.

With a heavy sigh, Petra looked around the foyer. Well, that hadn't gone according to plan. In spite of the living room fiasco, she was still tempted to see what the rest of Vorador's house looked like. His bedroom would be an especially fascinating place to begin.

She actually had one foot on the steps leading upstairs when her common sense reappeared. She needed to get out of here before she got herself in big trouble. Spying a phone in a small alcove under the stairs, she called a cab. Luckily they had caller

ID, since she didn't have a clue what Vorador's address was. Deciding even the fifteen-minute wait would be too big a temptation, she headed for the front door.

"Please, ma'am, step away from the door."

Petra jumped back. "What the—?"

She looked around, but there wasn't a soul in sight. For a second she'd been afraid the armor had escaped. This voice had been English, too. With a shrug, she reached for the doorknob.

"Please, ma'am, this is your second warning. Kindly step away from the door."

That skunk had left a spell on his front door.

Well, there was more than one way to skin a cat. Moving carefully, she tried the other doors in the hallway. None of them issued warnings. She found a library with floor-to-ceiling bookshelves. Next she discovered a spacious bathroom with a large sunken tub. That gave her pause for a moment. Why would anyone have a bath in a downstairs powder room? Most houses only had a half-bath on the main floor.

Eventually she located the kitchen. At last here were the gleaming stainless steel and stark modern designs she'd anticipated finding in Vorador's house. Everything was spotless, not a crumb or smudge in sight. Either the guy had one heck of an efficient maid or he knew how to work a whopper of a cleaning spell.

After a few more minutes' exploration, Petra passed through a laundry room and found the back door. It opened into the garage, which held a battered Jeep. Another door led directly outside. Taking a deep breath, she grabbed the knob. Nothing happened. It was a surprise when she easily managed to exit.

She supposed the wizard had left in too big a hurry to remember to secure all the doors and windows. For which she thanked her lucky stars as she hurried down the driveway when the taxi arrived a few minutes later.

Chapter Eleven

Petra ran into her house, grabbed her purse, then dashed back out to pay the cab driver. Without even a grunt of thanks for the large tip, he sped off as soon as the money touched his palm. Back inside, she didn't see Bosco. Hurrying down the hall, she cursed Vorador for not liberating her poor cat. She stood clear of the open door, expecting him to streak past. Nothing happened. She peered around the corner, fearing the worst.

The cat sat imperiously on the bath mat and glared at Petra.

"Sorry," she told him, squirming under his unwavering stare. "Come on, kitty. What more do you want? Blood?"

"Yeow."

Petra started to chuckle, then stopped uneasily. It had sounded eerily like the cat had said yes. He turned his back to her and started washing a paw. Boy, she was losing it. Cats talking? Wizards could do a lot, but not that.

She headed to the kitchen but stopped in the front room. The hole was still there, black and menacing in the middle of her rug. Bosco strolled into the room. She'd better cover the hole or he could end up down there again. At this point, the last thing she wanted was another visit to that creepy hotel.

She flattened two empty packing boxes and laid them over the opening. She anchored the cardboard with boxes full of books. She knew she was right to cover it up when she had to shoo Bosco away several times during her labors. For some reason she felt like he disapproved of her actions.

"What?" she finally demanded, staring down at the cat, hands on her hips. "Not stylish enough for you?"

"Neow."

Petra shook her head. She needed a nap . . . or something. This time it had distinctly sounded like the cat had said no.

"Tough luck, Mr. Boss Man. After the day I've had, I'm not in the mood for your attitude."

Bosco hissed at her.

Petra chuckled. "Obviously you're not in a very good mood either." Once more she headed for the kitchen. "Come on, let's share a can of tuna. Then I'm going to take a nice long shower and go to bed early."

Bosco only hissed at her again.

"Suit yourself."

As she made a tuna salad, Petra wondered how far she would get in her plans for the evening before a certain dark-eyed wizard showed up and put a major kink in them.

Done with her shower, she was just drying her hair when Bosco scratched her on the ankle. "Ouch, you little monster."

Guess the cat had been out for blood after all. Turning off the noisy dryer, she heard the knocking on her front door. She slanted a glance at the cat sitting there looking rather smug. "You couldn't find a less painful way to let me know someone was at the door?"

"Neow."

Not quite as startled this time, Petra plainly heard the no. Reassured only a small mark marred her ankle, she hurried into her thick terry-cloth robe and went to the door. She took a deep breath for courage, having a pretty good idea who was calling at this hour.

She opened the door, deciding on a strong offense. "What do you—Oh!"

"Hello."

"You're not—" Petra stared at the strange woman standing on her porch. "Sorry. I was expecting someone else."

The woman smiled. "I'm sorry to disturb you."

Figuring she was a neighbor, Petra smiled back. "What can I do for you?"

"I wonder if I could ask you a few questions?"

"I guess. What about?"

"My name is Fytch and I'm with Rapid Renovations."

"Rapid Renovations? But I didn't use your company."

"I'm aware you decided to use our competitor. If for any reason you're dissatisfied with the service you received, we would be more than happy to step in and offer you an alternative."

Petra decided that had been a pretty little speech. Wonder how successful it normally was with dissatisfied customers? Rapid Renovations must be losing a bundle to ERG to make these follow-up visits.

"May I take a few moments of your time, Miss Field?"

"Well . . . I suppose." Petra knew she couldn't let Fytch inside her house. Not while she still had a large hole in the middle of her living room floor. And not after the things Vorador had said about Fytch—whether they were true or not. "It's a nice night. Let's sit here on the porch."

She thought Fytch looked a little disappointed but decided that was only her overactive paranoia. Once they were settled in the wicker chairs, Fytch pulled some papers and a clipboard out of her briefcase. Petra took the opportunity to study the woman a little more closely.

Fytch was of average height, slender but curvaceous. She wore a lightweight pumpkin orange sweater. The matching skirt showed off her shapely legs. Her long hair reached past her shoulders, full and thick, curling on the ends. In the porch light it looked brown, but Petra had a feeling in sunlight it would be a rich chestnut color.

"All right," Fytch said in a businesslike voice, "what made you decide to go with ERG's services?"

Petra shrugged. "They got here first."

"But you called us."

"Listen, I'm sorry, but I was desperate. They promised to get the job done before my party started. I didn't know anything about either of your companies."

"Then why—"

"I spent a long time on hold when I called your office. I couldn't risk the rest of your service being that slow." Petra almost regretted her blunt honesty when Fytch sent an irritated glare in her direction.

Still, she managed a civil smile before saying, "Yes, I admit we have a problem with our answering system. As a prank, some students from the university put a spell on it a few weeks back. We haven't been able to remove all the bugs yet."

"Sounds like your wizard needs to get some help if he can't even remove a student spell." Petra knew she sounded petty, but she wasn't in the mood to be courteous. It had been a rough day.

"I am their wizard."

Oops. Petra winced. Well, the way her luck was running lately, that just figured. Why hadn't either of those dorks in green robes bothered to share that particular tidbit? When Vorador called Fytch a witch she'd thought he'd been politely saying she was a bi—

"Sorry," Petra said.

There was an awkward silence before Fytch spoke. "Yes, well . . . Have you been satisfied with the work Emerald Renaissance Garments provided?"

Now there was a loaded question, Petra thought. On the one hand she was completely dissatisfied, since they hadn't removed the spot/hole. On the other hand, she hesitated to say anything negative to Fytch. Now that she'd spent these few moments with her, there was something about the woman, something that simply rubbed Petra the wrong way. It was more than being jealous of an attractive woman. This entire visit didn't feel right.

81

She settled for replying, "I have no complaints about Vorador's abilities."

"Vorador?" Fytch's voice was sharper than before. "Dugan sent his senior wizard in for a simple cleaning job?"

How did Fytch know it was a *simple* cleaning job? Why should Vorador be above such assignments? That was it, Petra realized. That was the something in Fytch that set her teeth on edge. Fytch obviously held the opinion that wizards were superior to mere mortals. It came through in her voice, her body language, her whole attitude. She thought she was better than everybody else. Therefore, all wizards were better.

It was a struggle, but Petra managed to keep her tone noncommittal. "You know Vorador?"

"Yes, of course."

There it was again—that smugness, as if Vorador only deemed to socialize with the wizard elite. Which of course included Fytch, but definitely excluded Petra. That really rubbed Petra the wrong way. She wondered if Fytch's name had been on Vorador's short list of enemy wizards.

"He seems to be an adequate wizard," Petra said, meaning it more as a dig at Fytch than any complaint about Vorador.

Fytch gave a disbelieving laugh. "Miss Field, he's one of Seattle's best."

"Really?" Petra felt perverse enough to enjoy pulling this woman's chain. "Well, it wasn't apparent last night."

Fytch leaned closer in sudden interest. "Then you aren't satisfied with ERG's service?"

Petra silently cursed her runaway tongue. She'd backed herself into a corner now. She might not be totally happy with ERG's progress, but there was no way she intended to let this woman into her house to try her hand at casting yet another spell on that rug. No telling what she would end up with. Something far worse than a hole, she suspected. A demeanor of tainted intentions seemed to hover over Fytch. Vorador was right about this woman, and Dugan was wrong.

"Well, that isn't what I meant, exactly." Petra danced around the truth. "His spell was efficient, but he seemed rather rude."

"I've always found him to be immensely charming."

"How nice for you," Petra managed to say.

Was there something between them, as Fytch seemed to imply? Something more than a professional relationship? Now she had one more reason to dislike Fytch. Much as it pained her to admit it, Vorador was a lot like Harold. For one, he preferred another wizard to her. She should have known. All wizards were the same. Lying, cheating scum, the lot of them. At least this time her eyes were wide open to the truth. This time she wouldn't fall in love and plan a wedding. It should be easy enough to nip her early attraction to Vorador in the bud.

Wait a minute—what about Vorador's comments about Fytch? His obvious dislike hadn't appeared fake. Much as she'd like to group all wizards together in the same disgusting lump, fairness demanded she give Vorador a chance to prove himself innocent. Perhaps he'd spoken the truth about Fytch. Or could he be involved with her but covering it up? Maybe. If he didn't want Dugan to know, wanted to avoid any jealousy between them.

"So, was he able to get the blood out of your rug?"

For a moment Petra panicked, wondering how Fytch knew about the blood. Then she calmed down, remembering the phone call last night. Dang, how to answer that? She'd already admitted Vorador's spell was efficient. Why couldn't she be a better liar?

"Ahhh . . . yeah, the blood's gone."

"I hope you weren't hurt seriously?" Fytch asked, obviously fishing for more information.

Petra answered truthfully. "No, I wasn't hurt at all. Turns out it was an old stain. Left by the previous owner, I presume."

"How fascinating. Blood from an old crime. Have you talked to the police?"

Petra gritted her teeth. "No."

Fytch made a noncommittal sound.

Before the wizard could continue, Petra cut her off. "Do you have any other questions? It's been a long day and I was getting ready for bed."

Taking the hint, Fytch put away her clipboard and stood up. "Thank you for your time, Miss Field. I hope if you have future magical needs you'll give Rapid Renovations another chance. I can assure you that you won't be disappointed."

Petra hoped her smile didn't look as fake as it felt. If she never saw this woman again it would be too soon. "I'll keep that in mind. Good night."

Once back inside, Petra watched out the peephole until Fytch got in her car and drove away. Even through a closed door she didn't want to turn her back on the wizard.

Making her nightly rounds, locking doors and windows, turning off lights, she refused to let herself think about a certain other wizard. Much as he had dominated her thoughts for the past twenty-four hours, it wasn't easy. Unless she wanted her heart broken—for the second time—she'd better put Vorador out of her mind.

In bed, snuggled under the blankets, Bosco curled up at her feet, it was even harder to banish Vorador. She kept waiting for his knock on her front door. When he hadn't arrived by midnight, she told herself she was every kind of fool. Why had she been so certain he would come after her? He didn't care in the least—not about her and not that she had trashed his house. She finally drifted off to sleep, her mind still insisting she didn't care either.

Petra jerked awake, her heart pounding. Disoriented, she fumbled for the bedside clock. Five o'clock. She moaned and buried her head under the blankets. She didn't need to be up for another hour. Memories of a bad dream flitted through her sleep-fogged brain. With a shudder she peeked out to make sure nothing lurked in the predawn darkness of her bedroom.

Gad, what a dream. Monsters and demons and freaks had come pouring out of that blasted hole in her rug. One in particular—sort of a cross between a vampire and a werewolf—stood out in her mind. A huge, hulking, hairy beast, with an enormous mouth full of needle-sharp teeth, slimy drool dripping from his fangs, his eyes had glowed red in the night as he lumbered down the hallway toward her bedroom.

Petra jolted upright as a thud sounded near the door. What was that? Her heart racing, she clutched the blankets to her chest as if they would shield her from danger. She listened more closely. There it was! The barest whisper of hair rubbing against wood. Out of the corner of her eye she caught a flicker of movement.

Something landed on the bed and she screamed. She flew out from under the covers and across the room. Grabbing the nearest object, Petra flipped on the light switch and turned to confront the monster on her bed.

With a shaky laugh, she lowered the leaded crystal pig. "Bosco, you horrible animal."

Knees shaking, she managed to make it back to the bed before they gave way. "Damn it, cat. You nearly scared me to death."

Looking totally disinterested and unaffected, Bosco began grooming himself.

Her heart was still pounding. She felt lightheaded. She leaned over and stuck her head between her knees. After a few minutes the room stopped whirling. Sitting up, she realized she still clutched her unlikely weapon. She had to practically pry her fingers off the glass pig to put it down.

"Not exactly the way I planned to start my day, kitty."

"*Yeow.*"

Petra scratched him behind the ears. "Apology accepted."

Looking at the clock, there wasn't much sense in going back to bed. She had to be up soon anyway, and she sincerely doubted she'd be able to sleep again. She probably wouldn't even be able to do that tonight. Not as long as that rug remained in her house. She would lay there, imagining all sorts of things crawling out of that blasted hole.

She jumped to her feet, startling Bosco, sending him hissing into the corner. "I've had enough."

Petra stomped out of the bedroom and down the hall, flipping on lights as she went. Stopping at the edge of the rug in the front room, she glared at it. "I was right yesterday. I want this dang thing out of my house."

She knew exactly who could have it. And where he could put it.

Chapter Twelve

Pushing rain-damp hair out of her eyes, Petra entered the lobby of Emerald Renaissance Garments. Suitably impressed, she took a moment to look around. The dark green carpeting was thick and plush. A tasteful grouping of sofa and chairs sat off to one side. The walls were painted a soothing pastel green. The artwork—if not very original—matched the decor. Plants added a final touch of elegance. All in all, it was low-key and under-stated. Not what she had expected. She'd thought to find something as tacky as those green robes they wore.

She didn't know whether to be relieved or irritated when she saw who sat behind the receptionist's desk.

"Good morning, Caylin," Petra said, even though it was about as far from good as she'd had in forever.

"Where?" the young blond wizard said.

"What?" Petra asked.

"Who?"

Frowning, Petra decided to cut to the chase. "I need to talk to Vorador. If he isn't here, I guess Dugan will do."

"Where—"

"Is Vorador here?" Petra asked before they started playing newspaper reporter again.

"Nope."

"Is Dugan here?"

"Nope, and neither is Caylin."

That stopped Petra. "You're not Caylin?"

"No, silly." The girl giggled. "I'm Zaylin."

Petra stared at the girl. Tiny and petite, with long blond hair and wide blue eyes, Zaylin appeared to be an exact duplicate of the young wizard. She was even wearing the obligatory green robe. Looking closer, Petra noticed something strange. Fine blond fuzz covered all of Zaylin's skin.

"Ahhh . . . pleased to meet you, Zaylin."

The girl giggled, then leaned across the desk and whispered in a loud voice, "I've got a secret."

"Really?" Petra wasn't sure she wanted to know what it was.

Zaylin beckoned her to come closer.

Looking around for either rescue or escape but finding neither, Petra took a step forward.

"I've got scissors!"

Petra rubbed at her ear, sure Zaylin's shout had deafened her. Scissors? That sounded familiar. "How nice for you."

Bouncing up and down in her chair and clapping her hands, Zaylin sent a cloud of fuzz wafting through the air. "Thank you."

Coughing, Petra waved her hand in front of her face, hoping to clear the air. Now she remembered. Yesterday, the page Dugan received had been about Zaylin—and scissors. "So, tell me, Zaylin, they left you here by yourself?"

"Who?"

Petra rolled her eyes and sighed. "Do you work here?"

"Ye-ah." She said the word with two syllables. "I'm the receptionist."

"Listen, I have something—"

"Scissors?" Zaylin clapped her hands again.

Petra massaged her temples. "No, it's a rug."

"Oh." Zaylin's whole body drooped in disappointment. "I don't like rugs. Vacuums scare me."

She just bet they did. "This rug is for Vorador. I'll leave it here and he can call me later."

Zaylin shrugged. "Whatever."

Petra wrestled the rolled-up rug out of her car and into the office. By the time she was done, she was dripping in sweat and panting for breath. Boy, if this wasn't a prime indication that she needed to find a gym and start working out, she didn't know what was. Leaning against the desk to catch her breath, she was grateful that at least the rain had slowed to a drizzle.

"Are you going to leave that there?"

Not about to move the darn thing one more inch, Petra slanted a glare at Zaylin. "Yes, I am."

"I don't like that rug."

Petra snorted. "I'm not real fond of it myself anymore."

Zaylin's expression brightened. "I have scissors."

"Yeah, I know."

"Can I cut it up?"

Petra blinked slowly. "You want to cut a rug—"

"No, silly." Zaylin giggled again, the high-pitched sound aggravating Petra's already frazzled nerves. "There's no music."

"Of course not."

How in the world could Zaylin be familiar with that saying? The only other person Petra had ever heard use "cut a rug" had been Grandma, when she wanted to go out dancing and reminisced about doing the jitterbug in the 1940s. It didn't make sense that Zaylin knew such an outdated reference, yet didn't have enough brains to know when her bosses got to work?

Petra started walking backwards to the door, uncertain about turning her back on this nutcase. She could very well end up with that pair of scissors stuck between her shoulder blades.

"Oomph." Petra froze, her spine pressed against something solid and warm. Barely a heartbeat passed before she realized it was a person. Probably a man, since he was taller and broader than she. Oh, please, please don't let it be Vorador.

She wasn't in any state to see him right now. Her hair hung in sweaty, rain-damp clumps. Dirt and dust streaked her baggy sweats. At this moment it didn't count that she had nice clothes in the car to change into once she got to work. Her face was undoubtedly still red from her physical exertions.

She glanced over her shoulder and offered a silent, "Thank you." Turning around and stepping back, she tried for some dignity. "Good morning, Dugan."

"Good morning, Miss Field. What a pleasant surprise."

"Not really," Petra muttered. He was dressed in regular clothes—khaki slacks, white shirt and a worn bomber jacket—and his charming spell seemed more potent than ever. He really was a very attractive man.

"Are you looking for Vorador?"

"Huh?" She shook off the effects of his spell. "No, I was just—"

"Come on into my office and we can have a nice chat."

Petra didn't want to go anywhere with Dugan. His overbearing charming spell grated heavily on her last nerve. She glanced at her watch. Unfortunately, she still had plenty of time until she had to be at work. She could lie to him, but it didn't seem worth the effort.

"Fine, but only for a few minutes."

Dugan turned and led the way down a short hall. Unlocking a door, he motioned Petra inside. The office was simply furnished with a large wooden desk, some file cabinets and several chairs. The Magic 8 ball on his desk made her smile. A closed door in the corner probably led to a storage closet, or perhaps a private bathroom. The first thing he did was go to his desk and check the drawers. With a sigh, he excused himself.

Curious, Petra followed him as far as the door and shamelessly eavesdropped.

"Zaylin," Dugan said in a stern voice, "give me my scissors."

Petra heard some mumbling, then footsteps. She hurried and sat down, hoping she looked nonchalant by the time Dugan came back. Once he was settled, she simply had to ask.

"What is it with her and scissors, anyway?"

Dugan put the large pair of scissors in his drawer. "She saw somebody wearing one of those joke T-shirts one time that said, 'Runs with scissors.' For some reason it stuck, and now she

90

thinks that's what you're supposed to do with scissors. She's already been to the emergency room twice for stitches."

Nobody could be that stupid, could they? "Why on earth do you have her working here? Is she Caylin's sister?"

"It's a long story."

Obviously one Dugan didn't want to share, which only increased Petra's curiosity. "But—"

"You mentioned you were short on time, Miss Field. Perhaps you should tell me what brings you here this morning."

Not happy about it, she let him change the subject. "I dropped off that blasted rug."

"So I saw. Did Vorador ask you to bring it here?"

"Since it's connected to Medora's murder, I thought he'd want it. Otherwise I would have just thrown it away."

"He told you? About Medora?"

Petra wondered why he sounded so shocked by the possibility. "Not everything he knows, I'm sure."

"How did Vorador find out it was Medora's rug?"

Now that was an interesting question, full of hints and clues. Especially taking into account Vorador's revelation that Dugan had lied to him. Just how closely were all these people involved with each other?

"I think it was Kitoka who told him."

"Kitoka! He ran into Kitoka? And she didn't kill him?"

"Not hardly." Petra snorted, remembering the seemingly fond reunion the wizard and Amazon had shared.

"Where was she? Nobody's seen her around town for weeks."

"Down that blasted hole."

"What? She was down there? How'd she get there?"

"You know, I never thought of that. I just assumed she was part of the whole hotel business."

"Hotel? What hotel?"

"Haven't you talked to Vorador? Didn't he tell you?"

"I haven't seen him since yesterday at your house."

"Really?" That surprised Petra, and worried her, if the truth be told. "So you don't know where he is?"

"He left a message on my machine, but I haven't talked to him."

That relieved Petra. She'd been envisioning Vorador laying in a ditch all bloody. Then she reminded herself that she was mad at the wizard because he hadn't bothered to call her.

"Back to this hole, Miss Field. Why don't you tell me what happened after I left yesterday?"

She hesitated for a moment, trying to think of a graceful way to refuse. None presented itself. So she gave him a brief synopsis of what had transpired at the Hotel California.

"You just left Kitoka down there?"

"Oh, my gosh!" Petra sat back, stunned by Dugan's outraged question. "We did. I can't believe I didn't think of that. We just left her down there. But—"

When she didn't continue, Dugan asked, "But what?"

Petra frowned, not at all happy with her thoughts. "Why didn't Vorador try to get her out? I mean, she was standing right there beside us. He somehow managed to grab my cat. Why did he leave Kitoka behind?"

"I'm sure he had his reasons."

Petra couldn't believe her own part in this. She'd been so wrapped up in her own selfish concerns that she hadn't even considered Kitoka's welfare. Taking an instant dislike to the Amazon was not a good enough reason to be so self-centered. Nor was the excuse that her attraction to the wizard had clouded her judgment.

"Where is Vorador?" she demanded.

"Last I heard from him, he was working in his lab. I guess he's still there."

"Well, why don't you go get him? I think he should roll that rug out right now and get Kitoka out of there."

"I don't think I should interrupt him at this point. He's working on a very sensitive spell. I'll be sure and give him your message as soon as possible."

"But—"

Dugan stood up and smoothly dismissed her, "I won't detain you any longer, Miss Field. I wouldn't want to make you late for work."

Petra sat there for several more seconds, long enough to make her displeasure plain. Jerking to her feet, she snapped, "Just be sure and give him my message."

"Oh, don't worry, Miss Field. He's gonna hear from me."

Chapter Thirteen

Vorador didn't turn around when he heard the door to his lab open. He kept his attention on the potion he was concocting. Only one other person had the access code. "Good morning, Dugan."

"You look like shit."

Vorador grinned at Dugan's honesty. Massaging the bridge of his nose, he said, "I've been up all night."

"Any problems I should know about?"

"No. Things are better now."

"She's okay?"

Vorador didn't need to ask who they were discussing. The topic had been Medora from the beginning. "She's stabilized."

Hands in his pockets, Dugan meandered around the room. Finally, he asked, "How much longer can you keep her that way?"

Vorador finished measuring out the dark blue liquid before answering. "At least a couple of weeks. Maybe longer."

Dugan walked up and down the aisles separating the long

tables cluttered with supplies and equipment. Another lengthy silence passed before he spoke again. "Good."

Vorador added a few drops of thick amber liquid to the blue and swirled the glass tube, carefully watching the color change. He could tell Dugan had something on his mind—something else besides Medora's condition. It wouldn't do any good to come right out and ask. Dugan would tell him in his own good time.

Dugan broke the drawn-out silence. "What're you making?"

"A potion."

"Is it for Medora?"

"No. I told you, she's stable for now. This"—he held up the flask—"is for our friendly neighborhood mugger."

"What mugger?" Dugan looked as confused as he sounded.

"Oh, that's right. I haven't told you about Petra's adventure yesterday. Sorry."

"She got mugged, too?"

Something in Dugan's voice made Vorador pause. "What do you mean *too*? Has something else happened?"

"I just meant on top of everything else. You know, the whole hole business."

Vorador set his work aside. "How do you know about that? I haven't had a chance to fill you in yet."

"That's what I came to tell you. We had a visitor this morning."

"Petra was here?"

Vorador wasn't sure why that piece of news left him feeling off-balance. Yet it did. She'd been one floor above him and he hadn't known it. Why should he expect to sense her presence? Then he had another thought that worried him even more.

"What did she want?"

"She left you a present," Dugan said.

Considering he hadn't contacted her since he'd left her locked in his house, he could pretty much surmise it wouldn't be a pleasant gift. "What is it?"

"She brought Medora's rug. And I can tell you, she's not real happy with you, buddy."

"Yeah, I know," Vorador muttered.

He went back to work on the potion, not wanting it to grow cool or he'd have to start all over again. Only part of his mind focused on the formula. What did it mean that she'd brought him the rug? Was she merely trying to be helpful? More likely it was an attempt to get him out of her life. Without the rug at her house he really had no reason to see her again.

What she didn't realize, and what he had only realized this moment, was that he would be seeing her again—whether he had a plausible excuse or not. His attraction to her was more than casual. He fully intended to end up in her bed. He wanted to discover if she brought the same passion and joy to love-making as she did to arguing with him.

"Vorador!"

Coming back to reality with a jerk, Vorador dropped the smoking beaker in a nearby sink. With a wave of his hand, the mess vanished. "Sorry," he said over Dugan's coughing.

Catching his breath, Dugan grinned. "You have got it bad, my friend."

Vorador didn't bother to deny it. He grabbed another flask and started over.

"She's not your usual type."

Once again, Vorador couldn't argue with Dugan's observation. She was entirely different from the kind of women he normally pursued. As a rule, he preferred tall, leggy model types, with more charm than wits. Petra definitely lacked any great abundance of the first, he thought with a smile.

No, that wasn't exactly accurate. True, she bordered on rude, but it was charmingly refreshing. She was like a breath of fresh air—brisk and bracing. He chuckled. Yeah, like a blast of take-your-breath-away, make-your-lungs-ache Arctic air.

Maybe his attraction was so strong simply because Petra was unreadable. He couldn't quite get a fix on whether she was even attracted to him. Sometimes he thought she wanted to wrestle him to the floor, other times her distaste for him was plainly evident. Most women were only too eager to fall into his bed. If they were shy, a simple spell took care of that. However, he was enjoying the chase too much to use any sorcery tricks on Petra.

However, there was her whole nonmagical element to consider. Most of the time he tried not to think about it, since it raised those damn memories. While she'd been surrounded by magic as a child, he'd grown up in a house totally lacking. Not only magic, but tolerance and acceptance of his differences. Not for the first time, he wondered if his parents would have gone a step farther and forbidden him to use his magic if they'd known the outcome.

"Vorador? Earth calling Vorador."

Snapping out of his trance, it took a moment to put aside the past and recall the topic of their discussion. "Petra told you about our adventure at Psycho Hotel California, huh?"

Dugan nodded. "It raises some interesting questions. Like, how did Kitoka get there? And why did you leave her there?"

"Which brings me to a few questions of my own," Vorador shot back. "Such as, why didn't you bother to mention that it was Medora's rug in the first place? Why didn't you tell me she was conscious long enough to place a spell? And why didn't you let Kitoka know what you'd done with Medora?"

When neither of them made any attempt to answer the other's questions, Vorador focused on his work. Finished, he set the potion aside to cool before he looked at his friend. He didn't like what he saw. "Listen, Dugan, we're supposed to be on the same side. So why're you hiding the truth?"

Dugan shrugged and looked away. Vorador waited with as much patience as he could muster. For whatever reasons, he could see his friend was struggling with something. He didn't know what, but he meant to find out. There had never been lies between them before. Well, not on Dugan's part, anyway.

"It really threw me that night," Dugan said in a low voice. "Walking in and seeing Medora's blood. There was so much of it."

Vorador assumed he was talking about entering Petra's house. Then again, maybe he did mean the night he'd found Medora in her apartment.

"At first I thought Petra might be involved," Dugan admitted.

"She isn't," Vorador said in a quiet voice.

"No, that's obvious. She doesn't have a clue who Medora is.

She just wants the blood gone. I do, too. Maybe if it was gone, then Medora would be fine."

Dugan went on in a rush before Vorador could speak. "I know that just wishful thinking, but I can't help clutching at any hope at this point."

"You should realize," Vorador said in a soft voice, "finding that rug is the first break we've had in solving the crime."

Dugan nodded and looked miserable. "Yeah, but then you did your spell and the spot disappeared. Maybe it was my imagination, but Medora seemed stronger that night when I came to visit her. Somehow in my head I connected the two events. Then that hole appeared and I knew I had to tell you the truth, but the only time I saw you was at Petra's and I didn't want to say anything in front of her. Then Medora got weaker and I was afraid to interrupt you and . . ."

Vorador moved closer and briefly rested a comforting hand on his friend's shoulder. "Okay. We can't change what's past. But I think it's time for the complete truth between us now. I can't help anyone unless I know all the facts."

Dugan nodded, then indicated the beaker of dark liquid. "What about that?"

Vorador acknowledged his eagerness to use the potion on Petra's mugger. "It'll still be potent an hour from now."

Settled upstairs in Dugan's office with coffee, the two friends eased the tension by first talking about mundane business matters. Finally, Vorador put aside his cup.

"Start at the beginning. We never have gone over it in detail. Tell me exactly what happened that night at Medora's." He'd been trying to spare his friend further pain. Knowing the basic events had seemed sufficient. Now it looked like he'd been wrong.

Dugan drained his own mug, then took a deep breath. "We had a date that night. I was running a little late. I remember I had flowers. I was whistling.

"When I got there, her front door was open a crack. I figured she'd left it that way for me. I went in and saw her—laying there in a puddle of blood."

Dugan's voice cracked and he had to stop. He got another cup of coffee while he composed himself. Instead of sitting down, he stood staring out the window, his back to Vorador.

"She was barely conscious. I called 911. She was bleeding from . . . There were wounds on her chest. I got towels from the bathroom and applied pressure. She was mumbling softly, under her breath. I couldn't understand any of it. I asked who did this to her, but she didn't seem to hear me.

"Then I heard a noise from the hallway. It sounded like the fire escape door slamming shut. I didn't know what to do. I didn't want to leave Medora alone. But what if whoever had done this escaped? I checked with 911 again, and they said the ambulance was only a couple of minutes away. Medora seemed to be holding on. She could still talk . . ."

"She must have been chanting the spell," Vorador said when it looked like Dugan was too choked up to continue. "That's when the Hotel California spell must've gotten on her rug."

Dugan took a deep breath, gathering himself to finish the story. "I decided to check out the hall—just for a minute. I went down to the exit door. It wasn't locked. I only meant to look inside and see if anybody was there, but as I opened the door and stepped inside, I saw Kitoka get off the elevator. I knew she would take care of Medora, so I took the stairs down to the parking garage but didn't see anyone or anything out of place. When I heard the ambulance arrive, I went back down to Medora's apartment.

"When I got there, Kitoka was gone. Medora was alone with the paramedics. They said she was dead. That's when I called you. You zapped in and we brought Medora here to your lab.

"And that's it." Dugan turned around to face his friend. "Petra said you guys talked to Kitoka. Did she tell you her version of what happened?"

"Just the basics. She got there, found Medora, called 911 again, found some clue that pointed to the murderer and left just as the ambulance arrived."

"She knows who did it?"

Vorador hated to ruin the hope he heard in Dugan's voice.

Somebody put an amnesia spell on her. Besides, I have a feeling that whatever she found was something you left there."

"Why did you leave her down in the hole? I mean, I'm not real fond of Kitoka either, but isn't that kinda harsh?"

Vorador chuckled in spite of himself. "Actually, I didn't."

"Petra said—"

"Oh, I'm sure she believes I did."

Dugan frowned. "What's going on?"

"I probably shouldn't be telling you since I'm breaking a confidence. But—"

"If you don't," Dugan cut in, "I may have to break both your arms."

"You can try."

The two men shared a smile, both relieved to have their relationship back on more normal footing. Although Vorador knew neither of them would ever voice such feelings.

"Kitoka did come out of the hole with us. Because"—Vorador made a sound like drum roll—"somebody turned her into a cat."

Dugan's mouth dropped open. "A cat?"

Vorador nodded and waited. It didn't take long before a gleam of understanding appeared in Dugan's eyes.

"You can't mean . . ." Dugan started to snicker. "So that's why Petra's cat tried to kill me. Oh, man. Poor, poor Kitty."

Vorador couldn't help smiling, too. "Better be careful. Use that nickname around her and cat—or not—she'll find a way to kill you."

"Don't I know it," Dugan got out between chuckles. "She never let anyone but Medora call her Kitty."

Vorador knew it was callous, but it was funny in a twisted sort of way. Kitoka had never been on either of their top-ten favorite people lists. She was a mean-tempered, vicious-tongued, man-hating Amazon who hadn't been happy about her sister's choice of dating partners or business associates.

Dugan's expression turned pensive. "I'm sorry about Kitty's dilemma, but how does this get us any closer to Medora's killer?"

"We know for certain now that it was another wizard."

100

"How do you figure that?"

"Only another wizard could have overcome Medora."

Playing devil's advocate, Dugan said, "If it was a burglar . . . who just broke in and stabbed—" His voice cracked on the last word.

Vorador shook his head. "Even in her own apartment she probably had standard personal safety spells in place. They're not the kind of thing you take on and off every time you come home or leave. A common burglar wouldn't have been able to penetrate her shield. Only another wizard, of equal or greater power, would have the strength to overcome Medora's magic."

"I feel like the dunce in the corner," Dugan said with a frown, "but didn't we already suspect a wizard?"

"Not a hundred percent. Now we know it had to be a stronger, more powerful wizard. Somebody turned Kitoka into a cat. And gave her amnesia. Those aren't easy spells."

Vorador paused, then said, "Kitty must have definite proof about who did this. Why else the double whammy? The murderer must have come back to Medora's apartment while you were checking the basement."

Dugan straightened in his chair. "You're right." He suddenly paled. "If Kitoka hadn't come along—"

Letting the sentence hang there in the silence, Vorador felt no need to finish it. If Kitoka hadn't arrive when she did, the murderer probably would have finished the job and killed Medora. Instead, by taking the time to put spells on Kitoka, Medora's life had been spared.

Somewhat recovered, Dugan went on. "It must have been a trick—the exit door slamming—to get me out of the way. The murderer must have hoped I'd check out the entire stairwell before returning to Medora. Unless there were two of them. Maybe the murderer hired a wizard to put on the spell—"

"No, that's too complicated," Vorador said. "When more than one person knows a secret, somebody always talks. There's not a word out on the streets or anywhere about who did this. I think we can safely assume he, or she, worked alone."

Actually, Vorador saw now, they needed to rethink the entire slant of their investigation. Up until now they'd been focusing on another Amazon as the murderer. Medora held a high position in the Amazon Congress, her official title Royal Adviser. She consulted mostly on magical matters, but the queen valued Medora's opinions and advice. They had considered someone jealous of her power as the main suspect. That was no longer an option. Unless it was a high wizard from another district who wanted to move in and take over Medora's position. No other Amazon wizard in Seattle had the power to work those spells on Kitoka.

"What about this mugger?" Dugan wanted to know. "What happened? How does he tie in?"

Vorador told him briefly.

"He used a knife?"

Since he'd had the same gut-wrenching reaction himself, Vorador allowed Dugan a few moments to recover from that shock. It had taken him longer than that. He would never forget the bone-deep terror he'd felt when he'd seen that knife at Petra's throat. Even now, he didn't remember stopping his car or getting out. Nothing was clear until the moment he'd felt Petra's hand on his arm.

Never again would someone close to him, someone under his protection, be harmed. He knew Dugan understood. That was why Dugan was always the one who explained ERG's protection policy to new customers. The horror from their past had forged a bond stronger than blood ties. Although sometimes it still amazed him that Dugan didn't hate him. Vorador shut the past away. Today seemed to be overrun with memories.

"So you think whoever killed Medora is after Petra now?"

Vorador thought for a minute, then said, "Maybe there's still some clue on the stupid rug that could point to the murderer. What I don't understand is how it got out of Medora's apartment in the first place."

"Did you ask Kitoka about that?"

"Didn't get a chance. Petra came back and, for obvious reasons, Kitty doesn't want her to know that she's, well . . . her kitty."

"When did you figure out it was Medora's rug?"

"Those stupid pigs." Vorador shook his head. "It looked vaguely familiar, but I didn't recall until later I'd seen it in her apartment."

"It's quite a coincidence that Petra collects pigs, too."

"Yeah, but who else besides somebody obsessed with pigs is going to put that butt-ugly thing on their floor?"

"Got a point there." Dugan smiled. "I didn't know what to think when I saw Petra's collection in her bedroom."

"Which reminds me," Vorador growled, "what the hell were you doing in her bedroom, anyway?"

With Vorador glaring at him, Dugan chuckled. "It's evident by your rotten and rather distracted mood that you haven't been invited into the inner sanctum yet."

Vorador stood up.

Dugan shot out of his chair and got out of the wizard's reach. "Hey, can I help it if she finds me more charming?"

Vorador was not amused. His voice was deadly serious as he warned, "Don't play games with this one, Dugan."

Dugan held up his hands in surrender. "No problem." He gathered their coffee cups and put them in a small sink in the corner. "So, when are you going to introduce her to Orwell?"

"Not until after I've got her in my bed."

"Want to make sure she ends up there because of your own limited charm and not because of your big—"

"Look who's talking," Vorador interrupted. "I distinctly remember you borrowed Orwell to impress Medora."

"It worked, too," Dugan said. "Now, get out of here and stop wasting time. We've both got a lot of work to do. Don't forget to check the schedule. I added an appointment at five o'clock."

Nodding, Vorador left Dugan's office. He was exhausted from his long night in the laboratory, but he had a full itinerary today. Plus he had to fit in a visit to the police station to continue his interrogation of Petra's mugger. The man had been strangely resistant to all Vorador's spells. Maybe that explained why he'd ended up in a police broom closet instead of the nice solid jail cell Vorador had envisioned.

Anyway, the guy kept insisting he worked alone, that he wasn't under anybody's orders, that no one had paid him to target Petra specifically. Vorador didn't believe him. The potion should do the trick, and he would get to the truth.

Going to the lobby, Vorador hefted the rug onto his shoulder and headed toward the elevator down to his lab. Now that he had it, and if the magic worked here, there were a few tests he could perform that might provide some answers. Which reminded him—he needed to do further research on ways to break the spells on Kitoka. He hadn't found anything promising in his own library so far. If he could get to the university, he might have better luck.

He also needed to see Petra today. His heart beat faster at the thought of seeing her again. Sadly, it didn't look like he'd have much time to spend with her. Maybe he could steal a few minutes during lunch—if his eleven o'clock appointment didn't run long. First he wanted to swing by his house. He hadn't even had time to go home. He wondered what damage she'd done during her escape.

Not that he'd made it very difficult. He'd only left a locking spell on the front door and the French doors in the living room. Plus one on his bedroom door. He didn't want her exploring that room until he was there to act as her own personal guide. He hadn't intended to keep her prisoner, only slow her down a bit so she wouldn't follow him to the police station. Although, considering her reticence concerning the authorities, that seemed pretty unlikely.

Chapter Fourteen

Carrying her tray, Petra carefully wound her way through the crowded deli, looking for an empty table. She spotted a couple of the decorators from work but veered in the opposite direction. Good grief, what were they doing here? She'd thought she was far enough from the office that she wouldn't run into anyone she knew. They must be in the area on a job. She wasn't familiar enough with the city yet to keep track of where everybody was working.

She didn't want company for lunch. Not that they weren't nice people, but today she preferred to eat alone. She intended to indulge in a full-blown pouting and self-pity session. She hadn't heard a word from Vorador. Not even a message on her answering machine. Not even a thank-you for the rug.

She found an unoccupied table against the back wall. As she sat down, Petra saw a startling sight and nearly missed the chair. There, at a table by the front window, sat Dugan and Fytch. They were talking and laughing, their heads close together.

Fytch laid her hand on Dugan's forearm in a casual manner that indicated familiarity.

Realizing she was gawking like a Peeping Tom, Petra focused her attention on her sandwich—for about ten seconds. Then she simply had to adjusted her chair for a clearer view of the couple. It might not be polite to stare, but it was a heck of a lot more entertaining than eating with her own gloomy thoughts.

Munching on her chicken salad sandwich and potato chips, Petra watched the couple. They were obviously good friends and at ease around each other. There were no awkward silences or lags in the conversation. However, no long smoldering looks or intimate caresses were exchanged either. Fytch seemed comfortable touching Dugan. He never touched her in return, though.

Truthfully, Petra was surprised to see them. Even after Dugan's statement yesterday that he and Fytch had a past, she hadn't expected them to be on such good terms. This morning he'd given the impression he was romantically involved with Medora. Unless she'd misread the entire situation.

Dugan stood up, catching Petra off guard. Before she had time to duck her head and hide, he spotted her. With a cheerful wave, he pointed her out to Fytch. Her gesture wasn't nearly as friendly. Petra forced a smile and waved back. She watched them clean up and gather their belongings. Just when she thought she was safe, they reversed direction and headed toward her table.

"Hi, Miss Field," Dugan said. "I didn't realize your office was around here."

It wasn't. Petra wasn't about to admit she'd come to this specific restaurant because it was the closest one to ERG's office and she'd been hoping to run into a certain wizard. Gad, that made her sound so desperate and pathetic.

"Hi, Dugan." Petra nodded a greeting at Fytch. "It's not really, but this place looked good when I passed it this morning."

"You made an excellent choice. This is the top-rated deli in the downtown area." Dugan smiled, seemingly totally unaware of the tension building between the two women. "We were just going to get some ice cream. Mind if we join you?"

Fytch's expression plainly stated what she thought about that idea. Condemning her own perverse nature, Petra pasted a smile on her face. "Sure. I'd enjoy the company."

He pulled out a chair for Fytch. The minute her back was toward Dugan, she glared daggers at Petra. But her voice was friendly when she said, "Thanks, Dugan."

"Can I get some for you, Miss Field?"

Petra indicated the large chocolate chip cookie on her plate. "Thanks, but no."

Once she was alone with Fytch, it felt like they were isolated on an island of hostility in the ocean of conversation that filled the deli. Why was Fytch's attitude so antagonistic?

"I didn't know you and Dugan were friends," Petra said, hoping that was a neutral enough topic, if not the whole truth.

"Why wouldn't we be?" Fytch snapped back. "And why should you have any knowledge of who Dugan is, or isn't, friends with?"

"Well, I don't, but—"

"You only met him two days ago, didn't you?"

Did she sound jealous, or what? "Yup, just met the guy." Petra tried to keep her voice casual, even though she was growing more and more uncomfortable. "Don't know him from Adam."

"Make sure you keep it that way," Fytch warned.

Maybe Dugan thought his relationship with Fytch was over, but it obviously hadn't ended in Fytch's mind. Petra glanced over to see if Dugan was on his way back yet. Unfortunately, he was still three people away from even placing his order. With a sigh, she turned back to her sandwich. Although trying to eat under Fytch's glower could give even a vulture indigestion.

Petra almost told the wizard to back off but stopped. She sensed that elusive *something* again. It seemed to hover over Fytch like a cloud of toxic gas. Petra was familiar enough with magic not to fear it—most of the time. She discovered, with sudden startling clarity, that Fytch scared the hell out of her.

"What's the matter?" Fytch demanded.

Fytch must have seen some physical reaction to her distressing thoughts. Petra scrambled for a lie. "Ah . . . I bit my tongue."

"Too bad," Fytch said with a nasty smile and fake sympathy. "Maybe you'll bleed to death."

Petra shot to her feet. "I'll be right back. I've gotta go to the rest room." Not waiting for any response, she escaped. If she was really lucky, Fytch would choke on a mouthful of ice cream and keel over dead before she came back.

Petra peeked out the bathroom door, checking to make sure Fytch no longer sat alone. Still, it was with more than a little reluctance that she rejoined Dugan and the witch—ah, wizard. Sitting down, she smiled brightly. "So, did Vorador get the rug?"

The instant she saw the look on Dugan's face Petra knew she'd made another mistake. Although she wasn't exactly sure why. Fytch already knew about the bloody rug.

"Why did you take your rug to Vorador?" Fytch asked. "I thought he got the stain out."

Petra's tongue froze as her mind raced to come up with a plausible explanation.

Dugan beat her to it. "Oh, he did. The police asked him to run some tests. You know, routine stuff."

After that bombshell, conversation seemed to be dead in the water. Since she'd done so well the first time, Petra hesitated to try again. As the silence stretched on, she just couldn't stand it.

"You know, if Medora wants her rug back, she's more than welcome to it."

"Ah . . ." This time Dugan was obviously at a total loss for words. "I'll, ah . . . be sure to pass that along. Thanks."

Fytch looked sharply from one to the other. "I thought Medora was dead."

In that instant, Petra saw her life flash before her eyes. If Dugan didn't kill her for spilling the beans, Fytch would gladly do the deed. And Vorador would help her. Good grief, why hadn't he mentioned that Fytch thought Medora was dead? The wizard had been as closemouthed as a clam, only saying nobody had died. She had assumed it was public knowledge. Therefore, it made perfect sense—to Petra—that Medora might want her property back.

"The news reports said she was dead." Fytch's voice sounded a touch too shrill for mere polite interest.

When Dugan didn't reply, Petra plunged in against all better judgment. "Well, you know how reporters tend to exaggerate the facts to make their story more sensational. Gotta up those ratings. Appease the masses."

Petra glanced sideways at Dugan, her look pleading for some help here. He appeared to be off in his own little world, not even following their conversation. What was wrong with the man?

"So, you're telling me that Medora isn't really dead?"

"I never said she was and I never said she wasn't."

Fytch's face turned red, and Petra began to get worried. Would the wizard forget about showing only her good side to Dugan and reveal her true personality? Was she unethical enough to use her magic to harm people? Petra would bet money on it. She had a feeling Fytch didn't have *any* scruples. No wonder Vorador had warned her about Fytch.

When she saw Fytch's lips start to twitch, Petra knew it was time to retreat. "Well, I gotta get back to work." Scrambling to her feet, she slung her purse over her shoulder. She left her trash and backed away. "Ah . . .'bye."

Not caring that she abandoned Dugan to deal with Fytch's anger, Petra made a speedy exit. She didn't breathe freely until she was in her car. That had been too close for comfort. Gad, was Dugan deaf and blind, as well as dumb, to think Fytch was a nice person? Or maybe he tried to stay on her good side out of fear of what she would do if he ever crossed her.

Petra knew she'd just made a formidable enemy, and probably one with a long memory. Fytch would undoubtedly view this little incident at lunch as a major attack on Petra's part, with Dugan as the prize. That comment about bleeding to death had been too creepy. She needed to convince Fytch she wasn't the least bit interested in Dugan.

Last night Fytch had gone out of her way to give the impression she was involved with Vorador. Did she want both men? Somehow that rang true with Petra's assessment of Fytch's possessive, power-hungry nature. Still, Petra got the sense that Dugan was the main focus of Fytch's affections.

*   *   *

Petra came in through the kitchen door and barely made it to the table before she dropped the grocery bags. Pushing wet hair out of her eyes, she checked to make sure she hadn't broken the eggs. Why had she tried to unload the car in one trip? Maybe because she didn't want to go out in the pouring rain again.

"Hi, Bosco." She greeted the cat as he rubbed against her ankles. "So, you've forgiven me for this morning?"

"Neow."

Hearing what sounded like no, Petra rolled her eyes. "Gonna hold a grudge, huh?"

"Yeow."

She put the milk in the fridge. He'd been one ticked-off kitty this morning. Once he realized she meant to take away the rug, he had yowled and hissed like a little feline maniac. When she tried to pass him, he'd scratched her again.

It had been an appropriate beginning to a pretty cruddy day.

"Hope your day was better than mine, Bossy Boy."

"Yeow!"

Petra didn't even blink when it sounded like the cat said yes.

She got a can of cat food and fed him. As she moved around the kitchen putting things away, Bosco followed close behind her, meowing up a storm. It was the most vocal he'd been since he had shown up on her doorstep the day after she moved in. Thankfully, it only sounded like typical cat noises. Hearing yes and no out of him was bad enough. Recent events had her questioning her sanity already, without adding a talking cat to the mix.

Petra hadn't expected magic to affect her life so much here in Seattle. True, she'd grown up around magic, but since moving out of her parents' house she'd tried to avoid it whenever possible. She'd been surprised, and somewhat dismayed, when she finally came to the realization that she missed the excitement and spice wizardry added to an otherwise boring life. Not that she would ever admit as much to Mom and Dad.

After the debacle with Harold, it was a wonder she hadn't sworn off magic completely. Or been tempted to enter one of those freaky techo-fanatic cults. Since she hadn't, maybe she'd matured beyond the need to hold a grudge against all magic just because of one rotten wizard.

However, after only a few days here, she might be getting too large a dose of magical excitement. She'd dealt with wizard's blood on her rug, met the most powerful sorcerer she'd ever encountered, visited an enigmatic hotel in an alternate reality, been frightened by the Wicked Witch of the Northwest and taken in a talking cat. All in all, it was definitely more than she'd bargained for.

"Ow!" Sharp, needlelike claws shattered Petra's thoughts. "Hey, you mangy beast."

"Yeow."

Petra rolled her eyes. "I had a feeling that would be your opinion on the matter."

Petra went back to fixing dinner, chatting with Bosco while she cooked. It beat being alone in an empty house and talking to the walls.

When she sat down to eat, the cat settled by her feet. He seemed to have an air of expectancy about him, as if he was waiting for her to discover something. If she didn't figure it out, he would probably use those sharp claws on her again.

Finishing her dinner, she gathered her dishes and tidied up the kitchen. While she stood at the sink, she felt Bosco butt his head against her ankle. Bending down she scratched him under the chin.

"Why, thank you. That's a much nicer way to get my attention."

Bosco batted a paw at a crumpled scrap of paper by Petra's foot.

"You are just so cute."

She flicked the paper away, laughing when he chased after it. He grabbed it in his mouth and brought it back. When he dropped it, she sent it scuttling across the floor again. This game continued for several minutes. She was a little surprised at the length of his attention span. She got tired of it before he did.

Grabbing a carton of raspberry frozen yogurt, she headed into the front room. She'd see what was on TV, or maybe read a book. What she wouldn't do was sit by the phone and wait for it to ring. She'd given up on Vorador calling. He must have been even less interested in her than she feared.

She smiled when Bosco jumped onto her lap. "Aren't you being the sweetie tonight? Trying to make up for your rotten attitude this morning?"

"Neow."

She rolled her eyes when he dropped that stupid piece of paper in her lap. "Good grief, bossy, I thought it was elephants who never forgot."

Petra leaned over and dropped the paper in the small trash can beside her desk. "Ouch!"

She jerked her hand back and stared at the bloody welts across her knuckles. In spite of his tendency to scratch at her ankles, this was the first time Bosco'd actually drawn blood. Grabbing him by the scruff of his neck, she stood up and marched to the bathroom. "Okay, Slash, I've had enough of your psycho ways. Just for that, you can spend the night in here."

She set him down, then slammed the door. He immediately started raising a ruckus, but she refused to relent. "If I let you out, you'd probably slit my throat in the middle of the night."

In the kitchen, she washed the scratches. She should put some antibacterial cream and bandages on them. Only problem was, all her medical supplies were in the bathroom. She wasn't opening that can of worms just yet. Back in the front room, she turned on the TV to drown out Bosco's meows. They eventually faded from furious to just plain pathetic.

"No," she yelled, as much to herself as to the cat, "You can cry and whine all you want. I am not going to let you out."

Chapter Fifteen

Half an hour later Petra felt so guilty she couldn't concentrate on anything. She turned off the TV and slammed her book down on the table. She might as well go to bed. She hadn't gotten much sleep last night. But she was not going to let that cat out. Even if he had been quiet for the past fifteen minutes.

"Do you hear me?" she shouted in the direction of the bathroom. "I am *not* letting you out."

She made her nightly circuit through the house, turning off lights, locking doors, talking to Bosco. "You can't go around attacking people whenever the mood strikes you. You need to control your anger and find more acceptable ways of venting—"

Petra stopped. Gad, what was she doing? Standing here lecturing a cat—a cat, for heaven's sake—on the nuances of interpersonal dynamics was plain wacko. She had stepped over the line from being charmingly eccentric into seriously loony.

Stomping into her bedroom, Petra changed into a baggy sleep shirt. She had just turned down the sheets when a loud banging came from the front of the house. At first she thought it was Bosco flinging himself against the bathroom door. No. Somebody was yelling and pounding on her front door.

Holey moley, she would recognize that bellow anywhere. She dashed down the hallway, but skidded to a halt in the front room. Did she really want to confront Vorador when he was in this mood? At least he'd stopped beating on her door. In the ringing silence, she waited breathlessly to see what he would do next.

"Petra, open the door! I know you're in there."

How could he know that for sure? She could be gone. The house was dark. She wished she *was* gone. She hadn't expected him to be quite this angry. In all fairness, she supposed she couldn't blame him. She had trashed his living room.

"Petra, let me in. I'm not going to tell you again."

Good, she thought. She jumped backward. The whole house seemed to vibrate under his renewed attack on the front door.

"Open up!"

Maybe she should let Bosco out and sic him on the wizard—attack cat to the rescue. She clamped her hands over her mouth to stifle her nervous laughter.

"I heard that," Vorador yelled from the porch.

Amazed, Petra took a step back. No, he couldn't have heard that tiny little giggle—not from across the room and through the door. It was impossible.

"You're not helping your case," he said, his voice muffled, as if he had his mouth close to the door, "by laughing at me."

She tiptoed to the door and peered through the peephole. He glared right at her, as if he knew she was checking. Shifting nervously from one foot to the other, she reviewed her options. She could hope he got tired and went away. Extremely unlikely. He could break the door down. Quite likely. She could open the door and let him in. Not likely.

She leaned a shoulder against the door. "Listen, Vorador, I'm really sor—"

"What the hell did you do to my house?"

"Redecorated?" She pressed her ear against the door. Was that

114

hushed laughter she heard? That was probably wishful thinking on her part. Who would have thought her cool, calm, collected wizard had such a fiery temper? Without warning, he whacked the door again, making her jump back.

"Damn it, Petra. Let me in. I promise I won't kill you."

"Oh, yeah. That's reassuring," she muttered. Out loud, she said, "I don't think so, Wiz Boy."

"I need to talk to you. About something important."

"Talk away. I'm listening."

There was a pause, then he said, "I don't think you want your neighbors to hear. Lights are going on all up and down the street."

"And whose fault is that?" she demanded.

"Yours," he shot back.

"In whose universe?"

"Mine."

She smiled, knowing he couldn't see her. "Arrogant jerk."

"Destructive brat." His voice sounded like a caress.

Checking that the security chain was latched, she opened the door a crack and peeked out. He stood in the shadows, one broad shoulder leaning against the doorjamb. His arms were folded and he had his ankles crossed. His pose looked entirely too casual for somebody who had nearly splintered her door.

"What do you want?" she asked.

His eyebrow elevated in that Spock imitation. "I don't think you're anywhere close to being ready to hear what I really want."

Petra shivered, and it wasn't because of the cool night air slipping in through the open door. It also brought in that clean tangy ocean scent of his. She breathed it deep into her lungs until she felt light-headed. No, she stopped herself, getting drunk on Vorador was not an option.

"Open up, Petra." He didn't sound angry. He sounded like he had seduction on his mind.

"Go home. It's late."

"It's not that late. Although"—he inspected her from head to toe—"since you're ready for bed, it must be later than I thought. But still not too late to let me in."

115

Petra swallowed with an audible gulp. Gads, the man could set a bucket of water on fire with a look like that. Afraid of falling down, she leaned against her side of the doorjamb. Only a few inches of wood separated them.

"You are a wicked, wicked man."

"I aim to please."

She released a trembling breath. "Satisfaction guaranteed?"

"What do you think?"

Petra eased the door shut and unhooked the security chain. Moving back, she waited. Vorador stepped in and shut the door with barely a whisper of sound. The only illumination came through the windows from the porch lamp and streetlights. He was little more than a dark outline. With any other man Petra might have felt intimidated. In spite of his earlier threats, she knew he would never hurt her—physically. No telling what kind of emotional damage he could inflict without even being aware of it.

"Sorry about your house. Things kinda . . . got out of hand."

"I should have known better than to leave you unsupervised."

"Yeah, you should have."

"What I don't understand is how you managed to wreak quite so much havoc."

"All I did was touch the suit of armor. Everything else just kind of snowballed."

"It looked like an avalanche hit the room."

"I'm sorry," she repeated. "I'll pay for the damages."

"That's not necessary. Everything is repairable or replaceable." He paused, then asked, "Just the armor? You didn't touch anything else?"

"No. Well, I tripped and knocked over a couple of tables, but that wasn't my fault. That homicidal armor chased me."

"It chased you?"

"Yeah, with the ax. It tried to chop me into little bitty pieces."

"You weren't the one who left the ax buried in my door?"

"No!" Geez, if that was what he thought, no wonder he'd come over here ready to smash her door.

"I wonder . . ."

"What?" she prompted when he didn't go on.

"I've never had a protection spell react like that. It should have only repeated the warning. I don't know why it became mobile."

"You mean that wasn't part of your spell?"

"No, of course not. Do you mind if I turn on the light?"

His abrupt question startled her. Petra hesitated. It was easier talking to him in the dark, where she could pretend anything she wanted. In the light, reality became too clear. Although tonight reality might not be so bad. Tonight a handsome sexy man was standing in her living room.

"Go ahead." When he stumbled into a chair, she said, "Here, let me," and found the switch.

Blinking in the bright light, her breath caught in her throat. He was gorgeous. He wore a black brushed silk shirt buttoned up to his neck, tight black jeans and black cowboy boots. No wonder she'd only been able to see his outline in the darkness. His long dark hair was pulled back in a neat braid. Talk about sinfully delicious.

"Cute pigs."

"Huh?" Petra felt as stupid as she sounded. "What pigs?"

"On your shirt."

Oh, crud. Face hot, she stared down at the squadron of flying pigs soaring across her chest. She crossed her arms, doing her best to cover them. The movement reminded her that she wasn't wearing anything except the shirt. Just the thought that she was practically naked in the wizard's presence was enough to make her nipples tighten in anticipation. She crossed her arms tighter and wished she could do the same with her legs.

"Do you ever sleep in anything else?" Vorador asked in a low husky voice.

"Huh?" She'd gone terminally feebleminded.

"The pig shirts. You were wearing one yesterday, too. Is that what you always sleep in?"

If he didn't stop talking about sleeping—in other words, going to bed—she would soon be nothing but a whimpering basket case curled up in the corner. "Stop it!"

Vorador quirked that deadly brow at her. "I'm not doing anything. I'm just standing here—"

"Yeah, you're about as innocent as a kid in a candy store."

That made him smile, his lips parting just enough to show a hint of teeth. She nearly swooned. He stepped toward her and her eyes glazed over. The dull gleam of rough black silk moved across his chest, reminding her of flowing midnight water. He came another step closer and she could practically see the power building in him. It was like a flood piling up behind a damn, swirling and battering against the barrier in its path.

Part of her mind screamed *Danger! Danger!* The rest of it was a seductive whisper—*Go for it.*

With one last step he was close enough to touch. She literally felt his power burst over the top. It rushed forward, sweeping aside all obstacles as if they were mere matchsticks. She couldn't resist any more. Didn't want to resist.

"Oh, the heck with it." She grabbed him, pulled his face down and kissed him.

For those first astonishing moments she wondered if she'd gone into shock. Her lips felt numb. Then she became aware of something amazing. He tasted wonderful! Oh, the extraordinary, deeply satisfying, glorious taste of him. As he kissed her back, she decided she'd never be able to get enough.

She kissed him again, becoming acquainted with his texture. His lips were firm and resilient. Could a person have muscular lips? The thought made her smile. She ran her tongue along the lower curve, mesmerized by the satiny skin. He felt luxuriant.

She wished he would put his arms around her. Tempting him, she ran her hands over the soft texture of his shirt, rich beguiling silk laid over supple yielding steel. Oh, no. She didn't want to, but she couldn't hold it back. Breaking the kiss, she laughed.

"What's so funny?" His deep voice poured over her like warm honey.

She giggled. She had to stop this.

"Tell me," he whispered.

His mouth hovered a fraction of an inch from hers. His breath hot and moist against her face like—"Stop it!"

He didn't move and she raised her gaze to meet his. They were so close, she could see where the rich warm chocolate of his eyes gave way to the black pupil. Amusement lurked in their depths as he waited to share the joke.

"Tell me," he repeated. His fingertips stroked her forehead and down the sides of her face.

Finally! At last he touched her. She closed her eyes, savoring the erotic sensations.

"What thoughts are rattling around in there, Petra, that you want to put a stop to them?"

So, he knew her well enough by now to understand what she meant. First she wanted to kiss him again, to see if it was as incredible as she remembered. She groaned when he retreated the exact fraction of an inch she advanced, keeping his mouth just out of her reach. She was drowning in the dark limpid pool of his eyes—the mood was spoiled when she giggled.

He inhaled deeply, as if trying to breathe in the sounds of her amusement.

Petra's laughter caught in her throat. Oh, what this wizard could do to her. She didn't care if it was a spell or the real McCoy. She simply didn't want it to stop. She buried her fingers in his long silky hair, pulling it loose from the braid.

"Tell me."

She wondered how he could make the words into a demand without raising his voice. A man of many talents. She smiled and her knees went weak when he responded with a smile of his own.

"I was thinking . . . about your lips, and your eyes," she said.

"Yes?"

"My thoughts—they sound like a cliched romance novel."

His smile widened into a grin. "I like romance novels."

She gave a sigh of relief. "Oh, thank heavens."

He prompted, "About my lips?"

"Silk over steel."

He rubbed his mouth over hers, making a humming sound of satisfaction. He gathered her into a closer embrace. "Your mouth tastes like a ripe juicy peach."

Laughing with him, she felt his amusement rumble in his chest. "Do you like peaches?"

"I have a passion for them." He nibbled at her lips.

She sighed again. "That's nice to hear."

"In fact"—he swayed slightly from side to side, rubbing his entire body against hers—"I bet if I look hard enough I can find a whole fruit salad."

She gasped at the sensations rocketing through her body. She gloried in the titillating feelings but tried for one last moment of sanity. Steadying herself, she pulled away slightly. "This probably isn't such a good idea."

He shook his head. "No, this is a great idea."

Fighting her doubts and old fears, she searched his face, looking for reassurance. Pressing herself against him, she murmured, "Oh, what the—"

"—heck," he finished for her, then covered her mouth, claiming her laughter for his own.

She was drowning. If it meant she could stay in his arms for the rest of her life, she didn't care if she ever breathed again. With a shiver of delight, she felt his hand leave her back and slowly, too slowly, follow the curve of her ribs. She almost forgot to kiss him back as she waited for him to reach that final destination.

When his fingers touched her breast, Petra jumped backward like she'd been shot from a catapult. Her feet slipped on the bare wood floor. She landed on her butt with a jarring thud. Gazing up at Vorador, she felt as dazed as he looked.

"Petra, what's going on? Why—"

"You shocked me!"

He looked insulted. "Well, sorry. But I thought it was a mutually satisfying moment and we were both ready to take it to the next level."

"No. You *shocked* me." His look was still uncomprehending. "You know, like electricity."

Now he was the one who looked shocked. Still feeling the trembling aftermath of those blazing kisses, she needed some help to stand up. "Give me a hand, will you, please?"

When he didn't move, she realized he was staring at her. It took a couple of seconds to perceive what he was staring at. The hem of her shirt was practically up to her hips, leaving more than was polite bare for public viewing. Scrambling to her knees, she jerked the fabric down, covering what shouldn't have been showing in the first place. Her face felt hot enough to ignite into spontaneous combustion. Where was a convenient hole when she needed one? Darn! She'd left it at Vorador's office.

"Petra?"

She kept her gaze on the floor, embarrassed beyond words. When his hand appeared in her field of vision, it startled her and her gaze flew upward. It never made it to his face. In fact, it never made it as high as his belt buckle. Her attention remained focused slightly south of there. A sound that was part sigh, part moan and part whimper rattled in her throat.

"Hello there," she said in a raspy whisper.

"Petra," his voice was an urgent warning, "if you don't stop looking at me like that, you're going to end up being a whole lot more than shocked."

She heard him and understood him. She just couldn't make her eyes behave. What would it be like to unleash all the power straining the metal buttons of his fly?

"Do you hear me, Petra?"

"Uh-huh."

"But are you listening to me?"

She sighed wistfully and licked lips gone dry. "Only if I have to."

With a vile curse, Vorador moved to the other side of the room, his footsteps echoing loudly on the wood floor.

Petra drooped in disappointment. "Spoilsport."

With the enticing view gone there was no reason to stay on her knees, and she rose shakily before plopping down on the couch in a comfortable sprawl. When she remembered she

121

wasn't alone, she wiggled into a more proper position and tugged on her shirt until it covered her knees.

"Okay, now what?" she asked, not sure if the question was for herself or the wizard.

Chapter Sixteen

Vorador shoved his hands into his pockets. It was the only way he could keep them off Petra. He couldn't believe how quickly things had gotten out of control. One moment they had been playful, kissing, laughing. In the next heartbeat he wanted her with a passion he'd never experienced before.

He sucked in a deep breath, feeling his overly sensitive skin stretch, remembering her touch—on his chest, in his hair, caressing his face. He watched Petra try for a dignified pose on the couch. He clenched his hands, nearly ripping the seams of his pockets. Spinning away, he headed for the door.

"Where are you going?"

He didn't break his stride. "I'll be right back."

Then he was out the door, into the cool night air. It did nothing to quench the fires burning inside. He stood by his Jeep and raised his face, hoping the misty drizzle would clear his mind. His skin felt tight and fever hot. The fine droplets seemed to sizzle and evaporate as soon as they touched him.

Leaning against the Jeep, Vorador raked his hands through

his hair. What the hell was wrong with him? He'd been furious when he'd finally seen what she'd done to his house. Not in his worst nightmare could he have envisioned such destruction. His fury hadn't faded while driving to her house. But when she called him an arrogant jerk in that breathy, sexy voice, his anger had metamorphosed into a passion that nearly sent him to his knees.

Luckily he had managed to collect himself by the time she opened the door. Crossing his legs, trying to appear nonchalant, he'd fervently hoped she wouldn't notice what she'd done to him. Otherwise, she never would have let him in her house.

The mere thought of Petra sent blood pounding to his groin. Not even when he'd used a potent sexual spell had his erection ever been that swift or that intense. He felt thick and heavy, and imminently unsatisfied. His harsh bark of unamused laughter spilled into the night. Hell yes, he was unsatisfied.

"Vorador, what the heck are you doing out there?"

"Shut up, Petra. Go back in the house."

He didn't expect her to let that insult pass, let alone obey him. There must have been something disturbing in his voice. For once, she actually did what he asked. Watching her go back inside, for some reason he felt disappointed. Seemed to be his night for it.

After several minutes of fierce concentration, he felt minimally in control. It was his job to protect Petra, not take advantage of her. She was a client, he reminded himself. He adjusted his pants, trying for a more comfortable fit over a hard-on that just wouldn't go away. He wasn't certain he was ready to face her, but any further delay wouldn't help. If he had a lick of sense, he'd go home.

Instead he opened the back of the Jeep. Lifting the rolled-up rug onto his shoulder, he marched back into the siren's den.

"What'd you think you're doing?" Petra demanded the instant he entered the house.

He dumped the rug at her feet. "Returning your property."

"You keep it." She transferred her glare from him to the object in question. "I don't want it back."

"Tough luck." Stepping away from her—it was either that or

124

grab her—Vorador fought his desire. "You win the prize."

Kicking the rug with her bare toes, she said, "No thanks. I gave it to you."

"Why such a big rush to get rid of it? If you'd called, I would've come and got it."

She shifted uneasily from side to side.

"Did something happen, Petra?" Sometimes she was remarkably easy to read. It was all the other times that drove him crazy.

"I had nightmares last night."

"Sorry, I don't see the connection."

"Nightmares about horrible creatures crawling out of that," she pointed to the carpet, "and coming to get me."

He looked at her, then looked at the rug. "You've had this rug for—what? A week now? Surely if there was some evil connected to it, it would have affected you earlier."

"So it doesn't make sense. Tough luck. I still want it out of my house."

When he made no move to obey her command, she put her hands on her hips and scowled at him, as if that alone could force him into submission.

He really wished she hadn't done that. It made him want to replace her hands with his. Her posture defined the curve of her hips, hiking the pig shirt up past midthigh. He liked her legs. They weren't too thin or too muscular. They looked feminine and soft. He could imagine how they would feel wrapped around him.

He nearly doubled over as lust hit him right between the legs. This wasn't right. Something was wrong here. Ignoring Petra's concerned questions, he sent his senses out, searching the air around her for unusual waves and patterns.

He could see her new co-workers' auras, but they weren't strong since she hadn't known those people very long. He saw the bright emerald green he recognized as Dugan. He even found traces of Fytch's menacing orange and burnt umber. The stark black and white of Kitoka stood out sharply.

There were a few frayed strands woven around her, hinting at childhood friends. He discerned an ugly dark brown thread with muddy glints of weak power. It wasn't very long, but it

125

wrapped tight around the area of her heart. That must be the bastard who had made her leery of wizards.

The most prevalent influence was from her parents. One thick rope of warm earth tones had the intermingled metallic sparkle of magic. That had to be her mother. The other matching coil was exuberant jeweled colors, brilliant with the inner glow of powerful magic. Her father's influence twined about Petra in love and total support.

Nothing seemed out of place. Nothing hinted at contact with an unfamiliar wizard, but he couldn't be sure. In his current state he could barely see past the passion blurring his vision.

"Petra, did you hire another wizard to cast a love spell?"

Her reaction took him by surprise. She burst out laughing. In fact, she collapsed on the couch, lost in fits of giggles.

"This is no laughing matter, Petra."

"Oh, yes," wiping tears from her eyes, she insisted, "it is."

He waited for her explanation. If she had gone to someone for a spell, they hadn't done a very good job. While lust had him nearly incapacitated, she obviously felt only mild attraction to him. True, she had kissed him first, but it had been more of a curious exploration than a desperate need. He didn't know what to think about the shock he'd inadvertently given her.

Finally, Petra said, "You don't know how glad I am to hear you ask that."

"Why? Because you want to confess?"

"No." Her grin was impudent and unrepentant. "Because I thought the same thing. Practically since the second I met you."

"What?"

"Only I thought you had cast a spell on me."

Vorador wasn't entirely sure what he felt at that moment. Relief that he wasn't alone in this aroused state. Insulted that she thought he needed a spell to attract women's interest. Guilty because he had used such spells in the past. Mostly he felt intense interest. He wondered how far she would let things go if he took up right where they'd left off—with Petra on her knees in front of him.

"I've used no magic on you." He couldn't be sure if his statement caused her relief or concern. "Since you claim you've had none cast on me—"

"Trust me, I haven't."

Something in her tone made him suspicious. Did she look guilty? True, she couldn't have done it, since she had no magic. If not her, then—"Could somebody else have cast a love spell on you?"

Her gaze darted away from his.

Yup, definitely guilty. "Who, Petra?"

She glared at him. "I don't know . . . for sure."

"Who?"

"Okay, maybe my parents," she confessed. "But only because they want me to settle down and be happy. And I'm not positive. I mean, it could just be some random—"

"I don't think so," he interrupted. Would her parents have really cast such a spell on their daughter? He supposed it was possible if her love life was as dismal as she seemed to think. "So, where does this leave us?"

"Nowhere," Petra said in a rush.

Acutely disappointed, Vorador hoped his face didn't show how much her denial affected him.

"Yet."

That one short word sent his hopes flying and his blood pounding. His erection was so painful he could barely walk. He made it to the couch and sank down, having to adjust a bit before finding a tolerable position. He did nothing to hide his state from her—as if he could. Even wearing his robe it would have been difficult to conceal.

He glanced at Petra to judge her mood. She was staring at the bulge in his jeans. Breathing through her mouth, she had a death grip on the sofa cushion. Her nipples poked through the flying pigs in interesting locations. He couldn't keep a slow, purely self-satisfied smile off his face.

"Are you sure not yet?" he asked, his voice low and gravelly.

"Huh?" Her eyes didn't even flicker.

It shouldn't have been possible, but he got even harder. Great googgly-mooggly! What was happening between them? He hadn't been this out of control since his sex-crazed, hormone-induced, wild-and-woolly teenage years. He had to touch her.

Reaching out, he cautiously captured just a strand of her hair. When no sparks flew, he deepened the caress, burying his hand in her hair. He gently spread his fingers across the back of her skull and eased her head up, urging her to look at him.

Her expression destroyed his seduction plans. Much as he wanted to ravish her, he couldn't do it. Not like this. Not because some possible outside force controlled their emotions. When they made love, they would both be in full control of their senses.

He forced himself to think rationally. Damn, but it hurt. "Petra, we need to do something about this."

"What?"

He wasn't quite certain of her meaning but plunged on. What—she didn't understand? Or, what should they do? "We have a problem here."

"Oh." Her gaze darted down to his crotch, then back to his face. She grinned. "All of my problems should be so big."

He grinned back. Petra's impudent humor had obviously returned, which helped him regain a bit more control. He gently massaged his fingers against her scalp. "I'm going to try a dampening spell. We have some serious matters to discuss."

"More serious than—"

"Yes," he said before she could finish.

He couldn't quite bring himself to remove his hand from its warm cozy spot cradling her head. He could smell the faint fruity scent of her shampoo. In fact, he could detect all the scents of a delicious fruit salad as he breathed in. She had strawberries in her hair; peaches on her face and neck; applesomething on her hands.

"Whatever." She shrugged, bumping her shoulder against his arm.

That simple contact made him realize he'd been building his dam out of straw instead of rock. Her soft touch sent him over the edge of the precipice. There was no more stopping his passion than holding back floodwaters. His hand fisted in her hair and he dragged her across the space separating them. Then he

128

kissed her, devoured her, nipped at her lips, ravenous for more. She moaned and he gathered her closer.

He groaned, not knowing if it was because her tongue boldly explored his own mouth or from the exquisite feel of her breasts pressed against his chest. He wanted to caress them, but after the last time, he hesitated. He settled for sending his hands lower across the small of her back.

Never breaking their kiss, he lifted her onto his lap, turning her to straddle him. Her weight settled on him, driving him crazy. His hands moved down to squeeze and caress her bottom. She arched her hips against him and cried out. He rediscovered what he'd known before; she wasn't wearing any panties. Her skin was as silken soft as he'd dreamed.

"Vorador." She murmured his name against his lips.

He deepened the kiss, using his tongue to silence her, not wanting to hear the voice of reason. She tasted more delicious than anything in his experience. Her arms wrapped around his neck and she pressed herself closer to him. With his lips he traced a sizzling path down her neck. She jerked against him when he bit her earlobe. His own hips lifted upward, grinding their bodies together.

"Vorador."

This time her voice sounded like a plea. To stop or not to stop; he didn't know. He used his teeth where her neck met her shoulder, then licked away the sting. She shuddered, her fingers digging into his shoulders. She arched her back, offering him her breasts, but he didn't dare accept, still rational enough to remember that shock.

"The dampening spell." She gasped as his hand stroked her inner thigh. "Use it."

"No." He increased his assault, daring to bite the upper swell of her breast through the shirt. He desperately wanted to kiss her puckered nipples, but with all the power flowing between them he just might electrocute her. His fingers brushed against the hair between her legs.

"Vorador!" Her voice was nearly a scream. "The spell. Do it." She gasped and shuddered when his palm cupped her. "This is too much. Too soon!"

He knew she was right, but he couldn't do it. He couldn't stop now. He eased a finger inside her. She was tight around him, slick with moisture and hot enough to burn. He pushed farther and her hips bucked against him.

One of her hands slid down his chest, across his stomach, coming to a halt pressed firmly against his erection. He nearly bolted off the couch. She rubbed up and down his length, sending shivers of pure sensation rioting through his body and mind. Had anything ever felt so good before? He didn't think so.

"Vorador. You have to stop this. I can't—"

Her words ended in a garbled sound when he flicked his thumb across her sensitized flesh. He knew she was right. This was wrong. Too fast, too strong. They needed to slow down. But not yet. Just a little more. He could tell she was close. He wanted to watch her shatter under his hands. He lowered his head, intending to kiss her, knowing that would push her over the edge.

"Please."

Again, one word, just one little word from her, changed everything. He couldn't quite bring himself to withdraw from her heat, but he gave in. He did what she asked of him. Even as he continued to stroke her, sending her higher and higher, he began chanting the spell that would douse their passion.

"Cool the fires—"

He stuttered to a halt when her inner muscles squeezed his finger. His body trembled at the incredible pleasure of her touch, wishing—He cut off the thought before it formed. With whatever was happening here, he feared even an unvoiced wish might become reality. He hurried to finish the spell.

"—that burn our veins."

He felt her clench around him again, then again. With one final caress, he sent her soaring over the edge.

"Dampen the desire—"

Her orgasm came crashing through her and she called his name. He held her close, absorbing her cries of fulfillment, his own flesh aching for the same.

"—and make us sane."

Suddenly, with a clap of thunder, water came pouring from

the ceiling. In seconds they were drenched. Stunned, Vorador raised his face, letting the cold water gush over him, trying to see where it was coming from. Petra squealed and jumped off his lap. He spared a brief appreciative glance at the way her wet shirt plastered against her body.

He sat there, the water getting more and more frigid, until the last of his passion shriveled and died, washed away. He uttered a few words and crossed his fingers, hoping the spell worked properly this time. The torrent of water slowed, became a trickle, then vanished, except for a few drops falling like liquid ice. They landed on top of his head and he shivered.

"Are you totally out of your mind?"

Vorador winced at Petra's shrill demand. He scrubbed his hands over his face, wiping water from his eyes. He shook his head, sending water flying from the ends of his hair, then slicked it back out of the way. He wasn't quite sure what to do next. Nothing like this had ever—ever!—happened to him before.

"Is that your idea of a proper dampening spell?"

Vorador could no more hold back his amusement than stop a runaway train. "Well, I'd say we're both pretty much dampened."

Petra gritted her teeth. He could actually hear them grinding together. "You were only supposed to tone down our emotions, not flood my entire house. Look at this mess."

She had a point there. The couch was a waterlogged disaster. Large puddles covered the floor and had probably ruined the hardwood finish. The rolled-up rug was drenched. Her desk had been splashed, papers were ruined, books damaged. He hated to think what condition her computer was in.

"If you want"—he flashed a grin at her—"I can cast a spell and clean it up."

She backed away from him. "Don't do me any more favors."

He chuckled, wondering when her sense of the ridiculous would kick in. Surely she saw the humor in their situation. "Okay, next time I'll just keep on—"

"There isn't going to be a next time. Trust me on that."

"I'm sorry, Petra." It cost his pride to admit it, but he owed

131

her the truth. He gestured around her dripping living room. "I don't know what happened."

She pushed wet hair out of her eyes and considered his words. "Okay. Fine. Apology accepted. I guess turnabout's fair play since I wrecked your front room yesterday." She pivoted and started down the hallway.

As soon as she turned her back, he quickly worked a general cleanup spell. It was a simple one, used by schoolchildren. He didn't see how it could fail. Still, he held his breath when he snapped his fingers.

She spun to face him, ready for battle. The fire in her eyes was replaced by surprise as she took in the spotless room. "You are one lucky wizard."

Vorador relaxed back on the dry couch. "It's pure skill and talent. Luck has nothing to do with it."

Smothering a snort of laugher, Petra looked down at her now dry shirt. "I think I'd better put on a robe. Then we'll talk."

When he was alone, Vorador blew out a cleansing breath. What a night! And it wasn't over yet. He could hardly wait.

Chapter Seventeen

Settled at the kitchen table with a soothing cup of tea, Petra was acutely aware of the man sitting across from her. He'd given her the most earth-shattering orgasm she had ever experienced and neither one of them had even taken their clothes off. Gads!

Harold had never touched her with such explosive results, that was for darn sure. Of course, Harold had been a selfish jerk.

"Petra, is there something wrong with your tea?"

"No." She took a sip to prove it but couldn't quite look Vorador in the eye. "Why?"

"You had a really sour expression on your face."

She had no intendion of discussing Harold with Vorador. She took another sip. "Tell me why you brought that stupid rug back."

Vorador sighed but did as she asked. "Because it doesn't work anyplace else. I intended to run some tests at my lab to see what information I could turn up. Nothing happened."

"The hole never showed up?"

"Not even the blood spot appeared. I thought the conditions might not be right, so I took it home. No blood. No hole. Just an ugly-as-sin rug."

"It's not ugly. It's unique."

"You can say that again." He held up his hand to stop her when she opened her mouth. "I want to put it back here at your house and see what happens."

Struck by a sudden thought, Petra leaned forward. "Why don't you talk to Medora? Ask her about the spell she used."

"That's not possible," Vorador said.

"Surely she won't refuse to help you. Better yet, take it to her place. After all, it's her rug. And her blood."

"Petra, she can't—"

"Well, I don't see why not. Sure, I guess it's a little morbid, but doesn't she want to find out who tried to do her in?"

"Petra, she isn't—"

"Well, she should. I can't believe she's not over here, banging on my door, demanding to be part of your investigation. I mean, I want to know who did this and I'm not directly involved."

"That isn't possible," Vorador stated in an emphatic voice. "She's—"

"Why not?"

"If you'd let me finish a sentence, I'd tell you."

Petra clamped her lips together, made the childish gesture of locking them, then motioned him to go ahead.

"Medora isn't available for questioning. Or anything else."

She couldn't stand it, couldn't stay quiet. "Why not?"

"Because she's mostly dead."

"*Mostly* dead?" Petra considered that outrageous claim for a moment. "I don't get it. Either you are or you aren't."

"She's not entirely dead, but not quite . . . actively alive."

"Okay," Petra said, irritated, "that's clear as mud."

"I guess the closest analogy would be that she's in a coma."

"If a medical doctor examined her, he'd say she was dead?"

"Yes."

"Wow!" What he was saying finally began to sink in. "I've never heard of any wizard doing such a spell before."

Vorador just shrugged and looked uncomfortable.

Curiosity quickly overtook wonder. Petra spoke in a rush, her words tumbling over themselves. "What spell did—? Where did you find—? How—?" She laughed at herself, then summed up her feelings. "Boy, you do have guts."

"Or luck."

Forgetting about everything else, she propped her elbows on the table, getting as comfortable as a kitchen chair allowed. "I want to know every detail."

He warily leaned back in his own chair, stretching out his legs under the table. "Not to be rude, but you don't have any magic. Why are you so interested in a spell?"

"Are you kidding?" She waved aside his skepticism. "I may not have any powers of my own, but you have to remember, I was raised around magic. Just by sheer osmosis, I probably know more spells and incantations than the average college graduate."

A fond tone softened her voice. "I have to hand them that. Mom and Dad never excluded me because of my lack of talent. Sure, more often that not I was their guinea pig—"

Vorador gave a short burst of laughter, then said, "Sorry."

Ever curious, hoping he would share, she prompted, "What?"

He hesitated, but finally said, "I just remembered using my friends for guinea pigs in some of my first spells. It wasn't always a pleasant experience." He shared a smile with her. "Lost more friends that way."

"I know how they felt." Petra chuckled, more at ease than she'd been since he walked in her door. "Anyway, no matter what, my parents always took pains to explain their spells to me, made sure I understood the principles behind them, even if I couldn't actually do the magic."

"Did you always know you didn't have any?"

"Yeah, but I held out hope my powers would suddenly appear." She smiled slightly. "I figured puberty was my last chance."

"I sense a story behind that statement."

Grinning, she teased, "Gee, and you're not even a psychic."

"So what happened?"

"The day I started my first period, I was positive my powers had blossomed forth. Just like my womanhood." She gave a self-mocking laugh. "So I worked a flight spell and jumped off the roof."

Vorador winced. "Didn't work?"

She shook her head. "Fell like an anvil. Broke both my legs and spent several weeks in traction. I'm still not sure who was more disappointed, me or my parents."

"In spite of that, sounds like you had a good childhood."

"You know, I never thought so." Petra tilted her head and studied him. This wasn't the first time he'd made such a comment. Maybe she should start listening to him.

He hunched forward, resting his forearms on the table. "Trust me, it had to be better than mine."

"How so?"

He just shook his head.

She lightly touched his hand. "It helps to talk about it." When he looked skeptical, she smiled. "Really. Trust me."

Vorador's answering smile was grim, the shadows in his eyes dark and full of pain. He cleared his throat before breaking the silence. "My family is very, very traditional."

Petra wished she could hug him, but the atmosphere between them was still too volatile. She wanted to comfort him, not arouse him. "So they don't approve of magic?"

"That's putting it mildly," he said with a wry twist of his lips. "They were extremely proud that their lineage was magic-free. Good genetic breeding, you know."

His cynical tone nearly ripped her heart out.

"I was the loser in the big game of DNA combination. I must have gotten all the magic that skipped all those generations in all those branches of the family tree."

"You're not a loser," she said, then realized he hadn't even heard her. He was far away in the past.

"I was only six months old when they began to suspect something was wrong with me. When I cried, things would fly off shelves. When I laughed, the whole room would brighten up, as if the sun shone inside."

Petra wished with all her might that his childhood had been

filled with such wonderful light but had already heard enough to know it hadn't.

"When I started walking, it got worse. If there was a toy I couldn't reach, it floated down to me. Or I levitated up to it. The twos really were terrible. My tantrums wrecked more than one room. When my parents couldn't hide their shameful secret any longer, they moved to another town. Then my training began."

"Training?" Maybe his childhood hadn't been as bad as she'd imagined. Not if his parents taught him how to use his magic.

"That's what they called it." His snort of laughter was harsh and grating. "They were training me to be normal."

"No." Her denial was a soft cry. All his years of pain were in that admission.

"Now that's a word I heard a lot growing up. 'No magic.' 'No, don't do that.' 'No. No. No.' By the time I was ready for kindergarten nobody would have guessed I was really a freak."

"Vorador, no." Petra wanted to smack herself when that word came out of her mouth. "You are not—nor ever were—a freak."

He ignored her. "We lived in a city where magic was banned. If I had showed the slightest sign of my powers, we would have been run out of town. My parents would have lost everything."

"How could they have done that to you?" Petra exclaimed in disbelief. "To put so much guilt and responsibility on a child? While forcing you to deny your very nature? It's inhuman!"

Her impassioned response seemed to drag him out of the past, back to the present. Shrugging, he said, "They were products of their own environment and upbringing. They did what they thought best."

"How can you defend them? After such cruelty and—"

"They're my parents, Petra."

It was a struggle, but she managed not to burst into tears at his simple statement. Of course he loved them, no matter how she might perceive them. Compared to his childhood, how could she not appreciate the way Mom and Dad had raised her? They had never done anything to exclude her, or make her feel like a freak. Her own feelings had made her act like an outsider.

"You're right, Vorador. I'm sorry."

137

"Apology accepted."

Petra leaned back in her chair and blew out a long breath. He looked as wiped out as she felt. At some point, she wanted to learn more about his past. What event had changed his life so he used his magic? But not now. Now it was time to make him smile.

"Geez, I feel like I just had a major breakthrough with my shrink."

"It goes both ways, Petra," he said in a solemn voice.

"How much do I owe you, doc?"

A slow, sexy smile spread across his face. "We could pay each other back to our mutual satisfaction." He lifted one eyebrow.

Petra scowled at him. Well, she'd gotten the smile—and then some. She could guess exactly what he had in mind. At the very least, a kiss. At the most—no, she warned herself, don't go there. "Never mind."

"I like that."

"What?" she asked, half-afraid to hear what he had to say.

"The fact that I can make you blush with just a few words."

Her face got hotter. "You do seem to have a talent for it. I don't think I've blushed this much in years."

"I like that, too."

Gads, she was probably bright red all the way down to her toes. "Let's get back on track. Tell me about the spell. I've never heard about somebody being mostly dead."

She thought she heard him mutter, "Chicken," before he answered. It was all too true.

"I first read the spell in an ancient grimoire," he said.

There was a term she hadn't heard in a long time. It sounded so much more romantic than "book of spells." "Where'd you find it?"

"I bought a box of used books for twenty dollars and there it was. Since it was in Gaelic I couldn't read it until I had taken some college courses. At first I thought my translation was wrong. I took it to Professor Helios and had him check it out.

"It was right. I'd found a spell that could return a person to life—if you managed to cast it before their spirit totally left their body. I never expected the opportunity to actually use it, but I made up the necessary potions and stored them in my lab.

"When Dugan called me about Medora—"

"Exactly how does Dugan fit into all this?"

"I thought you knew." When she shook her head, he went on. "He and Medora were dating."

Petra gave a low whistle. She'd guessed right. Which made that lunch encounter with Fytch all the creepier. "How serious was—is it between them?"

"They'd only gone out for a few weeks, but he likes her."

She couldn't quite imagine Dugan with an Amazon warrior/ wizard. What did the local Amazon ruling council think of one of their members dating him? True, a certain percentage of Amazons had to breed in order to continue their order. Somehow Dugan didn't seem suited to be the subservient male partner, staying home and raising the kids.

"So Dugan knew about the spell," Vorador continued.

"You guys are really good friends, huh?"

"I've known him since we were in grade school."

"One of your guinea pigs who didn't get away?" Petra asked with a smile.

"Something like that."

She had a feeling there was more to the story but let it slide for the moment. Instead she made sure she understood Dugan's part in the events. "So he was the one who found Medora. In her apartment. Bleeding on that rug."

She picked up her feet and tucked them out of the way. It gave her the creeps to think she'd walked all over that very same rug. Over the past few days the people involved had become more than just statistics. Now the flea market find seemed to give off a malevolent presence. She *really* didn't want it back in her house.

"Petra?"

She shook off the heebie-jeebies. "So Dugan called you and you worked your magic."

He looked like he wanted to question her mood, but instead finished the story. "We took Medora back to my lab. Dugan thought she was gone, but I could see the barest threads of her presence. When the paramedics shocked her heart, it must have

139

kept her hanging on. I used the potions, worked the spell and she's not quite dead."

"Is she still there in your laboratory?"

He hesitated for a long time, then slowly nodded.

"Considering somebody already tried to kill her, that's a big secret, isn't it?"

He nodded again.

Deeply moved by his show of trust, Petra hoped she hadn't already blown it at lunch with Fytch. She hated to think what that evil witch would do if she suspected Medora was alive. It would be better all around if—

"How come you just don't wake her up?" Petra had a horrible thought. "The spell did tell you how to do that, didn't it?"

"Yes," he reassured her. "But to work the final phase and bring her back to consciousness, I need blood from the person who did her the harm."

She nodded in understanding. Many of the most powerful, older spells called for such equality. "Blood for blood."

"Exactly. Until we figure out who did this, I can't bring her back."

"How long can you keep her in—What did you call it? Suspended animation?"

"As close a description as any. The spell wasn't specific. There have been some fluctuations in her condition, but I should be able to maintain her current status for at least two to three more weeks."

"After that?"

Vorador just shook his head.

Chapter Eighteen

Petra wrapped her arms around herself to ward off the chill that snaked down her spine. There was no mistaking Vorador's silent answer. If they didn't find the guilty person, Medora would die.

"You don't have any idea who did this to her?"

Vorador shook his head again.

Not sure she wanted to know, Petra still asked, "Exactly what happened? I mean, how was she—"

As if he understood her difficulty in saying the words, he quietly said, "She was stabbed. Thirteen times."

Petra clutched herself tighter, fighting the sudden impulse to vomit. She'd known it was bad, but hearing about it brought the horrifying reality too close to home. "Do you think it was just a random act of violence? A burglary gone bad?"

He didn't respond, as if waiting for her to say something more.

"You're working with the police, aren't you?" she asked.

"Yes, I am."

Dugan had been telling the truth at lunch. Vorador had gone

to the cops. She wondered if he'd tried the rug at the police station? "I suppose I can't blame you for not mentioning that."

"Care to tell me why you're so eager to avoid the authorities?"

"No."

"Well, that explains why you haven't asked about your mugger. You're afraid to get sucked into the legal system."

"Good grief!" Petra straightened with a jerk. "I can't believe it. I forgot all about him. What happened to him? Did he confess to having an accomplice? Or being an accomplice?"

"No. Not yet."

The wizard's dark tone sounded threatening even to her. "He *is* still in police custody, isn't he?"

"Yes."

At least that meant Vorador hadn't turned the guy into a bucket of slime, or something even more disgusting. It also meant the mugger would eventually be charged—if he hadn't been already—and start working his way through the legal process. Sooner or later she would have to become involved. Victims had to testify at some point, didn't they?

"You still think he's connected to Medora's attack?"

Vorador nodded. "It's too much of a coincidence otherwise."

"Because he used a knife." Petra swallowed hard, remembering the blade against her throat. She could almost feel Medora's panic, her terror and pain as the knife stabbed into her flesh. Over and over again. Thirteen times.

"Did the police find the murder weapon?"

"No."

"Do they have any suspects?"

He shook his head.

Wondering if she was doing the right thing, Petra paused, then plunged ahead. "Have you ever considered Fytch?"

"As the murderer?"

Petra didn't care for the disbelief in his voice. Why would he so quickly doubt Fytch could be involved? Maybe there really was a common past between the two wizards. A relationship gone bad would explain his animosity toward Fytch. Maybe Fytch had dumped Vorador to take up with Dugan. Old hurts and new suspicions curdled Petra's insides.

"Yes," was all the reply she could manage.

"Only briefly."

"And?" she prompted when he didn't volunteer anything else.

"She has an airtight alibi."

He didn't sound too happy about it. Or maybe that was only her imagination. Then again, the police had at least counted her as a suspect and questioned her. How else would they know she had an alibi?

"Besides," he added, "Fytch can't stand the sight of blood. Even animal blood makes her light-headed. She faints every time. There are a number of spells she can't work."

"Hmmmm."

"What does that mean?" he asked.

"It means . . . I guess it means I don't trust that woman. I would take everything she says with a huge grain of salt."

"You would, huh?" Vorador suddenly sat up straighter. "Wait a minute." His eyes narrowed and he looked at her suspiciously. "When exactly did you meet Fytch? I thought I told you to stay away from her."

"Yeah, right." Petra made a snorting sound, dismissing this latest display of masculine stupidity.

"I don't believe this," he said. "I even saw her influence around you and didn't realize the significance."

"Hey, that's not my fault."

"The fact remains that I told you to avoid her."

"It's not like I went looking for her. She stopped by the house last night. Then I was lucky enough to run into her and Dugan at lunch today."

He picked up on her sarcasm. "Lucky?"

"You were right about one thing, wiz boy: That woman is a certifiable witch." Should she tell Vorador about her slip during lunch? She'd hinted—all right, practically admitted—Medora wasn't actually dead. No, she was a coward. She didn't want him to yell at her again. Surely no harm would come from it. Surely Dugan had done damage control after she'd left and convinced Fytch that Petra didn't know what she was talking about.

"What happened?" He reached out and grabbed her shoulder, practically shaking her. "Did she hurt you?"

143

Patting his hand in a comforting gesture, she said, "It's okay." She gave him a quick synopsis of their encounter. "She didn't do anything overt, but she scared the snot out of me."

Vorador released her and leaned back with a loud sigh. "Thank you!"

"What for?"

"I've been telling Dugan for years that she's an evil, two-faced bi—"

"Speaking of Dugan, I might not know him well, but he acted darned peculiar around Fytch. During her ugliest behavior, it was like he totally zoned out."

"Thank you," Vorador said again. "It's as if he purposely ignores anything bad she does. I thought she might have cast a spell, but I didn't find any sign of one on him."

"Then you really do suspect she could've been the one to attack Medora?"

"No. Much as I might think she's capable of it, I have to admit it just isn't possible. Not only because of her alibi and the blood phobia, but because I don't think she's powerful enough to overcome Medora."

Petra wasn't sure his logic would hold water. Less power was only a limitation if a person let it be. She'd seen weaker wizards get the better of stronger ones by using shrewd thinking and cunning wit. She wouldn't trust Fytch even if the lady wizard was handcuffed in a straitjacket, strapped to a bed in a padded cell, with bars on the window and the door nailed shut. Fytch had seemed plenty powerful to her.

"Well, then"—Petra slapped her palms against the table for emphasis—"we'd better be darn sure and find the culprit before your spell conks out."

"I don't intend to fail."

Such certainty deserved a reward. Impulsively, she leaned across the table and kissed him on the cheek. "You're a good man, Charlie Brown."

He looked uncomfortable but teased her right back. "Not even close."

"What? You're not a good man?"

"Some people might say that's debatable. But if you're trying to guess my name . . . Trust me, it's not Charlie Brown."

"Okay, score one for you." Petra laughed and jumped to her feet. "Now let's get to work."

"So, it's agreed? The rug stays here?"

"By all means." Petra still wasn't completely happy with the arrangement, but there really was no other choice. She waved a hand toward the other room. "Be my guest."

She leaned back against the counter and watched him walk away. Man, oh man. Wiz Boy had a backside that could make the angels weep. Nice and firm, showcased beautifully in those tight black jeans. Add those broad shoulders, narrow hips, muscular legs—which also looked mighty fine in those jeans—and you ended up with a deadly package. If ERG put up a billboard of their jean-clad wizard, customers—female customers—would be tearing down the door.

"Petra, are you coming?"

"Not yet," she muttered even as she blushed. "But it won't take long if I don't get my mind out of the gutter."

"What?" Vorador yelled from the front room.

"Nothing," she yelled back. Tightening the belt of her robe, she took a deep breath and went to see what he was doing.

He already had the rug rolled out and was adjusting her furniture to make room for it. There was no blood. She didn't know whether to be relieved or disappointed.

Trying not to be too obvious, she watched him move her sofa. His silk shirt was just baggy enough to conceal his chest. Would he be suspicious if she asked him to take it off? Maybe she could spill something on it. Then he'd have to remove it.

"Petra."

"What?" She pasted on a grin, hoping it looked as innocent as she tried to make it.

"I want to re-create the situation as closely as possible. Did you have anything else sitting on the rug besides the couch?"

Oh, for the pleasure of watching him bend and lift, she would tell him every piece of furniture in the room sat on that stupid rug.

145

"Why're you staring at me like that?" Vorador looked down at his clothes.

She couldn't resist. "The desk. And the chair. Oh, yeah—and that bookcase, too."

Finding a good vantage point, she leaned a shoulder against the wall and watched him go to work. When he crouched and picked up one side of the desk, she sighed in appreciation. Mighty fine. Her earlier embarrassment over the episode on the couch was quickly fading. In its place grew a desire to give it another try.

"You know, Vorador, it would be a shame to ruin that lovely silk shirt with sweat stains. Maybe you should take it off. Just until you get done."

He slanted her a look that clearly said he suspected she was up to something but wasn't quite sure what. After a brief hesitation, he started unbuttoning the shirt.

Petra slid down the wall and collapsed on the floor.

Vorador looked at her in alarm. "What are you doing? Are you all right?"

"Just give me a minute." Burying her face in her hands, she said, "I'll be fine."

Holy Toledo. What the heck was wrong with her? She had never been like this around a man before. It was as if her sex drive had kicked into high gear and was stuck there. She couldn't have even one simple, innocent conversation with the wizard. Instead her thoughts, her words, her very actions even, all ended up wicked, and sinful, and full of lust.

He squatted beside her. "It's happening again, isn't it?"

She nodded without uncovering her face. "This is so embarrassing. I don't know what's wrong with me."

"I don't mind. It's kind of flattering."

She tried to be outraged, but her laugh spoiled the effect. "Okay, Mr. Ego, I hate to burst your bubble, but I can't take much more of this." She peered at him through the shield of her fingers, doing her best not to take any notice of his sheer masculine perfection. "Any suggestions?"

"Well . . ." His grin was pure original sin. "We could stop fighting it and go to bed for the next week. Maybe two."

146

She hoped he never suspected how deeply tempted she was by his offer. "Nope, not an option."

"Yet?" he said hopefully.

"Not an option," she repeated firmly and dropped her hands. "Any other bright ideas?"

His grin was too cocky by far. "Talking about it might help."

"Only if you're in another country and we're talking on the phone."

Vorador laughed and waggled both his eyebrows, leering at her. "Phone sex. Now that's what I call a suggestion."

In spite of her very real concern, Petra laughed with him. "Okay, forget this. Let's just get back to business. I'll deal with it—somehow."

He gave an exaggerated sigh. "Fine, you try ignoring it. Or are you hoping it will just go away? That hasn't worked too well up to this point."

"No," she said, "it's finished." She got to her feet by sheer willpower and determination. Staring at the rug, she tried to focus on that problem instead of the emotions raging inside her. "Done. Over. Kaput."

Chapter Nineteen

Vorador did the gentlemanly thing and didn't call Petra a liar. Rising to his feet, he headed toward the bookcase. A sound from her stopped him. "What?"

"Nothing."

He didn't believe her. Having learned a few things about her over the past couple of days, he merely looked at her and said her name. He really liked the way she did that. It wasn't often nowadays he got to see women blush. He tried not to gloat when he saw her mouth soften.

"Forget the bookcase," she said, not quite meeting his eyes.

"I want everything exactly the way it was. I don't mind—"

She threw up her hands in defeat. "I wanted to watch you lift heavy things, okay? Are you happy now?"

Looking at her in total incomprehension, he frowned. "I guess so."

He finished rearranging the furniture. Why would she want him to move something that didn't need it? Punishment? Revenge? Women! Who could ever understand the workings of the female mind? Not him.

He stepped back and surveyed the room. No blood on the rug yet. He hoped they didn't have to wait several days for it to appear. In spite of his announcement that he could safely maintain Medora, she might not hang on long enough. He had to find out who attacked her and restore her before it was too late.

Plus he had the Amazon Council clamoring for results, making him wish he'd never told the queen that Medora wasn't really dead. They didn't have a wizard powerful enough to work the spell and keep her alive, so they were counting on him completely. He hated to think what the Amazons would do to him if he failed.

"Hey." He suddenly realized something. "Where's your cat?"

Petra glared down the hallway. "Locked in the bathroom." She raised her voice. "And he's staying in there till morning."

"What'd she—he do?"

"He seems to think violence is the answer to every situation." She started yelling again. "I'm sick and tired of being used as his scratching post. Maybe a night in the bathroom will teach him some manners."

Vorador smothered a laugh. Looked like maybe Kitoka had met her match—at least while she was in cat form. When she regained human form she'd likely try to slice Petra open from top to bottom. Which reminded him . . . He needed to find a time to try that spell he'd discovered and get Kitoka back to normal. Although he'd have to be very careful; some of his spells showed a disturbing tendency to backfire since he'd met Petra.

"Surely he's learned his lesson by now. Why don't you go let him out?"

Petra didn't look convinced. "Speaking of releasing my cat, I thought you were going to send Caylin over here yesterday to let him out."

Damn. She would have to remember that. Trying for a sheepish look, he hoped to get off the hook. "Sorry. I forgot."

"You—" Petra stared at him.

The expression on her face was almost comical. He wondered

149

if she was stunned that he'd forgotten. Or because he apologized. Either way, it was in his best interests to keep her off balance. Because when she got flustered, she got that cute little frown—

Damn! There he went again, thinking Petra was cute. Okay, she was, but there was more to her than that. She was also sexy as hell. Naive and shy, but smart. He found her unique combination of traits damned lethal to his libido.

Pushing those worries aside, he spoke loudly enough to be heard down the hall. "I'm sure if you let him out he'll behave."

Stepping back, her voice wary, Petra asked, "You're not trying to work some spell, are you?"

It irked him that she didn't trust his magic. "No."

"Fine. I'll let him out." She went down the hall.

He'd better find time tomorrow to do some research. There had to be an explanation for his misfiring spells. It really was peculiar. He'd completed five jobs of varying difficulty and complexity today. None of those spells had gone awry. That only happened around Petra. Now why would that be? She didn't have any magic of her own to interfere.

Could that be it? Could her very lack of talent somehow affect his magic by making it less potent? No, that didn't make sense. She had grown up around wizards. If her presence disturbed spells, surely she would be aware of the phenomena. Yet she'd been as surprised as he was when his dampening spell hadn't worked.

A violent hissing broke into his thoughts. "Calm down, Kitty," he warned. "I'm—"

The cat stalked toward him and he backed up. He tried to ignore Petra's snicker. It wasn't that he was afraid of Kitty. Leery was more like it. "I brought the rug back."

That stopped Kitty in her tracks.

Petra asked, "How did you know Bosco got mad when I took the rug away this morning?"

Hell's bells, he'd forgotten Petra still didn't know who her cat was. "Just a lucky guess."

Stiff-legged, Kitty walked to the rug, haughty as any princess, and sniffed all around it. Laying down, she rolled, rubbing herself against the rough nap. She made a mournful sound over and over, then raised her gaze to Vorador with a questioning *"Meow?"*

Knowing Petra looked at him as if he'd gone crazy, he quickly explained the day's events to Kitoka. He had to find some way to be released from his promise not to reveal Kitoka's real identity. He'd already pushed the limits by telling Dugan.

With a satisfied purr, Kitty stretched, keeping a watchful eye on the spot where the blood would reappear.

"I should've known this isn't a normal, everyday cat. Plain old cats can't talk," Petra said.

"She can talk?"

"That's not the first time you've called Bosco a *she*."

He held up his hand to forestall any further questions. "I'm not at liberty to tell you."

"Excuse me? Not at liberty? Well, how convenient for you."

"Can she really talk? I haven't heard her say anything."

"Maybe she has nothing to say to you."

He turned to the cat. "How about it, Kitty? Can you talk?"

"Yeow."

Vorador was startled when he distinctly heard the cat say yes.

"Well, I'll be damned."

"Probably," Petra muttered. "Now, why don't you take your stupid cat and get out of here? I'm ready to go to bed."

As she uttered that last word, Vorador's desire slammed through the barriers like a rampaging elephant through a circus tent. Oh, he'd like to get her in bed.

He felt light-headed from all the blood suddenly rushing to his lower body. His reaction had to be the result of conflicting magic at work. Only another wizard's spell battling his own control could account for this overwhelming lust. Why couldn't he detect the spell?

Meaning to question her, he glanced at Petra. Her brown hair was tousled from their earlier encounter. She fiddled with the belt of her robe. He wanted to take her in his arms and watch her blue eyes go all soft and dreamy when he lowered his head to kiss her.

"Vorador."

151

"Yes?"

"Go home and take a cold shower."

He looked at her closely. She didn't appear even remotely affected. Did her parents' spell only arouse him to such heights? No, he recalled the way she'd slid down the wall when he'd started to take off his shirt. It just seemed to hit them at different times. Although they had come together quite nicely on her sofa.

He smiled at her. "Then I can't borrow your shower?"

She took a step back. "No."

He was burning up and wanted nothing more than to start stripping off his clothes. Petra was flushed as well.

"Petra, I want to stay."

"No." She shook her head—in further denial or to clear it? "I want you to go." She didn't sound very convincing.

"I don't mean I want to stay because of this." With a sweep of his hand he indicated the aroused state of his body. "I mean because of that." He pointed to the rug.

She shook her head again, not looking at him. "I can't."

"I promise"—it was the hardest thing he'd ever done in his life, but he finished the sentence—"I won't touch you."

Her expression turned skeptical, so he added with a wolfish smile, "Unless you want me to."

"I don't think that's such a good idea, Mr. Wizard."

Not for the first time, and probably not for the last, he found himself questioning her meaning. Was it that she didn't trust him? Or herself? Either one could lead to some interesting and pleasurable possibilities. "I need to keep an eye on the rug."

Playing dirty, he played his trump card. "I'll protect you from any more nightmares."

"Low blow," she said, disapproval in her voice.

"All's fair in love and war."

"It shows a decided lack of creativity on your part when you resort to cliches."

He arched an eyebrow at her. "Oh, I don't know. You gave me pretty high marks for creativity not long ago." He sent a significant look toward the couch.

Petra didn't disappoint him. She turned bright pink and

huffed in embarrassment. Damn, but he enjoyed making her blush. He could turn it into a lifelong pastime. Whoa! Where had that come from? Okay, he liked her. He enjoyed spending time with her. He relished crossing verbal swords with her. He wanted her—a hell of a lot. But a serious commitment? He wasn't ready to even start considering that.

"Go to bed, Petra. I'll sleep out here on the couch."

"Darn right you will." She stomped out of the room, only to return shortly. After throwing a pillow and blanket at him, she told him, "Turn out the lights and lock the doors."

He heard her bedroom door slam. He bet she locked it as well. Did she honestly think a piece of wood and a little metal would keep him out if he decided to join her? Grinning, he made his bed on the sofa. For all her experience with wizards, sometimes she was alarmingly naive.

Once the house was dark, he stripped down to his shorts. He supposed it might be tempting fate, but there was no way he could sleep in those tight jeans. Not tonight. Not in the same house with Petra, where her smell and presence infused the entire atmosphere. He rubbed a hand across his chest, trying not to dwell on the way her skin had felt, all soft and smooth as satin.

Finally finding a semicomfortable position on the too short couch, he called out, "Good night, Petra."

Waiting for her to respond, he dozed off.

Chapter Twenty

"Petra! Wake up. You're having a bad dream."

Petra jerked to consciousness with a gasp. A dream; it had all been a dream. No monster lurched down her hallway. A movement in the doorway caught her eye and she tensed. Then she smiled, remembering yesterday morning. It was only Bosco.

No! The shadow stretched up and up, until it loomed over her bed. She tried to scream. Nothing except little squeaks of fear came out. Reverting to childhood beliefs, she yanked the covers over her head.

A hand touched her shoulder. She imagined talons ripping through the blanket's thin defenses. She screamed, loud and long.

"Damn it, Petra. Knock it off before the neighbors call the cops."

Recognizing her wizard's voice, she cut off in midyell. Relief flooded her, leaving her weak, her heart pounding in reaction. She heard a soft click as he turned on the lights. She peeked one eye out of her cocoon. Yup, Vorador stood beside her bed. Yikes! She scurried back into hiding.

Great balls of fire! She winced, expecting the worst. Glory be for small favors. She hadn't been dumb enough to say the words out loud. Now she had to figure out how to get the half-naked wizard out of her bedroom before she suffocated. One good look at those black jeans riding dangerously low on slim hips and she just might die. A happy woman no doubt, but dead nonetheless.

"Petra, are you okay?"

"I'm fine. Go away."

He didn't respond and she was tempted to peek again. Just to see what he was doing, not to ogle him. Sure, and her eyes weren't blue either.

"Petra, come out before you pass out from lack of oxygen."

He had a point. But she wouldn't survive the sight of him. "Turn out the light."

"Why?" He chuckled. "Are you naked under there? Do you take off your pig shirts and sleep in the buff?"

"Just turn out the light." Admitting her cowardice, she added, "Then go away."

She heard his bare feet move across the rug, then the small click of the switch. She held her breath, waiting for the sounds of him going out and shutting the door. She squealed and nearly jumped off the bed when she felt the mattress dip. Gads, he was sitting right beside her.

Lowering her protective blanket, she could make out his silhouette in the darkened room.

She flinched as his hand came at her from the darkness. When he only stroked her hair in a comforting, almost impersonal gesture, she relaxed her death grip on the covers. In spite of the dark she could see intriguing glimpses. There was his muscled shoulder, the line of his torso where his chest narrowed down to his waist, the corded strength of his forearm. And she could smell him just fine. In fact, his clean, bracing scent was filling her head with all sorts of forbidden images.

"You know," she had to clear her throat before she could go

155

on, "you're using one of the oldest tricks in the book."

"How's that?" he asked in an amused voice.

She could almost see that one Spockish eyebrow climb upward. "This whole situation. If you read romances—"

"I do."

"The hero using a nightmare as an excuse to get into the heroine's bedroom has been written often enough to be a cliché."

When he shrugged one shoulder in a dismissive gesture, the faint light played across his body in an utterly provocative manner. She wanted to touch him. She closed her eyes against the temptation.

"I know I said I wouldn't touch you," his voice was serious in the darkness, "but would it be all right if I held you right now?" When she hesitated, he added, "That's all. Just a comforting hug."

Since she wanted the same thing, she allowed herself the luxury of saying, "Yes."

Expecting him to simply stretch out beside her, she frowned when he stood up. She heard cloth rustle. "What're you doing?"

"Taking off my jeans."

"Taking off—?" Her mind froze.

He lifted the covers and slipped into her bed. His hip bumped her and he gave a little push. "Don't hog the middle. Scoot over."

Her double bed had never felt so small. "I'm not sure this is such a good idea."

He nestled closer to her and wrapped his arms around her. "Sure it is." Before she could comprehend what was going on, he had her back snug against his front in cozy spoon fashion. One of his arms pillowed her head. The other draped across her stomach, his hand tucked under her rib cage. He nudged one of his knees between hers and their feet tangled together in a seductive embrace. She had never felt so safe and secure in her entire life.

But before long she couldn't ignore his increasing hardness growing where her bottom was pressed. "Vorador, I'm not sure this is such a good idea."

"Don't worry about it."

His breath blew warm and moist over her ear. She shivered in delight and felt a more insistent prodding from him. "But—"

"I'm not some sort of sex fiend, Petra. My erection is an involuntary reaction to being close to you, but I can control myself."

Closing her eyes, she drew in a long breath and held it. His words excited her at some primal level. Most men wouldn't be so honorable—or trustworthy—in his position. She did trust him, in spite of what had happened between them earlier. He was an exceptional man for more reasons than just his incredible magical power.

"We can put a pillow between us if it bothers you that much," he offered.

"No!" She wanted to smack herself as soon as the denial shot out of her mouth. In spite of her trepidation, she didn't want to lose the security of his closeness. "That's not necessary. I trust you."

His arm tightened briefly in a quick hug. "Gee, thanks for the rousing vote of confidence."

"I think you're already *roused* enough, Mr. Wizard."

"So tell me," he whispered in her ear, "what was your nightmare about?"

Shivering in spite of his warmth all around her, Petra said, "I'd rather not."

"Come on, you know as well as I do, holding something in is the worst thing you can do."

"Geez, this from the man who's as closemouthed as a Mafia boss under indictment by the FBI?"

"Don't worry, Petra." His voice was soft and seductive. "I'll keep you safe."

She realized if anybody could vanquish her personal monsters, it would be Vorador.

Of course, there was the possibility he would totally annihilate her in the process—if his interest was merely professional. Or if he wanted just a casual affair. She wasn't sure her heart could take another rejection. Harold had done far more damage than she cared to admit. Mainly because she didn't want to admit he'd ever had that much power over her. Power she had allowed him to gain.

She answered Vorador. It was easier than facing her thoughts. "Something was chasing me. It was huge and hairy. Sometimes it walked on all fours. Others it was upright, like a man."

"Like a cross between a werewolf and a vampire."

She nodded. "It had long claws and huge teeth. This time it ate everything it touched."

"This time?"

"I had nightmares last night. That was why I wanted the rug out of my house, remember?"

"I didn't realize it was the same exact one."

"That means something, doesn't it?" she asked, trying to turn around and face him.

Holding her in place, he admitted, "Maybe."

Settling back into place, she sighed. "A spell."

"Most likely."

"Whose?" she asked, even though she had a strong suspicion.

"Probably the murderer's."

Yeah, that's what she'd thought. Then something even scarier occurred to her. "Left over from when Medora was attacked? Or placed recently?"

"I don't know." He didn't sound happy about it. "I don't want to consider that the murderer knows you have the rug."

His words frightened Petra so much she couldn't speak. He must have sensed her reaction because his arm tightened around her. He brought his leg up over both of hers, tucking her closer to him, wrapping her in the warm security of his presence. His action didn't seem sexual. She snuggled in even closer.

She trembled. The moment felt hugely important and significant. It was much too soon, but she had suspected she could easily fall in love with this wizard. That both frightened and exhilarated her. Frightened her because Harold had been a wizard, too, and look how badly that had turned out. Exhilarated her because it seemed she'd waited her whole life for this man and finally found him.

"Petra?"

Too emotionally raw to answer him, she still nearly cried out when he loosened his embrace. She wanted it back—wanted his warmth, his nearness and all the implications of that touch. Her own uncertainty and timidity stopped her from inviting him back, or offering him even more.

A shadow of doubt crept in. Maybe he didn't feel the same. The same as what? she thought with a mental groan. She didn't understand her own emotions; how could she hope to interpret his?

Maybe because the darkness intensified the feeling of intimacy, she haltingly confessed, "I don't want you to—well, get the wrong impression. You know . . . what happened . . . before. That's not—I usually don't do that with a man I barely know."

"Really?" he asked in an interested voice while he nuzzled her ear.

"Absolutely."

She got a little breathless when his teeth nipped at her earlobe.

"I just want to make sure there's no misunderstanding between us," he said, his voice low and seductive.

The only sound she could make was a muffled humming when his tongue darted in her ear.

"Do you mean like when your nipples—"

She found her voice real quick. "Vorador!"

"Or maybe you mean when you straddle me and—"

"Stop it!"

"Or could you possibly mean being so wet and wild and hot as you climaxed in my hand?"

He finished the sentence in a rush even though she reached around and covered his mouth. "Geez, you make me sound like some sort of uninhibited, immoral floozy."

Laughter rumbled in his chest. He kissed her palm, then took her hand away. "Of course not."

"I've been called straitlaced, uptight. A frigid b—"

Now his hand covered her mouth, stopping the words. "Don't." His thumb caressed the line of her jaw. "If any man ever thought so, then the fault was his, not yours. Trust me. I have enough experience to know when a woman—"

159

She shoved his fingers aside. "Oh, and that's supposed to reassure me? To have you confess that you've slept around with hordes of women?"

This time he didn't bother to silence his chuckles. To think she'd been starting to feel sorry for him—both from his earlier lack of release and his current aroused state. She jabbed her elbow back into his ribs. Satisfied when she heard him grunt, she tried to squirm free from his embrace. Suddenly it seemed he had dozens of arms and legs.

"Let me go, you asinine octopus."

He laughed and easily held her. She froze when she accidentally shoved her butt hard against his crotch. He sucked in a sharp breath, going still himself. She could feel him against her bare skin since her shirt had twisted up around her waist during their struggles. Only the thin fabric of his underwear separated them. Were they boxers? Or briefs?

Petra knew she should move but just couldn't bring herself to do it. She wanted him and would probably give in if he pushed the issue. Strong morals? Who, her? Not tonight. She wanted to be the one out of control, the one whose passions burned so hot they couldn't be denied. She wanted him to be the strong one, the first to withdraw.

Because she knew she wasn't ready—emotionally or mentally—to have sex with him. No matter how much she might want it physically. She needed him to be the responsible one. To prove she could trust him. To keep his promise.

Vorador's entire body was rigid with tension. As illogical as it sounded, she knew if she accepted what he offered, she would walk away afterward. Any chance of a lasting relationship would be over between them. It simply wasn't in her to indulge in sex for sex's sake. While she hoped deeper feelings would grow between them in the future, they were barely a seed right now.

If he pressed the issue and they had sex tonight, she would never see him again. The relationship would end before it really started. She would lose respect for herself and probably for him as well.

What she needed right now was proof that she could believe

160

his promise—that in spite of her own weakness, he could be strong. For once she didn't want to say no first. She hoped he respected her enough to do what was right without making her defend her moral standards.

Chapter Twenty-one

"Petra, let go of my arm and I'll get up."

Somehow she managed to pry her fingers loose. "Sorry."

Vorador slowly got out of the bed, as if each movement hurt him. "No, I'm the one who's sorry. I thought I could handle it—being that close to you. Obviously I overestimated my control. Or underestimated your appeal."

She didn't know what to say to that without sounding terribly conceited. Watching his shadowy movements as he pulled his jeans back on, she did know she didn't want him to leave on this note.

She didn't want this awkwardness to swamp their fledgling friendship. She hoped it might grow into something larger.

"Maybe we could try this again. With the lights on." Realizing how that sounded, she added, "Maybe in the other room." Gads, that wasn't any better, considering what happened in there earlier. "You know, just talk."

He didn't reply but flipped on the lights. She assumed that meant he agreed. She plumped up a pillow and scooted back to sit against the headboard while he made a slow, careful examination of her bedroom. Oh, crud. She'd forgotten his seeming obsession with pigs.

"Nice pigs."

How could he make two such innocuous words sound lecherous? "What is it with you guys and pigs, anyway?"

He flashed a roguish grin. She knew exactly how a pirate's captive must feel—like she was ready to be locked up in his quarters to be ravished at his leisure.

"How come you like them so much?" he asked, bending over to examine a large bronze pig on the floor.

She liked his long hair. It was black as sin, absolutely straight, and hung loose past his shoulders. Speaking of shoulders . . . His were very nice. Well muscled but not too much.

He straightened and picked up a stuffed pig from a chair. "Pigs," he prompted.

She watched, mesmerized, while his long fingers stroked the soft pink fur. She already knew how talented those fingers were. Her eyes glazed over when he idly rubbed the pig up and down his bare chest. He had just enough hair on his chest. A narrow trail of it pointed down toward the waistband of his jeans.

"Never mind." Coming to the bed, he traced a pattern on her upper chest with a finger. "Tell me about this instead."

She swatted away his hand. "What do you mean?"

"Tell me about the bastard who broke your heart."

Drawing in a sharp breath, she flinched backward. "What?"

He prodded the area over her heart. "I can see him here." He drew the pattern again.

This time she recognized it as a heart. "Don't."

His finger moved, sketching that stupid heart again. It was as if she could feel his touch inside her, pulling and prodding at the remnants of her past relationship with Harold. It didn't exactly hurt. The sensation felt more like a cross between a tickle and an itch.

"How can you do that? *What* are you doing?"

He shrugged and sat on the edge of the bed. "Tell me about Mr. Mud."

He was obviously referring to Harold's psychic color. That

163

made her smile. It always had irked Harold that he didn't have a more flamboyant color, but now she knew the drab color suited him perfectly. "So tell me, Mr. Show-off-his-amazing-talents, what color are you?"

"You know very well that a wizard can't detect his own colors on other people."

She wondered why he avoided the question. He might not be able to see it, but surely he knew his own color. Maybe it was something awful—like chartreuse, or puce, or bubblegum pink.

"Don't try to change the subject." He poked her chest again. "Tell me what this guy did to you."

"I'd rather talk about my nightmares."

"We'll get to those in due time. What was his name?"

She sighed, knowing he would never give up. "Harold."

"Where'd you meet him?"

"I was working at a small college in Albuquerque as the president's administrative assistant. Harold's the dean of the magic department."

"Love at first sight?"

"Not exactly."

In truth, it had taken nearly six months of persistent pursuing on Harold's part before she agreed to even go out with him that first time. Looking back, she couldn't remember why she'd changed her mind. Guess he'd just worn down her resistance. In hindsight she realized she should have paid more attention to her first instincts.

"He won you over?"

"Yeah" was all she said, not wanting to tell Vorador how stupid she'd been.

"You were lovers?"

"We were engaged to be married."

He looked shocked, as if he hadn't suspected that serious a relationship. "Who broke it off? You? Or him?"

"Oh, I did."

"Good girl." A small frown appeared between his eyebrows. He tapped her heart again. "Then why all this?"

"Because I found him . . . Ah, let's just say I found him making magic with somebody else."

"So?" The wizard's frown deepened. "I mean, since you can't do magic, why would you object to him practicing his spells . . ." His words trailed off as he caught her meaning. "The son of a bitch!"

Hoping her smile didn't look as forced as it felt, she merely said, "Exactly."

"Hell, the man must have been a fool in more ways than one. Besides cheating on you, why would he be stupid enough to bring another woman to a a place where you could catch him?"

"Well, he thought he was safe. It was the middle of the afternoon." Biting her lip in an effort not to cry, she told herself she was the fool. Harold wasn't worth any more of her tears. "I never came home once I'd gone into the office, but it was the six-month anniversary of our engagement. I thought it would be romantic to celebrate. I knew he'd be home, working on an article. I thought I'd surprise him. I had champagne and roses. And . . ." Her voice faded away.

"Except you were the one who got surprised." Vorador reached out, briefly resting his palm against her cheek. "I'm sorry, Petra. The man was a first-class idiot."

She sniffed and nodded.

"This goes a long way to explaining why you hate the thought of being predictable," he said with a teasing smile.

Remembering her reaction down in the hole when he'd indicated she might be just that, Petra gave a dry chuckle. "Yeah, I guess you could say I've had an attitude adjustment. I'm much more inclined to do things on the spur of the moment."

Not commenting on that, he instead asked, "Who was the other woman?"

"One of the professors in his department. Turns out they'd been involved off and on for years."

"Then why didn't he marry her? Why did he ask you—? To make her jealous?" He examined her expression, then went on, "No, that wasn't his reason, was it?"

She shook her head. It still hurt too much to actually say it. Gad, how her pride had been crushed when the truth came out.

She would never forget Harold screaming at her that—

"It was because of your parents, wasn't it?" Vorador asked in a soft voice.

She hung her head, ashamed he'd figured it out so quickly. Was it obvious to everyone but her? Was she so unattractive and so unappealing that the only reason any man would want her was for the connection to her powerful parents?

"He thought marrying you would enhance his own standing in the magic community." Vorador sounded disgusted by the idea.

"That pretty much sums it up, sparky."

"I don't like nicknames."

"Well, you could tell me your real name and solve the whole problem."

"Nice try but no cigar. On the other hand, this means I get to pick a nickname for you, too. How about petunia?"

Petunia wasn't so bad. She'd been called worse. Sooner or later she would find out his name. It must be horrendous for him to guard it so jealously. "So, sparky, tell me—"

"Stop it," he snapped and got to his feet.

"Gad, you're cute when you're angry."

Folding his arms, he glared at her and spoke each word slowly and distinctly. "I—am—not—cute."

"Relax, sparky." Laughing in pure delight, Petra said, "Don't get all fired up about—"

"Damn it, Petra. You did it again."

Chapter Twenty-two

Flames immediately burst out on Vorador's shoulders and biceps. He slowly unfolded his arms. The flames raced down and shot off his fingertips. Petra leaned over the edge of the bed to see if her rug was singed. When she looked back at the wizard, a flickering blanket of fire covered his entire upper body.

She hunched her shoulders up around her ears. "Sorry."

"You are a menace, Petunia."

"Does it hurt?"

He sighed and shook his head, the ends of his hair dancing across the flames.

"Can I touch?" She thought he looked surprised by her request. "I figure if it doesn't hurt you, it can't hurt me."

He slowly spread his arms out to the sides. "Go ahead."

Making sure her nightshirt was pulled down, she climbed out of bed. She chuckled as she saw Bosco crouched in the open doorway, his eyes reflecting the firelight. His tail was poofed out to twice its normal size. Obviously the cat wasn't used to seeing flaming wizards in the middle of the night.

In spite of Vorador's reassurance, Petra held out her palm, testing for heat. She only felt the warmth of his body. She poked one fingertip into the fire dancing on his forearm. There was a slight tingling sensation but no pain.

"It tickles."

He released a pent-up sigh. "Yes, it does."

"You were worried," she said in a surprised voice.

"A little," he admitted.

"Why?"

He shook his head with a wry smile. "My magic tends to misbehave when you're around."

"Hey, that's not my fault," she protested. Gaining more courage, she boldly ran her hands up his arms, over his shoulders and down his chest. The tiny tongues of flame danced out of her way, flowing back over his skin in her wake. Reversing her path, she wrinkled her nose at the bubbling tickle of his magic.

"Has it ever happened before?" he asked.

"This fire? Why're you asking me?"

"No, you disrupting magic. Does it happen often?"

Still distracted by the wonder of his cool fire, she nodded. "Occasionally."

"You didn't think that was important enough to tell me? Maybe give me some warning?"

Her head jerked up at his sharp tone. "Hey, don't blame me for your own incompetence."

"It's not my fault my spells have gone haywire."

She stepped away, no longer quite so intrigued by his magic. "No? Gee, and all this time I thought you were the wizard."

"I repeat—you should have given me some indication—"

"You should have been able to figure it out for yourself, Wiz Boy. The same thing happens to most wizards when they're around nonmagical people unless they compensate."

That brought him up short. "You know," he slowly admitted, "I don't think I've run across one single person who didn't have at least a small amount of power. Not since I left—"

He must have come to Seattle right after he left home. It was a very progressive, liberal city. Lots of magic. Everywhere.

His face closed off in that expressionless mask she was really

168

coming to hate. It seemed like she routinely spilled her guts to him but had to drag every little scrap of information out of him. Would it hurt him to be just a tiny bit forthcoming? With a sigh, she realized that, yeah, it probably would hurt him.

"Ouch!" Petra glared down at the cat, one paw still out-stretched, as if ready to strike again. "I'm warning you, bossy, you're treading on shaky ground."

Bosco ran out the door with a flick of his—her tail.

"I've gotta find another name for him—her." Petra ran her fingers back through her hair. "Geez, this is getting confusing."

"Just call her Kitty," Vorador suggested. "It's an all-purpose name, suitable for either gender."

"Right." It irritated Petra that he wouldn't, or couldn't, tell her the truth about the mystery surrounding the cat. "Listen, if you're done goofing off, why don't you douse the fire?"

"Goofing off?" His voice sounded dangerous and his eyebrow shot up.

"It's three o'clock in the morning and I'm tired. A few more hours' sleep would be nice before I have to go to work."

"Meow!"

The demanding cry came from the hallway. Petra and Vorador exchanged a look, and she felt as though they were reading each other's minds. They both started forward. Petra laughed when they ran into each other at the doorway.

"Maybe I should call you Moe instead of Sparky."

"Get out of my way, Curly."

With a poor imitation of a Stooges laugh, she waved him to exit first. She didn't need to turn on any lights, since the wizard still merrily blazed away. She wondered how long it would be before he realized that, and if she could embarrass him when he finally did. Probably! She ran into his back when he halted abruptly.

His fire tickled her nose and she sneezed. "Hey, watch it."

"It's back."

She peered around him. Sure enough, there sat the hole. It loomed . . . No, something on the floor couldn't loom. It hun-kered there? Yeah, that sounded menacing enough. "Yipee."

"Such enthusiasm," he chided her.

169

"Hey, I'm not the one who wanted it back. I could live and die a happy woman if I never set eyes on the dang thing again."

"I don't understand your lack of curiosity. Don't you want to know—"

"Spare me the whole justice lecture again." She waved away any objections he had. "Now that it's back, what're you gonna do about it?"

"Go down there."

"Are you out of your mind?"

"Since meeting you," Vorador said, his eyebrow flicking upward, "I'm beginning to suspect I might be."

"Cute."

"Am not," he quickly denied.

"I might be able to take you a little more seriously if you weren't blazing like a marshmallow that got dropped in the fire at a 'Smores party."

Vorador quickly snapped his fingers. The flames vanished with a final crackle and a loud pop. He grabbed his shirt off the chair and slipped it on.

Petra hoped her disappointment didn't show when he buttoned it up, covering his oh-so-lovely chest. She sighed when he tucked the shirt in and fastened his jeans. He efficiently gathered his hair and wrapped a cord around it, making a neat ponytail. She knew the competent wizard was back and intended to get down to business when he pulled on his socks and boots.

"Guess I might as well get dressed, too."

He stopped at the edge of the rug. "Why?"

"You don't think I'm going down there like this, do you?"

"I didn't think you were going at all."

"Well, think again," she informed him. His tone seemed to imply he hadn't so much thought she wasn't going as he wouldn't allow her to go. It was childish in the extreme, but she couldn't help adding, "You're not the boss of me."

"If you stick out your tongue at me," he warned, "I won't be responsible for what happens next."

Unable to resist the challenge, Petra did just that, then ran for her bedroom. Slamming the door, she leaned against it. She wondered what his threat involved. Undoubtedly something dark and dangerous that included kissing and tongue sucking. Her hands shook as she pulled on jeans and a T-shirt, socks and hiking boots. Knowing it was pure vanity, she took the time to run a brush through her hair, put in earrings and slick on lip gloss.

"Ready as I'll ever be," she declared, stepping back into the front room. "What on earth are you doing?"

Vorador had dumped out the trash can by her desk. Paper was scattered from one end of the room to the other. Kitty attacked each piece, bringing them to Vorador, who was sitting cross-legged on the floor.

"Have the two of you lost what little minds you had to begin with?" Petra demanded, starting to pick up the mess.

"Leave it."

"I will not." Hands on hips, Petra glowered down at him. "I may not be the best housekeeper in the world, but—"

"There's something in here Kitty wants."

"Oh." She remembered the stupid piece of paper the cat had played with all through dinner. She looked at the scratches on the back of her hand. The cat had gotten very angry when she'd thrown the paper in the—"Okay."

Helping them search, it wasn't long before she found a familiar crumpled-up scrap of paper. "Here it is."

"*Yeow.*"

"Sorry," Petra said, "but you could have told me it was that important."

The cat hissed at her.

"All right. What's so all-fired important about it, anyway?"

"Damn it, Petra!"

Petra groaned. She'd done it again. She slowly swiveled around until she could see the wizard. His entire body was engulfed in flames. "Oh, geez, Vorador, I really am sorry. I didn't mean—"

"I think I'm going to muzzle you."

She sheepishly held out the paper. "Here." She jerked it back just as he reached to take it.

"Stop playing games, Petra."

"I'm not. But you're—Will your fire burn paper?"

"What do I have to do to prove—"

She could tell he was angry. Her first clue had been how strained his voice sounded. Added to the fierce expression on his face. And the smoke coming out of his ears.

Still, when she held out the slip of paper, he made his fire vanish before he accepted it. She found the gesture oddly endearing. Trying to keep her mind focused on the matter at hand, she watched while he flattened the wrinkled scrap on his thigh and silently read it.

He looked at the cat. "Sorry, Kitty. This isn't a clue."

The cat hissed and spat.

Petra accepted the paper from Vorador. It read, *Wildflowers for my wild warrior wench. Yours, Dugan.*

"I'm assuming this was a note to Medora," Petra said.

"*Yeow.*"

"Where did it come from? How did it get here in my house?"

Both humans looked at the cat, who could only look back at them in mute frustration.

Vorador smoothly rose to his feet. "That doesn't really matter. It's not a clue, Kitty. We know Dugan brought Medora flowers."

"*Yeow meow meow meow meow—*"

Vorador interrupted the tirade, since it was impossible to understand. "I know how much you want to believe in Dugan's guilt, but I know for a fact he isn't."

Another flurry of meows was his answer.

"This is impossible," he declared. He grabbed Petra's hand and stepped toward the hole. "Let's move this downstairs."

Petra leaned back against his pressure on her arm. "Wait a minute! Why are you so eager to head on back to Hotel Psycho California?"

"I want to look for clues. Medora must have left some hint there. Otherwise, why would she have used the last of her breath to construct the spell? Something important has to be down there."

Petra gasped in disbelief when Kitty took a flying leap, directly into the hole. The cat hung in midair long enough not to

172

look natural, then fell straight down and vanished. Off balance, Petra didn't resist when Vorador tugged on her hand again, bringing her close to his side. Before she could think, speak or act, he picked her up and stepped off into nothingness.

Throwing her arms around his neck, she held on for dear life.

"Think happy thoughts," he told her, "and maybe we can manage to land closer to the hotel this time."

She was all for saving herself another long hike through that weird desert. Although she had enjoyed the scenery quite a bit the first time around. And her wish had come true. Vorador was wearing jeans instead of that tent of a green robe. She was glad the darkness hid her lecherous grin.

Chapter Twenty-three

Vorador flexed his knees, absorbing the shock of landing. Petra clung to his neck tight enough to strangle him. One corner of his mouth kicked up in a grin when he noticed that she had her eyes tight shut. She obviously didn't travel well.

"You can open your eyes now. We're safe and sound on solid ground."

He reluctantly disengaged her arms from around his neck and set her on her own two feet. He kept his hands around her waist only long enough to make certain she had her balance. Okay, it was longer than that. Long enough to regret that her shirt was tucked into her jeans so he couldn't sneak underneath for a feel. It would have been a most pleasant foray. She wasn't wearing a bra.

"Do you see Bosco—Kitty?" she asked.

Finally letting go of her, he looked around and saw familiar paw prints in the sandy dirt, but no sign of Kitty. Or Kitoka. Raising his gaze, he saw the hotel's outline about a half-mile in the distance. "No, but I bet we'll find her there."

Petra looked in the direction in which he pointed. "Oh. It's not far away at all, is it?"

Was that disappointment on her face? Why? She'd done nothing but whine and complain about the long walk last time. "Notice anything weird?" he asked.

"Come on, let's go see what we can find."

Surprisingly, she followed along in his wake without further argument. Time passed, and the hotel grew larger on the horizon. The longer Petra was silent, the more nervous he got. What was she doing back there? He could hear her walking behind him but wasn't picking up any vibrations as to what her mood might be. He couldn't remember her ever going this long without speaking since they first met.

Finally he couldn't take it anymore. Spinning to face her, he demanded, "What are you doing?"

She jerked to a halt and swiped a damp hank of hair out of her eyes. "Huh?"

She looked hot, sweaty and so sexy it was all he could do to keep his hands off her. She also looked guilty as hell. "Don't play stupid, Petra."

"Stupid? You think I'm stupid?"

"I want to know what you're up to." He could practically see her mind racing as it concocted, then rejected, insults to lob back at him. He nearly grinned in anticipation. "Don't act naive. I know—"

"Oh, now I'm unsophisticated? And stupid? What a charming compliment. Let me return the favor—Orwell."

Orwell? He felt a moment of panic. How had she found out about Orwell? No, he calmed himself, she was just being her usual smart-aleck self. George Orwell was the author of *Animal Farm*, where pigs ruled their little corner of the world. "Wouldn't it be more appropriate to call me one of the pigs? Instead of the author? After all, do you have any proof that Mr. Orwell was in any way swine-like?"

"Oh, shut up."

"Can't remember any of their names, can you?" He grinned. "If memory serves, there was Major. And Napoleon. And I think the other main characters were Snowball and Squealer."

"You just have to rub it in. Further proof I'm not as clever as you, English Lit Boy."

"Now that's an interesting observation."

"Don't you mean a *stupid* observation?"

"I'm not the one genetically lacking in logic. Women are traditionally the more emotional—"

She threatened him with her foot. "How'd you like me to put this size-seven boot somewhere the sun don't shine?"

"Now who's falling back on clichés?" Vorador suddenly realized he was enjoying himself. The atmosphere no longer seemed oppressive and lonely.

"This is the thanks I get for trying to be cooperative?"

That outrageous comment made him laugh out loud. Petra cooperative? Only if she couldn't squirm her way out of a situation. Or if she was using some form of compliance to throw him off track. Or was trying to sweet-talk him into doing what she wanted against his better judgment. "Sorry, babe."

"Babe?" She had her hands on her hips and looked like she wanted to use real matches to set him on fire instead of just magical words. "Either you just called me a pig, or used some sexist endearment—"

His fingertips actually itched to touch her. He rubbed them against his thighs and hoped she would think he was wiping off sweat. "You won't accept my apology?"

"No," she shot back.

"Well, that's okay, then. Since I'm taking it back."

He turned and started walking again, feeling much better. It was a sad state of affairs when he could only be happy picking a fight with a woman. Wouldn't it make more sense to try to woo her? Maybe. With another woman. But not Petra W. Field. Oddly enough, that thought cheered rather than depressed him. He really was losing his mind.

They reached the hotel before he felt the need to start another argument. He led the way onto the porch, looking for any sign of Kitoka. Nothing had changed since their earlier visit. The neon Hotel California sign still blinked over the door. The place had the same deserted ambience as the *Psycho* motel.

"I'm just all aquiver, waiting to be filled by your wisdom, O

176

Great Wizard," Petra said when he paused to look around, "but can we just go inside and get this over with?"

"Place giving you the willies, huh?" he asked with a grin.

"What about Bosco—Kitty?"

"I'm sure she'll show up." He wondered how much longer it would be before Petra put the pieces together and figured out who Kitty really was.

He opened the door and entered the cool interior. An ugly orange plastic chandelier provided dim light. Cheap roadside motel furniture, with a decidedly Spanish flavor and upholstered in worn red velvet, lay scattered around and did little to alleviate the gloomy atmosphere.

The Formica-covered front desk was deserted. Three corridors led out of the lobby. The place was much bigger than it appeared from the outside. Picking the hall on the right, Vorador motioned Petra to follow him.

"What are we looking for?" Petra asked in a whisper.

"I don't know." His own voice was just as quiet. Something about the place seemed to demand stealth. "Just keep your eyes open."

"Yes, sir."

He didn't need to glance at her to know she'd given him a wise-ass salute. "Behave yourself."

He thought he heard her mutter something about eyes in the back of his head. Let her think so. Maybe it would keep her in line. Yeah, right, he thought, like that was a realistic possibility. Or like he really wanted her to be well behaved. Where was the fun in that?

"Hey, Sparky."

He barely restrained himself from showing her how much he disliked that damn nickname. "What?"

"Aren't you going to try any of the doors?"

He glanced at a door as he passed it. "No. I think we'll know when we find whatever it is we're looking for."

"Well, as long as one of us knows what that might be."

He heard the quiver under her sarcasm. Vorador slowed down until Petra came up beside him. Wordlessly, he reached out to her. He knew she was more frightened than she would ever admit when she immediately grabbed his hand and held on for dear life. "Don't worry, Petunia, I'll keep you safe."

"Yeah. My hero."

Her words should have warmed him, but he couldn't take them as a compliment when she used that mocking tone of voice. "You don't think I can protect you?"

He regretted the words as soon as he said them. Hell, was he really that needy for her approval? Sad to say—yes, he was. Downright desperate for it, if he was totally honest with himself. The best way he knew to earn it was to protect her. He would never let anything happen to Petra. He would never fail like that again. Never.

"How handy are you with your fists, Wiz Boy? 'Cuz that's what you'll have to use, since your magic doesn't work down here."

"I know how to take care of myself." Wanting to end this conversation, he tugged on her hand. "Come on. The sooner we finish our search, the sooner we can get out of here."

At the rear of the building there was another long hallway. It, too, was lit with candles. Turning down it, they came to the center hall and followed that back to the lobby. There still wasn't a soul in sight. With a shrug, he led the way into the final corridor on the left.

They'd only gone a few feet when Vorador halted. "Look at that room number."

"Yeah, so?"

"The doors in the other hallways didn't have any numbers at all. That's the same number as Medora's apartment. We must be on the right track."

"And about to be run over by a train."

"All aboard," he said with a smile. He reached for the doorknob. A jerk on his other arm from Petra stopped him.

"Vorador, be careful."

"Hey, I have a fifty-fifty chance. Nothing will be there—"

"Or," she interrupted, "you'll be greeted by a knife-wielding maniac."

"Only one way to find out." Without any further hesitation, he pulled her close, kissed her hard and fast, then grabbed the knob and swung the door open. Steeled for any attack, he took one step inside, careful to keep Petra safely behind him.

He whistled softly when he got a clear view of the room. "Somebody order room service?"

Peeking around his shoulder, Petra whispered, "As long as we're not the main course."

Agreeing with her, he cautiously inspected the cavernous banquet hall. It looked ready for a horde of starving conventioneers. Several buffet tables were piled high with every kind of food imaginable. Just when he'd decided it was as deserted as the rest of the hotel, he heard what sounded like silverware clinking against china. It came from a far corner of the room.

Jerking backward, he pushed Petra into the hallway. "Somebody's in there."

Taking a stance in the doorway, he set himself for an attack. Long agonizing seconds ticked by. He heard Petra behind him doing something but didn't turn his attention to find out what. No other sound came from the room.

"Here. Take this."

He nearly jumped out of his skin at Petra's whisper. He looked down at the object she urged him to take. It was a tall iron candle holder from the lobby. He was touched. "Thanks."

Moving with caution, he slipped back into the room, his makeshift weapon at the ready.

"It's about time you got here. I've been waiting for you."

He lowered his arm, the tension flowing out of him. Motioning Petra to join him, he said, "Hello, Kitoka."

The Amazon warrior sprawled in a chair at the head of one long banquet table. She had a large pineapple chunk in one hand and a cup of wine in the other. "Have a seat."

Chapter Twenty-four

Petra groaned and leaned against the wall. Wasn't this a fine kettle of fish? Kitoka was the last person she wanted to run into, here or anywhere else. She wanted to smack the wizard on the back of his head when he took a chair next to the Amazon in her skimpy leather outfit. Did he have to grin like that?

"Food's not bad," Kitoka assured them.

"Of course," he said, "I imagine anything would taste good after—"

"Shut up, wizard." Kitoka glared at Petra, even though she spoke to Vorador.

"I think it's time to spill the beans," he said.

"If you do that"—Kitoka set down her wine and picked up a large steak knife—"I might have to take action."

Petra didn't like the sound of that. Stepping forward, she asked, "Have you seen a big black-and-white cat?"

Kitoka stabbed the knife downward, plunging the tip into the table, right though the tablecloth. "No."

Staring at the knife swaying there, stuck at least an inch deep in the wooden table, Petra merely nodded. In spite of her earlier thoughts that the Amazon wouldn't actually hurt another woman, maybe it was time to rethink that assumption.

"Sit down, Petra," Vorador invited.

"No, thanks. I'm not hungry."

"Really?" He surveyed the table. "Look—here's a lovely bowl of fruit salad."

His tone of voice warned her that he was up to something. She wasn't quite sure what. "No thanks."

"Then how about this peach?" He plucked it out of another bowl and tossed it lightly from hand to hand. "It looks nice and ripe and juicy." He licked his lips and winked at her.

Gadzooks! He was referring to that embarrassing moment when she'd kissed him and all those stupid romance novel cliché had made her laugh. "You're such a pig."

"Not a bad thing where you're concerned." He took a bite of peach. "With any luck I'll end up plastered on your chest."

"Vorador!"

"Like those shirts you sleep in," he clarified. His innocent facade crumbled when he licked juice from the peach.

Petra slanted a glance at Kitoka, but she seemed absorbed in feeding her face. Sidling around the table, Petra took a seat on the opposite side. She wanted to keep both of them in plain view.

"At least have something to drink," he insisted.

She politely refused the pitcher of deep red wine Kitoka offered, hoping the Amazon wouldn't throw it at her. She settled for a plain glass of water. There was no way she wanted to muddle her wits with alcohol. "Well, isn't this cozy and civilized?"

Ignoring Petra, Kitoka gave her full attention to Vorador. "If you don't take Dugan's note to the police, then I will."

"Kit—"

"How did you know about that?" Petra interrupted. "Are you able to eavesdrop from down—" Petra remembered some of the things that had gone on in her front room. "Oh, gads!"

Vorador threw back his head and burst out laughing.

Petra had lovely visions of grabbing another of those steak

knives and cutting off his braid. "If you had a lick of decency, you'd be embarrassed, too."

"You're both disgusting," Kitoka announced with a hiss.

Something in the Amazon's voice captured Petra's full attention. It sounded vaguely familiar. Like she'd heard it often in the past few days, though she'd only met the warrior once. She studied Kitoka. "Do you have another sister or something?"

"Or something."

Suddenly it clicked into place. Petra jumped up to her feet and pointed at the Amazon. "Great balls of fire! It's you!"

"Petra!" Vorador yelled.

She spun back to him, expecting to see him engulfed in a ball of fire. She barely had time to register that he wasn't flaming when he launched himself across the table and knocked her to the floor. As she fell, she heard a whishing sound go overhead. Vorador landed on top of her. After that, everything went black.

"Petra? Can you hear me?"

How weird, she thought. It sounded like Vorador was calling her from a tunnel. His voice had all these strange echoes and distortions. Why was it so hard to breathe? Her ribs ached, as if she'd been tackled by an entire football team.

"Petra? Damn it! Answer me."

Even in her groggy state, Vorador's demands made her smile. Bossy man.

"She isn't hurt if she can grin like that," another voice said.

Petra frowned. Who else was here with her wizard? It was a woman. It seemed there was something she should remember.

"Shut up," Vorador said. "Or I'll do worse things to you than turn you into a feline."

"Oh my gosh!" Petra managed to pry her eyes open. Squinting against the light, she saw Vorador hovering over her. Behind him she saw an Amazon in a black leather bustier and thigh-high boots. Kitoka. Kitty. Bosco. "You're my cat."

"Are you all right?" Vorador pushed Kitoka out of the way, as if trying to keep her away from Petra.

Events were beginning to focus. She should have set Vorador on fire. No, he had no magic here. Kitoka was Bosco. He had tackled her. But what had made that whooshing sound? Petra craned her head around and looked behind her. A lethal-looking knife was buried in the wall. It hadn't been there before. Kitoka had thrown it at her. Vorador had saved her life.

Sitting up, brushing aside Vorador's helping hands, Petra glared at Kitoka. "You tried to kill me."

"If I wanted you dead, you would be."

"Scaring me to death doesn't count?" Petra asked.

The Amazon shrugged one shoulder in a negligent fashion. "Not to me."

Finally accepting Vorador's assistance, Petra allowed him to help her to her feet. Once she was upright, a wave of dizziness swept over her and she gratefully sank onto a chair. She even took a drink when he shoved a glass of water in her face. When he tried to feel her forehead, she'd had enough.

Pushing his hand aside, she demanded, "Will you stop?"

He went down on one knee beside her chair and gently took her hand. "Petra, she almost—"

"That's okay, sparky." Taking pity on him, she patted his cheek with her free hand. "I understand."

"No!" He brushed away her hand as if it was a pesky fly. "Let me finish."

She graciously gestured for him to continue. Then she leaned back in the chair to enjoy the show. She didn't imagine the wizard found himself offering apologies very often. No wonder he wasn't very good at it and couldn't seem to find the right words. He just kept getting cuter all the time.

"I'm sorry, Petra." He heaved a big sigh, as if relieved he'd managed to get out the words. "I didn't mean to hurt you. I was only trying to protect you."

"I thank you for a job well done, Mr. Wizard." She looked over her shoulder at the knife embedded in the wall. That very well could have been buried in her.

A loud belch made them both look over at Kitoka. She had reclaimed her seat at the head of the table and was devouring a bunch of grapes. She said, "Don't let me stop you now. You two are better entertainment than most soap operas."

Petra groaned and let her head fall back against the chair.

Thank heavens, she—the cat—had been locked in the bath-room during one specific encounter.

"Petra, are you sure you're all right?" Vorador asked.

"Yeah, I'm fine." Never admit to weakness in front of an enemy. "So, how did she get turned into an animal?"

Attacking a plate of carrots, celery, cauliflower, broccoli and olives, Kitoka indicated with a jerk of her head that Vorador could go ahead and tell.

"Whoever tried to kill Medora did it to her," he said. "Plus gave her an amnesia spell. She knows she was at her sister's apartment that night and is sure she found a clue, but she can't remember any more than that."

"I guess a cat makes sense," Petra said. "Kitoka. Kitty."

"I vow, if either of you call me that again, it will be your last word."

Petra watched Vorador, who was still kneeling beside her chair, to see how he took the threat. She knew it scared the crud out of her. A corner of his mouth twitched, as if he struggled to hold in a smile. She leaned closer and whispered, "You're not afraid of her?"

He shook his head.

"Why not?"

"Her bark is worse than her bite."

Vorador placed his hand on Petra's knee. She supposed he meant it as a comforting gesture, but it had the totally opposite effect. The heat of his touch burned through her jeans in seconds flat.

"Please tell me you guys aren't getting all sickeningly mushy again. You're going to spoil my appetite."

At Kitoka's harsh voice, Petra tried to jerk away from Vorador. He firmly held her in place. "Don't let her intimidate you."

She nodded, agreeing in principle. It wasn't so easy to be tough with a disgruntled Amazon glaring daggers at her from less than ten feet away. Especially since real ones could soon follow. "Okay, back to the spell. This wizard attacker . . . he must have expected Kitoka to show up."

"Why do you say that?" Kitoka demanded around a mouthful of coleslaw.

"Because he obviously had the spell prepared in advance," Vorador explained before Petra could answer.

"It's not a simple thing for most wizards to turn a person into something else on the spur of the moment."

"Could you do it?" Kitoka asked the wizard.

Vorador nodded, his gaze never leaving Petra's.

Without warning, Petra's mouth went dry and she could barely swallow. Yes, he could work such a spell—easily. She didn't know why his admission disturbed her. But it did. Deeply.

Petra squirmed in her chair, uncomfortable with the direction in which her thoughts were heading. Suspicions were growing faster than weeds in an untended garden. Why was Vorador staring at her so intently? He looked cautious. Of her? She hadn't done anything.

It was almost as if he expected her to . . . what? Suspect something? She rolled that thought around in her mind. Yes, of course. She *should* suspect him. If anything, he was the guilty one! The unexpected vehemence of that mental statement gave her pause. Guilty of what?

She supposed it was possible Vorador had something to hide. There could even be more to his involvement than assisting the police and helping Dugan. Here was an off-the-wall theory: Maybe he got involved in the case merely to make it easier to hide his own guilt. Heck, go all the way. Just come right out and say he was the one who attacked Medora.

"Petra?"

She shook her head, barely hearing him. She needed to think this through. Why would he try to kill Medora? Then turn right around and save her? Another of those horrid suspicions popped up and wouldn't go away. *Was* he trying to save Medora?

The whole almost-dead spell could very well be a ruse. It was the perfect cover-up. Medora needed blood to be revived. If it was Vorador's blood she needed, he would make darn sure that was the last blood in the world she ever received.

Gads! Maybe Medora really was dead. Had anybody seen her since he'd taken her to his lab? Petra's head felt ready to explode. How could she be sure he wouldn't do something so horrendous? She knew very little about the wizard. He'd been consistently closemouthed, telling her only what he wanted her to know. He wouldn't even admit his real name. Oh, this was absurd.

"Petra, what's wrong?"

Shaken by all these sudden doubts, Petra glanced around, looking anywhere to keep from meeting Vorador's gaze. She was struck by the number of knives in the room. There was a steak knife by each place setting. A complete carving set stood at the end of each banquet table. Decorative swords and ancient knives hung on every wall.

Vorador had gone berserk when he'd seen the mugger with one measly knife. He'd nearly killed the mugger. While Kitoka only got a verbal reprimand.

Which raised another pertinent point: Why had the Amazon tried to kill her? Simply because Petra figured out who Bosco was? It seemed a bit excessive—even for Kitoka. Petra rubbed her forehead. Everything had gotten so confused. Shifting uneasily in the chair, Petra tried to unobtrusively ease away from Vorador's touch. Something was very wrong here.

One big question jumped to the front of her mind: Was the problem with her? Or with Vorador? Was she going crazy? Or was he really guilty? Okay, that was four questions. She was sure they were all valid. What was that famous saying? Something about after you eliminated all logical possibilities, then the impossible must be true.

"Petra, can you hear me?"

It seemed unlikely that Kitoka and Vorador were partners in crime. As far as she knew, they had no reason to kill Medora. Well, other than the age-old, time-tested reasons of jealousy, revenge, power, money or love. Any one could be the truth. Which brought her back to where she'd started.

Had Vorador been the one to turn Kitoka into a cat? It was a surefire way to protect the Amazon and keep her away from the police. Of course, it didn't explain why in the world she returned to her true form while down in this hole. Once again Petra could only see one logical answer. If they were lovers, they could continue to have romantic rendezvous here. That certainly explained Vorador's lack of fear toward Kitoka.

No, that scenario was too preposterous. She needed to back up to make sense of things. Okay, start when Bosco turned up on her back porch. Considering what she knew now, only one explanation made any sense—Vorador had sent Kitoka to spy on her.

In hindsight, the explanations about how ERG managed to show up for her cleaning job instead of Rapid Renovations now sounded contrived and false. Instead, it had been the perfect excuse to get inside her house. What better way to find out what she knew? As if she knew anything! She supposed they wanted to know if she would be a problem in their continuing efforts to cover up the crime. Gads, her brain hurt.

It boiled down to one thing—Vorador and Kitoka. Whatever the reasons behind the attack on Medora, she was absolutely positive the wizard and the Amazon were in this together. How foolish to suspect Vorador and Fytch were an item. All along, Kitoka had been the one Vorador really wanted.

"Damn it, Petra! Answer me."

Petra tried to tell herself she was being silly, that she was letting her imagination run wild. But after the lesson learned from Harold, how could she blindly accept everything Vorador told her? There were too many things he wasn't telling her. Her skin crawled with the recollection of how close she'd come to letting him seduce her.

Unable to face all the questions and suspicions, she jumped to her feet. "Listen, you guys do whatever it is you came to do. I'm going back home."

"Petra?"

She ignored the wizard's call and hurried across the room. It was impossible to ignore the prickling sensation between her shoulder blades. At any second she expected to feel a knife plunge into her back. By the time she reached the door she was

187

covered in cold sweat. Not until she was safely in the hall did she unclench her fists and her teeth.

Running for the lobby, her only hope was that the checkout process would work for her and not just the wizard.

Chapter Twenty-five

Petra looked around her front room, blessing whatever lucky star she'd been born under. Now that she'd escaped from Vorador she had to decide what to do next. It would be too easy for him to track her down at work. She needed time to think, time to try to straighten out this mess. At least in her own mind. Grabbing her purse and a jacket, she left the house that no longer felt like her safe haven against the world.

Fifteen minutes later she settled into a corner booth at a small diner. She finished her first cup of coffee before letting herself think. What was she going to do? She had hoped her crazy suspicions about Vorador would fade. No such luck. If anything, they were stronger. The thought of coming face-to-face with him petrified her.

Until she could either give her complete trust to the wizard or prove him guilty, all she wanted to do was run, as fast as she could, as far away as possible. But what did she know about hiding? She had no friends, no family here, only a new job she

189

didn't want to quit. Plus, how could she search for the truth if she was hiding?

Taking out money to pay for the coffee, she realized she only had fifty dollars in cash. Sure, she had money in the bank, but it wouldn't open until 9:30. If—*if* Vorador was the bad guy she suspected and he realized she'd run for cover, one of the first places he'd stake out would be her bank.

ERG obviously had a talented computer system. With the right instructions, they could track her within seconds if she used her credit cards. Was Vorador already out of the hole? Already tracking her? She didn't dare use her ATM card and find out. Rubbing her temples as a headache began to form, Petra signaled the waitress for another refill.

Was she overreacting? Gad, she suspected him of murder! But if she chose wrong, she could end up dead, dead, dead. Part of her still insisted, *He's innocent, you fool.* The more cautious part of her couldn't accept that as the final answer.

Right now she just wanted to hear a friendly voice. She went to the pay phone by the rest rooms and placed a collect call.

Her dad answered on the first ring, and accepted the charges immediately.

"Dad, what're you doing home? Shouldn't you be in class?"

"Petra! What a pleasant surprise. How's Seattle?"

"Rainy." Petra nearly burst into tears, hearing her father's rich, warm chuckle. By the time she recovered, he'd gone on speaking.

". . . blew out all the windows! The university had to cancel classes until they can get the worst of the mess cleaned up."

She made the appropriate sounds, then asked, "How's Mom?"

"She's fine. Off on one of her feminist retreats. She'll be sorry she missed your call."

"Tell her I said hi, okay?"

After that, Petra was at a loss as to what to say. It was so tempting to ask for Dad's help. If she accused Vorador and he turned out to be innocent, she could ruin his career. The wizard brotherhood was a tight-knit group.

"What's wrong, Petra?"

A nostalgic smile pulled at her mouth. He always had been able to read her mind.

"Things not working out to your expectations?" he asked.

She made a sound that was part laugh but almost a sob. "Oh, things are working out just hunky-dory."

"Want me to lend a hand?"

There it was. If he offered, it wasn't the same as her running home, asking her parents for help, was it?

He softly said, "You know I can be there in two seconds."

Deeply touched by his support—which he'd unconditionally given her entire life—tears filled her eyes. "I know, Dad."

"But you think you ought to be all grown-up and handle whatever mess you've gotten yourself into?"

"Yeah, that about sums it up. I promise I'll holler if I really need help. Guess I was just feeling a little lonely out here in the big old Pacific Northwest, so far from home."

"Petra—"

"So, anything else exciting going on?" She cut him off, afraid if he offered his support again, she wouldn't be able to turn him down.

He sighed but followed her lead. "As a matter of fact, there is. Harold was here last week."

Petra froze, then finally managed to ask, "What did he want?"

"Wanted to know where he could reach you."

"Gads, you didn't tell him, did you?".

"No." There was a long pause. "Although after the story he told us, I was tempted to come hunting for you myself."

"Dad! You didn't believe him?"

"No, of course not." He sounded impatient with her for even asking. "You should have told us what a horse's ass he is. Instead you just sat here like a whipped puppy and took all that crap from your mother about working through a relationship instead of giving up and running away."

"Well, since running away is basically what I did . . ."

"You had good cause."

Yeah, she supposed she had. Why in the world was Harold trying to find her? Surely he didn't think they could patch things up and still get married. She had a horrible thought.

"Dad, Mom didn't try anything, did she? You know, to get me and Harold back together?"

"I don't think so," he said, not sounding at all certain.

"Gads, if she cast a love spell on me and Harold, you darn well better let her know it backfired. Get her to remove it."

Her dad chuckled, not without some sympathy. "That what's troubling you, Petra? Man problems?"

Changing the subject again, she asked, "Are the cops still looking for me?"

He gave a disgusted snort. "Some detective came snooping around. Told him what he could do with his charges."

"What a mess." Maybe if she went home and handled the predicament with Harold . . . It wouldn't be like she was running home so her parents could protect her.

No. As tempting as it was, she couldn't go home. Vorador would be sure to look for her there. Good grief! Where had her life gone so wrong that she had two angry wizards chasing her?

"Dad, I need to go now. It was nice talking to you."

"Petra, if you need anything—"

"I know, Dad. I'll call. Oh! But don't call me, okay? Don't call my house."

"What the hell have you gotten yourself into?"

"Gotta go, Dad. Love ya." She gently placed the receiver in its cradle, silencing the rest of her father's demands.

Getting another cup of coffee, she planned her strategy. The first order of business was avoiding Vorador. She didn't doubt he would come looking for her. Secondly, she needed information. She couldn't make a decision without all the facts. She thought finding out more about Vorador's past would shed some light on how trustworthy he was now. And she knew the perfect place to start.

Hours later, Petra was ready to ban all technology and enter a back-to-nature commune. Grubbing in the dirt, eating nuts and berries and making her own clothes had to be preferable to dealing with recalcitrant computers. After calling in sick to work, she'd come to the university's main library. Confident she would be able to sweet-talk the school's system out of the information she wanted, she'd blithely entered Vorador's name. After all, she'd worked with numerous university computers over the years. She might not understand business computers but college machines were more accommodating, since they were programmed to teach the students.

She feared she'd lost her touch. She'd found absolutely nothing. No, that wasn't entirely true. She found prior addresses dating back to the time he'd started at the university. She found grades from his six years at the school. No big surprise there. He'd been the top of his class.

She'd managed to get into files from his counselors. His personality profiles made for interesting reading. Words like *brilliant*, *powerful*, and *intuitive* were liberally used. *Proud*, *arrogant* and *impulsive* were no more helpful in finding out where the heck he came from.

She knew he'd paid his tuition with student loans—which had since been paid off. She'd tapped into his credit history, discovering wizards in private practice in Seattle earned very handsome salaries. Plus he'd made some wise investments. If it made a difference, the guy was loaded.

Expanding her search, she found his exam for admittance into the Wizards Guild. He'd passed with flying colors on his first attempt. However, the guild's records were too well protected for her to get any more information than that.

While she'd found no trace of Vorador's identity prior to college, she had discovered one interesting tidbit. While there was no mention of family—not even distant relatives—on every report, file and record that asked for next of kin or guardian, the same person always popped up. Professor Helios.

With a sigh of frustration, she glanced at her watch, surprised to see it was nearly eleven o'clock. No wonder she was hungry. The caffeine rush from her early morning coffee had long since worn off. She could find some cheap food here on campus. Maybe after she'd eaten her brain would start working again and she would think of another path of attack. Vorador's past had to be in the blasted computer somewhere.

"Petra!"

She froze. That voice! She'd know it anywhere. Gads, how had the wizard managed to find her?

"What a wonderful coincidence."

Turning in her chair, she prepared to run. Oops! It wasn't Vorador after all. Guess his voice wasn't that familiar. She hadn't realized before that the two men sounded so much alike.

"Hello, Professor Helios. How nice to see you."

The man who bent down to kiss her on the cheek looked like a wizard straight out of a fairy tale. In spite of his age, which had to be somewhere on the far side of ninety, he stood straight and moved with youthful grace. His long white hair flowed down to mingle with the white beard that reached halfway down his chest. His blue eyes sparkled with intelligence.

Petra had known him all her life. As far as she remembered, he'd always looked the same. He said spending so much time around his students kept him young. Petra thought it more likely that he'd perfected some sort of fountain of youth spell.

"My dear, I just got off the phone with your father a few hours ago. He told me you'd moved to Seattle and here you are."

"Yup, here I am."

Dad had interfered after all, called the cavalry to charge to her rescue. No big surprise. Wasn't that more or less why she'd called home in the first place? How the professor had known to look for her at the university library she could only guess. If asked, he would probably wink and say, "Magic." It was his standard answer when he didn't want to explain.

"How're you doing, Professor? You look wonderful, as usual."

"I'm doing just fine. And you, Petra dear?"

She didn't miss his sharp inspection. "Oh, I'm just swell."

"Really? You look a little frazzled this lovely morning."

"Guess you're right about that." She had a feeling there would be no avoiding him, so she invited him to lunch. "I was just going to get something to eat. Care to join me?"

"I'd love to. I don't have a class until this afternoon."

"Then you can treat me to the best the cafeteria offers." Might as well save money where she could. She turned back to the computer. "Let me shut this down."

"I see you're researching Vorador. Have you met him yet?"

Petra mentally said all the swear words she'd learned not to say out loud. Her mind raced for a plausible explanation. She wasn't ready to confide in anyone yet, especially not Professor Helios, Vorador's closest thing to family. She had nothing but a brain full of suspicions and no hard facts. Drat! She hoped the professor didn't feel obligated to tell Vorador about her search.

"Oh, I was just . . . checking out the local competition. You know, seeing if anybody could give Dad a run for his money."

"Laszlo and Vorador? Two of my most promising students." Helios chuckled. "Now that's a showdown I'd pay money to see."

Petra wondered how Dad would react to being described as merely *promising* after more than thirty years as a practicing licensed wizard, with twenty years' teaching experience of his own. "Well, family loyalty demands I bet on Dad."

"Yes, quite commendable, my dear." Helios held her chair out of the way while she gathered her belongings and left the desk. "You didn't say whether you've met Seattle's Grand Wizard yet."

Darn, darn, darn. Grand Wizard? Of course he was. Heaven forbid that she should get involved with some nice, normal, low-level industrial wizard. No, she went straight from Harold, a college dean of magic, right to Vorador, the city's highest wizard. She knew better than to lie to the professor. He'd probably already seen Vorador's influence wrapped all around her.

"Tall man? Long black hair? Hokey green robe?"

"Yes, that certainly sounds like him." Helios smiled fondly. "I can still remember the first time I saw him."

Petra couldn't believe her good fortune. He would drop the information she wanted right in her lap. "When was that?"

"He was already tall, skinny as a rail. You know, all elbows and awkward angles. Could barely walk without tripping over his own feet or bumping into things."

In spite of herself, she was entranced by this picture of Vorador as a boy. Especially since it was at such odds with the man he was now. "How old was he then?"

"Couldn't have been more than thirteen. Maybe fourteen.

Zounds, that boy had more power than sense." Helios seemed to get lost in some memory, then recovered himself. "Enough about ancient history. You said you've met him?"

Disappointed not to get more, she said, "I've seen him around town a time or two."

When the professor didn't come right out and call her a liar, she decided to take advantage of this opportunity. She'd start out with some innocuous questions before working around to what she really wanted. "What's up with that stupid robe he wears?"

Helios took her arm as they strolled out of the library. "You can blame that scamp, Dugan. Vorador only tolerates it because they're friends as well as business associates."

Petra made a noncommittal sound. She couldn't act too eager. The professor might be old but was still sharp as a tack. She didn't want him sending some magical message to Vorador to join them for this little tête-a-tête. "How long have they worked together?"

"Seems like they've always been a matched set. Dugan got them into trouble and Vorador got them out of it."

That fit. Dugan had found himself in a mess and called Vorador to help him clean it up. However, that set up Dugan as the villain. What about her suspicions that Vorador had committed the crime? She needed something more before casting her doubts aside.

"You knew them even before they started at the university?"

"Oh, yes. I've known them for years."

"How'd you meet them? Were they neighbors?"

"No, not at all. Vorador's uncle sent the boy to me for training. As always, Dugan simply seemed to tag along."

Ah ha! "You knew his uncle?"

"We'd met. Unpleasant man. Hated magic. Was particularly zealous in campaigning against it back in the old days."

"Must have been hard then, having a nephew with magic."

"Luckily he died not long after Vorador came to town." Helios seemed to realize what he'd just said. "Sorry. Not very charitable of me, is it? But he was a sour, unhappy man, who tried to make everybody around him as miserable as he was."

"What happened to Vorador after his uncle's death?"

"I brought the boy to live with me. Made it easier to continue his training. He was woefully ignorant on how to handle that much power. Should have started training before he learned to walk. Stupid, blind, ignorant—" Helios cut himself off with a wave of his hand. "Enough about the past. Tell me about your new life here in Seattle, my dear."

Deciding she could try during their meal to learn Vorador's family name, Petra reluctantly did as he asked. She only hoped the professor wouldn't call Vorador to tell him of their encounter until she was long gone.

Chapter Twenty-six

Petra stood in the airport phone booth, wondering if she'd gone totally insane. This cloak and dagger stuff might make her look pretty ridiculous, but if she wasn't crazy, then what did several hundred dollars on her credit card matter? At least she'd be alive to sort it out later.

With a deep breath, she pushed the button and sent the command zapping out into cyberspace. Barely thirty seconds later she received confirmation. Her purchases had been approved.

A quick but thorough scan of her surroundings reassured her that no one was paying any attention to her.

Moving to the next step of her plan, Petra dialed ERG's number. She cut off Zaylin's cheerful greeting. "Is Vorador there?"

"You're rude. I'm not gonna tell you."

"Is he in his lab?"

"No, but—"

"Is he out on a call?"

"Yes, but—"

"When do you expect him back?"

"Six o'clock, but—"

"Thanks." Petra slammed down the receiver, then wiped her sweaty palms on her shirt. If her ploy worked, they would track her call to the airport. Vorador would come running after her like a hound chasing a fox.

Grabbing her purse, she hurried to her car. While Vorador was busy, she felt safe going back home. Now if only she could get what she needed from her house before he realized she'd led him on a wild-goose chase.

A computer check at the airport would tell him about the five separate plane tickets she recently purchased. With any luck, he would think she'd used one of them to leave town and would waste lots of time running from one gate to another. With a bit more luck, she would be long gone, tucked into some cheap anonymous hotel. Just to be safe, she also intended to leave her car in a downtown parking lot. She would walk or take the bus to her final destination.

She wasn't about to admit that part of the reason she ran from Vorador was her own lack of self-control. He scared the crud out of her—emotionally. Didn't say much for the strength of her moral fiber, did it, now? Gads, she'd succumbed to his seduction so easily. Which raised another issue—why had he tried to seduce her? After only a few days?

She knew better than to think she was irresistible. Men hadn't exactly chased her in great numbers over the years. Harold hadn't had any trouble resisting her charms. In fact, he'd found them so lacking, he had looked for satisfaction elsewhere. How could she believe a man like Vorador had been overcome by passion for her? No, there had to be darker, more sinister reasons for his supposed infatuation.

Arriving home, she cautiously parked half a block away. Using the neighbors' backyards, she snuck in her rear door. Standing inside the kitchen, she waited, listening for any sound of another person. She heard her answering machine beeping. After several nerve-racking minutes, she decided she was alone.

Not even Bosco—Kitty—seemed to be around.

Tiptoeing to her bedroom, making a wide detour around the hole in that stupid rug, she grabbed a suitcase and crammed in

199

a bunch of clothes. She hesitated a moment, then also put in her oldest stuffed pig. She could use whatever small comforts she could find. Stopping by the bathroom, she loaded up all her toiletries. As she made her way down the hall the phone rang. She froze in terror and held her breath until the machine picked up.

"Petra, if you're there, answer the damn phone!"

She cringed and almost retreated down the hall when the wizard's angry voice boomed into her silent house.

"I don't know what game you're playing, but I'm not amused."

Yeah, well, she wasn't exactly laughing either.

"Once I get my hands on you . . ." His voice ended on a choked sound of frustration.

Gee, that was enticing. She wished she dared pick up the phone and tell him exactly what she thought of him.

"You'd better have a damned good explanation." The sharp sound of him hanging up made her flinch.

She needed to get out of here before he showed up and demanded that explanation in person. That wouldn't be a pretty scene. Well, if her plan was working, he ought to be on his way to the airport soon. Maybe he'd even called from the airport. That was a happy thought. Moving to her desk, she found her bankbook. She still wasn't sure how she could withdraw money or use a check without being caught, but she felt better having the means available if the opportunity arose.

On the way back to the kitchen, she noticed an envelope on the floor by the front door. Somebody must have slipped it under the door. Who? Did she want to take the time to find out? She knew she couldn't afford not to. Too many questions remained unanswered. It might be an important clue. Leaving her suitcase in the hall, she crept back to get the envelope.

Ripping it open, she didn't immediately recognize the handwriting. Both sides of the single sheet of paper were full. Turning it over, she almost threw it away when she saw the signature. It was from Vorador. Blast her curiosity. She had to read it.

There was a P.S. below his signature. *P.S. Try giving Kitty—*

Bosco—some different food. She's a vegetarian. She'll thank you in the end.

Petra nearly choked on a laugh. Kitoka, the fierce Amazon, was a vegetarian? Right! Who was he trying to kid? Although, now that he mentioned it, she remembered Kitoka had only eaten fruits and veggies while she'd been gorging herself down at the hotel. An Amazon who didn't eat meat?

Petra almost tossed the letter then. If he was going to ask her to look after the stupid cat, who was probably his lover, then he could just stuff it. She had better things to do. Such as protect herself. And find out if he was really a murderer. Or an innocent bystander. She started to the trash can. Once again common sense lost out. She turned to the front of the paper.

Petra, Sorry I missed you this morning. Why did you leave in such a hurry? I thought maybe you were late for work. Then I found out you called in sick. Why aren't you at home? I checked all the hospitals but haven't been able to find you. Are you sick? If you're reading this, call me immediately.

He must have left the note sometime this morning while she'd been wading through computer files at the university. Did he really have no clue why she was avoiding him? No, more than likely it was a trick.

I have some news. After you left, Kitoka and I explored the hotel further and we found the murder weapon.

Petra gave a snort of disgust. Yeah, they'd probably been searching for a bed. After all, if they were lovers, it had been a couple of days since they'd had an opportunity to be together.

In the bedroom next door—

Ah ha! Petra thought with triumphant glee, then wondered what she was so happy about.

—we found the knife laying in the middle of the bed. I won't go into all the gory details, but it had obviously not been tampered with since the crime. I've turned it over to the police.

That gave Petra pause. If he was guilty, that didn't make sense. Unless . . . unless he had already removed any clues that might point in his direction. Perhaps he'd even planted the weapon, with fake evidence on it. What better way to cast sus-

201

picion on someone else and throw the cops off his trail?

"I'm so confused," she wailed, not caring that she was talking to herself.

"That makes two of us," a voice said from behind her.

Chapter Twenty-seven

Petra screamed and threw her hands up in the air. The letter went flying. Spinning around, she saw Vorador standing in the kitchen doorway. She screamed again and lunged for the front door, frantically trying to open it. Her finger slipped on the knob. A glance over her shoulder told her that the wizard was advancing on her. With another scream, she yanked on the door. It rattled but wouldn't open.

"Petra, what the hell is wrong with you?"

He was close enough now that he could grab her if he wanted to. Choosing to face him, she turned and pressed herself back against the door. Gad, what would he do to her? Panting as if she'd just finished a marathon, she managed to gasp, "What're you doing here?"

He tipped that one mocking brow up at her. "I could ask you the same thing."

Mind racing, she couldn't come up with an answer that would satisfy both herself and him. When she didn't say anything, he blew out a noisy sigh. She flinched, expecting the worst.

"Why did you take off this morning without any explanation?"

Afraid to tell him the truth, she could only stare at him, feeling like a rat caught on a sinking ship.

"Then would you care to explain what you were doing at the airport?"

"How'd you know—?" Dang, he'd worked faster than she'd anticipated.

"That you didn't go to L.A.? Or Dallas? Or Miami? Or Chicago? Or New York? Is that your question?"

She couldn't move, too afraid of what he planned to do now he'd found her.

He made an angry sound and started pacing back and forth in front of her. He was wearing a tight black T-shirt, tucked into black military style pants, which were tucked into ankle-high combat boots. All in all, he looked like a deadly efficient assassin ready to go to war.

"What the hell *are* you doing, Petra?" He raked his hands back through his hair, pulling it loose from the neat ponytail. It fell around his face as he continued pacing. "What possessed you to buy five tickets to five different cities? Then not use any of them?"

She pressed herself farther back against the door, wishing she had just a tiny bit of magic so she could make herself disappear.

He stopped in front of her, hands on his hips. "Or do you mean, how did I know you were here?"

She cringed away from the fury crackling in his eyes.

He bent and picked up the discarded letter. "When I left this, I told myself I was being foolish. For some reason I listened to that little voice telling me to put an alarm spell on it." He waved the paper under her nose. "Just a tiny little spell to warn me when it was opened." And to make sure nobody else but you could open it. After all, you're the only one I can trust with such sensitive information. Or so I thought."

Her gaze darted down to the note, then back to his face. Well, crud—an alarm. He was even more conniving than she'd suspected. The dirty, rotten sneak.

"Imagine my surprise. There I was at the airport, worried sick, thinking you'd left town. Because of some family emergency, or some horrendous catastrophe. Then boom!"

He tossed the paper into the air and it burst into flames. They both watched the ashes slowly drift to the floor. "My alarm goes off. And here you are."

She swallowed hard and waited.

Placing one hand on the door beside her head, he leaned in close. He nuzzled aside her hair to whisper in her ear, "What's going on, Petra?"

His lips delicately nibbled at her earlobe and a shiver ran down her spine. Not entirely sure if it was fear or attraction, not wanting to believe it could still be the latter, she turned her face away. That exposed the column of her throat. He didn't hesitate to take advantage. Her head thumped against the door when he nipped the skin over her jugular vein.

"Stop it." She hated how weak and breathless she sounded.

"Stop what?"

He put his other hand on the opposite side of her head, effectively caging her in. He leaned closer, rubbing his body against hers in the lightest of contacts. Just enough to send her heart racing and her blood pressure soaring. From fear, she insisted. Not from desire. No, not that. Doggone it. How could she suspect him of being a murderer yet still want him so darn much?

"Talk to me, Petra."

He moved even closer to her, totally covering her body with his. He raised his chin; she was short enough that her head fit snugly beneath it. Her nose pressed against his throat. With every breath she inhaled his brisk scent. He rubbed harder against her and she felt his erection grow. Her senses whirled until she was dizzy and confused. What was he doing? Why torture her like this? Why not just kill her and be done with it?

"You have no idea—" He groaned low and soft and seemed to almost collapse against her, as if he would have fallen if her body and the door weren't supporting him. His words came out in harsh fragments. "When I couldn't find you—I never want to go through—"

A loud knocking from the other side of the door made them both jump.

Petra clutched her chest, not sure she could withstand many more shocks. Vorador leaned over, hands on his knees, breathing deep. His hair swung forward, hiding his face so she couldn't judge his state of mind. She had to wonder exactly what he'd been trying to say before they were so rudely interrupted.

Another knock came, this time hard enough to rattle the door.

"Who is it?" Vorador asked her softly without looking up.

"How the heck should I know?" Petra whispered back to him.

"This is your house, isn't it?" he shot back, turning his head to peer at her through the curtain of his hair.

Giving him a dirty look, wishing she dared do more, she tiptoed forward and peeked through the peephole. She didn't know the woman standing there. It could be a neighbor. Acting on impulse, she opened the door before Vorador could tell her not to. Of course, now it opened without a hitch.

"Hi," Petra said with a smile.

The lady standing on her porch was short and rather stout, her bulk buttoned into a flowered shirtdress that looked a couple of sizes too small. She carried a large black purse that clashed with her pastel dress. Her hair was—Good grief, it was pink! It was teased and poufed into a style dating back to the 1960s.

"Well, howdy there," the lady replied in a thick Southern accent. "I was beginning to think nobody was home."

Petra shrugged and resisted the urge to give more information than she needed to. "Can I help you?"

"I certainly hope so," the lady gushed in a breathless voice. "I've been looking all over and I hope I've finally found the right person."

"Yes?" Petra prompted, wondering what the wizard inside her house was doing. She didn't want to turn and look. Maybe he would leave. Yeah, right! She would win the next Miss America contest before Vorador would voluntarily leave her house.

206

"I've been out of town for a few weeks," the woman said. "You know, visiting my sister's youngest daughter."

Petra was beginning to feel trapped in a bad dream with an escapee from a trailer park asylum. "Uh-huh?"

"Well, while I was gone, Wendell—he's my own dear sweet hubby, he decided to clean out the garage and attic and earn himself some extra money. He took a bunch of stuff out to the fairgrounds. Where they have those big flea markets and garage sales about every month or so?"

Petra nodded beginning to have a great big hunch where this might be leading.

"Well, darned if he didn't up and sell my favorite rug."

Not totally taken by surprise, Petra nodded again, waiting to see where this whole bizarre episode was heading.

"If you're the one I'm looking for, then you know what I'm talking about. It's a darling rug. With lots of pigs all 'round the border and kinda pale blue."

"How did you get her name?" Vorador stepped up beside Petra and pulled the door open wider to reveal himself to the woman.

With a squeal of surprise, the woman tottered backward. For one horrible long second, it looked like she would tumble off the porch. Acting quickly, Vorador jumped forward and grabbed the woman's arm, pulling her to more stable footing. She was gasping and squealing in fright. Petra slapped her hand over her mouth, barely holding in hysterical laughter. The woman sounded exactly like an overexcited pig.

Just as suddenly another thought slammed into Petra's mind. This was her opportunity to escape! While Vorador was busy with Ms. Piggy, Petra could get away. Not stopping to think any further, she stepped back from the door, into the house. Vorador was still trying to keep the woman on her feet.

Petra slammed the door shut, locked it, then ran for the kitchen. Snagging her suitcase, she darted out the back door. Running hard, she was nearly three houses away before she heard the wizard's enraged bellow. Then she was in her car and pulling away from the curb. In her rearview mirror, she saw him plow through a hedge and barrel into the street.

He started running after her, but she accelerated faster than was safe for neighborhood streets and quickly lost him. She hoped he didn't try to zap himself into her car. On the other hand, maybe that wouldn't be such a bad thing. Maybe she could screw up his magic enough to send him somewhere else. Somewhere totally disgusting. Like a stinky pigpen. Or an overflowing sewer.

She didn't draw an easy breath until she made it downtown. There was no sign of the wizard. Without a backward glance, she abandoned her car at one of those park-it-yourself lots. There was a bus stop on the corner.

Chapter Twenty-eight

"Oh, my! What happened, sir?"

Vorador brushed past Caylin on his way down the hall. His voice was low with warning. "I'm fine. Don't worry about it."

Caylin trailed after him to Dugan's office. "Dugan's not here, sir."

"Well, hell! Where is he?"

"He had to leave." Still not venturing into the room, Caylin's voice barely carried inside. "He told me to wait here until you arrived."

Hands on his hips, Vorador tried some deep breathing, searching for a center of calm in the sea of insanity his life had become. He nearly gagged as he breathed his own stink. Without another word, he started stripping off his filthy clothes. As long as Dugan wasn't here, he couldn't object to Vorador using his private executive washroom.

Caylin squealed in shock, her head darting out of sight.

Seemed to be the reaction of the day—the mere sight of him

sent women screaming and running for the hills. First Petra and now Caylin.

At least he understood the behavior from his timid junior wizard. Caylin was so shy she rarely managed to string five words together in a coherent sentence whenever he was around. Her magic was strong enough, and she seemed knowledgeable about spells, but she lacked the confidence to execute many of them. Stepping into the shower, he wondered if she'd still be there when he got out.

Eventually he felt clean again. Emerging back into the office, dressed in the spare robe Dugan kept on hand, Vorador was glad to see Caylin had disposed of his rank clothing. It was probably ruined anyway. Some things were beyond even magic. He would miss those boots, though.

Caylin slipped into the room, looking everywhere but at him. "Are you all right, sir?"

"If you know what's good for you, you'll leave now."

"I'm sorry, sir, but . . ." Her fingers twisted in a painful-looking knot. She dropped her gaze to the floor. "It looked like somebody threw you in the sewer."

Eyebrow climbing in surprise at her daring, he grunted in reply.

She flinched but sat down in the chair by Dugan's desk.

He growled, "Mind your own business."

Caylin made a sound like a soft sob and hunched further around herself. He was surprised she didn't run wailing from the room. He threw the wet towel in the corner, disgusted at himself for venting his frustration on such a helpless creature. Slicking his hair back from his face, he quickly braided it, securing the end with a rubber band from Dugan's desk.

To appease his own guilt, he tried not to sound as surly as he felt. "Nobody threw me in the sewer. I did it to myself."

She didn't look up. Her voice barely louder than a whisper, she asked, "Were you looking for clues about Medora's case?"

"In a manner of speaking." Settling on a corner of the desk, he said, "I was trying to talk to Petra."

Caylin's head snapped up. "*She* threw you down a manhole?"

"No, of course not." The idea amused him, until he realized

210

that that was basically what had happened. The more he thought about it, the madder he got—again. Vorador slammed down his fist, rattling everything on Dugan's desk. "I swear, she's doing it on purpose."

"Doing what, sir?"

"Trying to drive me crazy." And in the process making him doubt his own magic . . . and turning him into a coward. How else to explain why he'd taken a shower instead of simply snapping away the filth?

He started pacing.

"What happened, sir?"

That was a good question. Too bad he didn't have any good answers. Vorador leaned his hands on the desk and rotated his neck, trying to work out the kinks. For the first time since his childhood, things were out of his control. He hadn't liked the feeling then and he didn't like it now.

"It's as if she's some kind of nonmagic black hole. Sucking in my sorcery. Then spitting it out somewhere else. Twisted, so I hardly recognize it." With a sigh, he admitted, "In other words, I don't have a clue what happened."

For one thing, he sure didn't know where to find Petra again. Most likely, her nonmagic prevented him from locating her. Why in the hell was she hiding from him in the first place? Something must have happened after she came out of the hole this morning. It had certainly changed her attitude toward him. For some reason she was afraid of him now. He could still hear her screams as she'd tried to claw her way out the front door. What had happened to the brazen flirt who had boldly asked to play with his fire?

His mind skittered off on that tangent. The memory of her touch gave him chills. No other woman he'd been involved with had ever—ever—wanted to touch him when he was blazing. Of course, most of them weren't foolish enough to disregard his warnings and actually set him on fire. At least not more than once. Trust Petra to be unafraid.

The feel of her hands skimming over his chest remained fresh and vivid in his mind. He had seen only innocent wonder in her expression, but it had been incredibly erotic to him. For the

211

first time in years, he wondered what it would be like to make love to a woman . . . to Petra, while his fire burned around them.

"Sir?"

He looked up, trying to recall what they'd been talking about. Right—the sewer. "I tried to zap myself into Petra's car. I ended up in the sewer instead."

Caylin's mouth fell open in an *O* of amazement.

He could practically hear the wheels turning inside her little blond head as she processed that information. Not wanting to discuss Petra any further, he asked, "Why did Dugan want you to wait for me?"

"Oh!"

He didn't care for the look on her face.

She took a deep breath, held it for a moment, then said in a rush, "Somebody broke into your lab."

At first the words simply didn't register. "What did you say?"

"Somebody broke into your lab."

He stood there for a moment, struggling to comprehend. Then, with a sudden jerk of his head, he disappeared in a poof of smoke.

Materializing in the center of his laboratory, he stared in disbelief. Caylin had been telling the truth. Every piece of equipment had been destroyed. Broken glass sparkled dangerously on the tables and floor. Nothing had been left intact. Dazed, he turned toward the door as Caylin skidded to a halt there.

"How?" was all he could manage to say.

"We don't know yet," she said, her voice laced with dread.

He could understand her fear. If he allowed free rein to his anger at this moment, he could probably bring down the entire ERG building. Who could have overcome the locks and spells on the door to his personal laboratory? He didn't know of one single wizard who had enough power to commit such an act.

"Medora?" His voice sounded distant even to himself.

Slowly turning, afraid of what he might find, he faced the wall that concealed his secret workroom, where Medora was hidden. His shoulders sagged in relief when he saw that the other wizard hadn't breached those safeguards. Speaking the entrance codes, he moved into the dim cool room, Caylin by his side.

Medora looked like the princess from *Sleeping Beauty*. Her complexion hadn't faded; her skin remained rosy and healthy. Her long black hair curled around her like a living blanket. There was an air of expectation about her, as if she might awaken at any moment.

Vorador knew her body was distressingly cool. If she was breathing, it happened so infrequently as to go unnoticed. Nor did she have a heartbeat or detectable pulse. However, she wasn't dead. He knew she clung to life. Her soul still resided, trapped inside that virtually lifeless shell.

Only the blood of her enemy had the power to restore her to full life. Otherwise she would die completely, her flesh at last starting to decay and rot. He had vowed to Dugan that he wouldn't let that happen. For the first time in his life Vorador began to doubt his own powers.

The facts were inescapable. A wizard with more magic had overcome his most powerful spells. Mingled with the anger such an invasion caused, a kernel of fear grew. It was a concept so foreign to Vorador that he could hardly grasp it. Somewhere in his city another wizard commanded more magic than he himself was capable of calling forth. And this other wizard was a criminal. Or insane. Or both.

"Is she all right?" Caylin whispered.

"She's unharmed."

Burying his bleak thoughts, he stepped back into his ruined lab. When Caylin was clear, he reset the spells guarding Medora. Then reinforced them with the strongest magic he knew—death to the uninvited. Uncomfortable with such drastic measures, fearing accidents, he also placed warnings. That would keep away anyone who accidentally stumbled into the wall. He didn't know who that might be, but he couldn't use deadly force indiscriminately.

"Where's Dugan?" Surrounded by the destruction, Vorador had an insane fear his friend had been hurt during the break-in and Caylin wasn't telling him. "Why isn't he taking care of this?"

"He is. I mean, he was. Here, that is." Caylin made a visible effort to get herself under control. "He went down to the police station to finish the paperwork."

"Was this the only room damaged?"

"No, several storerooms and supply closets were searched."

He felt a small measure of relief. Yes, it had been a search, some method behind the madman's actions. But not a search specifically for Medora. If he'd come for her, he would have gone straight to the lab and not wasted time searching elsewhere. Only in a wizard's lab could the magic be strong enough to hide such a treasure. Whoever had broken in hadn't even been aware she was here. So, if he hadn't come for Medora, then what?

"The rug." It had to be. None of ERG's other jobs involved this level of risk. Only Petra, and that damned ugly rug. Somehow, the attacker knew Petra brought it here. Which meant it was even more important than he thought.

With a snap of his fingers, a broom sailed out of the closet and began sweeping up broken glass. How had the murderer known the rug was here and not still at Petra's house?

No, the leak could have come from the police department. There were even a couple of reporters nosing around, although he and Petra had been lucky enough to avoid them. Anybody could have seen Petra dropping off the rug this morning—but only the murderer would realize the significance.

Damn! He banged his fist down on the counter and a pile of junk disappeared. The woman at Petra's house. She'd come for the rug. Had it been the wizard in disguise?

If that had been the wizard on Petra's porch, he hadn't suspected a thing. For a moment unfamiliar feelings of inadequacy almost swamped him. No, he'd deal with all this emotional crap later.

First things first. He sent a mop over to clean up some spilled chemicals. After he put that blasted rug in a safe place, he would tell Kitty about this latest development. Damn. There was another of his failures. He still hadn't been able to restore the Amazon to her rightful shape.

He had to find Petra before anyone else did. What if the other

214

wizard suspected she had some knowledge—that would lead to solving the crime. She could be in real danger. Everywhere he turned this other wizard's power mocked him. With a determined scowl, he pushed aside the insidious self-doubt. He didn't have time for this nonsense. He needed to start searching the city for Petra.

Once he had her, she *would* explain why she ran away. She *would* tell him why he frightened her. She damn well *would* tell him everything he wanted to know! Even if he had to scare her to death to convince her how serious he was.

"Caylin, I've got work to do. Finish cleaning up for me."

By the time his words faded, only a lingering wisp of smoke remained to show he'd even been in the room.

Chapter Twenty-nine

"Petra."

Snuggling deeper into the pillows, Petra tried to ignore the insistent whisper. It seemed like she'd barely gone to bed.

"Petra. Time to wake up."

She pulled the covers over her head. Fifteen minutes. That's all she wanted. Then she'd get up. Really she would.

"Come on, Petra. Don't make me come in after you."

Something about the voice made her crack one eyelid open. Did she know that voice? She drifted back to sleep before an answer came to her.

"Petra!"

This time the demand snapped both her eyes wide open. Everything snapped back into focus. Vorador! He'd found her. Lowering the blankets, she peeked out. She'd drawn the heavy curtains, not wanting to be disturbed by sunlight come morning. The hotel room was pitch black. She couldn't see Vorador, but she heard him breathing. It raised the hair on the back of her neck.

"Did you really think you could hide from me, Petra?"

"All right. Bonus points for you, Mr. Wizard. You found me. Now stop messing around and turn on the light."

"You're not in any position to give me orders."

The chill in his voice sent a shiver down her spine. He didn't sound amused. All her fears and suspicions came crashing down like an avalanche. Up until this point her heart hadn't believed 100 percent he would actually harm her. Now, here in the dark, he sounded extremely dangerous.

"It's time to end the game, Petra. You lose."

She screamed and scrambled for the opposite side of the bed. Safety hovered temptingly close—another person, a passing car, the motel manager, a handy phone booth. If she could only make it to the door. She collided with a chair. Crying out in pain, she sprawled on the thin rug, momentarily dazed. Icy fingers closed around her ankle.

Still hoping he was playing some kind of warped game, she said, "Stop it, Vorador. You're scaring me."

An eerie, hollow-sounding chuckle filled the room. "Oh, Petra my dear, I haven't even started."

Driven by pure terror, she screamed. Kicking to free herself, she clawed at the rug, desperate to reach freedom.

"Settle down, you devil's spawn."

The whispered curse came out of the darkness and her limbs went slack. She couldn't move a muscle, not even a finger. For one panicked moment she thought she couldn't breathe, then managed to suck in a desperate breath. She tried to speak, to reason with him, to plead and beg with him, but her vocal cords were as paralyzed as the rest of her body.

Closing her eyes, wondering if a person could drown in her own tears, she waited for the pain of a blade in her chest.

When she opened her eyes again, Petra realized she wasn't dead. Not dead, but where? Disoriented by the total absence of light, fear and shock sent adrenaline coursing through her body and momentarily she couldn't tell if she was standing, sitting or upside down. She reached out in the inky darkness, desperate

217

to connect with something, anything. There was nothing. Gads, where had he put her?

The utter silence further confused her. It was as if she'd gone deaf and blind. At least she hadn't lost her voice. She screamed for help until she was so hoarse she could do no more than whisper.

A long while later she regained enough strength to explore her prison. After her screaming session she had crouched on the ground in some semblance of the fetal position, her arms wrapped around her knees. Now, she leaned forward and placed her hands beside her feet. She winced as rocks scraped her fingers. A dirt floor could mean a cave.

Straightening up, her arms stretched in front of her, she carefully shuffled forward. She flinched when her toes squished in a patch of frigid mud. A few steps later, her fingertips encountered a dirt wall. Trying hard not to panic, she moved sideways, keeping her hands in contact with the wall.

It didn't take long to realize the wall curved, going around in a circle. How big a circle? How could she tell when she got back to her starting point? Taking a deep breath, she turned and cautiously crossed the open area. Barely ten baby steps later, her fingers brushed against another dirt wall. Not a cave. An underground chamber. Had she been buried alive? She couldn't help it; she started screaming again.

She could only guess how much time passed before she managed to get herself under control. She discovered she could almost reach both walls with her arms fully extended from her sides. By jumping as high as she could, she also knew there didn't seem to be any ceiling. That gave her a first glimmer of hope. She had been deposited in a pit—she might be able to escape, to climb out the top of it. If only it wasn't so dark. So quiet. So cold.

Huddled on the driest spot of dirt, she pulled her knees up to her chest and wrapped her arms around them to preserve body heat. Why couldn't she have slept in a nice warm pair of sweats instead of one of her stupid pig shirts? Eventually she could lose enough body heat to die of hypothermia.

However, *why* she was here worried her even more. Why

hadn't Vorador murdered her at the hotel? Not that she was complaining. But if he had killed Medora, it didn't make sense for him to get squeamish now. It was stupid of him to leave a loose end laying around. One expected some logic—even from a homicidal maniac.

Did that mean she should give up? Just sit here in the mud and wait for death? Out of the darkness, she heard a voice as plain as if the person huddled in the pit with her.

"Are you done wallowing in self-pity, Petra? If you are, get up off your butt and find some way out of this mess."

"Mom?" It sounded just like her. Biting her knuckles to keep from crying, Petra wished her mom really was here.

"Feeling sorry for yourself won't solve anything. Use the mind you were blessed with and help yourself."

"Darn it, Mom!" Petra jumped to her feet. "If you can see the mess I'm in, then why the heck don't you zap me out of here?"

Only silence and blackness answered her. It had been bad enough to be left here by Vorador. To be abandoned by her own mother was nearly unbearable.

She shook her fist at the heavens, starting to get angry at her shabby treatment. "You asked for it, Vorador."

On hands and knees, she searched the floor. She found and discarded several rocks before finding the right one.

"One way or another, I'm going to make you pay for this."

Taking the fist-sized rock, she pounded the sharp edge into the hard-packed dirt wall, making a hole. A hole just big enough to accommodate fingertips or toes.

She made another indentation several inches above the first one.

She started her climb. Hanging precariously onto the wall, she pounding more toe- and handholds.

"If it takes me the rest of my life. I'll crawl my way out of this pit."

She kept her grip on the wall through sheer tenacity.

"Once I get free—"

She heaved herself upward another step.

"—I'm gonna nail you to the wall, Mr. Whatever-your-real-name-is."

Stretching up, she started the process again.

Eventually she stopped issuing threats at the absent wizard. Instead she concentrated her efforts on making her way ever and always upward. Just as well, she thought, that it was totally dark. That meant she couldn't look down and be terrified by how high she might be. Or how much farther she had to go to reach the top. And reach the top she would. Or die trying.

Trembling from fatigue, Petra clung to the wall. She wasn't about to give up, but she didn't know how much longer she could keep banging away at this cliff. Why, oh why, hadn't she followed through on that blasted New Year's resolution to work out at the gym three times a week?

She had to be nearing the top. It was no longer pitch black. Gray light had gradually replaced the dark. With a weary sigh, she tightened her grip on her hammering rock, ready to start the next hole.

"No!" Her fingers cramped and the rock slipped from her grasp. She tried to grab it even as it fell. She missed and nearly lost her tenuous position. Instinctively, her fingers and toes dug into the dirt. She pressed herself flat against the cliff face.

Cheek crushed against the earth, silent tears overflowed and ran down her face. Now what? How could she continue upward without a digging rock? She couldn't—wouldn't go back down. No, never back down into that black pit. Besides, she doubted she had the strength to repeat the journey.

"If you're going to give up, Petra, you might as well let go and simply fall."

Sniffing, she tried to wipe her eyes against her shoulder. "While I appreciate the sentiment, don't you think you could give me a little more help?"

She waited but heard only silence.

"Fine! I'll claw my way out. I'll use my fingernails. Teeth. Whatever. But a little helping hand would be appreciated right about now."

"Petra! Take my hand!"

It took several moments to realize this voice hadn't come from inside her head. Nor had it been her mother's voice. Dazed from

220

emotional stress and confused by physical exhaustion, she whispered, "What?"

"Take my hand."

Careful of her precarious position, she craned her neck to look up. A face peered down at her from only a few feet away. It startled her so much, she almost let go in surprise. She hugged the wall again, trying to control her panicked breathing and trembling limbs. Gads, could things possibly get any worse?

"Petra." The voice was softer now, as if Vorador realized he'd almost scared her into falling. "It's okay. Take my hand."

"Yeah, right!" she challenged the wizard. "I'll let go and you'll drop me."

"Why would I do that, Petra?"

"How convenient that you arrived just in the nick of time. I'm almost to the top, and free. I don't need your help, wizard."

"What the hell is wrong with you? Just take my damn hand and let me get you to safety."

"No." She desperately wanted to believe him, yearned to give in to the temptation of his strong arm so close above her. But only because she was exhausted. Not because she was ready to forget all her suspicions.

"I swear, if you don't take my hand on the count of five"— he leaned down farther, stretching his arm closer—"I'm going to use a spell to levitate you up here."

"No!"

"Yes! Now just remember, my magic isn't its most stable around you. The choice is yours, Petra. My hand." He shook it at her. "Or my magic."

She glared up at him as best she could from her awkward position. "Go screw yourself."

"Is that any way to talk to your rescuer? One."

"Take a flying leap—"

"Two."

"—off a short pier."

"You're mixing metaphors. Three."

"Stuff it—"

"Four."

"—up your a—"

"Five!"

Petra's arm shot up. She grabbed Vorador's wrist. For one panicked moment she thought he meant to let her fall. Then strong fingers wrapped around her forearm, holding her secure. She felt herself being raised through the air. She lost her last toeholds. Her feet dangled over nothingness. Her life was literally in his hands. She prayed she was wrong about him.

It felt like her arm was being ripped out of its socket. She nearly screamed in pain when he jerked her up the final few inches. Collapsing facedown in the dirt, she gasped for breath. She was safe. She'd done it . . . well, with a little help.

"Petra? Are you okay?"

Feeling too weak to move, she still told him, "I'm fine."

"I don't know whether to paddle your butt for scaring the shit out of me or kiss you senseless."

"Neither, thanks just the same," she said, her equilibrium returning now she was back on solid ground.

Grinning like an idiot, he pulled her into his embrace. Before she could utter another word, he kissed her. His heat warmed her chilled body inside and out. It felt so good. Letting herself sink into the moment, she kissed him back. Until she remembered she shouldn't be doing this with him.

Pushing at his shoulders, she squirmed away from him. Even though her hand was filthy, she wiped the back of it across her lips, showing him how distasteful his kiss had been. "Don't ever do that again."

The passion in his dark eyes turned to immediate anger. "Damn it, Petra. You need to get it through your thick head that I'm not Harold. Don't judge me by his standards. I expect you to treat me with the respect I deserve."

"Respect? Ha! The only thing you're going to get from me is a nice long stay in a jail cell."

With a lightning quick move, he pinned her to the ground. "Is that what you did to poor Harold? Turned him in to the police when he didn't live up to your expectations?"

"Get off me, you big jerk!" Even as she struggled to get free, she asked herself what the heck she was doing. Should she really be antagonizing him? He'd already kidnapped her once.

With one hand, he easily restrained both her hands above her head. "Afraid I might make you feel something? Don't worry, I have no intention of making love to you until these"—leaning back slightly, he flicked a finger against her heart—"are gone."

"Ha! We'll make love when pigs fly!"

His anger vanished as abruptly as it had appeared. He smiled down at her. "Now there's a promise I intend to hold you to."

"Don't hold your breath. No, on second thought—do hold your breath. Hold it till you pass out and die!"

"Doesn't work that way. Once you pass out, you automatically start breathing again." Chuckling, he rolled off her. "I'm sorry, Petra. I should have saved this conversation until you'd had a chance to recuperate."

She scooted away from him. "Don't think you can apologize, you Benedict Arnold."

Pushing himself into a sitting position, he frowned. "You think I betrayed you?"

"Don't play the innocent." If he was acting, he was doing a darned fine job of it. No, she couldn't weaken now. He had kidnapped her. Stuck her in a hole! "I'm on to you."

"Petra, you're not making any sense." Vorador rose to his feet and held out a hand to her. "Let's get out of here. We can discuss matters in the morning, after a good night's sleep."

She turned away from his offer. What she saw made her frown in confusion. "Where are we?"

Chapter Thirty

Dazed, Petra searched for the dirt floor and fuzzy gray sky. Instead they were on some sort of metal platform. Iron girders crisscrossed above her head, supporting the ceiling. She sat on thick steel plates bolted together.

"How did we get here?"

Vorador frowned. "This is where I found you."

She carefully peeked over the edge of the platform. She couldn't even see the bottom. A ladder snaked up through the maze of supporting girders. Had she climbed that? Utterly bemused, she could only stare at the wizard.

He squatted beside her. "Are you all right? Should I take you to the hospital?"

She shook her head. "Where are we?"

"Inside a service area of the Space Needle."

Tipping her head to one side, she jiggled it, hoping to shake that information into place inside her mind. The Space Needle? Was this metal enclosure the hallucination? Or had the dirt wall been the fantasy? She didn't have a clue which was reality. If

Vorador had the power to confound her senses so completely, she might never know.

Obviously she couldn't trust any of her perceptions. "How did you find me?"

"The maintenance crew have been hearing a banging since yesterday. They couldn't detect where it came from. They were afraid it was some poor soul who'd committed suicide in the Needle. To be on the safe side, they called in a wizard to perform an exorcism."

Had she died and was she now haunting the place of her death? In a small voice, she asked, "Am I a ghost?"

"You're as real as I am, Petra." He gently took her hand. "I found you hidden behind an invisibility spell. That was why the workers couldn't see you."

She winced as she flexed her battered hand inside his grip. "I was climbing a cliff. To get out of the pit."

He nodded as if he understood. "You were hanging on to one of the girders for dear life."

She stared down at the steel beams as if she'd never seen them before. Which she hadn't.

"Come on, let's go home." He didn't wait for her permission, but simply helped her to her feet, holding her steady when she swayed off balance.

"Yes," she said in a faint voice, "home sounds good."

She didn't protest when he swung her up in his arms. At the moment, getting out of here seemed more important. If she ended up somewhere even worse . . . Well, then she'd have time to regret trusting him, wouldn't she?

Watching as he closed his eyes, she realized he meant to use a spell to zap them home. Gad, she hoped he knew what he was doing. Otherwise, they could end up in the middle of Pioneer Square. What the heck. It would be an improvement over here.

He finally whispered one word. "Home."

Petra looked around the immaculate foyer of Vorador's house and heaved a sigh of relief. She wiggled herself out of his hold and immediately complained, "I thought you were taking me home."

"Your house isn't familiar enough." He let her go but kept one arm around her waist. "This was the only place I dared try."

"Fine." She took a moment to steady herself, then stepped away from him, determined to stand on her own two feet. "Didn't you say something about a bath?"

Taking her arm, as if he guessed she was near collapse, he lead her toward the stairs. "I think I can accommodate you."

He seemed to be awfully eager to please. Self-preservation made her tug free of his hold. She couldn't just follow him like a mindless sheep. If he wanted her upstairs, then that was precisely where she wouldn't go. She headed toward a door across from the stairs.

"No. Not in there."

"Why not?" She stopped with her hand on the doorknob. A frown pulled her brows together. "That is a bathroom, isn't it?"

"You can't use that bathroom."

"Why not?" she repeated with less patience.

"Because it's Orwell's bathroom."

"Who's Orwell?"

After the briefest of hesitations, he said, "My roommate."

"You're worth about a gabillion dollars, but you still have a roommate?" She shook her head, unable to cope with his oddities right now. "Just show me where I can clean up."

She followed him up the stairs, into what was obviously his master bath. Without another word he left. Curiosity made her regret that the door to his bedroom was shut. Good manners dictated she didn't go exploring.

Half an hour later, Petra was nearly asleep in the tub with water and bubbles up to her chin. In fact, she was about to slide under when Vorador knocked on the door. She didn't have enough energy left to protest when he invaded her privacy.

When he lifted her from the tub she roused enough to slide an eye open, her body practically boneless in his arms. She knew she should raise a fuss about him seeing her naked, but the effort didn't seem worth it. He bundled her into a large towel, then wrapped another one around her dripping hair before he carried her into his bedroom.

She tried to open her eyes, but it was too much work. Instead she snuggled her head in the crook of his neck. He smelled so good. Evil wizards should smell like rotten eggs and putrid frog's lips, not like expensive aftershave and sea-foam shampoo.

Gently placing her on the bed, he removed the wet towel and pulled the covers up over her nakedness. She cuddled into the soft mattress and softer pillows. In her sleep, she felt him join her there. She dreamed he held her safely all through the night.

Petra yawned and stretched, feeling more rested and contented than she had in a long time. Morning sunshine streamed in the windows. Seattle must be having another sunny day. Either this was a rare streak of good weather, or everyone lied about how much it rained here. Rolling over, thinking to doze a few more minutes, she smacked into something hard and unyielding. Oh, crud! Scooting to the far side of the massive king-size bed, she stared at the wizard sprawled facedown in peaceful slumber.

For a moment she couldn't remember how she'd ended up in bed with Vorador. Then it all came crashing back—her suspicions, the kidnapping, the rescue. She really must be a glutton for punishment. Why else would she be in his bed after all that? Or else her subconscious didn't believe in his guilt.

The pale green sheet covered him from the waist down, but one muscled leg hung outside. The sight of his bare back would have been enough to make her swoon, if she had been the kind of woman who did that. She never had been before, but now she might have to take it up. His long dark hair spread out over the pillow in wild disarray. What a delicious sight to wake up to.

She was tempted to sneak out of bed and run away again. With a sigh, she knew the futility of such an action. Last time she'd ended up in a much worse situation, and he'd found her anyway. She might as well confront him and get it over with. Stretching out a leg, she poked him in the ribs with her toe.

Without warning, his hand closed around her ankle. Flashing back to when the same thing had happened in her hotel room, she freaked out. Kicking wildly, screaming, she tried to break free. The next thing she knew, she was underneath him, unable to do more than wiggle her fingers and toes.

"Settle down, you little hellcat."

She froze. That was almost the same thing he'd said in the hotel. Gad, that saying about frying pans and fires was true.

"That's better." He looked down at her with a sleepy grin. "Good morning, Petunia."

He must be trying to lull her into submission. Okay, two could play that game. It took all of her limited willpower to keep her voice steady. "We need to talk."

Lowering his head, he nuzzled her neck, his only answer a low humming sound.

"Vorador, I mean it." She tried to pull away from his invading lips. "We have some serious issues—"

"Oh, I agree," he mumbled while kissing her chin. "Very serious."

Gasping when he rubbed his leg against hers, she remembered she was naked. So, it seemed, was he. Other concerns melted away, replaced by burgeoning passion, and not just on his part. She shoved at his shoulders.

"Get off me, you big lug."

He rolled, taking her with him. "You prefer to be on top?"

Her legs fell apart and she ended up laying on the naked wizard in an extremely intimate position. Mind turning to mush, she valiantly struggled to recall what she wanted to discuss with him.

He ran his hands down her back.

No, not exactly discuss, she thought. Argue about something?

His hands cupped her bottom, pulled her hips even closer to his.

She should be afraid of him. What was it he'd done?

"What do you want, Petra?"

She didn't have a clue.

"Shall I tell you what *I* want?"

Shivering, she nodded.

"Sex," he whispered in her ear. "With you. Lots of it."

That brought her back to reality with a thud. "Vorador, I can't sleep with you."

"That's okay," he said, his hands busy exploring up and down her back. "I don't want to sleep either."

"No, you don't understand." Placing her palms against his chest, she levered herself up. Until she realized that gave him quite a view of her naked breasts.

Plopping back down, she made a sound of frustration and buried her face against his chest. Oh, that was a mistake. Once there, it was impossible to resist the temptation to taste him. After that, she simply had to discover the texture of the black hairs on his chest. That wasn't enough to satisfy her. She explored till she found his nipple, then teased it with her tongue. When it tightened, she lightly bit him.

Suddenly he flipped her off him. She flew through the air and bounced several times on the bed. By the time she had her wits back and had covered herself with the sheet, he was across the room and had pulled on a pair of sweatpants. He still looked good enough to eat. She licked her lips. He backed up, moving even farther away from the bed.

Rolling onto her side, she propped her head on her hand. She wondered what had caused the abrupt change in his behavior? One second he'd been as intent on seducing her as she'd been on arousing him. Why had he bolted out of bed? The man was nearly as perverse and contrary as she was.

"You're driving me insane," he said.

"Good."

That startled him. "You mean you're trying to?"

"Not on purpose. But it seems only fair that I'm doing the same thing to you that you're doing to me."

"You are? I am?"

She laughed at his confusion. "I think I like you in the morning, Mr. Wizard. So cute and rumpled, not quite awake yet and just a tad slow."

For an answer, he stomped over and disappeared inside a large walk-in closet. He came out a few minutes later dressed in a black T-shirt and jeans. He threw some clothes in the general direction of the bed. "Get dressed, Petra. Then come downstairs to the kitchen. We'll talk over breakfast."

Laughing as he nearly ran for the door, she got out of bed. They might still have a lot of problems to work out between them, but she no longer doubted Vorador's honor and integrity.

Just like that. Poof! Whatever madness had possessed her before, it was gone. She knew they still had to sort everything out. As he said, over breakfast.

She inspected the wardrobe he'd selected. The royal blue silk shirt was so huge it would hang nearly to her knees. The baggy black sweatpants would literally fall off if she tried to move while wearing them. Seemed he wanted her covered from neck to toes. Tossing aside the pants, she settled for the simplicity of the shirt. The tail was long enough to preserve her modesty. She had to roll up the sleeves several times to free her hands.

She took her first good look around Vorador's bedroom. Once again she was surprised at what she saw. The place was nice, but totally generic. The king-size bed had a dark green comforter, with light green sheets. There were a couple of perfectly unremarkable dressers, one with a mirror. Several fairly insipid landscape prints hung on the walls.

There was a total lack of personal clutter. Not one item identified this space as belonging specifically to Vorador. Why weren't some of his collections in here? She would have figured his favorite ones would find a place in such a private room. It was too bizarre to contemplate on an empty stomach.

Padding on bare feet, she quickly used the bathroom, borrowing his brush to try to tame her hair. It had dried in all sorts of weird shapes since she'd slept on it wet. She finally gave up. He'd already seen her at her worst. If that hadn't sent him running for the hills, he was strong enough to handle a bad-hair day.

Chapter Thirty-one

Entering the kitchen, Petra sniffed appreciatively, then admired Vorador's offering of orange juice, strawberries, melon slices, bacon, blueberry pancakes, several varieties of syrup, milk and coffee. He even used good china. There wasn't a dirty pot or pan in sight. She slanted a look at the wizard. Not a hair out of place, he looked cool and collected. It was hard, but she resisted the temptation to walk over and kiss him.

"Where are the rest of your clothes?"

Too bad he didn't sound as agreeable as he looked. "The pants were too long. You wanted me to trip and break my neck?"

He stared at her bare legs, his hands clenching and unclenching at his sides. Finally he said, "Sit down and eat."

Trying not to read too much of her own emotions into his actions, she slipped into a chair. He seemed to be as attracted to her as she was to him, but they had a lot of matters to clear up. It wouldn't do to get her hopes up only to have him crush them—as he was sure to do once he heard her story. She decided to play it safe and keep her mouth shut.

It took less than a minute to break her resolution of silence. "So, Sparky, did you actually cook this? Or use magic?"

"Does it matter?" He took a seat across the table from her. "It tastes the same either way."

"It may not affect the taste, but it reveals a lot about the person doing the cooking . . . or the hocus-pocus."

"I cooked it."

Sipping orange juice, she made a noncommittal sound.

"Well?" he demanded after she'd tasted several of the dishes.

"What?" She did her best to maintain an innocent air.

"After your snide comments, you aren't going to give me your opinion about the fact that I cooked?"

Hiding her smile by taking a bite, she shook her head.

Once he stopped staring at her mouth, he attacked his own breakfast.

She nearly burst out laughing as he tried to conceal his bruised masculine ego. It felt so good to be rid of those nasty suspicions. Until this very moment, she hadn't realized how liberated he made her feel and act. Although he might growl and grumble, he showed considerable tolerance for even her most outrageous behavior.

She wished they could just wave a magic wand and everything would be resolved. She might have forgiven him, but she still wanted an explanation for why he'd stuck her in that pit— or rather, in the Space Needle.

He didn't say another word until they were finished eating. With a sweep of his hand, he ordered, "Be gone."

Petra flinched as the dishes disappeared. The sound of breaking china came from the laundry room. "Oops. Sounds like you sent them to the washing machine instead of the dishwasher."

With a heavy sigh, he leaned his elbows on the table and studied her. Long, uncomfortable seconds ticked by. Well, uncomfortable for her. He looked perfectly at ease, darn his hide. It was hard, but she somehow managed to keep her mouth shut. Let him make the first move. Although as more time passed, remaining silent became downright painful.

Finally, he said, "So, tell me, Petra. Has running away from your problems always been your way of coping with them?"

"I do not run away—"

"What about Harold? And the police? And more recently, me."

"Okay, I guess you have a point."

Knowing she was probably destroying their fledgling relationship, she told him everything—about her suspicions and her fears. She doubted he could forgive her for suspecting him of murder, but she was totally honest. She made no effort to paint herself in a more flattering light. She took full responsibility for her actions—no matter how stupid they had been. She only hoped he would be as honest when he confessed.

When she finished, he asked, "Why did you run away from Harold?"

Surprised by his question, unsettled by his bland tone, she hesitated. He wasn't going to give even one little outraged bellow about how deeply she had wounded his pride and honor?

"I think we're getting off track here."

"Maybe I want to take the scenic route."

Scenic for whom? Her romantic past wasn't a pretty sight. She sighed. "I ran away from Harold because he filed a complaint with the police. They issued a warrant for my arrest."

"For what?"

She hemmed and hawed, played with her place mat, squirmed in her chair, got more coffee, until she realized he could—and would—outwait her. With a sigh, she finally said, "Assault."

His only response was that one raised, questioning brow.

Feeling like a rebellious teenager undergoing the third degree from exasperated parents, she obeyed his silent command to continue. "Well, the night after I found him in bed with that other woman, I snuck into our house. He's a sound sleeper, so I managed to—" She rubbed the back of her neck, uncomfortable confessing how jealous she'd been.

"What?" His demand was uncompromising.

"I had some spell-resistant handcuffs and rope. I guess, I sort of, you know . . . handcuffed him. Then I . . ."

"In other words, you trussed him up like a pig in a poke?"

Laughter snorted out her nose. "That about sums it up."

233

"And then?"

"Then I woke him up."

"And then you beat the crap out of him?"

"No! I threw all his clothes out the window."

"That's all?"

"Well, not exactly." She didn't want to tell him the rest. It was sure to make him angry. "Dang it, can't you leave me any privacy?"

"No. So tell me what you did to him."

"I cut off his hair."

Vorador's face stayed blank, but she saw the shudder pass over his body. She'd committed a cardinal sin where wizards were concerned. Long hair was an outward manifestation of their inner power. Of course, Harold believed the longer the hair, the more powerful the wizard.

"Okay," Vorador finally said. "Is that all?"

"Yes. Then I packed up all my stuff and left."

"Then why did he charge you with assault?"

"Well, I guess after I left, he was trying to reach the phone to call for help, and he fell off the bed. From what I heard, he got a black eye, broke his nose and his arm."

Vorador frowned while he considered that. "I don't see why he charged you with assault. He was uninjured when you left."

Petra could only shrug since she hadn't exactly talked to Harold about his motivations.

She obviously hadn't ever had a clue how Harold's twisted mind worked.

"Tell me, Petra, what did you ever see in him?"

That was something she'd pondered more than once and had yet to figure out an intelligent answer. Whatever justification she had for getting involved with Harold didn't paint her in a favorable light. "I guess I was lonely. And he was a good liar."

Although in hindsight she realized the tone and meaning of Harold's comments had changed subtly, bit by bit, after their engagement. Once certain he'd captured her affections, his compliments had shifted into criticism. Looking back, she didn't understand why she'd put up with it. Why had she allowed him to undermine her confidence so badly? Didn't say much for her strength of character.

She wanted to suspect he'd used a spell, except Harold simply didn't have the talent. No, she hit the nail on the head the first time. She had succumbed to loneliness, tired of seeing all her friends getting married and starting families. Depressed at being alone night after night, she'd convinced herself Harold was the man for her.

"Maybe I wanted to believe what he was telling me. Out of desperation."

"You don't strike me as the desperate type."

She smiled her thanks for that small compliment. "Listen, can we just move on? I've already beat myself up about the whole episode."

He reached across the table and placed his hand over hers. "Trust me, Petra, if I ever meet this idiot, he'll be lucky if all he ends up with is a broken nose and arm."

Wondering if the warm fuzzy glow she felt inside showed on her face, she merely said, "Oh, aren't you just mad, bad and dangerous to know?"

"You bet your ass, sweetheart."

Turning her hand over and clasping his, she gave it a squeeze of thanks. "Okay, now that you've satisfied your curiosity about my sordid past, what about my more recent behavior?"

"Why did you run away from me, Petra?"

Jerking her hand out of his, she leaned back in the chair. "What? Once wasn't enough? You want me to recite the whole list of my moronic behavior again?"

"No," he said with an impatient gesture. "You explained your actions. What I want to know are your reasons."

"Doggone it! I don't know why." She lurched to her feet and paced around the kitchen. "I had plenty of time to think while sitting in that damned pit—where you put me, I might add—and where I really wasn't in the first place—for which I'm still waiting for an apology—and I still don't know why I ran. One second you were innocent. The next, a stone-cold killer."

He looked her full in the face, holding her gaze with his. "I hope you know I wasn't the one who kidnapped you."

Feeling surly, she wasn't ready to admit any such thing.

"I would never do anything to harm you. You're under my protection. I don't think you know what that means to me." His voice tense, he said, "I want to tell you, Petra. I want you to understand."

He was silent for so long she thought he'd changed his mind.

"It happened," he finally said so quietly she could barely hear him, "when I was twelve.

"It was getting harder and harder to control my magic. The temptation to use it was nearly unbearable. Especially to impress girls, or make myself popular. But the threat to my family was still very real. If I exposed my talent, they lost everything.

"But being a teenage boy full of raging hormones, I didn't always think about the consequences. Dugan and I would sneak away to our private clubhouse and make up spells. He didn't have as much power, but his organizational skills were impressive."

"If he had magic," Petra interrupted, "then why was his family living in that town? Were they like your family and hated all magic?"

Vorador shook his head. "No, they'd lived in the town for generations and had a large, profitable family business there. Dugan had only recently started showing signs of his abilities and they were already talking about moving, but it took time to make the financial arrangements."

He paused, then took up the story again. "Anyway, we had tried a few love spells on the most popular girls in school. But we were kids and not as careful as we should have been. My father found out I had used magic. He kicked me out, disowned me. I didn't have anywhere to go.

"I was hiding at our clubhouse. Dugan brought his dad there. He offered to let me stay with them until something could be worked out. He helped carry my stuff to their car. Dugan's mom was waiting there. I nearly lost it when she hugged me. I couldn't remember a time when my own mother had ever hugged me."

He fell silent, but Petra guessed that wasn't the end of the

236

story. She wished it was. What she'd heard so far was enough to break her heart.

When he continued, his voice was devoid of all emotion. "There was an accident. Both Dugan's parents were killed. We tried . . . I tried to save them, but I didn't know how. I had all that damn power but not enough skill to save the lives of those good people. From that day on, I swore I would learn everything I could. No one under my protection would ever be hurt again."

Chapter Thirty-two

Petra slumped against the counter. This explained so much about the man Vorador was today. She also understood what he wasn't saying—how he had suffered and worried when she'd disappeared. "Vorador, I'm sorry. After everything we'd been through in the past several days, I should have trusted you."

"Apology accepted. Now, about this kidnapping business—"

"I didn't want to believe you kidnapped me but it was your voice. It sounded exactly like you."

"I think we can logically assume it was some sort of spell."

"A spell?" Petra smacked herself on the forehead. How had she managed to overlook the obvious? And probably not one spell—the fake kidnapping—but those ridiculous suspicions must have come from another one. "Would you believe that possibility never even occurred to me? I must be losing my mind."

"It's possible the spell aroused your suspicions, then blinded you to their origin. Once you gave your doubts full reign, it would be an easy matter to make you hear my voice."

"Wonder why this spell only affected me? It started down in that stupid hole. You and Kitoka were there, too. It didn't do zip to either of you."

"There's no way of knowing unless we can find the spell and I can examine it."

"Was I just the lucky one it latched on to?" She shivered and rubbed her hands up and down her arms. "Or do you think it was aimed specifically at me?"

"I'm afraid you were the intended target." He filled her in on the break-in and destruction at his lab and his speculation about the woman who had tried to buy the rug. "More than likely Medora's attacker is responsible for everything that's happened."

"Oh, gads! Petra the incompetent strikes again."

"What do you mean?" he asked.

"It's all my fault your lab was trashed."

"How do you figure? Unless you were the one who did it."

She supposed she couldn't blame him for the suspicion creeping into his voice. "No, I didn't do it. Remember when I saw Dugan and Fytch at lunch the other day?"

Vorador nodded.

"I didn't exactly tell you every little detail." Petra flinched when that evil eyebrow of his arched upward. "I sort of—well, I kind of hinted—you know, let it slip that Medora might not be dead after all."

"Damn it, Petra! Why didn't you tell me?"

That had to be the dumbest question he'd ever asked her. He was angry enough to scare all the Devil's minions to the South Pole. "Take a look in a mirror, Wiz Boy."

"Point taken."

"Are you okay with this? It must've been a big shock to find out a more powerful wizard is putzing around in your city."

"I don't know what you're talking about."

She sensed his withdrawal even though he hadn't moved a muscle. The very essence of stillness surrounded him, reminding her of that old saying about still waters running deep. Maybe she shouldn't have raised such a personal issue with him. No, the heck with that! He'd poked and pried into every corner of her psyche. The least she could do was return the favor.

"Right," she said in a mocking voice. "It didn't faze you when you saw somebody had broken into your lab, that he overrode all your locks and safeguards."

He stared at her, giving nothing away, admitting nothing.

"It must be especially galling that he has enough power and skill to hide himself from you. He's free as a bird. Breaking and entering, committing murder, who knows what else. Even knowing about him, you still can't—"

Vorador surged to his feet, sending the chair crashing to the floor. "Enough!"

"You can dish it out, Wiz Boy, but you can't take it?" She pressed against the counter, tucking her hands into the small of her back. Otherwise she might be foolish enough to reach out and try to touch the power swirling around him like a whirl-pool. "Isn't that just like a bully?"

Two long strides brought him face-to-face with her. "I am not a bully."

She could practically hear his power crackling around them. "I notice you didn't refute the rest of it."

"I don't like being psychoanalyzed."

"Deal with it. Or kick me out."

His expression went blank. Holding up his hands, he stepped back, taking himself out of her personal space.

He looked so solitary. It occurred to her that he needed a hug. Did she dare? Of course she did. Raising her hand, she slowly caressed his cheek. The skin below his eye was soft in contrast to the rough texture where his whiskers grew. Aware of his power swirling around them, she could practically feel the floor shifting beneath her feet like a sandbar being washed away.

"Don't bully me, Petra."

"I'm not." She smiled up at him and stroked his cheek again. "I'm teasing you. There's a big difference."

He swallowed hard, then looking deep into her eyes, spoke in a harsh whisper. "You're playing with fire."

When he burst into flames, she laughed and threw her arms around his neck. "Oh, I certainly hope so."

Pressing herself even closer, wanting more, she felt the tingle as cool flames zinged across her body.

"Petra, you'd better get the hell out of here unless you're damned serious."

She tugged the hem of his T-shirt out of his jeans, loving the way the flames leapt from his body to hers, then back again. Running her hands up under his shirt, she caressed his chest, almost drooling as she watched the ebb and flow of blazing light. His whole body stiffened. She could practically feel him vibrate.

She simply had to taste him. She yanked his shirt over his head, then tossed it aside. Using hands and mouth, she explored all the wonderful textures of his chest. Unable to resist the temptation, her hands circled his waist, slipped down and came to rest on his butt.

Squeezing him there, she grinned when he jumped and gave a startled squawk. She'd bet her whole pig collection he'd never made such a sound before in his life. Did she shock him so much? It made her sad to consider the alternative—that none of his other lovers had ever teased him. He was too serious by far.

"Petra, do you have any idea what you're doing?"

"I certainly hope so." Keeping her hands on his butt, she pulled his hips closer and rubbed her body against him. Her eyes closed and she exhaled a shaky breath, loving the smell of him, the feel of him. "Be sure and tell me if I'm not getting it right."

With one last wiggle, she suddenly lost control of the situation. His mouth claimed hers in a greedy kiss. His hands seemed to be everywhere at once: fisted in her hair, skimming down her waist, cupping her breasts, squeezing her bottom, tweaking her nipples until she thought she would scream from the sheer pleasure of it all. Over and around each touch, the flames of his magic enhanced the sensations to incredible heights.

He rubbed against her, as if trying to climb right inside her skin. Losing her balance, she stumbled backward. Never breaking contact, he followed her, until she felt the kitchen counter behind her. Her hands went to the zipper on his jeans.

It seemed to be stuck. "Help me here, Sparky."

He made a sound that was half laugh, half groan and pure passion. He brushed her clumsy hands aside, then picked her up. She squealed as her shirt rode up and her bare bottom made contact with cool porcelain.

"Yikes!" She grabbed at him as she slid down into the sink.

A shudder rippled through his body when her nails lightly raked across his chest. His entire body was encased in swirling, dancing flames. Sparks shot out from the ends of his hair. She'd never seen such a magnificent sight in her entire life. It didn't matter that she looked ridiculous herself, sitting in a sink, her legs sticking out at an awkward angle. Capturing a lock of his hair, she tugged him down for a kiss.

The harsh lines on his face gentled and he smiled down at her. "I hope you don't expect me to climb in there with you."

She wiggled her bottom, testing the roominess of the sink. "Just how creative are you, Mr. Wizard?"

That one brow of his slid upward, even more effective with tiny little flames twisting out of its way.

Laughing, she ran a fingertip over that sleek line of hair. "This should be declared a lethal weapon."

His hands went to the front of her shirt. Mesmerized, she watched his long, lean fingers work each button free. She wanted to tell him to hurry but didn't trust her voice. By the time he finished she was nearly panting.

Using the barest touch, he eased the sides of her shirt open, revealing her body. The hungry look in his eyes made her feel giddy. Her nipples tightened when tiny tendrils of his fire stole across her skin. For the first time in her life she felt truly beautiful.

The moment was shattered by a ringing telephone. Neither of them moved as it rang twice, three times. It rang again. He reluctantly pulled away with a wry smile, then answered the insistent phone.

Petra slumped against the porcelain, trying to recover her equilibrium. Staid, uptight Petra W. Field making whoopee in a kitchen sink. Grinning, she wiggled her way out of her uncomfortable position. Back on her feet, she glanced at him. His fire was gone. She rebuttoned her shirt. Playtime was over.

Not wanting to eavesdrop on Vorador's conversation, she went to the laundry room. Peeking inside, she saw her earlier observation had been correct. She started picking pieces of broken china out of his washing machine. She wondered how long it would take until he got used to the way she disrupted his spells. Startled when Vorador came barreling into the small room, she dropped the china back into the washer.

"Petra, take my car and go to ERG."

"You're gonna let me use your car?" was her first reaction. Her second was to look down at her attire. "You want me to go dressed like this?"

"Yes, and yes." He thrust some keys at her. Hands on her shoulders, he turned her and herded her into the garage. "Go."

"What's going on?"

"That was the police on the phone. They finished testing the knife we found at the hotel. I can run some tests of my own now. I'm going to pick it up from the police station and then take it to my lab at ERG."

"Wouldn't it be better if I went home? If I'm at ERG, I might interfere with your tests."

He shook his head while he opened the Jaguar's door. "No, it isn't safe, Petra." He practically pushed her inside. "From what I've observed, it's only when you're in the same room, or in my sight, that you make my spells behave unnaturally."

"But—"

He gave her a quick hard kiss, then slammed the door.

Before she recovered from the kiss and gathered her wits enough to fit the key into the ignition, Vorador was in the Jeep and backing down the driveway.

Starting the car, she listened to the expensive purr of the powerful engine. It was amazing that he trusted her with his hundred-thousand-dollar toy.

Chapter Thirty-three

Vorador eased the knife out of the plastic evidence bag. Medora's blood stained the blade and the handle. The attacker must have been covered in blood. He could have only escaped using an invisibility spell. There had been too many people on top of the crime scene. First Dugan, then Kitoka, followed quickly by the paramedics.

Fighting down his distaste, he studied the knife. It was a normal butcher knife, the kind used in many kitchens. The police hadn't found any fingerprints. Either the killer had removed them or worn gloves.

As he gathered various chemicals and magical components for his tests, Vorador wondered what Petra was doing. He had the rug stored someplace safe, but he didn't want her wandering around. So he'd forbidden her to leave ERG. That order had gone over like a two-ton truck driving across thin ice. But she'd stayed. She might be independent, but he'd never accuse her of being stupid.

Some time later, waiting for one of the more complicated tests to finish running through an analyzer, he stretched, trying to work the kinks out of his back. He wondered if Petra gave good massages. It was too bad they'd been interrupted this morning. Otherwise, they would be in his bed right now. Damn, what lousy timing. He checked the mixture, but it wasn't done yet.

His thoughts went back to Petra. How could she think him capable of murder? On the other hand, it made sense for the killer to try to convince Petra of Vorador's guilt. Divide and conquer was a good offense. Whoever this other wizard was, he was damned clever.

When had she become so important in his life? Even now, he could hardly believe he'd confided his past to her. Nobody but Dugan and Professor Helios knew about that dark period. Thank heavens it hadn't scared her away. The thought of a future without her was bleak and dreary. That didn't alarm him as much as it should.

Could he be falling in love with her?

He'd almost taken her right there in the kitchen sink. Having her touch him while magical flames consumed them both had been every bit as erotic as he'd always imagined. If not for that phone call, he would have been inside her in a matter of seconds, promise or not. With a groan he leaned against the counter. When had he turned into a masochist?

The analyzer beeped, signaling that it was finished. He checked the results. Dissatisfied with his findings, he began the next test. Once it was under way, his mind returned to the puzzle of the mystery wizard.

Only five other wizards in Seattle had enough power to do the spells he'd witnessed over the last few days. None of them were psychopaths—to his knowledge. Nor were there any new high wizards in town. Of course, it made sense that this person would keep a low profile.

A knock on the door interrupted his thoughts. "Come in."

"Is it safe?"

Just the sound of Petra's voice brought a smile to his face. "I don't think you'll blow anything up."

She stuck her head around the doorjamb. "Sorry to disturb you, O High Mouthy Mucky-muck, but I'm going across the

245

street to get some sandwiches. You want anything?"

Looking at his watch, he was surprised to see it was mid-afternoon. "I'll take a turkey on rye, with mustard and pickles, coleslaw on the side and a large iced tea."

Petra pulled a face. "That's disgusting. Who in their right mind eats mustard with turkey? Normal people use mayo."

"Well"—he winked at her—"I've been telling you all along that you're driving me crazy."

She stuck out her tongue, then disappeared. An instant later, she popped back in. "How's it going? Any progress?"

He shook his head. "Nothing definitive yet."

Giving him a sympathetic smile, she left.

He called her back. "Petra," he said when her head reappeared, "take somebody with you, okay?"

She looked ready to argue but agreed with a sigh. "I'll be back in a flash," she said and ducked out.

He chuckled and snapped his fingers. The flash fire that had engulfed his body at her words disappeared. He would have to break her of that bad habit. Checking to make sure the flames hadn't interfered with his tests, he smiled. Well, maybe he wouldn't try to change her. Not if she wanted to play with his fire every time she sent him up in flames. Now, that was a masochistic thought. At this rate he'd be hard forever.

Crossing the street to the deli, Petra wondered how much protection Zaylin would be. At the first sign of trouble the fuzzy clone would probably shriek like a banshee, run and hide. Well, that was about all a car alarm did and they were pretty effective.

Glancing at the girl trailing behind her, Petra smiled. Zaylin was wearing one of those stupid green robes. It had to be at least three sizes too large for her. She kept stepping on the hem and tripping herself.

Of course, Petra didn't have much room to be the fashion police. After listening to half a dozen of Dugan's smart-mouth remarks about who was sleeping in whose bed, she'd decided a green robe was marginally better than parading around in the wizard's shirt.

246

Petra entered the deli, glad there wasn't a line. She placed their order, then sat down to wait.

"Well, hello. How nice to see you again."

Petra spun around with a startled jerk. Oh, crud! Fytch! Did the lady wizard hang around the deli, waiting to bushwhack unsuspecting victims? Forcing a polite smile, she said, "Hi."

Fytch sat down in an empty chair at their table. She didn't seem to notice Zaylin cringing away from her with a whimper. "Have you gone to work for ERG, Miss Field?"

"Nope, just had a minor clothing mishap." Some devil made her add, "Dugan was kind enough to lend me this."

Fytch's eyes narrowed and her mouth pinched into a thin line.

Petra was reminded she wasn't yanking some harmless kitty cat's tail. It was more like poking an alligator to see if it was sleeping—and not using a ten-foot pole but her finger. Zaylin slid out of her chair and hid under the table. At least the girl had enough sense to be frightened. Petra doubted her own sanity.

"Your parents should have taught you not to play with fire, Miss Field. You could get burned."

In spite of the circumstances, Petra smiled. Gad, when she'd touched Vorador's flames . . . "Oh, I don't know. Guess it depends on the fire. Actually, I think it kind of tickles."

Steam was practically coming out of Fytch's ears. Her lips began to move in a soundless chant.

Because she didn't want the deli damaged, Petra warned, "You need to be careful what kind of spells you use around me."

"Is that a threat, Miss Field?"

"What possible threat could I be to you?" Petra tried her best innocent look. "But Vorador complains that I—"

"Vorador is too weak and cautious for his own good."

Totally surprised by that faulty analysis, Petra could only sit there and blink. Finally, she rallied and said, "As Seattle's Grand Wizard, I'm sure—"

Fytch's mocking laughter cut her off. "The only reason he got that antiquated title is because those with genuine power don't want it. Why be a figurehead?"

Petra didn't care for the darker implication of Fytch's words—that there was a substrata of wizards, working out of view of the public eye. Doing what kind of magic?

"Authentic wizards prefer to keep a low profile," Fytch said.

Gad, could that be the reason for Medora's attack? Maybe she discovered the underground organization and threatened to expose them. Petra's gut insisted Fytch had been involved in the attack in some way. In spite of Vorador's protests of her innocence.

"I'll be sure and give Vorador the update," Petra said.

Fytch leaned across the table. "If you know what's good for you, you won't say anything." Her voice turned even more menacing. "Repeat one word of this conversation and you won't be around to regret it. Do you understand?"

Hoping she looked a whole lot calmer than she felt, Petra said, "As I said before—be careful what spell you put on me. It could turn around and bite you on the butt."

This time Fytch's laughter sounded just like the Wicked Witch's cackle from *The Wizard of Oz*.

"Yeah, that's real low profile," Petra said.

Green bilious smoke started swirling around Fytch.

Waving away the smoke that remained after Fytch disappeared, Petra bent down to see how Zaylin was doing. The girl was huddled into a fetal position but appeared to be in one piece. "You can come out now."

"Is the bad lady gone?"

"Yup, all gone."

Crawling out of her hiding place, she said, "She's mean."

Maybe Zaylin had more brains than Petra had first suspected. "I don't like her."

Zaylin's bottom lip was quivering. "She chased me with a vacuum. Said she was gonna suck my head off."

Petra patted the girl's arm, surprised at how soft her fuzz felt. It was like petting a baby chick. "Well, she's gone now."

"Good!" Obviously made braver by that fact, Zaylin said, "Vorador oughta turn her into something slimy. Like a worm. Then I'd take her fishing. I'd catch a big old fish with her. Then I'd cut him open and stick his guts—with that nasty old Fytch-worm in his stomach—I'd stick them right down the garbage disposal and grind 'em into tiny little pieces. Then I'd—"

Her bloodthirsty tale was interrupted when their order was called. Petra paid, then herded Zaylin out the door, glad to leave the deli. She wasn't sure she'd ever go back again. Their food might be delicious, but she couldn't say much for the caliber of their clientele.

Chapter Thirty-four

Petra finished her sandwich and threw away her trash, waiting for Vorador to take his attention off the notes he was studying. They were alone in a small lunchroom at ERG. She'd been patient for the last fifteen minutes. When he started to gather up his things, she couldn't stand it anymore.

"Have you found anything?"

Looking up from his papers with a distracted frown, he blinked, as if noticing her for the first time. "Did you say something?"

His expression looked so much like her dad's when he was deep in some mystical realm. No wonder Mom was always kissing Dad. Petra settled for repeating her question.

He shook his head. "Nothing useful."

"Are you done with your tests?"

"Just about."

She hesitated briefly, then plunged on. "In anything you've found, even the smallest thing, the remotest probability . . . Could there be any clues that point to Fytch?" She held up her hand to stop him before he spoke. "I know you said it isn't possible, but I think you're wrong."

He sighed and rubbed the back of his neck. "I told you, Petra. Much as we might want to believe her guilty, she—"

"Forget her alibi. Those can be faked. People lie all the time. Heck, she could've used a spell. They might not even know they're lying to cover her tracks."

"She was at a meeting. At least a dozen people—prominent citizens—came forward after the police questioned her."

"Okay, that might be hard to fake." Petra thought for a moment. "Why was she questioned in the first place?"

"Long before Medora dated Dugan, the two of them disliked each other. Questioning Fytch was standard police procedure. Once I verified her blood phobia she was in the clear." This time Vorador gestured Petra to remain silent. "Believe me, one drop of blood and she's out cold on the floor."

"That could be faked too," Petra stubbornly insisted.

"If it's a charade, she's sustained it for years. Give me one reason why she would do that?"

"It would be a perfect cover."

"I never would have pegged you for a conspiracy nut."

"Doggone it. At least pretend to take me seriously."

"Okay," he said in a tone obviously meant to pacify her, "a cover for what?"

"For everything. Because I also think you're wrong about how powerful she is."

"Petra, let's not waste time going over this again." He sounded weary and impatient. "I've worked with Fytch for years and felt her magic. Trust me, she isn't that strong."

"How can you be so sure? I mean, this wizard we're looking for has the ability to camouflage his power. So, if it is Fytch, then of course you wouldn't know." She was proud of her reasoning, until she got a good look at Vorador's face. Oops, guess she'd bruised his ego again.

He pushed to his feet. "Stop harping on this. You're wasting my time."

"What do you know about a secret organization of wizards who prefer to work their magic out of public view?"

She held her breath, waiting for his reaction, plus in fear that Fytch's spell might work after all. It would be rather inconvenient if her tongue fell out. Or she disappeared in a poof of green smoke. When nothing happened, she sighed in gratitude.

"What're you talking about? Black magic?"

"I don't know anything for certain, but . . ." She repeated the brief but unpleasant encounter she'd had with Fytch.

After a long silence, he asked, "Why would she tell you any of this?"

"I don't know. Maybe I tend to bring out the worst in her."

"I can believe that. You're maddening enough to drive a saint to drink and debauchery."

She gathered up the rest of his trash. "Do you think she was telling the truth? Or only trying to scare me?"

"A few days ago I would've said she was bluffing. Now, I don't know." He leaned one hip against the table. "I'm honest enough to admit I don't want to believe I could have been so blind and stupid all these years. If Fytch is guilty."

She sighed, beginning to wonder if they would ever catch this psycho. No, they had to, or Medora would die. Gad, what had she done for excitement before moving to Seattle? She'd gladly leave the crime-fighting to professionals. She would prefer to keep a certain wizard with killer looks and a heart so tender he tolerated all of her foolishness—within reason—happy for the rest of his life.

"So, sparky, tell me about the tests you've been running."

He rattled off reams of information, detailing the tests and their results. Sorry she'd asked, her eyes glazed over. Not even trying to follow him, she merely nodded and made listening sounds at what seemed appropriate intervals. He was so earnest . . . and cute. She repressed a smile, since he was talking about blood-splatter patterns.

At length he said, "The most interesting things I've found so far are some strange strands of magic on the murder weapon."

"About that weapon—I've been meaning to ask you. Where did the knife come from?"

"What?"

"Was it Medora's knife? Or did the killer bring it?"

Vorador just stared at her for the longest time. Finally, he asked, "Why do you want to know?"

"That can tell you things about the killer and the crime."

"Go on."

"If it was from Medora's kitchen, then the crime probably wasn't premeditated. The person was there for some other reason, and got so angry, he grabbed the first available weapon."

He was looking at her strangely. "And?"

"If the killer brought the weapon, then he fully meant to kill Medora. Shows planning and previous intent. Whichever scenario, this was a crime of strong emotion. You can't kill from a distance with a knife. It's an up close and personal weapon."

"How the hell do you know all this?"

Startled by his cold anger, Petra sat back. "Geez, I watch the news. I've seen my fair share of crime movies. I've even been known to read a mystery now and then."

He held up his hands. "Sorry. It's a touchy subject. The knife's origin has been kept out of the papers."

Petra nodded her head. "Yeah, keep a few things secret. When they catch the bad guy, they have hard facts to nail him."

He looked startled again.

She rolled her eyes. "Will you stop looking at me like that? Police procedures are no big secret. Only the specific details. So, tell me"—she leaned closer and lowered her voice to a whisper—"whose knife is it?"

He just shook his head. "That information is not currently available for public release."

Laughing good-naturedly, she let the matter slide. "So, back to those strange fibers you found on the knife. Strange how?"

"I've never seen fibers this color before. They're white, but iridescent, almost translucent. I compared them to the guild's membership records and there's no match."

"I always get confused. Is white what you get when all the other colors are mixed together? Or is that black? Seems like it ought to be black, but it is white, isn't it?"

"You ask the most unrelated questions. Why does it matter—"

"No particular reason." She shrugged. "Just making idle conversation. Never mind."

Silence descended once again. Petra tried not to fidget since it was obvious his mind was occupied. She was picking at her cuticles when he spoke.

"I was wrong when I said I hadn't seen these fibers before."

"Oh, yeah?"

"I found a few of them in your hotel room."

"Well, that makes sense. I mean, if it was the same wizard who attacked Medora and kidnapped me. Which seems like a very good possibility—especially since the same fibers were in both places. Right?"

"I just realized something else. The only magical threads I found in your hotel room were these white ones."

"Yeah, so?"

"Most places are littered with threads people shed in everyday passing. I'm so used to seeing them, most of the time I just tune them out. Your room was remarkably clean. I figured I didn't find more threads because you were nonmagical, therefore you wouldn't leave any traces.

"There should have been piles of stuff in a motel that old. There was nothing. It was clean as a whistle."

"So, what does this mean?"

"Maybe those strange white fibers were formed because the wizard tried to remove any trace of his presence by removing *all* magic from the room. As you said, all colors mixed together make white. He must have gathered up every strand, twisting them into one compact thread that he could more easily make disappear."

"A wizard can't see his own influence. How—"

"With a"—Vorador gestured like an old-time stage magician finishing his best trick—"magic vacuum."

Petra grimaced as she recalled Zaylin's story about Fytch threatening to suck off her head with a vacuum.

"The killer must have tried the same thing with the knife. Yet both times, because he was in a hurry, afraid of being caught, he didn't double-check. A few minuscule pieces remained."

"This helps you . . . how?"

He was grinning now. "If I can use the electron microscope at the university, I can isolate each filament that makes up this

254

strand. The hotel sample could be a problem, since it's bound to contain threads from dozens, if not hundreds, of people. The knife is a different story. With the Amazon Council's help, I should be able to identify nearly all the strands."

"The one that doesn't fit—"

"That has no reason for being there—that will be our villain. We can verify his identity if the same strand shows up in the sample I took from your hotel room."

Laughing, he grabbed her face between his hands and kissed her hard. Then he snatched up his papers and ran out of the room.

"Shit."

Vorador's curse instantly caught the attention of everyone in the room. Dugan and Petra hurried over to his position at the electron microscope. Kitty—Bosco—trailed in their wake.

"What?" Petra asked.

He turned away from the machine and stood up. "I'll be right back." He couldn't say anything to them. Not yet. First he had to confirm his discovery. Then he needed a few moments to come to terms with it himself.

He pushed past them and went to an office in the corner of the university lab. Professor Helios had allowed him access to the college's expensive, up-to-date equipment. He'd needed it for a full-scale examination of those strange fibers. Once inside the professor's office, Vorador shut the door. Through the window that overlooked the main lab he watched Dugan and Petra exchange a troubled look. Then Petra shrugged, and it looked as though Dugan uttered his own curse. Kitty began washing a front paw. Petra wandered around the cavernous room, studying the various experiments but not touching anything. Dugan paced back and forth in front of the microscope, his hands nervously shoved in his pockets. Vorador moved away to perform one final test.

Nearly half an hour passed before he was done. When he emerged, Petra, Dugan and Kitty all turned toward him in expectant silence.

"I've identified a common strand in both specimens. There's

no other reason for these orange threads to be in Medora's apartment. Or at Petra's hotel room."

"Orange threads?" Dugan was the first to make the connection. "Are you crazy, Vorador? You think Fytch did it?"

Petra didn't disappoint him. She pumped a fist in the air. "Yes! I told you she had a hand in this."

Yowling at the top of her lungs, Kitty dashed to the exit and scratched frantically at the door, trying to get it open.

"Vorador, you can't seriously believe Fytch is capable of murder. I know she's not your favorite person, but . . . murder?"

Dugan had never allowed anyone to speak against Fytch, had always been her champion. In the beginning, Vorador had suspected Fytch of putting a spell on Dugan, to charm him, to blind him to her faults, to bind him to her. However, he'd never been able to detect any of Fytch's magic on his friend. Now, that didn't seem to be as good a judging tool as he'd thought it was in the past.

"I'm sorry, Dugan. It's not as if Medora would have freely invited Fytch in. They despised each other."

"You can be darned sure I didn't want her anywhere near me," Petra stated.

Suddenly there was a loud boom, like thunder exploding inside the room. A blinding zigzag of brilliant light followed. Several beakers shattered. Shards of glass shot through the air.

With a curse, Vorador extended his personal safety spell until it encompassed Dugan. Petra was too far away. Reaching out his hand in her direction, he closed it into a fist, then jerked it to his chest. "To me!"

With a startled yelp, Petra flew through the air, straight toward them. He realized he'd miscalculated again. Instead of floating into the safety of his spell, she was rocketing at them as if she'd been fired from a cannon. "Watch out!"

Dugan ducked, but Vorador spread his arms and tried to slow her approach. There wasn't enough time. She slammed into him. They went down in a jumble of arms and legs. He let himself fall straight back, absorbing the worst of the impact. For a few seconds he could only lay there, dazed. He didn't stay that way long. Not with Petra squirming on top of him like a demented lap dancer. He grinned, even in the chaos of the moment able to take pleasure in her unique abilities.

"What in the blue blazes do you think—Oh, Fudgcicle!"

Vorador couldn't help it. He started laughing when Petra banged her forehead down on his chest while she muttered, "Stupid! Stupid!" With each thump, the blue flames covering him raced up the strands of her hair, shooting blue sparks in all directions.

Soft applause cut off his amusement. "Very entertaining. But then, you always were good for a few laughs, Vorador."

Chapter Thirty-five

Vorador shoved Petra aside and surged to his feet, snapping away his fire as he moved. Petra scrambled up seconds later. Fytch stood amid the broken glass and wrecked equipment, an almost bored expression on her face. How sweet, Petra thought as Vorador positioned himself between her and Fytch. She moved slightly to the side, wanting a clear view of this show-down.

"Good evening, Fytch," Vorador said in a calm voice. "So good of you to join us."

"Yeah," Petra added, "so we can send you to jail where you belong."

Vorador murmured for Petra's ears only, "I was hoping this one time you had enough sense to keep your mouth shut."

She pressed a smile against his shoulder. "Hope springs eternal," she whispered back.

"Petra," he warned. "Now that her crimes are out in the open, there's no telling what she might do."

Fytch had moved close enough to hear them. "I see you've

figured out my little secret. Score one for idiot boy wonder."

"Fytch, is it true?" Looking shell-shocked, Dugan took a step toward her. "Why?"

"Dugan honey, I love you madly." She smiled. It wasn't a pleasant smile. "But I'm afraid your elevator doesn't go all the way to the penthouse."

That knocked Dugan even further off balance. "You love me?"

Petra decided to give poor Dugan a clue, but addressed her words to Fytch. "Medora was moving in on your territory. So you decided to get rid of the competition. Didn't quite go according to plan though, did it?"

The first signs of anger showed in Fytch's facade, her lips pulling back in a snarl. She glared at Dugan. "I could have killed *you* when you started dating that Amazon bitch."

Vorador's voice cut like an ice scalpel. "Just as you were afraid Dugan would kill you if he ever knew the truth about—"

"Shut up," Fytch yelled.

"I'm tired of keeping this secret, Fytch. No more."

Fytch waved her hands around, trying to cast a spell on Vorador. With a flick of his fingers, he protected himself.

"It's time for Dugan to know you tried to seduce me."

"It's a lie," Fytch screeched, her face bright red.

Petra recalled Fytch's attitude that first evening they'd met, her proprietary manner toward both Dugan and Vorador. Now she understood why Vorador hated Fytch so much. He would never betray Dugan's friendship for a woman, and would hold any woman who proposed such a thing in contempt.

Dugan looked as if he'd been run over by a tank. "You? And Vorador?"

"Don't believe him, Dugan. He's a lying snake."

Vorador's hair turned into a writhing mass of snakes. He snapped his fingers and they vanished. Obviously tiring of the games, he bluntly asked Fytch, "What did you hope to gain by killing Medora? Dugan broke up with you long ago."

An ugly sneer further distorted Fytch's features. "Is that what he told you?"

"You know," Petra butted in, "that's one thing I wondered about. How Dugan managed to break up with you, yet remain

259

on friendly terms. It took me a while to figure it out."

Fytch said, "How ironic. You've known me the shortest time, yet know me better than either of these two bozos."

Dugan and Vorador were suddenly dressed in clown outfits. Full white makeup covered their faces, with oversized red lips and blue stars around their eyes. Orange rubber balls on their noses and matching orange fright wigs appeared as finishing touches.

Once she stopped laughing, Fytch flipped her hair out of her face and smugly announced, "Dugan didn't break up with me. I broke up with him."

"Why?" Vorador asked, showing no reaction to his wardrobe change. "You said you loved him."

Petra marveled at how calm he sounded. She wondered why Fytch's spells weren't going all wonky like Vorador's usually did. In fact, even some of his were working. It couldn't be easy for him to stand here and have Fytch rub his face in his short-comings. Not that Petra thought they were shortcomings, but she knew Vorador was in full "protection" mode and probably thought he'd failed in that duty.

Petra answered before Fytch could. "Basic relationship strategy. She must have sensed Dugan was losing interest. If he broke up with her, then pride would demand she never see him again. Because she ended it, they could still be pals. And she had hope that his interest might be rekindled at some time in the future."

"He spoiled it all," Fytch complained, sounding like a whiny two-year-old whose favorite toy was broken.

An offensive odor permeated the room. Petra sniffed and re-alized Dugan smelled like spoiled meat. Gross!

"He was supposed to come back to me. He wasn't supposed to go out with some no-talent Amazon bimbo."

"I can't believe this." Disbelief dripped from Vorador's voice. "You mean this was all because of petty jealousy?"

"It almost worked, too," Fytch admitted with no apparent remorse.

Recalling Dugan's strange behavior at lunch, Petra asked, "With a little help from your spells?"

Fytch's nasty smile was back. "They really were exquisite spells. Vorador didn't even suspect I had my magic wrapped all around Dugan so he couldn't hear or see a single negative thing about me. To him I was all sweetness and joy. He was turning to me for sympathy and support." She pointed at Petra. "Until you started nosing around and screwed it all up."

"Me?" Petra held up her hands. "Hey, all I did was buy a rug. You were the one who kept casting spells right and left."

Vorador looked at Fytch like she was a bug under a microscope. "Is that why you sent a mugger after Petra?"

"What mugger?" Fytch's confusion looked real enough.

Petra smirked at Vorador. "I told you it was just a coincidence."

Ignoring her, he addressed Fytch, "You showed incredible irresponsibility by using so many different spells. Didn't you care what kind of chaos you created?"

Fytch shrugged. "If I could have gotten rid of that blasted piece of rug, I would have been home free."

"You know," Petra butted in, "you really blew a prime opportunity when you searched Vorador's lab."

"What do you mean?"

"That was you, right?" Petra asked.

"Yes," Fytch admitted in an impatient tone. "Explain yourself."

"Guess you didn't catch on that Medora was right there in his lab all along."

"What?" Fytch shot a frown at Vorador.

"You not only missed the stupid rug, you lost the big prize. Now, how could that have happened?" Petra paused, tapping her finger on her chin. "Hmmm, could it be that you're not the Big Bad Pooh-Bah of the Dark Forces that you thought?"

Fytch looked ready to explode.

"But then, that whole rug business was a fiasco from the beginning. How did I end up with it anyway?" Petra asked, more to keep Fytch talking than with any real interest in her answer.

"Why don't you ask little sister?" Quickly rebounding from her anger, Fytch's laugh rolled through the room like a vile fog, raising the hairs on the back of Petra's neck.

Petra realized Kitty was nowhere in sight. She hoped the cat hadn't been hurt in the initial explosion. She might be their only chance of getting out of this alive.

"Here, Kitty, Kitty, Kitty," Fytch called, than laughed.

The sound was so ugly, it actually turned Petra's stomach. "You're despicable."

She leaned against Vorador's back, drawing on his strength. Gad! What was she doing? She needed to get as far away from him as possible. Otherwise he would never dare use his magic. Standing this close, there was no telling what her influence would do.

"About the rug," Petra said, inching backward.

"Oh, that was easy. After the police finished, the apartment was no longer classified as a crime scene. The building manager called in a cleaning company to tidy up." Fytch grinned. "My cleaning company. I convinced him the rug was beyond repair and hauled it away."

"Well, somebody obviously found it, cleaned it up and sold it at the flea market." Petra just realized something. "You caused my nightmares, didn't you? You cast the spell that night you came asking if I was satisfied with ERG's services."

Looking proud, Fytch said, "Actually, I did it that afternoon when I left my card in your door."

"What about that lady who showed up, trying to buy it?"

Fytch giggled like a maniac. "That was a pig I borrowed from a local farmer."

"You—" Horrified, Petra didn't want to give voice to Fytch's abhorrent deed. She had used her magic on a poor defenseless animal, forcing it to do her evil will. "Gads! What about your alibi? What did you do to all those people?"

Fytch shrugged. "Oh, that was easy. I picked up a homeless bum off the street and cast a spell to make him look like me. As far as everyone was concerned, I was at that meeting."

"All this trouble over a stupid rug. Why didn't you zap it out of existence? Or just burn it?"

"I tried. All I could do was make the blood disappear for a short time. Medora put some sort of protection spell on it. Since it was deathbed magic I couldn't override it." Fytch turned the full force of her anger on Vorador. "Except you tricked me. Somehow you managed to keep her alive."

Petra rolled her eyes. "Yeah, we're back to that again. He did it by hiding her in only the most obvious place—his lab. Duh! Didn't you even think to look for her while you were there searching for the rug?"

"I'm not sure," Vorador said, "if you just complimented me. Or insulted me."

Petra flashed him a grin. "Well, obviously a compliment since your plan worked. Brilliant in its simplicity."

Fytch's smile wasn't as pleasant. "I never thought you were simple-minded, Vorador . . . until now. Dumb as dirt and arrogant as hell, but—"

"But nothing," Petra interrupted. "He outsmarted you, plain and simple."

"Shut up!" Fytch buried her hands in her hair.

Wanting to keep Fytch further off balance, Petra said, "Which raises another interesting question: why go through that elaborate ruse of kidnapping me and sticking me in the Space Needle?"

Fytch took a deep breath and made an effort to calm herself. She smoothed down her hair. "Pretty darn clever, huh?"

Petra knew she was asking for trouble, but she had to know. "Why didn't you just kill me when you had the chance?"

Fytch flinched, as though Petra had slapped her. "I might have wanted to torture you for all the problems you caused, but I wouldn't kill an innocent person."

Afraid to ponder Fytch's lack of logic, afraid of getting sucked into whatever bizarre alternate reality she lived in, Petra couldn't speak.

Vorador said, "Or maybe you aren't as all powerful as you want us to think."

Petra had never seen so much hatred in a person's eyes. Fytch looked ready to tear out his throat with her bare hands. Then, somehow, she managed to rein in her fury. With a crackle of green lightning, Vorador's clown outfit vanished. Now he stood there in a schoolboy's uniform of knickers, white shirt and black tie, with a dunce cap on his head.

Once again, he refrained from making any comment.

Crud, Petra thought, maybe instead of moving away from Vorador, she should try moving closer to Fytch.

"Well," Fytch sneered, "I'm still a hell of a lot more powerful than you."

"You think?" Vorador asked.

Petra cut in. "You know, I never did quite figure out the exact chain of events. How did you pull it off, Fytch?"

Fytch spun to face Petra, quickly shifting moods. "Of course your puny brain couldn't grasp the beauty of my plan." She preened like a peacock in full display. "It was so simple. Once that Amazon troublemaker was down, I used an invisibility spell."

"Because you were covered in blood?" Petra felt sick.

"She totally ruined my favorite suede jacket."

"I take it your blood phobia is as fake as everything else?" Vorador asked.

"Actually," Fytch admitted in a conversational tone, "blood is one of my favorite spell ingredients. But since I didn't want any of you do-gooders to know what I was up to, it seemed best to—"

"That's it," Petra broke in. "That's how you controlled Dugan and hid it from Vorador. You used a blood spell."

Looking very pleased, Fytch nodded. "A little of this. A little of that. Add some of his blood," she pointed at Dugan, "and a little of his," now she pointed to Vorador, "and voilà! I had them both eating out of my hand like well-trained lap dogs."

"Until Medora showed up," Petra pointed out. "I wonder . . . did she used magic to counteract your hold on Dugan? Or was it simply her own innate goodness that attracted him?"

"That damn woman ruined everything," Fytch snarled.

"What a pity," Petra said.

"I was all set to finish her off. Then you showed up, Dugan." Fytch made a disgusted sound. "Damn it, you cried over her body! I almost killed you for that. But I wanted you to suffer." Her face took on a look of mock sympathy. "I would be right there at your side, comforting you, offering you solace in your sorrow."

Fytch's expression hardened. "I went into the hallway and kicked a door, knowing you'd hear it. When you left, it was the perfect opportunity to end her, but then her sister showed up. Ridiculous Kitty. Kept telling Medora"—Fytch spat the name out as if it were poison—"to hang on. I had to get rid of her so I could finish the job for good.

"So I turned her into a cat. A male cat!" Fytch nearly doubled over with laughter. "Isn't that just too ironic?"

"Why the amnesia spell on top of that?" Petra asked, intent on keeping the other woman talking.

"Because I had to become visible to cast the spell. So I gave her a double whammy." Fytch's laughter died away. "By then it was too late. I barely got my cloaking spell back in place before the paramedics arrived. I knew I couldn't get away with killing the whole lot of them. So I had to leave, trusting Medora was too far gone to save."

To hear Fytch so casually discuss killing more people chilled Petra to the bone. What happened to not harming innocents?

Fytch turned to Dugan, her expression a terrifying mixture of sadness, pleading and fury. "Why did you interfere and bring in this fool?" She pointed at Vorador. "He ruined all my plans."

Deciding it was time to change the topic, before Fytch got worked up into a rage, Petra asked, "Did you really put a spell on me at the deli this afternoon?"

"What?" Fytch frowned.

"This afternoon. You said I'd be sorry if I told anybody about our conversation. Did you put a spell on me?"

"Yes!"

Vorador glanced over his shoulder, looking startled to find Petra so far away from him. Even from clear across the room she could practically hear the wheels turning in his head. She hoped he came up with a good plan. She was sick of listening to Fytch spew out her hatred. Her face was turning the most amazing puce. Petra expected hairy warts and oozing pustules to erupt at any moment.

If she could keep wacko witch babbling long enough, maybe

265

Vorador could deal with her. If his magic was strong enough. If her own nonmagic didn't screw everything up.

"Well, Fytch"—Petra pasted on a smile—"your spell didn't work. Trust me on this. I told everybody! Yet here I am." She spread her arms. "Unharmed. Undamaged. And all in one piece."

Fytch's face went through an incredible rainbow of colors. Petra had never seen such a sight. Not even when she'd hogtied Harold on his bed.

"You saccharine-sweet, sickening little Goody Two-shoes!"

"Oh, Fytch," she said with pity, "that was a downright pathetic endeavor. Even Zaylin came up with something more original. Her little Fytch-worm fishing story was—"

"Petra!" Vorador stormed across the room until he was right in her face. "Are you out of your ever-loving mind?"

"No," she hissed at him, "but you must be. Get the heck away from me. I'm gonna screw up your magic."

"So what? I'm supposed to stand aside like a weak, helpless fool and let you sacrifice—"

"Shut the hell up!" Fytch's scream was loud enough to rattle the windows. "Both of you." She pressed her hands over her ears. "You're driving me crazy."

"Now that's a short trip," Petra muttered.

That was the final straw for Fytch. She flung out her arm, one finger pointing straight at Petra's chest. Vorador stepped in front of Petra barely in time. Whatever magic Fytch threw must have bounced off his personal protection shield, because Petra felt nothing.

She watched Vorador send a bolt of energy at Fytch. When she went flying several feet, the wizard stepped back as though startled by his own power. He landed on Petra's toes.

"Ouch! Watch what you're doing, you big oaf."

Ignoring her, he quickly sent another jolt of magic outward. Fytch was hit again. Her body twitched, but she held her position.

"Damn," Vorador muttered.

Petra stopped examining her bruised toes. "What?"

"If she recovers enough to retaliate, I could be up shit's creek without a paddle." Another series of bolts flew at Fytch. They had even less effect.

"Why isn't my presence sending them flying all over the lab?"

"I don't know. I'm not about to question our good fortune."

Power seemed to swirl around and into Vorador like water going down a drain. Petra could feel it like static electricity sliding and crackling along each strand of her hair. It looked as if he actually grew larger. Slowly, deliberately, he stretched out his arm toward Fytch, who was busy with her own incantations.

His power hit Fytch. She staggered back, tripping on an overturned chair. Under the onslaught of Vorador's magic, an aura formed around Fytch like a bubble. It began to shimmer and spark. Petra could actually see it! It must be a physical manifestation of Fytch's personal protection shield. Was that a good sign? Or a bad one?

Keeping up a steady, unrelenting bombardment, Vorador blasted more of his energy at Fytch, never giving her a chance to recover enough to launch her own attack. She could only defend. Soon the whole lab was bathed in the strange flickering light coming from around Fytch. She fell back several more steps.

All this time Dugan had been frozen in place. The poor guy had obviously been stunned by Fytch's revelations. Now he moved to stand beside Petra. "What's he doing to her?"

"I don't know," she admitted. "He could merely be draining her power. Or he could be killing her."

"Vorador—" Dugan started.

"Sorry, Dugan," Petra interrupted, afraid he was on the verge of stopping the wizard, "but at this point I don't much care. If she dies, we'll all have to deal with the consequences—later. But she has to be stopped."

The tendons in Vorador's neck stood out with the effort he put into battling the evil wizard.

Fytch's body began turning translucent. Soon it was nearly transparent. Petra could see the other side of the lab right through her body. Reaching out with both hands now, Vorador prepared to deliver what would obviously be the final blast.

"Vorador! No!" Dugan's cry cut through the eerie silence.

The wizard paused. "Dugan, it has to be done."

"Not yet," Dugan insisted. "We need her blood."

Vorador actually staggered as that truth hit him squarely between the eyes. "Oh, hell. How could I have forgotten?" He closed his fist, halting his attack.

"Vorador," Petra warned, "she's still fading."

All three of them stared at Fytch in horror. Even though Vorador had stopped his assault the other wizard continued to vanish. Bit by bit, little by little, she became more and more see-through. Vorador flung out his arm again, clearly trying to draw his power back into himself. It didn't have any effect.

"I know what's happening!" Petra tugged on Vorador's sleeve to get his attention. "It's that blasted spell."

Not stopping, he demanded, "Which blasted spell?"

"This afternoon, in the deli." She ticked off the high points. "I saw Fytch, we chatted, I insulted her, she cursed me, I warned her it would probably come back to bite her on the butt."

"And this means?" Vorador demanded, the majority of his attention remaining on Fytch.

"Gads, you're dense." Petra took a deep, calming breath. "She cursed me that I would disappear. It took a while, but it obviously bounced off me and is now"—she waved her hands in Fytch's direction—"doing that to her."

"Obviously," he said in a dry tone, that brow doing his best Spock impression. "I'd be happy to let her go. Especially if she ends up wherever she planned to send you. I doubt it was a very pleasant destination. But we need that blood."

"Can't you do something? Use a blood removal spell? Turn into a vampire? Gads, just bite the witch!"

Before Vorador could reply, an unearthly yowl split the air. A black-and-white ball of fury vaulted from table to table and rocketed toward the barely visible Fytch. Her personal protection spell must have weakened along with her physical body. There wasn't much left of the woman, but Kitty, teeth bared and claws extended, managed to sink all her available weapons into the unprepared wizard.

Everything happened so fast, Petra could barely follow the action. She watched as Fytch tried to shake off the snarling, clawing cat. For her part, Kitoka fought valiantly, latching onto different body parts as the wizard tried to dislodge her. It was an uneven match. Even in her weakened state, it was only a matter of time until Fytch overpowered the feline.

"Vorador," Petra pleaded, "do something."

"To protect the cat," he chanted in a measured voice.

"Speed it up," Petra moaned when Fytch gave Bosco's tail a vicious yank.

"My spell is pat," Vorador continued.

Bosco managed to get a firm grip on Fytch's little finger with her teeth, making Petra wince.

"To trap a rat."

"Spit it out, wiz boy." Petra watched in dismay as Fytch used her free hand to wildly swing at the cat hanging from her finger. "Hit her with a bat!"

"No!" Laughing maniacally, Fytch spoke for the first time since Vorador's attack began. "She flew like a bat."

Suddenly, silence filled the laboratory.

Chapter Thirty-six

Fytch was gone. For several heartbeats Petra couldn't believe her eyes. The truth was too terrible to contemplate.

"Vorador?" Petra's gaze flew to him, silently asking the question: *Where* had Fytch gone?

Instead of answering, he snapped his fingers. Normal black T-shirt and jeans replaced his schoolboy outfit. Dugan's clown suit vanished, leaving him dressed similarly. Only then did Vorador shake his head in response to her question.

"You didn't send her to jail?"

He shook his head again. "I didn't complete my spell."

Petra winced. There was no condemnation in his voice, but she felt guilty nonetheless. If she hadn't been screaming at him, he might have been able to finish it.

"So, where'd she go?" Dugan asked, stumbling his way toward them across the wrecked lab.

Once more Vorador shook his head. "I don't know."

"Isn't there some way of tracing her?" Petra said.

"Hope springs eternal?" Vorador said, in a weak attempt to

lighten the gloom. "I wish I had a better answer, but we may never find out where she is."

"Surely she isn't going to get away scot-free?" Petra didn't like what she was hearing. "After everything she did?"

"The Wizards Guild will send out a JAWA. If she uses her magic, they'll know about it."

Petra cocked her head to one side. "They're going to send those little *Star Wars* creatures in the robes to catch her?"

"No." He smiled. "Judicial Announcement Worldwide Alert." He gently tucked a strand of hair behind her ear. "Don't worry, she'll get what she deserves. At some point in time."

Petra nodded. They all seemed to be avoiding the obvious, sort of like not mentioning the rhinoceros in the bathtub. With Fytch gone, there was no way to save Medora. It just didn't seem right that evil should prevail. They had come so close. Good was always supposed to win.

Dugan looked around. "What about Kitoka? Did she vanish with Fytch?"

"Gads, I hope not," Petra said with real horror. "I wouldn't wish that fate on anybody. Not even that foul-tempered b—"

"How nice of you to say so."

They all spun toward the voice coming from behind an overturned table. A figure slowly rose, sending equipment clattering to the floor.

Petra held her breath. Then released it with a whoosh. "Kitoka."

Brushing bits of broken glass from her hair, there stood the Amazon in all her leather-clad glory, a feral grin on her face. "Glad to see me?"

Backing up a step, Petra hurried to assure her, "I was going to say beast. Honest."

Stalking toward them, Kitoka made a noncommittal sound. She tossed something to Vorador. "See if you can make use of this."

He caught the item, then held it up for inspection.

"Eeeuuwww!" Petra put her hand over her mouth. "Please tell me that isn't what I think it is."

271

Even Vorador appeared slightly shaken when he got a good look at Kitoka's trophy.

Dugan's face paled and he turned away with a gagging sound.

Kitoka licked her lips and said, "Yup."

Laying there in the palm of Vorador's hand was a severed finger. Petra knew, but had to ask. "Fytch's finger?"

Kitoka looked like the cat who ate the canary, Petra thought, suppressing a hysterical giggle. She covered her mouth with her hand. Cat got your tongue? Gads, look what the cat dragged in!

"Petra, stop it," Vorador said, as if he knew exactly what warped path her mind had taken.

"Sorry," she managed to say without laughing.

"Can you use that?" Kitoka asked, a jerk of her head indicating the gruesome prize.

"Yes," Vorador reassured her. "It should provide me with exactly what I need."

"Then why are you still here, wizard? Go restore my sister."

"You'll excuse me then, if I go on ahead?" Vorador turned to Dugan, who still didn't look as if he'd recovered his equilibrium. "You'll bring the ladies to my lab?"

Dugan nodded and made an effort to pull himself together.

Petra had to feel sorry for him. He'd been friends—and lovers—with Fytch for a long time. His foundation had to be severely shaken. Their entire relationship had been based on lies, deception and worse. Fytch had attempted murder, justifying it with her twisted love for him. He didn't look in any condition to get behind the wheel of a car.

She patted Dugan's shoulder. "I've still got the keys to Mr. Wizard's Jaguar. You can ride shotgun."

Vorador shook his head, then vanished in a puff of smoke.

Feeling better now that the gross Fytch souvenir was gone, Petra steered Dugan toward the door.

"I'm not riding in back." Kitoka stomped after them.

Dugan gave a snort of laughter. "I see you're back to your old charming self."

"Stuff it, slug boy, before I'm tempted to stuff you down the nearest small hole."

Petra unlocked the car. "Oh, I can tell you two are gonna be more entertaining than watching a handyman with a truckload of free duct tape.

Kitoka pushed Dugan into the backseat. She settled herself beside Petra.

Starting the engine, Petra eyed the Amazon. "While we're being so open, I'm curious how you ended up at my place to begin with."

"I followed the rug," Kitoka said, the condescension evident in her voice.

Of course. It was so obvious—now. "That note you tried to give me. Where did it come from?"

Kitoka rolled her eyes and looked ready to hit something. "I went and got it from Medora's apartment. Now shut up and drive."

Deciding she'd already pushed her luck, Petra did just that.

When they pulled up in front of the ERG building, the Amazon immediately jumped out and strode through the front door.

Dugan was a bit slower. He paused on the curb when he noticed Petra still sitting in the car. Tapping on the window, he asked, "Aren't you coming in?"

Rolling down the window, she said, "No, I don't dare."

He nodded. "I understand. Although I doubt Vorador will."

Not quite sure what he meant by that, or in any frame of mind for emotional spelunking, she changed the subject. "What's his real name?"

"Who?"

Okay, so she hadn't raised the issue in a graceful manner. "Vorador. I figure you must owe me at least one little favor out of this whole mess."

Squatting beside the Jaguar, he studied her face. "Are you planning on sticking around?"

"No. I'll probably go home and grab a shower—"

"Not right now. I mean on any sort of permanent basis."

"Oh." Sticking around. As in a serious relationship—with a wizard. Petra waited for the sense of panic such a question should raise. It never came. Instead she felt excitement, anticipation and . . . just plain happiness. "Yeah, I'll be here."

"Good." He grinned with satisfaction. "Then if you still don't know his name a year from now, I'll tell you."

"Hey, that's not fair," Petra said.

"Consider it an anniversary present." He kissed her cheek, then stood up and sauntered through the front door.

Putting the car in gear, she headed home, feeling all warm and cheery inside. She might not know a certain wizard's real name, but the future looked promising. This was more fun than Rumpelstiltskin. She didn't have to worry about spinning straw into gold. All she had to do was wait, and hope it wouldn't be too long until her wizard showed up. After all, how long could it take to bring a mostly dead person back to life?

Medora was laid out on a long table, numerous white candles casting the only light. Vorador hadn't been this nervous since he'd tried his very first trick in his secret clubhouse. So much rode on the successful outcome of this spell. His confidence had been shaken by the encounter with Fytch. Time enough later for recriminations and guilt.

Checking one last time that everything was at hand, he took a deep breath and began chanting the revival incantation. The unfamiliar rhythms of Gaelic filled his workshop. Keeping a steady pace, he used the earthen bowls one at a time, brushing their contents on the appropriate places on Medora's body. One potion went on her eyes, another spread on the palms of her hands, one on her chest over her heart, one smeared across her forehead, one on her stomach, another dusted on the soles of her feet.

Finally he picked up the silver bowl containing the concoction made from Fytch's blood. The viscous dark red fluid looked black in the flickering candlelight. Chanting the last phrase of the spell, Vorador dipped his finger in the liquid. As he spoke the final word, he drew his wet finger across Medora's sealed lips, anointing her with the blood of her enemy.

He stepped back, never taking his gaze off the motionless woman on the table. Seconds ticked by, each seeming like an eternity. He wished the ancient text had specified how quickly the spell would work. He didn't know if he needed to wait a few minutes until she showed signs of life, or hours, or even days. If it failed, could he repeat it with any hope of success?

Abruptly, a gasp burst from Medora's lips, her back arching up off the table.

Relief swept over Vorador like a tidal wave. She gasped again, nearly choking in her attempt to breathe. He grabbed a rag and wiped the distasteful potion from her mouth. Immediately her struggles eased. He quickly rid her body of the rest of his marks. As each one vanished, her chest rose and fell more steadily. By the time he cleaned her feet Medora was breathing normally.

At Vorador's gesture, Kitoka and Dugan stood on either side of him. He felt their excitement and impatience, but he couldn't rush this final phase. Medora needed to come back to full consciousness in gentle stages or the remembered terror of her attack could send her into shock. He took her hand, encouraged by the warm suppleness of her skin. Before she'd been cold and stiff to the touch.

Fingers on her pulse, he softly called her name.

She stirred somewhat, a frown creasing her forehead.

"Medora, can you hear me?"

Her head moved slightly. The barest hint of a groan slipped past her parted lips.

"It's Vorador." He touched her cheek. "Kitoka and Dugan are here with me."

Eyelids fluttering, Medora seemed to respond to the names.

Encouraged, Vorador nodded for the others to join in.

Kitoka moved around the table and took Medora's other hand. "Dorrie, it's Kitty. Everything's okay. You're gonna be fine."

"Come on, Medora." Dugan leaned down and pressed a gentle kiss on her forehead. "Time to wake up. Open your eyes."

They spent the next several minutes coaxing her, reassuring her.

Finally her eyes flickered open, her look one of pure confusion.

"Everything's fine," Kitoka said. "You're okay now."

Medora seemed to roll that comment around in her mind,

testing it for truthfulness. After several moments she nodded. "Where am I?"

"You're in my lab," Vorador told her.

"What's the last thing you remember?" Dugan asked.

She frowned at him. "You were late."

The two men smiled at her accusatory tone.

Kitoka added her frown to her sister's. "Typical male."

"I'm sorry." Dugan lightly brushed Medora's cheek. "I can promise you it will never happen again. I learned my lesson."

"And nearly cost my sister her—"

"All right, children," Vorador interrupted before too much was said too soon, "play nice."

Medora smiled. "Whatever happened, I can see not much changed while I was gone."

She seemed stable. They should be able to proceed without risking her fragile state. It had actually worked! "What do you remember?"

Brow furrowed, Medora took a moment to respond. "I was waiting for Dugan. Kitty called and said she was stopping by to pick up a book. I was listening to the radio while I . . ."

When her words faded away, Vorador simply had to know. "What song was playing on the radio?"

"I think . . . 'Hotel California,' " she said after a brief pause.

He nearly laughed out loud. That explained the weird landscape down that damn hole.

"There was a knock on the door," Medora went on. "I thought it was Dugan. I was busy looking for Kitty's book, so I just called out for him to come in." Staring at Dugan, her frown deepened. "It wasn't you, was it?"

"No, I'm sorry to say, it wasn't."

Medora's gaze shifted to Kitoka. "It wasn't you either?"

She shook her head.

"Holy Athena! It was Fytch!" Medora's whole body spasmed as memories slammed through her.

Vorador placed a soothing hand on Medora's forehead, murmuring a calming spell. "Be calm, sweet Amazon. All the pain is past. She has no power to hurt you again."

Gradually the tremors shaking her body faded. She might

276

have been weakened physically, but strength radiated from her eyes as she demanded, "Tell me. Everything."

Between the three of them, they managed to give her a complete picture of events. As they ran through the facts, it overwhelmed Vorador how logical it seemed now. Yet at the time, they'd been totally blind to Fytch's evil manipulations. Well, all except Petra.

Vorador made a determined effort to push Petra out of his thoughts. If he let himself think about her, he was bound to go all mushy and sentimental. Not exactly his normal emotional state, he mocked himself.

"Vorador, are you listening?"

"Sorry, Medora. You were saying?"

"What happened to Fytch?"

He finished telling her the story, taking full credit for his failings. In the end he had been so focused on revenge, so intent on rendering harm, that he'd forgotten a wizard's first rule: *Use magic only to do good to others.* He hadn't spared a thought for Medora. Such selfishness didn't say much for his moral superiority.

"I'm afraid she's vanished. But we'll find her—sooner or later."

Medora sat up. "It's an astonishing tale. I can remember Fytch arriving. She was furious, screaming that I'd stolen Dugan from her. I tried to stay calm, but I admit before long I was yelling right back at her.

"She suddenly stormed out of the living room, into the kitchen. I thought she was trying to leave and had gotten confused. Even when she ran out of the kitchen with the knife, I just stood there like a stupid lamb waiting to be slaughtered."

She rubbed her hand across her chest. "I still can't believe she actually tried to kill me."

"Are you in pain?" Dugan asked.

Palm pressed over her heart, she shook her head. "The next thing I remember, I was on the floor, gazing at the ceiling."

Kitoka looked ready to break down, but Vorador knew Medora needed to talk and get it out of her system. "What then?"

"I was cold, but I didn't hurt. I remember being really pissed off Fytch'd gotten blood on my favorite rug." Medora chuckled through the tears in her eyes. "I know you hated it, Dugan, but—" She sniffed and gladly accepted the tissue Vorador produced.

"With the last of my strength, I put a spell on the rug. Or maybe on my blood. My mind got all confused with Fytch, then Dugan, and then you, Kitty. I was so scared. I kept trying to chant a spell, cursing my blood, the rug. I managed to make an alternate space and send the knife there."

Vorador ran a soothing hand across her forehead. "Do you recall making it so magic wouldn't work down there?"

She nodded. "I hoped she would go there looking for the knife and get trapped. Things were blurring together. I didn't know who'd done what, or who I could trust. I kept trying to leave clues in case Fytch got away before anyone arrived."

"Suspicion and fear," Vorador suddenly said.

Medora nodded. "Yeah, that about sums it up."

Now he understood what had happened to Petra that second time they'd gone down the hole. Those two strong emotions had influenced Medora's spell. Probably because of her non-magic nature, only Petra had reacted to them. Why they hadn't affected her the first time, he could only guess. Maybe the effect was cumulative. He was glad to have a plausible explanation for her suspicion that he could commit murder.

Medora smiled at each of them. "I thank you, my friends and dear sister, for seeing me safely through.

"How can you thank me when this was all my fault?" Anguish colored Dugan's voice. "If I hadn't been such a blind fool about Fytch, none of this would have happened. I'm an idiot. A spineless dupe. A witless buffoon. I'm—"

"Too cute for words," Medora finished for him. She held up a hand to silence him when he looked ready to continue the list of his faults. "None of us suspected her true evil nature."

"And," Vorador added, "you were trying to break free from Fytch's influence."

Kitoka snorted. "Which explains why you subjected everybody to that ridiculous hit-us-over-the-head charming spell."

"Okay, I'm convinced." Dugan turned to Vorador. "Make it go away."

"Definitely," Medora agreed. "You don't need it anymore. I think we'll get along just fine without it from here on out."

Kitoka made a gagging noise when Dugan kissed Medora.

With a wave and a snap, Vorador said, "To a long and uncomplicated future."

Dugan looked relieved.

Medora looked very pleased as she rested her head on Dugan's shoulder. "I do have one other thing to say." She winked at Vorador. "I can't wait to meet this Petra."

Vorador silently groaned. Hell, was he that transparent? That even a woman barely off her deathbed could tell how enamored he was? He feared he was blushing but managed to smile. "I'm sure we can arrange that."

"Good. Because I want my rug back."

This time his groan wasn't silent. Oh, crud. He hoped Medora didn't have a battle on her hands. All things considered, his money was on Petra.

Chapter Thirty-seven

"Petra. Wake up."

Ignoring the seductive whisper, Petra snuggled her head deeper into her pillow. For some reason, it didn't feel as soft as usual. She punched it, trying to get it into the proper shape.

"Ooof!"

That wasn't right, her groggy mind insisted. Pillows didn't talk. Well, not normally. Lately there was no telling what might—or might not—end up talking. Burrowing deeper, she sneezed when something tickled her nose.

"Now that's romantic," said a voice in her ear.

With a squeal, Petra scooted across the bed, but she was too close to the edge. Landing on her butt brought her fully awake. She glared at the shadowy figure leaning over the side of her bed. "Are you trying to seduce me? Or scare me to death?"

"The first." Vorador helped her back into bed.

Wrapped in his embrace, Petra sighed happily. Of all the weird ways she'd been awakened in the past few days, this was by far the most pleasant. "How's Medora? Were you successful?"

"It worked like a charm."

"Cute." She wiggled slightly, simply to torment him. Or maybe herself. "I think I'm rubbing off on you."

"Yeah, something's rubbing, all right," he muttered.

Petra snickered and repeated her action, this time pressing a little harder. Which in turn made him a little—"Stop it," he ordered.

"I think it's too late to stop."

"Got that right."

She smiled at the restraint evident in his voice. "Tell me about Medora."

He kissed the top of her head. "She's fine. Kitoka and Dugan took her home."

"Good."

He went on, giving her a play-by-play account of Medora's recovery and recollections.

She laughed out loud when he told her Dugan had dropped the charming spell. "Do you think they'll get their very own 'happily ever after'?"

"They looked well on their way last I saw. Or at least they will be once they ditch Kitoka."

"Yeah, it would be kind of hard to get romantic with her standing there growling and reaching for her sword every time Dugan got too close." Petra smiled at that mental picture. "Now, tell me the rest."

When he told her about Medora's fears and suspicions being part of the spell, Petra gave a huge sigh of relief. "I knew there had to be a logical reason for my behavior."

"My thought exactly. Well, as logical as things ever get around you, Petunia."

"By the way, what did you do with my rug? I was surprised to finally get back home and find it gone."

"Technically, it's Medora's rug."

"You gave it back to her?" Petra made a disgusted sound. "That's not fair. I paid good money for that rug."

"Do you really want it back? With all the spells Fytch worked on it, we may never be able to completely clean it."

"Good point. Medora can keep it. Now, are you ever going to make love to me, Mr. Wizard?"

"What?" he croaked.

"I thought you were one of those manly men who took charge of every situation. I'm beginning to think you're a tease." She pressed a kiss on his bare shoulder. "What are you wearing?"

"Wearing?"

"Boxers? Or briefs?" Keeping him off balance, she slipped out of his arms and out of bed. "I simply have to know."

"I'm not the tease."

"Please don't yell," she told him. "You're going to wake up Mom and Dad."

She was glad she chose that exact moment to flip on the light. Catching the expression of shock on his face was well worth all the trouble she'd suffered the past few days.

"What?" he bellowed.

"Shhhh." Gad, this was more fun than watching Fytch play catcher for a dart team. "They were here when I got home."

"Your parents are here? In your house?"

She nodded, anticipating his next reaction. He didn't disappoint her.

Leaping out of bed, he grabbed his jeans and had them on in seconds flat. Not before she finally saw what kind of underwear he wore—black silk boxers. Very tasteful. And sexy.

"Don't worry," she told him while he yanked his T-shirt over his head, "they don't know anything. They probably don't even suspect that much."

"What the hell is that supposed to mean?" He was on his hands and knees, looking under her bed for his boots.

Petra slumped against the wall for support. All she could see was his butt waving around as he searched the floor. "Gad! Have you registered that with the police as a lethal weapon?"

"What did you say?" he asked suspiciously, getting up and trying to tame his hair into a ponytail.

"You wanna meet them?"

"Now?"

She bit her lip so she wouldn't laugh out loud. "Do you have any idea how adorable you are?"

"I am not." His eyes narrowed. "Are your parents really here? Or are you playing one of your sadistic games?"

"Oh, they're here. Which is why I think it would be a good idea to go to your house if we're going to make love. That was your plan when you slipped into my bed, wasn't it?"

His gaze darted to the closed door. "Petra, stop it."

She really should, she supposed. He was acting like a ten-year-old, caught smoking cigarettes out behind the barn. That thought sobered her. Of course that would be his reaction to any family situation. He hadn't been much older than ten when he'd had to leave his family. He'd never had a chance to establish an adult relationship with his parents. Suddenly she felt like Snidely Whiplash tying the heroine to the railroad tracks while demanding the deed to her ranch.

"I'm sorry, Vorador." She put on her robe, covering up her pig sleep shirt. She'd almost worn a slinky negligee but had decided against trying to pretty herself up at this late date. Besides, he seemed to like pigs as much as she did. Sitting on the bed, she promised, "I'll be good."

He hesitated, as if not totally trusting her.

"You okay with what happened tonight?" she said.

He reluctantly sat, keeping the width of the bed between them. "You care to narrow it down a little bit more?"

"The whole Fytch business."

"I'm fine," he said, in a tone of voice that plainly told her he didn't want to discuss it.

Which was precisely why she intended to do exactly that. If she didn't force him to talk about it, he would bottle everything inside. There it would fester with all his other secrets and old hurts.

"And still as arrogant as ever, I see."

"So much for sympathy," he muttered.

"Yup," she confirmed, "cocky as all get out. Not at all bothered. Self-confident's the word for you, all right."

"Knock it off, Petra. You're not funny."

"Not trying to be. I'm simply impressed that finding out you're not the all-powerful top dog wizard hasn't affected you in the least."

"That's not what I meant," he insisted.

"Then what?"

"Just let it go. I'll work it out."

"How? When?" she pushed.

"Whenever," he snapped.

She laughed that he'd stooped to such a cliché. "No time like the present."

"Damn it, Petra. What do you want from me? You want to hear that yes, I'm an arrogant bastard who got exactly what he deserved? That it was ultimately my fault this whole disaster happened? That I was so blinded by pride that someone nearly died?"

"So now you're going to add self-pity to your list of faults?"

"I'm obviously not going to get any from you."

"How about some truth? Instead of pity?" She gently caressed his cheek. "You do realize none of this was your fault."

"No," he said, his tone surly.

"No matter how strong your magic, Fytch had you beat. She was using blood spells, Vorador. Nothing is more powerful. Or more evil. Yes, she fooled you for a while, but in the end good triumphed." She stroked his cheek again. "I know you don't want to believe that it wasn't your fault, but will you at least promise to think about what I've said?"

He nodded.

But she wasn't done yet. "Has anything like that ever happened before?"

"Like what? he asked, his voice wary.

"Have you ever purposely harmed someone with your magic?"

"No! Damn it, what kind of man do you think I am?"

"One of the finest I've ever met," she promptly answered. "But you're kidding yourself if you think making somebody disappear isn't going to affect you in the least bit."

"I'll deal with it."

The very grimness of his words brought instant tears to her eyes and nearly broke her heart. She scooted across the bed and knelt beside him. "You don't need to do it alone."

His face went totally blank and his eyes wouldn't meet hers.

She pulled back slightly. Had she misread him? Maybe she was the only one who wanted to deepen their relationship. Maybe he didn't want to confide in her. Never one to feel overly confident about her interpersonal communication skills, Petra started to get off the bed. One look at Vorador changed her mind. No, she wasn't about to give up that easily on him. He was worth fighting for. This time she had no intention of running away.

In that same second his hand reached out and settled atop hers. "Don't go."

Those two words promised unending joy. The future looked bright indeed. "Trust me, Wiz Boy, I'm not going anywhere."

"Except straight to my bed."

She threw her arms around his neck. "What're you waiting for? Let's get out of here. Your car is still parked out front."

"Thanks for the reminder." With a quick flick of his wrist and a quick snap of his fingers, he mumbled, "Home," just before he kissed her.

Gads, she hoped he'd put enough concentration into his spell. Or they could end up sitting on the bronze pig statue in front of Pike Place Market.

Vorador didn't stop kissing Petra, but he did open one eye to check their location. They sat on the front steps of his house. Close enough. No car in sight though. He hoped it had landed where it was suppose to—safe and sound in the garage.

He wondered if he would ever get tired of kissing her. When they were both old and wrinkled, with gray hair and no teeth, would the mere touch of her lips still excite him? He was inclined to think the answer was yes. He sincerely doubted life with Petra would ever be boring.

Maddening as a poison ivy rash he couldn't scratch perhaps, but not boring. She might drive him crazy with her incessant prodding and questions, but she would never bore him. She might force him to look at himself in new and painful ways, but he'd never tire of her. She made him a better man. A less arrogant man. A more humane man. A man burning up with wanting her.

"What're you grinning about?" she asked as his mouth curved upward against hers.

"You," he told her, kissing the tip of her nose.

"Oh, so you think I'm funny?"

He knew he was grinning from ear to ear like some demented fool, but for once in his life he didn't give a damn about maintaining control. "Yes, you are funny, Petunia. Funny, and wonderful, and adorable, and bright, and wonderful—"

"You already said that," she interrupted him.

He bent down and gave her a quick peck. "And sexy."

She fairly hummed under his touch. "I like that one. Even if it isn't true."

He pulled back in surprise. "You don't think you're sexy?"

"I *know* I'm not sexy."

He gave a harsh laugh. He grabbed her hand and pressed it against his erection. "That's what you do to me every time I even think about you."

She gasped and made a brief attempt to pull away. Then she relaxed against him, her fingers curving around his hardness.

He groaned from a pleasure so sharp it was nearly torture. "Trust me, Petra, you're deadly."

Rubbing her breasts against his arm, she purred.

"You're welcome," he teased her. It was either that or take her right here on the sidewalk for the entire neighborhood to see. With that in mind, he reluctantly removed her hand from his lap. He kissed her palm before releasing it. "Now I've handled that misconception, there's something you can do for me."

"What?" she asked, her voice and expression immediately wary.

He couldn't help smiling again at such a typical Petra reaction, always suspicious of ulterior motives. "Release me from that damn promise so we can get on with it."

"Get on with it? I bet you didn't learn that from any romance novel." She punched him in the shoulder. "What promise?"

"That promise I made not to do anything but comfort you."

"Holy crud, you mean that's what's been holding you back?" She shook her head. "Here I thought you were such a shy, considerate fella."

Yeah, he was, but he suspected her words mocked him. That was okay, as long as she set him free. Feeling ready to explode, he kissed her again. And again. His tongue invaded the warmth of her mouth in imitation of what he really wanted to do. He skimmed a hand under her robe and up her leg. She wiggled her bottom against him. His fingers convulsively dug into the tender flesh of her thigh.

"Damn it, Petra. Say it."

"I want you." She wrapped her arms around his neck. "Forget that damn promise before I go up in flames."

He groaned loud and long as magic fire consumed his body.

She leaned back slightly. "Oops, sorry."

"No, don't apologize." He pulled her close. "I want this. I want you."

He thought he had died and gone to heaven when she ran her fingers through his hair, sending a shower of sparks swirling up toward the stars. Which reminded him; there was one other item to take care of before he could bury himself in her heat. He got to his feet, carrying her up the steps.

"Open," he ordered the front door. Inside, he told it to shut while he continued on. Instead of climbing the stairs, he went into the bathroom. There was a door in one corner.

"What the heck are you doing?" she asked, wiggling in protest. "You're going to put me in the closet?"

He merely raised an eyebrow at her misconception. Opening the door with another command, he stepped inside. She went still once she got a good look at where they were. Releasing her legs, her body slowly slide against his until she stood on her own feet. He enjoyed it, even if she was too dazed to appreciate it.

"Where in heaven's name are we?"

He stood behind her, his hands on her shoulders, proudly surveying the landscape. "This is where Orwell lives."

"Your roommate lives on a farm? In your bathroom?"

Vorador glanced around, seeing it through her eyes. Rolling hills stretched out into the distance and a full moon frosted the gentle curves with a silvery light. Close by was a small tidy barn, surrounded by various pens and enclosures. "You want to meet him?"

"Don't wake him on my account."

Her voice sounded choked and he smiled again. Petra might have grown up around wizards and have vast knowledge about magic, but she was still easily disconcerted by unusual events. "You have to meet him before I can make love to you."

Her head twisted around until she glared up at him. "Is this some sort of test? I have to pass muster first?"

"Nothing like that." He slipped an arm around her waist and pulled her closer. A thrill shot straight to his crotch when his fire, still burning brightly, flowed out to encompass her. The softness of her bottom cradled his heavy arousal. Damn it, if he didn't get her in bed soon, he would be permanently crippled.

"What're you doing?" she demanded, but didn't try to escape.

"Nothing." That was the truth, for the moment. He simply felt like having her close. It was exhilarating to be free to indulge himself, to know she wanted him, to no longer be held to his promise not to make love to her.

He explained, "You were a bit . . . ah, distracted at the time, but I remember a particular promise—or threat—you made. In the Space Needle."

Frowning suspiciously, she looked over her shoulder at him. "I don't recall any—" She jerked out of his embrace and spun to face him. "Wait a minute. Oh, please! Tell me you didn't."

"I didn't what?" he asked, striving to maintain an innocent expression. Had she figured it out that quickly? He shouldn't be surprised. She always did seem to be one step ahead of him.

"If you plan on telling me you fulfilled my stupid flying pig remark, I may have to kill you. That's just plain cruel and—"

He gave a sharp, piercing whistle, cutting through her words. She turned toward the barn. She should have been watching the pen on the other side. He nudged her head in the right direction at the right moment.

"Holy moly!"

Pride and amusement warred inside him while the small rotund figure flapped across the short distance. The startling sight was silhouetted perfectly against the silver circle of the moon.

He shook his head. Orwell always had been a show-off. Vorador smiled as Orwell did a loop, then landed at their feet.

"Holy sh—" Petra sounded properly stunned. "What the blue blazes have you done, Vorador?"

He laughed when his fire flashed from orange to blue.

She poked him on the chest. "How could you do such a horrible thing to a poor defenseless pig? It's inhumane."

"Settle down, Petunia. I didn't make Orwell just to get you in bed. I've had him for years."

Still looking skeptical, she darted a quick glance at the creature. "Really?"

"I created him when I was thirteen. Before I knew any better. Once he was here, there was nothing Professor Helios could do. Not knowing enough about magic, I didn't leave a way to undo the spell. Orwell was here to stay."

"Orwell—for *Animal Farm*?" She put her hands on her hips and scowled at him. "What about that grief you gave me about the pigs' names? And all the time, you'd named your pig after the author?"

Not looking the least bit repentant, he asked, "Can you see a thirteen-year-old boy using any of those names? Squealer and Snowball were never even contenders—too girly. Napoleon and Major were too representative of the military and I was extremely anti-authority at that age. I thought about George, but Orwell just seemed to fit him."

He watched as Petra squatted beside his pet. Another side effect of his youthful spell had stopped Orwell's growth. He was still the size of a small piglet. Which was probably a good thing. Wings would never have been able to support a full-grown hog. Or else he would have been the size of a Cessna. No, Orwell was permanently tiny, pink and cute. An impression his elegant white feathered wings only enhanced.

Petra held out a hand, allowing Orwell to sniff it. Vorador watched her pet the pig, scratch behind his ears, coo baby talk to him and generally make a fool of herself. For his part, Orwell soaked up all the extra attention. For obvious reasons, Orwell didn't get a lot of visitors. With all the craziness lately, Vorador knew he hadn't been spending enough time with him.

Helping Petra to her feet, Vorador broadly hinted, "He needs to get back to his beauty sleep."

With a soft oink of farewell, Orwell took to the air and flew away. Further proof that pigs were highly intelligent creatures. Vorador smiled at the bemused expression on Petra's face. He hoped she looked just as dazed when he finished making love to her. Lust hit him right between the legs and he nearly doubled over with need.

With a snap of his fingers, he envisioned his bedroom. Petra appeared in midair, then dropped with a squeal. Luckily his aim wasn't totally off. She shrieked again as she bounced on the bed.

Pushing her hair out of her eyes, she scowled at him. "You could give me some warning. Or at least provide a parachute."

Stretched out on the mattress beside her, his fire still burned, casting a romantic bluish glow over the room. Appreciating the fine view, he merely raised an eyebrow, waiting for her to realize the rest of it. Truthfully, he was pleased with the success of his spell. He'd been working on it practically since the first day he met her. Finally, he had her right where he wanted her: in his house, in his bed, both of them naked and ready to make love.

"Where the heck are my clothes?" Petra dove under the protection of the sheet with a flash of legs and breasts.

He rolled onto his side and propped himself up on one elbow.

"You're naked!" she told him.

Amused, he watched her struggle between modesty and curiosity. He knew which one would win. Only seconds passed before her gaze lost the battle and darted down his body. He resisted the urge to suck in his already flat stomach. Nor did he make any effort to hide his erection. She'd felt it often enough. She'd better get used to seeing it, too.

"Now that's a banana," she said in a breathless voice.

For a moment his disappointment almost deflated him. Banana? That's the only thing she could think to compare him to? Then he relaxed as he recalled the first time she had kissed him and his comment about fruit salad. "So, little girl, you like bananas?"

Her gaze still hadn't moved on and she licked her lips. "I think they just became my favorite fruit."

"Then how 'bout you show me your peaches?"

She started to lower the sheet she had clutched to her chest but stopped. She twisted the cloth while she hemmed and hawed. "Vorador . . ." Her voice faded away.

She was so bold in many ways, he was surprised by how tentative she suddenly seemed. Then he reminded himself that her last sexual experience had been with Harold, a man who probably hadn't done a whole lot to satisfy her. He closed the distance between them and tenderly took her in his arms.

"I love you, Petra."

Chapter Thirty-eight

Petra jerked backward so she could see Vorador. She wondered if her face had the same expression as his. If so, they both looked like cows who'd just been zapped with a stun gun on the way to the slaughterhouse. "Did you plan on saying that?"

He swallowed hard and shook his head.

"Planning on taking it back?"

There was a long pause before he slowly shook his head again.

"Sure about that? It's not too late to escape."

"I meant it, Petra."

Okay, so where did that leave her? She released a gusty sigh. Love, huh? In spite of her earlier calm acceptance, right about now she felt like a plague of locusts had overwhelmed her when she wasn't looking. After Harold she'd thought it would be years before she would be ready for another serious relationship. Instead it was mere weeks.

"I guess you know what this means," he said.

Gads, she was as clueless as a kid on the first day of kindergarten. "Not really."

Vorador gave her a long, slow, sweet kiss.

Oh, so that's what it meant. Okay, she liked that. She could handle more of the same. "Hey! Where are you going?"

He got out of bed and disappeared into his closet.

Feeling very discombobulated, she covered herself with the sheet. When he reappeared dressed in his typical black T-shirt and jeans, she was disappointed but couldn't quite bring herself to say, "I thought we were going to make love."

He tossed her a black silk shirt. "Put this on."

"Why?"

"Because I don't think you should go talk to your Mom and Dad naked. I have a feeling parents frown on that kind of behavior."

"We're going to talk to . . . Why?"

He whipped back the sheet, then kissed her before assisting her out of bed. "Because I love you, that's why."

She felt like she was in the Twilight Zone and he was following a different script than the one she had. "Yeah; so?"

"You're a bright girl. I'm sure you'll figure it out."

She wasn't so sure about that. Having Vorador help her get dressed at this point was not how she'd expected the night to turn out. As he buttoned the shirt, his knuckles brushed against her breasts and she shivered. She didn't protest when he led her into the hall, down the stairs and into the kitchen.

She balked when he headed for the garage. "What's going on?"

He handed her some keys. "I want you to drive yourself home. I have some business to take care of first. I'll meet you there."

"As much as I've been driving your car lately, you might as well sign the title over to me."

He grinned and kissed her.

Holy smoke, if he didn't stop doing that she would never be able to concentrate. Then she'd never figure out what the heck was going on.

He unwrapped her arms from around his neck and held her at arm's length. "Drive safely, Petra."

"Interesting you should say that. Since I'm driving without a license."

"What?"

She explained, "I left my purse in that hotel room and never got it back. Or the rest of my stuff. If the police stop me, they'll probably throw me in jail for car theft."

"You're quickly accumulating quite a criminal record."

"Guess you're just gonna have to take me with you to keep me out of trouble," she said with a sweet smile.

"Nice try." He turned her toward the garage door and gave her a gentle push. "Go home. I'll see you there."

Petra stuck her tongue out at him over her shoulder, then squealed when he swatted her on the butt. "Bully."

Rubbing her behind, she cast one last look over her shoulder. Vorador was already gone. Whether he'd popped himself out or left by more conventional means, she didn't know. He must be getting better at counteracting her non-magic since he'd managed to safely zap his car home. Sliding into the Jaguar's soft leather seat, she noticed a note stuck on the steering wheel. It said: *Look in the trunk*. With a sigh, she got back out and opened the trunk.

"Smart aleck," she muttered. There was her purse, her suitcase and her stuffed pig, Pork Chop. He must have retrieved them from the motel at some point. With everything that had been going on, she supposed she could forgive him for not telling her sooner. Feeling all warm and mushy inside, she got back in the car and drove home. She couldn't wait to see what her wizard had planned. Gad, he loved her!

The look on Petra's face when she walked in was priceless. Vorador knew he would carry it in his heart until the day he died. Obviously, the last thing she ever expected to find in her living room was her parents, in their pajamas, chatting with him at three o'clock in the morning.

"What took you so long?" he asked. "Did you get a ticket?"

For one of the few times since he'd met her, she was speechless. Truly a moment for the record books.

"We've been waiting for you," he went on, cocking an eyebrow.

She gaped at him, then at her parents, then down at her legs, barely covered by his shirt. Her face instantly went beet red.

Gillian Field came up off the couch with her arms extended and embraced her daughter. "Petra! Such wonderful news! I'm so happy for you."

Petra hugged her mom back. "It is? You are?"

Vorador just smiled when she shot him a pleading look. No, he wasn't going to help her out. Not when he'd gone to so much trouble to arrange things. The temptation to spill his guts was nearly irresistible. It was time to get this show on the road before he spoiled the surprise.

Laszlo Field rose to his feet, taking his cue from Vorador. "Petra, why don't you go with your mother? Junior here and I need to have a little talk."

Vorador nearly laughed at the expression of pure panic on Petra's face. Seeing her beside her mother gave him a suspiciously warm, fuzzy feeling inside. That was how Petra would look thirty years from now, her soft brown hair mixed with silver, her figure more voluptuous but still trim.

"If it's all the same, Dad, I think I'll stay right here."

Laszlo straightened, his long white hair making him appear almost regal—even dressed in a ratty plaid bathrobe. He didn't need to say anything, he simply gazed down at her.

She rolled her eyes but started toward the bedroom. "Please, Dad. Just don't turn him into a frog. Remember what happened last time."

When the two men were alone, Vorador said, "Thank you for your assistance, sir."

"I'll help, as long as you intend to do right by her. I won't see her hurt again."

"If you're referring to Harold, have no fear. If I ever cross paths with that weasel, I'll make him pay for what he did to Petra."

"Good man." Laszlo clapped him on the shoulder. "And when

the time seems right, you might let her know that all legal charges have been dropped. I made him see the error of his ways."

"Someday—when we aren't as rushed—I think I'd like to hear that story, sir."

"And I'll enjoy the telling. Can't have weasels hurting my little girl."

Vorador grinned, thinking of the future. Someday would he get to play this same role with his own daughter? He certainly hoped so. "Shall we go, sir? I don't imagine she's going to be patient much longer."

Laszlo nodded, and both men disappeared in puffs of smoke.

Pacing beside her bed, Petra tried to hear what was going on in the front room. She didn't hear any furniture breaking, so they must not have resorted to violence. Yet. Could happen any second, though. Vorador was arrogant enough to try a saint's patience. Dad never had claimed to be either a saint or patient.

"Petra dear, perhaps you should put on something a bit more appropriate."

Cringing, she faced her mom. "It's not as bad as it looks."

With a noncommittal sound, Gillian went to the closet and flipped through Petra's clothes. She brought out a dress. "Here, why don't you put this on? It's always been one of my favorites."

Petra was beginning to suspect her mom was suffering from jet lag, or sleep deprivation. The garment in question was an elegant ivory lace dress more suited for a formal wedding than an early morning confrontation between her parents and her soon-to-be lover. "I don't think so."

"Just humor me, sweetie." She laid the dress on the bed, then went through dresser drawers, finding matching lingerie. As the final touch, she pulled out a pair of ivory heels. "Hurry and change. We don't want to keep the men waiting too long."

Petra tried to protest again, but her mom overrode every objection. Before she could marshal her defenses, Petra found herself being zipped into the ivory dress. Her eyes widened when she was handed a pearl choker. "Aren't those Grandma's pearls?"

"Why, yes, they are," Gillian said as she fastened them around Petra's neck. "How very observant of you."

She could hardly think when her mother started brushing her hair. She hadn't done that since Petra was a little girl. "When I was in the pit . . . ? Was that really you?"

The hairbrush hesitated, then continued. "I'm not sure I want to know, if this is about something kinky—"

"Then you didn't see me? Didn't scold me?"

"I could do it now, if you really feel the need."

"That's okay." Petra smiled at this typical Mom answer. "And by the way, have you been casting any love spells lately?"

"Why, no, dear. What makes you ask?"

Not quite sure what to think, Petra frowned. If Mom hadn't . . . And Dad said he hadn't . . . So did this mean all that burning, seething lust between her and Vorador had just happened? It wasn't the result of some spell? Just simple old-fashioned mutual attraction? Well, that put an interesting twist on events. It meant he really had fallen in love with her. Just her. Plain, slightly pudgy Petra. No magic—other than love—involved.

Gillian stepped back and surveyed her daughter. "You look lovely, my dear."

Petra gazed at herself in the mirror. She did look nice. But she felt like she had slipped—not into the Twilight Zone, but a Stephen King novel. Normal things were slightly off kilter and circumstances seemed about to slide into an even scarier reality.

"Shall we go?" Gillian asked.

"Go where?"

"To join the men, of course."

"Of course," Petra muttered as they disappeared in a swirling mist.

"Oh, dear." Gillian's dismay was plain in those two words.

Petra looked around and echoed her mother. "Oh, my!"

Vorador grimaced as he took in their surroundings. "Damn, it happened again."

"If this is your idea of a joke, young man . . ." Laszlo left the rest of the threat unvoiced.

"Hell, no," Vorador answered. He'd thought he'd taken Petra's influence into account when casting his traveling spell. Obviously not. They were way off target. Her parents must have more practice because they arrived appropriately dressed—her father in a sedate tuxedo, her mother in a satin dress that looked too sexy for the mother-of-the-bride.

"At least we seem to be in the correct town," Gillian said.

Suddenly Petra started to giggle. "Gads, they're playing 'Suspicious Minds.'"

Looking around the room that was a complete and utter shrine to Elvis, the King of Rock and Roll, Vorador listened to the tinny music coming through the cheap overhead speaker. She was right. It was "Suspicious Minds." Not exactly what you expected to hear in a wedding chapel—even in Las Vegas. He felt the beginnings of a smile tugging at his lips.

"Well, Petunia, not quite what I had planned, but what do you say?" He angled up an eyebrow, waiting for her reaction.

Her lips twitched as she took note of the black velvet paintings of Elvis, the ceramic Elvis-head lamps, the hip-swinging Elvis clock and countless other Elvis treasures. "I take it this is a proposal, Porky?"

He nearly laughed. She'd finally made the connection that Petunia was Porky Pig's girlfriend. "T-t-t-that's right, folks."

Petra laughed and threw her arms around his neck. "Gee, I think that's what I love most about you, Mr. Wizard. You're so darned romantic." She kissed his cheek. "Besides which, you look totally spiffy in that pale blue velvet tuxedo."

Suddenly it didn't matter that his plans had gone awry. Why would he want a dull, traditional black-and-white tuxedo when she liked him in blue velvet? Feeling ridiculous moisture filling his eyes, he tenderly kissed her forehead. "You love me?"

"Yeah, I do." She sighed and snuggled her head on his shoulder. "How could I not love a man—a wizard—who fulfills all my fantasies?"

He buried his face in her hair until he managed to get control of his emotions. "We could go find someplace nicer. We were supposed to be at the Rose Arbor Chapel. It's quite—"

"No." She chuckled and rubbed her cheek against the soft nap of his velvet coat. "This will do just fine."

"Well, folks. Ready to get the show on the road?" a voice asked from the doorway.

They turned, and all four of them burst out laughing. Vorador didn't think he'd ever been happier in his entire life. It seemed appropriate that the minister was dressed in full Elvis regalia, from his gravity-defying Elvis pompadour wig to his white spangled jumpsuit split open to his waist showing his hairy chest and stomach in all their overweight glory, right down to his high-heeled white patent leather disco boots. The moment was complete when his friends arrived from Seattle. They were all there: Dugan, Kitoka, Medora, Caylin, Zaylin and Professor Helios. He could only hope and pray Fytch didn't show up.

With all the laughter, it was a wonder he and Petra managed to make it through the ceremony. The only rough part came when Monsignor Elvis asked for their names.

"Do you—speak up, boy."

Vorador hesitated, waiting for the old hurt and pain that came when he thought about his family. It was there, but distant. He was starting a new family. "Gerome Adam Pierson."

"That's not *that* bad," Petra said in an accusing tone.

"I never said it was bad." He grinned at her. "You just assumed it was, since I wouldn't tell you."

"Dork." She poked him in the ribs with her elbow.

Preacher Elvis went on. ". . . take—what's your name, honey?"

"Petra W. Field."

"You gotta tell what the W stands for," he informed her.

Now Petra was the one to squirm. She hemmed and hawed.

"Wing," her mother finally said. Seeing everybody's looks, she defended herself. "It was my grandfather's name."

That business taken care of, the ceremony proceeded quickly. In the end, Petra's "I do!" warmed Vorador's soul until he thought he might spontaneously burst into flames. He only hoped Petra approached this marriage with half as much gladness in her heart as he had in his. Looking into her blazing sapphire eyes while he spoke his vows, any lingering doubts vanished. She loved him. In spite of his faults and shortcomings, in spite of his arrogance and magical ways, she was committing

299

the rest of her life to him. He wanted to shout his happiness from the top of the Stratosphere Tower for all of Vegas to hear.

When the Elvis minister told him to kiss his bride, he did; then he spoke one word, taking his bride to the only place on Earth he wanted to be with her.

"Home."

Chapter Thirty-nine

Petra bounced on the bed. "You really need to practice your landings, Mr. Wizard."

He bounced beside her. "I intend to get lots of practice putting you in my bed, Mrs. Wizard."

"Oh, I do like the sound of that." She held out her hand to admire the deep blue sapphire ring on the third finger of her left hand. "A lot."

"You wouldn't rather have a diamond?"

"Nope, that's too traditional."

He chuckled. "That's the last thing anyone would ever accuse you of being."

"Yeah, like you're Mr. Respectable Normal Business Dude."

He caressed her cheek. "I really do love you, Petra."

She nuzzled against his palm. She could hardly believe he had proposed to her. No, that wasn't what had her so stunned. What amazed her was that he'd gone through with it. Right up until he said, "I do," she had expected to see his back walking out the door. Instead, she was now Mrs. Gerome Adam Pierson. Not bad at all.

"You're my very own hunk of burning love."

Bursting into flames, Vorador groaned. He kissed her, licking at her lips. "Thank you, Petra."

She scooted closer to him. Determined not to let her shyness hold her back, she hooked a leg over his hips. "What for?"

"For this." He held up a hand merrily blazing with magical fire. "No one—"

She nudged him, stopping that train of thought before he went any further. She'd just as soon he didn't mentioned other women on their wedding night.

He tried again. "I've always wanted to know what it would be like to make love like this, but none—"

Raising up on an elbow, she glared down at him. "You're on treacherous ground, Swamp Boy."

Wrapping an arm around her, he drew her back down. "All I'm saying is that I've never had the opportunity to make love inside this magical fire. You're fulfilling all my wildest fantasies."

Petra smiled and ran her hand over his chest, creating whorls and eddies in his fire. "Guess I'm just the adventurous sort."

"Thank all the heavens above for that," he mumbled and pulled her over on top of him. His fingers fumbled until he managed to find the zipper on the back of her dress. He slowly slid it down.

She practically purred when his hands slipped inside and caressed up and down the length of her back.

"Does it hurt?" he asked when she gasped and twitched her shoulders.

"No." She wiggled even closer to him. "I told you before, it tickles, it tingles and it's very arousing."

He pulled the material forward off her shoulders, revealing her lacy bra. Just knowing he looked at her made her nipples tighten into hard pebbles under the ivory lace. He slid her up his body, until he could reach the temptation. When his mouth closed over her, her back arched and she cried out.

He paused. "You didn't get another shock, did you?"

"No! Don't stop." Gads, it felt as if his fire had leapt right

302

down inside her body and was burning her to cinders. Glowing, pulsing, throbbing cinders.

Still, when he fumbled with the hooks on her bra, she panicked. Pulling away, she tried to cover herself. She wanted to ask him to put out his fire so they could do this in the dark, but she wasn't quite heartless enough to do that. But she really didn't want him to see her out-of-shape body. Why, oh why hadn't she invested in whatever had promised those buns of steel? Her abs could use a lot of work, too. Should only take about five thousand situps. Her legs were a disaster. What was that thigh gizmo hawked on late-night TV?

"Petra, what's wrong? Not getting cold feet, are you?"

At this point, her feet were about the only thing she was willing to let him see. Well, her boobs weren't bad. Not too small, and not big enough to droop. They just had the misfortune to be right above the slight bulge of her stomach. That stuff could be hidden in the dark, but not with him blazing like a torch. She might not feel as bad about revealing her less-than-perfect body if only he wasn't such a poster boy for the exercise generation.

Under that baby blue velvet tux, she knew he had the ultimate washboard abs, shoulders King Kong would envy and pecs a bodybuilder would—Oh, now, wasn't that an inspiring fantasy? Vorador wearing one of those tiny bikinis that barely covered the pertinent equipment, his gorgeous body slathered in oil, while he flexed and preened. Nope, her dress was staying on.

"Petra, what's going on?"

She considered all her options but knew he would be able to discern any lies she told. In the end, she had no choice but to blurt out the truth. "I'm fat and flabby and disgusting."

Half-expecting him to burst out laughing, she jerked when he gently brushed her hand aside and cupped her breast. Her death grip on her dress loosened when he kissed her with mind-numbing tenderness. What had she done in her life to deserve this man?

"Shall I tell you a secret?" he whispered in between kisses.

"Sure." She shivered in delight when he bit her earlobe. "Whatever."

"I had a secret obsession when I was a teenager."

The phone beside the bed rang and Petra screamed.

"No," she whined when he reached to answer it.

He grinned. "Patience." He picked up the receiver.

Not able to get any clues from his abrupt, "Yes," and, "No," answers, she poked him in the ribs to get his attention. "What?" she mouthed.

With a frown he waved aside her question.

When he finally hung up she was nearly bursting. "Well? What was that all about? What could be important enough to interrupt our wedding night? Surely, whoever it was could have waited until—"

"They caught Fytch."

"Oh." That had been much quicker than Petra expected. "Where?"

"She was on the *Titanic*."

"The *Titanic*! On the bottom of the ocean? Like a fish?" Petra started to laugh. "I can't wait to tell Zaylin that part of her wish came true."

"Actually, she was trapped there."

"Oh, my." Petra considered that. "Do you think that's where she meant to send me?"

"It's a good possibility. She probably intended to sink you and whatever plans we had. But because of your effect on spells, you were the massive iceberg that destroyed her instead."

Petra rubbed her throat, imagining being trapped in that cold watery tomb, not able to breathe, drowning. "Is she dead?"

"No. She managed to create an air bubble."

"Where is she now?"

"The Guild wouldn't say. But now they're aware of her skill and unbalanced state, they promised she won't ever escape."

"Good to know." A shiver ran down her spine, but she pushed all unpleasant thoughts aside, determined to recapture the earlier mood, unwilling to let Fytch spoil one more second.

"Now, tell me about that secret teenage obsession, Mr. Casanova."

Seemingly just as willing to pick up where they'd left off, he kissed along her collarbone. "Professor Helios wouldn't allow any dirty magazines in the house. You know, *Playboy* and—"

"I get the idea." This time she didn't stop him when he removed her bra. She made sure her dress went no lower than her ribs.

He gazed down at her, idly rubbing his thumb back and forth across her nipple. "But he didn't object to art books."

Petra grinned. "What a resourceful child you must have been."

He didn't answer until he had paid thorough attention to her breasts. He seemed to be especially fascinated by the way a tiny flame shot out from his fingertip to the point of her nipple when he got within a couple of inches of it. Each time the magical fire stroked her, she gasped and arched a little higher off the bed.

"Anyway," he finally continued, "I still have a great fondness for the paintings of Rubens. Your body reminds me of the Great Masters' best works of art. You're lush and womanly, even more beautiful in the flesh than any of the pictures I used to daydream about."

Petra thought his statement was a total exaggeration, but it was nice to hear such flattering words, and from her husband no less. She wanted to believe him.

"You are the most gorgeous woman I've ever met." He took her hand and placed it on his erection. "What more proof do you need, Petra?"

She needed to break that bad habit of his. On second thought . . . Pushing aside her reservations, she rubbed up and down his heavy arousal. "You certainly make a compelling case."

"Then in closing, let me remind you that I've already seen you naked. More than once."

"You have?" She snatched her hand away and gave him an accusing look. "When, Tommy boy?"

"It wasn't peeping through any windows." He counted on his fingers. "One—when you sprawled on the floor at my feet. Two—when you fell asleep in my tub and I rescued you from drowning. Three—in the kitchen sink. And four—just a couple of hours ago, right here on this very bed."

He had a point. He had seen her body before and hadn't run screaming into the vast unexplored reaches of the Cascade Mountains. And there was the way he got hard every time she happened to be anywhere near his crotch. Fighting her modesty, she reached out and took off his bowtie, then started unbuttoning his frilly shirt.

"May I?" he asked.

She assumed he meant undress himself. Since her fingers felt about as nimble as a gorilla wearing boxing gloves, she nodded. A startled gasp flew out of her mouth when his clothes, and hers, disappeared in a great show of sparks. Gads, now she was totally on display. And so was he.

Seeing the admiring, almost dazed expression on his face, Petra finally had to believe he honestly did find her attractive. Okay, that was it. No more insecurities allowed. No more self-centered concerns about the way she looked. Instead she would focus on him. On showing him exactly how much she admired and appreciated his body.

She put out a hand to touch him but stopped short of contact. No, it wasn't just his body she craved. It was the whole man. She loved his goodness, his gentleness, his caring, his loyalty and so much more. No, her attraction went way beyond just the physical. Although she wouldn't deny he made her horny as—

"Petra." His voice demanded her attention.

"What?"

"Do I need this?"

She felt herself blush when he held up a small foil square. "No. I'm on birth control pills."

"Good. I don't want anything to come between us tonight. I want to feel every inch of my skin against your skin."

Tilting her head for a better look, her voice was husky. "That's quite an impressive bunch of inches you've got there, Mr. Diggler."

His dark eyes smoldered. "Did you know a pig's orgasm can last for up to thirty minutes?"

Snickering, she waggled her eyebrows at him. "Why do you think I like them so much?"

"Petra!" He sounded downright shocked.

"All my life I've been looking for a man who can be a real pig in bed."

"Hope springs eternal?" he asked in his best Spock impression.

Feeling like an inferno had just burst into being deep inside her, Petra knew she was more than ready. All shyness and objections forgotten, she rolled onto her back and pulled him over. He willingly followed, settling himself on top of her. Just the sensation of his whole body touching her was nearly enough to make her come.

"Please don't make me wait any longer, Vorador."

"What happened to the longest orgasm in history?" His voice was a harsh, grating sound as he tried to avoid her uplifted hips.

"Forget it." She gasped when he slipped a hand between them, smoothing his palm down over her belly.

"As you wish." His hand made its way between her legs. He groaned as he fitted his palm against her heat, finding her already wet and eager for him.

"See?" She raised her hips again, pressing herself against his fingers. "Come on in. No waiting necessary. We're ready and available for immediate service."

The strangled sound he made could have been a laugh. Or maybe a groan. He rolled onto his back, taking her with him, settling her astride his stomach. "I want to watch you, Petra. I want to see you go up in flames."

She nearly collapsed in a boneless heap but propped her hands on his shoulders and managed to maintain at least a tiny fraction of control. Looking down at the wizard engulfed in swirling flames, she knew she would gladly do this for him. Feeling bold and beautiful under his simmering gaze, she rose up on her knees and scooted back to sit on his thighs.

Mouth gone dry, she stared at the wonder of his arousal, rising firm and thick from dense night-black hair. Flames raced up and down his impressive length. Gadzooks! What would it feel like to have that fire inside her? Feeling faint, she closed her eyes, trying for at least some semblance of restraint, and took a deep breath.

"If it frightens you, Petra, I'll understand. I can make it go away."

"Don't you dare," she said, her voice fierce.

With just the tips of her fingers, she chased the flames up and down. His whole body went taut, his hands fisted in the sheets. When he gave an agonized groan, she relented and closed her hand around him. Stroking, fondling, caressing him, she didn't stop until he begged for mercy.

Kneeling over him, she leaned down and rubbed her breasts against his chest. His hands left the sheets and took possession of her. They touched her everywhere, igniting wildfire in their wake. Until she was nearly incoherent.

Watching his face, she slowly lowered herself. His heat entered her, filled her. Her climax exploded like a stick of dynamite. Trembling and gasping, she shuddered as wave after wave of hot pleasure whipped through her body. His fire twined around her thighs and hips, then up her torso to lick at her breasts.

"Gads! I think I'm dying," she gasped.

"Not yet." His hands gripped her hips. He pulled her down while he thrust up. She nearly screamed as she felt him go deep inside. Inside, where she could feel each flicker and flutter of his magic fire. With each slow, deep thrust, she felt his burning hardness and reveled in the friction he created.

"Faster," she demanded, her body rapidly building toward another climax.

"Not yet," he groaned. "It feels too good like this."

She let him have his way for the moment. Then she squeezed her muscles around him, glorying in the burning heat of him stroking inside her. His movements came faster, harder, deeper. Showers of sparks were shooting all over the bedroom, making it look like a miniature Fourth of July fireworks display. She could feel the same thing happening inside herself. Any second now—Oh, yes! Here it came. The grand finale.

Petra felt his climax deep inside her body. The hot, burning liquid kindled her own passion, intensifying and heightening her pleasure in ways she couldn't even begin to describe.

When it was all over, she collapsed in a limp heap on his

chest. Somehow she found the strength to whisper, "I'm never moving from this spot for the rest of my life."

Holding her in a loose embrace, his breathing harsh and rapid, Vorador said, "Try it and I'm bringing out the chains."

Petra grinned and pressed a kiss to his sweaty shoulder. " 'They were found by friends and relatives a month later, chained to the bed, their bodies wasted away, but with the biggest grins on their faces.' "

"They died happily ever after?" Vorador brushed her damp hair out of the way, then kissed her neck. "Frankly, my dear, I'd rather live happily ever after."

"Then so we shall," she said.

SHOCKING BEHAVIOR
JENNIFER ARCHER

J.T. Drake has always felt he pales in comparison to his father's outrageous inventions. But with the push of a button, one of the professor's madcap gadgets actually renders him *invisible*.

Roselyn Peabody's electrifying caress arouses him from his stupor. The beautiful scientist claims his tingling nerve endings are a result of his unique state, but J. T. knows sparks of attraction when he feels them. And while Rosy promises to help him regain his image, J.T. plots to dazzle her with his sex appeal. Only one question remains: When J.T. finally materializes, will their sizzling chemistry disappear or reveal itself as true love?